Bloodhunters v1: Bad Blood

Xine Fury

ISBN: 978-1-967029-02-0

Bloodhunters Volume 1: Bad Blood

Contents

Part 1

01.00 Prologue... 7
01.01 Disaster... 12
01.02 Aftermath... 17
01.03 Preparations... 23
01.04 Journey... 35
01.05 Transport... 45
01.06 Cargo... 51
01.07 Convergence... 61
01.08 Alliance... 72
01.09 Arrival... 83
01.10 Confrontation... 90

Part 2

02.00   Assignments... 109

02.01   The Chauffeur... 118

02.02   Gravity... 130

02.03   Science Experiments... 153

02.04   Safeguards... 167

02.05   Paradise... 175

02.06   POP... 184

02.07   Adrift... 194

02.08   Identity Politics... 216

02.09   Mindwipe... 228

02.10   Brimstone... 240

02.11   Blackmail... 252

Bonus Stories

03.00   Introduction... 275

03.01   Blood Hunt (Detanna)... 276

03.02   Blood Bond (Sekka)... 293

03.03   Blood Contract (Yeela)... 303

03.04   Blood Ties (Zak & Vex)... 311

03.05   Blood Frenzy (Panther & Yna)... 329

03.06   Blood Guardian (Whisper & Zhari)... 339

Note: The bonus stories were previously published as a free e-book called "Blood Samples." These stories are prequels that take place in the months leading up to this book. If you're the type of reader who prefers to read everything in chronological order, then you may want to skip ahead to these bonus stories. However, they aren't critical to the overall narrative, and merely provide some additional backstory to some of the characters.

Part 1

01.00 *Prologue*

ED.02499.12.31

Trasa was called the City of A Trillion Lights, but A'Tral currently fled through the darkest part. Pushing through crowds of diverse beings, he scanned for any source of refuge. He suddenly turned and dashed across the street, causing a beat-up hovercar to swerve into the wrong lane. The purple-skinned driver yelled out some very colorful insults, but A'Tral kept running. He vaulted over a floating garbage truck, barely straining his cybernetically-enhanced legs, and barreled into an alley between two restaurants. It was dark here, and his eye implants took a few seconds to adjust. He knew darkness alone couldn't hide him, as his pursuer was no doubt similarly equipped with expensive enhancements. He spotted a sewer grate at the far end of the alley and ran over to it. He set the grate aside and started to climb in. Then he paused for a moment, legs dangling in the shaft.

It was a gamble no matter what he did. What would the hunter be expecting? Was it safer to blend into the crowd, or hide in the tunnels below? His pursuer was a master at predicting the behavior of his prey, and A'Tral didn't want to go back to prison. Especially not now that he was so close to freedom. He patted his left thigh, where the stolen gem rested securely in a secret compartment. All he had to do was make it across town, then he could meet his buyer and leave this planet for good.

He heard the whine of a drone echoing through the alley. He turned his head, his visual software zooming in on it. The small disc hovered at the alley entrance, most likely scanning for movement. It was no bigger than one of A'Tral's pocket grenades, and colored in the hunter's signature shade of red. There was no more time for debate. He dropped into the sewer, ignoring the ladder and letting his cyberlegs absorb the impact of the lengthy fall. He was reasonably sure the drone hadn't detected him, but he wasn't going to hang around to find out. There was very little light in the tunnel, and once again he was thankful for his ocular upgrades. He picked a direction and ran, hoping to find a junction where he could orient himself.

He didn't get far. He spotted the device on the wall a split second after it was too late to avoid it. A red metal tube – the same shade as the drone had been – flipped out from the wall, firing a cylindrical projectile at A'Tral. It separated into four smaller discs as it soared through the air, and a thin net unfurled between them. Before A'Tral had time to react, the net pinned him to the wall, each disc magnetizing itself to the metal girders lining the sewer wall. He struggled to reach one of his many pockets. The netting was incredibly strong for something that thin, but it was elastic enough to keep from cutting him. He couldn't move much, but fortunately he had stowed a tiny AON blade in one of his cuffs. With a bit of effort he managed to retrieve it.

He pressed a button on the handle and the finger-length metal blade burst forth. The blade quickly heated up, glowing a bright orange. "I wouldn't do that," he heard a voice say. A'Tral stopped for a second, his eyes darting back and forth. His attention finally fell on the wall-mounted micro-cannon that had fired the net at him. There was a blinking red light on it, and most likely a camera as well. He also noticed something strange.

It's not the kind of detail most people would pick up on, but being a cybernetics enthusiast, A'Tral had an eye for new hardware. And the micro-cannon... well, it wasn't *clean*. It was covered in the same level of grime as the rest of the sewer walls, which meant the cannon had been here for a while. How long, he couldn't say, but probably longer than he'd been on the run. Why had it been installed here, if not for A'Tral?

Whatever, he thought. He could ponder the bounty hunter's methods some other day. For now, he had to get loose before the hunter showed up in person. He moved the blade to one of the thin strands of netting. As soon as the blade touched the strand, A'Tral cried out in pain as the net sent electric shocks through his body. The AON blade fell from his hands and clattered away. Then he heard footsteps echoing from down the tunnel.

"I did warn you," a voice said. It was deep and sounded electronically amplified. A humanoid shape approached, casually strolling toward the criminal. A'Tral easily recognized the famous bounty hunter. Every criminal feared that black-and-red armored jumpsuit. A drone zoomed into view, and docked onto one of the hunter's wrists. Then the hunter stepped closer, fiddling with a wrist-mounted control panel. "I'm going to release the net now," he said. "If you try to run, you'll regret it." The net fell off the wall, and A'Tral collapsed to the floor. The hunter pulled out a pair of wrist restraints. "Hold out your hands," he said.

A'Tral didn't like his chances, but his fear of returning to prison was greater than his fear of a single bounty hunter. From his crouched position, he jumped forward with the maximum power his cyberlegs would allow. His head caught the hunter in the stomach, where the hunter's armor was more of a flexible mesh, as opposed to the heavy red plates covering his chest. The impact hurt A'Tral's head - a lot - but he felt great satisfaction at hearing the supposedly untouchable bounty hunter say "Oof." Then he sprang past the hunter, sparing a second to drop a pocket grenade behind him. As he turned the next corner, he stumbled and skidded to a stop. His attention now focused on a shiny red cannon sitting on a tripod, tracking his every move. Still a bit dizzy from the head impact, he stepped backwards a few paces.

Would it fire if he ran? Would it fire if he stayed still? What if he slowly inched back around the corner? And... shouldn't he have heard an explosion by now? He had now backed up enough to turn towards the previous tunnel.

"Not. Wise." The bounty hunter stood just a few meters away, holding the now-deactivated pocket grenade. His body language was like that of a disappointed teacher, and though the hunter's blood-red visor was opaque, A'Tral imagined a stern expression on his face. A'Tral pulled out another AON blade, brandishing it menacingly, but the hunter just shook his head, unimpressed. A'Tral realized he wasn't going to win this, and made a snap decision. Better death than prison.

He moved to thrust the blade into his own throat, but the bounty hunter was quicker. He tapped an icon on his wrist pad, and the tripod-mounted cannon fired. A white ball of electricity hit A'Tral in the side, knocking him to the ground, once again causing him to drop his knife.

Straining to stay conscious, A'Tral watched the bounty hunter step closer. "At least," A'Tral said with exhausted resignation, "tell me how you knew where to set up the cannons."

"Trade secret," the hunter replied, in that electronically-enhanced voice. A'Tral flinched as the infamous bounty hunter reached toward him. But then something curious happened. A light flashed on the hunter's gauntlet, and he stopped to stare at the readout. He pressed a couple of keys on his wrist computer, his attention completely focused on the tiny screen.

Still concentrating on the screen, he absently reached for

A'Tral's left thigh, retrieving the stolen gem. "It's your lucky day," the hunter said, pocketing the gem. "I have bigger fish to fry. Now get lost."

01.01 *Disaster*

ED.02499.12.31

InterGalactic Police Sergeant Daniel Malis had a knack for finding himself in crisis situations. When terrorists had taken hostages at the Galactic Nations Embassy six months ago, it had been during his shift. Two months before that he had been on vacation on a luxury starship when it was hijacked. And, even though he lived hundreds of kilometers away, he just happened to be in Los Angeles when the big one hit. The infamous "Malice Luck" was legendary at the IGP training camps. Most officers would chalk it up to coincidence, but that didn't stop them from avoiding the sergeant whenever they could.

As a large, intimidating, bear of a man, Malis would have had trouble making friends even without his bad luck. Not that he considered his luck bad. He actually felt very fortunate for these chance events. He always managed to turn these tragedies into opportunities for heroism. Once, he was making a deposit at the bank when it was held up by two robbers. In less than five minutes he had them tied up and on their way to prison. It was opportunities like this that had earned him his rank as a sergeant.

Today was different. Today he was not on top of the situation. Today he was thousands of kilometers away from the danger zone, and he had never felt more vulnerable.

He viewed the transmission again. First it showed the outside of IGP EarthStation 1. Orbiting the Earth at a slightly greater distance than the moon, it was nearly as large as a moon itself. As this solar system's primary police headquarters, it was home to over fourteen thousand IGP officers. With its powerful shields and formidable weapons systems, as well as its sheer size, it was completely invulnerable to attack. But then, the designers had never expected an attack of this nature.

The scene suddenly changed to show the face of a woman. She appeared to be in her mid-twenties, with short black hair, pale skin, and crystal blue eyes. She announced without emotion, "This is Alterra Sarr. Your station is under my control. Unless you submit to my demands, this station will be destroyed, along with everyone in it. You have two hours to decide." The transmission ended there. The computers had downloaded a list of demands which included large sums of money as well as the release of several prisoners.

"Can she do it, Esh?" asked Malis. The "Esh" in question was Doctor G'Heesh Eshton, a tall, gray-skinned humanoid with large, black eyes. The doctor was every bit as anxious as Malis, though possibly a bit less bothered about being "stuck" on Earth during the crisis.

"I have connected to the station's computers," Eshton said in his stilted accent. "I am locked out as far as actually being able to take any kind of control, but I managed to sneak a peek at what she's been doing. Somehow she has reprogrammed the propulsion systems to backwash into the ventilation systems. In addition, the gasses used in the power core would be released. Apparently she knows which gas combinations will cause a massive explosion."

"And there's no way we can get in?"

For a second Eshton looked offended. "I helped design the station myself, sergeant. If there were any way past the weapons systems, I would know it. She has somehow even locked out our own security override codes."

"How did she do this? Where did she get these authorization codes? I thought our system was unbreakable. Alterra Sarr is just a patrol officer. She shouldn't have had access to any of these systems!" Malis was beginning to lose his temper.

"I do not know how she could have done it. She must have been setting this up for a long time. She could have had help from one of the station's engineers..." Eshton broke off, frowning. "...but, to accomplish all of this, she would have to have known passcodes that only a select few of us possessed, possibly even codes that only I know."

"We'll worry about security problems later. Right now we need to stop her. Have you read her file? Maybe we can talk her out of this."

"I have read her file, sergeant, but this takeover does not match her profile. She has always been an exemplary officer. She was even in line for a promotion. In fact, some of the prisoners she wants freed are ones that she captured herself. It does not make sense."

The video screen flickered on again. This time it was a split screen. On the left was Alterra Sarr, broadcast from the IGP station. On the right was the face of IGP Captain Trent Dellwood, broadcast from the IGP Earth Headquarters in Greenland.

"We can't submit to your demands, Alterra, you know this. We don't give in to terrorists. There is no way you can get away with this. If you destroy the station your life won't be worth spit anywhere in the galaxy. Start releasing the officers and maybe we can talk. If you give up now I'll look into reducing your sentence." Captain Dellwood had conducted terrorist negotiations before, but never one of this magnitude. He was visibly nervous.

Alterra Sarr still showed no emotion. "It was worth a try," she said, and that was all. Her transmission ended, and the left side of the screen now showed the outside of the station. Dellwood, still on the right half of the screen, had a look of confusion on his face. Then, at the stroke of midnight, the station exploded.

It was a spectacular sight as the station's exterior panels suddenly blew outward, one after another, while the burning gas and the vacuum of space caused some areas of the station to explode while others imploded. Huge metal segments blew out in every direction, while other parts of the station caved in. Bright flames flared out from the center for a few seconds and then vanished as the station's atmosphere dissipated into space. In less than fifteen seconds the entire station became a cloud of debris.

Sergeant Malis just stared, unable to speak.

Several solar systems away, in a squalid bar on Chirminon, the entire crowd became silent as the news came on. This was significant for two reasons. It was not the type of crowd that watched the news, and it was not the type of crowd that became silent. All eyes turned toward the large video screen as the reporter spoke.

"Tonight's top story: Over fourteen thousand InterGalactic Police officers were killed today when a terrorist destroyed the Earth IGP space station. The terrorist has been identified as former IGP officer Alterra Sarr. Officer Sarr, shown here, reportedly took control of the computer systems and used pirated codes to create a systems malfunction which destroyed the station. She is still at large.

"Due to the sudden extreme shortage of IGP officers, the United Galaxy Organization is encouraging all bounty hunters to participate in the search for this dangerous woman. A collection is being crowdfunded, and the governments of several planets have contributed large sums towards the reward for her capture. So far the total is up to seven million credits. Money is still rolling in, but one thing is clear. Whoever brings in Alterra Sarr is going to be very wealthy.

"If you have any information, or would like to make a contribution, please report to your nearest IGP terminal. For more information on this case, and complete files on Alterra Sarr, download file SarrAlt382 from our site."

Then it cut to commercial. At once the bar was no longer quiet. Boasts of "I'll be rich!" and "She's mine!" were heard as a room full of cutthroats all ran toward the computer terminals. There was one who did not run, however. This single figure stood in the back of the room, not speaking a word. Watching the crowd through a blood-red domed helmet, the figure contemplated this turn of events. When the bounty hunter finally spoke, it was just one word.

"Fools."

The few who heard him knew that he was correct. No one stood a better chance of finding her than Bloodstone.

01.02 *Aftermath*

ED.02500.01.01

On Earth, in a police dorm in downtown Chicago, IGP Officer Vik Lambert watched the news in horror. His face was pale, his jaw wide. He suddenly found himself unable to stand up, and shakily backed into his chair. All his friends… all his… Oh no. Oh. No. Zhari… she was covering his shift today, while he met with the minister. Was she still at the station, or out on patrol? "Comm. Call Zhari," he said. On the table by the door, a small black device blinked on. He reached out his hand, and the comm flew across the room into his grasp. The screen flashed "Connecting…" for several seconds, then flashed "Network Busy." Of course he wouldn't be able to get through. After what just happened, the entire world would be on the comm. He kept trying.

Between attempts, his comm's wallpaper reminded him of what he might have lost. Looking tiny in one of Vik's old T-shirts, Zhari held out her fuzzy hand. Her fingers were splayed wide, proudly showing off the ring he'd given her. Her catlike eyes gleamed with mischief, and her mouth was set in that lopsided smile that always made his heart flutter. The picture was less than a week old. Through watery eyes, he kept tapping the call button. Seventeen attempts later, one call looked like it might go through. "Network Found" it flashed. This brief, bright moment lasted only a few seconds before the comm displayed, "User Comm Not Found On Network."

It didn't mean anything. It didn't mean anything. Overloaded networks gave all sorts of error messages. It didn't mean anything.

On a swampy planet of Gleegha, a lime-skinned man with large, froglike eyes pulled on his temperature-regulating jumpsuit. Felreg Ninnor, who went by the professional name "Gekko," warmed up his ship's engine and did some pre-flight checks. He saw his people as a species of underachievers, content to spend their days warming themselves on rocks and eating the giant insects that were plentiful on this planet. *It's a miracle we even achieved sapience,* he thought. Gekko had always wanted more out of life, and saw bounty hunting as a means to see the universe. He did it for the travel, not the money, but a score like this one meant he'd be able to quit bounty hunting so he could travel indefinitely.

Not having the skills or experience the more reputable hunters possessed, Gekko was what they called a "carrion hunter" – someone who relies on the skills of other bounty hunters. He would try to glean clues from other hunters, follow the ones he deemed most likely to catch their prey, and snatch the fugitives out from under the noses of rival hunters. He wasn't above killing another bounty hunter just to take credit for their work. It was considered the lowest of the low among bounty hunters, but Gekko didn't care. He came from a cold-blooded species, both literally and figuratively. Prestige was of no consequence, only results.

His pre-flight checks finished, he blasted off and set a course to the nearest warp gate.

Jeke Skeeper looked up from his bowl of mint-mango beer and stared at the news on his wrist comm. He'd been relaxing in a rocking chair on the lawn, on a spot that would one day be a porch. He was about as far from Earth as one could get and still be in the Milky Way, but the news had traveled far. He almost ignored it until he saw the size of the bounty. "Sweet Feezles, that's a lot of credits." If he left now, with the homestead only half built, he knew the property would be overrun with creeping vines and nightbears by the time he got back. But if he was the one to sniff out Alterra... well that would be something. He wouldn't have to settle on this backwater planet, he could buy property anywhere he wanted. Wasn't the chance of a fancy plantation home worth losing the work he'd already put into this house?

And it's not like he had roots here. He didn't actually know where he was from, but he was far from any planet he'd ever considered home. He'd been raised as a slave, trained to be a bodyguard among a species that bore no resemblance to himself. He'd eventually escaped, and soon found he had a knack for tracking people thanks to his powerful nose. They called him "Berdawg" due to his canine features and the small yellow feathers that covered him like fur. He'd yet to meet another of his kind, and he preferred it that way. It meant nobody had any preconceptions when they met him. There weren't any stereotypes he had to disprove.

Jeke hemmed and hawed for a few more moments, and finally decided it was just too much money to pass up. He hurriedly lapped up the rest of his beer, grabbed his double-barreled energy rifle, and made a beeline for his ship.

Detanna Taush did an automated equipment check. All her weapons and gadgets were accounted for, and one hundred percent charged. Not one to blindly trust her computer, she performed the check again manually. And then, just because she could, she performed another automated check.

She did not allow mistakes to happen. It wouldn't do for people to start thinking she was capable of failure. Her reputation was too important to tarnish. It allowed her access to the highest-paid jobs, and it intimidated her captives into making mistakes of their own.

It had been a difficult road. She'd been born male - or at least assigned male at birth - but had known from an early age that she was a woman at heart. Her gender issues had led to her parents separating, and at fifteen Detanna found herself homeless. A street gang took her in, but when they found out she was transgender, they weren't any more accepting than her parents. She was lucky to have escaped with her life.

Later she managed to join a group of galactic pirates, presenting herself as male the entire time. She'd known that there was only one way she'd be able to truly be herself, and it would require more credits than she was going to earn working for the pirates. So, she became a bounty hunter.

Life is funny sometimes. It turned out she had a knack for bounty hunting. Her criminal background gave her a natural instinct for predicting the behavior of fugitives. Her success as a bounty hunter had allowed her to save up a lot of money, which she was planning to use for her transition. In truth, she'd already saved up enough to afford many of the surgeries most typical trans folk get. But Detanna didn't do "typical," it was the best or nothing.

There was a specific procedure she was saving up for, the most expensive transition operation available. Doctors on Cytrine Delta had a machine that completely rewrites your chromosomes, then regenerates nearly every cell in your body. It switches your glands to produce estrogen instead of testosterone. Unwanted hair follicles are permanently disabled. Facial features are feminized. Vocal cords are tweaked. The Adam's apple is eradicated. Down to a cellular level you become XX instead of XY.

It still wasn't perfect. She wouldn't be able to bear children, for instance, not that she necessarily wanted to. And she would still be the same height, which was tall even for a man. But it meant she could stop taking hormones, and she would look and sound like her true self from the moment she opened her eyes every morning. The operation was truly a miracle. The price of that miracle? Over six million credits. Not on a bounty hunter's salary, regardless of your reputation. But now there's Alterra...

She knew that every hunter in the galaxy was racing to catch this woman. But Detanna didn't believe in failure. This was a race she intended to win.

Letho Kragnar stood on his massive knuckles, his lesser arms busy securing his armor straps. Looking like a cross between an ape and an armadillo, his imposing frame was enough to cause most foes to surrender without a fight. But even braver enemies would falter when they saw the arsenal attached to his suit. The armor itself was mostly redundant, due to the protection provided by his natural plating, but it helped him carry his weapons. Not a centimeter was bare, with grenades, ammo clips, and every weapon imaginable covering his outfit. He examined his armor straps with both sets of eyes, confirming for the fifth time that they were strong enough to carry the weight of his equipment. It wouldn't do to have a strap break during a firefight.

It had now been two years since he'd gone AWOL from the Grunthian armed forces. He wondered if they were still after him. He faced a death sentence if they ever brought him back, but then it was a suicide mission that had caused him to leave in the first place. Letho didn't fear death, but he wanted to face it on his own terms. He sure as Krek didn't want to die following the orders of an incompetent commander who didn't recognize when a mission was doomed to fail. *Well, if they still want me, let them come,* he decided. He'd fought them off before, and he'd do it again. But this time, he'd have millions of credits backing him. He'd build himself an impenetrable fortress, armed to the teeth. Better yet, he'd use the money to fund an army of mercenaries to raze Grunthar until it was molten rubble.

Then maybe he'd get some peace.

And so it went on various planets all over the galaxy. On the aquatic planet of Nemur, a many-tentacled cephalopod donned a water-filled exo-suit, greed overcoming his fears of leaving his home planet. On Razgul Four, a reptilian stuntman decided to try his hand at bounty hunting, in hopes of finally paying off his student loan debt. On Treem Delta, a peaceful Sasquatch-like woman picked up a gun for the first time, hoping to give the reward to her church. On the third moon of Siktar, a sapient swarm of hornets powered up their HIVE (Humanoid Interface VEhicle), so that they could search for Alterra without looking conspicuous. On the mining station that orbited Asteroid Foth-Janik 137B, seven miners quit their jobs without notice, all banking on being the one to find Alterra.

A retired soldier on Armus. A schoolteacher on Dectalon. An escaped serial killer. A plastic surgeon. And of course, hundreds of seasoned, professional bounty hunters. Swarms of ships converged on Earth, looking for clues.

The IGP, already overburdened by the loss of staff, couldn't handle all the requests for information. They released all the intel they had on Alterra into a public database, but an in-depth background check revealed some inconsistencies. While her IGP bio claimed that she was from Earth, there was no actual record of her birth, her parentage, or even her hometown. It was as if she had sprung into existence the day she entered the IGP. Either she'd created a false identity to become an officer, or she'd deleted her records when she destroyed the space station. Either way she had to have hacked the public records database at some point, and that was no small feat. She either had incredible hacker skills or some powerful connections.

01.03 *Preparations*

ED.02500.01.01

It's ready for testing. Want to come see?

The thoughts entered Raven's mind as clearly as if they had been her own. Clearer, in fact, since her own thoughts were often a jumbled mix of words, images, and sudden painful memories. But Trenyn's telepathic message came through as distinctly as if they had been spoken words. *I'll be right there*, she thought back, and started moving.

"Chair. Come," Raven said, and a small chair floated over to her side. Then came the hard part. With no arms or legs, she had to wriggle her body off the couch and onto the chair. More than once she had fallen over the chair and onto the floor during this process. She still had a scar from when she'd hit her head on the coffee table.

But this time she made it with no problems. As she positioned herself in the cushioned seat, a restraining belt automatically slid around her waist. "Chair. Lab," she said, and the hoverchair whisked her out of the room and down the hallway.

Raven wasn't wealthy, but you would be forgiven for assuming she was after seeing her sprawling mansion. She held the patents for several medical implants and robotic prostheses, but she hadn't designed them to get rich. And she only retained those patents to keep the resulting products cheap for those who needed them. The last thing she wanted was for some lazy trillionaire to buy one of her patents just so they could up the price, screwing the poor people who relied on them.

Raven hated her house. Everything about it reminded her of her father, despite having only met him a couple of times. It was oversized and ostentatious, built to advertise wealth rather than for comfort. She probably would have sold it years ago, and moved into something smaller, but the many rooms had proven useful for her experiments. Besides, the house was paid for, and thanks to some shady loophole her father had set up, she didn't even have to pay property taxes. It would actually cost her more to move into a one-bedroom apartment.

Her hoverchair approached a closed door. "Open," she said, and it slid open. She hated that, too. Voice-activated doorways just seemed so inefficient. But it's not like she could press a button or turn a doorknob. Without arms or legs, she was pretty much stuck using voice commands.

As she passed through the doorway, she mused on other solutions. She supposed she could program the doors to open automatically when the chair approached them. But the thought dissipated as soon as she passed the kitchen, where multiple half-finished projects fought for her attention span.

Everywhere she looked, she saw things that could be improved. When she spotted outdated tech, her mind immediately went to work on how it could be updated. But her lack of mobility meant she had to work through other people's hands, and this meant most of her ideas had to be postponed or left unfinished.

Next she passed a suit of medieval armor in the hallway, another relic of her father's style. She'd sold off most of his garish art collection to pay for her tech. *If only his taste for decor had been the least of his crimes*, she thought. Even if she'd shared her father's tastes, art in general just didn't mean much to Raven. She preferred functionality to aesthetics. But the armor spoke to her. It reminded her of her current project. Well, Trenyn's current project. Credit must be given where it was due.

She thought about how fortunate she was to have met Trenyn. The fact that they were able to communicate telepathically was incredibly lucky. It was just random chance that Raven's non-human half could communicate with Navorans; she'd never been able to speak with anyone else in that manner. Their ease of communication made working together so much more efficient. She connected with them in a way that she never could have with anyone else. Trenyn was more than a friend, closer than family. It was like working with the other half of herself.

She then thought about how big a step, quite literally, she might be about to take. It had been six years since her so-called "accident," and since then she'd thought of little else. On that day she lost more than limbs. She lost her youthful innocence, her capacity for happiness, quite possibly even a piece of her soul. But today that could change. Once she solved her problem of mobility, she could work on her other losses.

She reached the robotics lab, where Trenyn stood at a computer terminal. *Ah, just in time,* they mentally projected. Trenyn was a thin, blue-green humanoid with a large bald head, who could only speak telepathically. *Ready to try it on?* They pointed to the other side of the room with two of their four hands. Raven saw what appeared to be a robot with no head. It was a perfectly proportioned female form, but colored an unpainted metallic silver.

"Here, robot," Raven called to it, but nothing happened.

Oh, thought Trenyn, *I didn't tell you. It doesn't accept verbal commands. I programmed it to recognize your thought projections.*

"Impossible," Raven said flatly. "We tried that with the chair, remember?"

I managed to make this one much more receptive to your brainwave patterns in particular. Our biggest obstacle was that we designed the interface to work with people, when we should have designed it to work with you.

"I don't know whether to be flattered or insulted," Raven replied.

What I mean is, you're not fully human. Our original interface was designed for humans. But having analyzed your unique brainwave patterns...

"I get it," Raven interrupted. Instinctively, she thought about raising her hand in a "stop talking" gesture, and to her surprise, the robot body did exactly that.

It reacts as if it were your own body. That's why the humanoid form instead of something more utilitarian. It will help if, instead of thinking verbal commands, treat it as if you were moving your own muscles. I couldn't have done it if not for the mental abilities you inherited from your father.

Her father. Raven shuddered at the thought. He was an evil man who had gained incredible wealth and power through mind control and thievery. Because she was half human, Raven only possessed a small portion of her father's mental abilities. It was because of her father's DNA that they were unable to clone or transplant new limbs onto her body. Her genetic makeup did not take well to medical implants.

But this new robotic body was different. It wasn't an implant so much as a human-shaped vehicle. It required no surgery, and with the thought interface, it would still have the control of a real body. As she stared at the form with her white-irised eyes - another side effect of her father's genetic makeup - she willed it to walk over to her, and it did.

It stopped as it came near her, and then the chest area split open. Inside, there was a padded hollow area large enough for her body. The arms reached out for her and lifted her from the chair. She was deposited into the hollow area and the chest doors closed around her. "It's a little tight, but I guess that will keep me from falling out. How do I look?"

Raven asked, as she willed the body to strike a feminine pose.

Trenyn was taken aback. This was not the Raven they knew. The broken woman whom they had befriended a few years ago in a moment of need, she was sullen and morbid, never perky, never vain. She did everything out of necessity, working towards her goals one step at a time, without emotion.

And now, here she was, her first goal finally realized. She was in a fashion model stance, and even smiling. And she looked... well, she looked like a metal woman with a human head. *Almost whole,* Trenyn answered. *Here, put this on.* They grabbed a long white lab coat from a peg on the wall, and helped her get her arms through it. It didn't fit very well, since it was designed for Trenyn, but it covered the robotic body almost completely. *You look... intact,* they told her. *With the right outfit, no one would ever suspect you were different.*

Of course Raven was no slave to fashion, even before her dismemberment. She kept her jet-black hair cut so short she was almost bald. This, however, was a different matter. If she was going to achieve her goals, she would need to look human all over. She did not want her weaknesses exposed. This device of Trenyn's would give her the strength she needed to get her revenge.

Raven smiled again and said, "Trenyn, you've done a wonderful job."

Trenyn's face turned purple with pride. It was how their species expressed emotions. These involuntary pigmentation shifts made it difficult for Navorans to hide their feelings, but telepaths rarely kept secrets anyway.

"Now," Raven said, "it's time to go see my father."

"Vik, you can not do this. Are you even listening to me? Vik!"

Vik looked up from the weapons case he was packing and glared into the huge black eyes of Doctor Eshton. "I was going to marry her, Esh. We'd set a date. And it wasn't just her. Some of those officers were my friends. Do you think I'm just going to stand by while some profit-driven bounty hunters let Sarr slip through their fingers?"

"Profit-driven bounty hunters are no worse than revenge-driven officers. Police resources are low enough as it is, criminals are becoming overconfident, riots have even broken out. We need you here, Vik."

"Bullshit!" Vik retorted. "You know as well as I do that if I stay here, I still won't see any action. You'll keep me here, running your little tests..."

"Well, that in itself is a reason for you to stay. You are not ready, Vik. You are the only one to make it this far in my experiments, and that makes you far too valuable to risk."

Eshton had a point there. Of the thirty-seven officers originally fitted with the Levatech implants, Vik was the only one who could be considered a success. Four had died, and most of the rest became ill and had to have the internal components removed. Vik was one of three agents who still had the implants, and he was the only one who could use them effectively. This made Vik a valuable commodity to the IGP.

"Look at it this way, Esh. If I manage to bring in Miss Sarr, and survive a few scrapes along the way, your experiment will be a success. Besides, you can't stop me."

"Untrue. Sergeant Malis will be very interested to hear of your desertion. As an IGP officer you are required to follow orders, and you are ordered to remain here." Eshton rarely pulled rank or gave orders, but this was important to him.

"The Sarge can fire me. After I bring in Sarr, I'll be a hero anyway." And with that, Vik picked up his case and walked out the door.

Eshton sighed. "Well," he said to the empty air, "if I can not stop you, I had better make sure you do not get killed."

It was a cloudy morning in the city of Trasa. In a quiet bar on the poor side of town, a group of patrons raised their heads as a police cruiser pulled up to the curb. An officer stepped out of the hovercar, grabbed his satchel, and headed for the bar.

The customers watched as the officer posted a large picture of Alterra Sarr on the wall of the darkened tavern. The poster was an oversized close-up of Alterra's face, with the message WANTED DEAD OR ALIVE, ALTERRA SARR, HUGE REWARD printed across the top and bottom. As the officer walked away, two of the gathering patrons stepped closer for a better look.

The first man stared at the picture in awe. "I hear the reward is already up to ten million. I could be free of this lousy planet and have a mansion on Valos."

"If you could take her," his companion snorted.

The first man yanked the picture down from the wall, studying the portrait. "She doesn't look so tough. That fancy police training doesn't mean a thing in a real fight."

"Well, I don't think you'll get your chance. I hear Bloodstone has decided to take the case."

Just the name sent shivers up his spine. Bloodstone was the galaxy's most respected and most feared bounty hunter. No one escaped him, everyone knew that.

"I guess that's that, then. It was a nice dream." The man holding the poster slumped his shoulders, giving the picture one last look before rolling it up. "Of course," he added, "it won't hurt to keep our eyes open." He was about to tuck the poster in his belt when a loud KRAK! sounded from behind him. Something cord-like wrapped bad around the poster and yanked it from his hand. It happened so quickly that the man had no time to react.

The two men spun around to face... nothing. Just empty shadows across the back wall. Then the shadows began to move. A tall, shapely woman stepped from the blackness. She was dressed in a sleek, skintight gray suit that covered her entire body, with black boots, wrist bracers, and a vest.

She wore a black helmet with a silver mirrored faceplate. In her left hand, she held a whip. Her right hand gripped the rolled-up poster. After unrolling and examining the picture, she folded up the paper neatly and stuffed it in her vest. Turning back around, she strode back across the room, her footsteps making no noise as she walked. Disappearing into the shadows, she was not seen again. After several minutes of stunned silence, the two men finally sat down at the bar and ordered doubles.

Elsewhere in Trasa, a lone figure trod swiftly down the sidewalk toward the edge of town. In one hand they carried a bag full of recently purchased supplies. Oblivious to all else, they appeared to be absorbed in their own ambitions.

A rodent-like creature named Siik watched the figure from a distance, scampering past them on the rooftops. Siik was fast, observant, and could leap from rooftop to rooftop with ease. He had been following Bloodstone all morning, from the bar, to the parking garage, to the supply shop. Knowing he'd most likely head back to the garage next, his allies had set up a trap.

Reaching the dark, abandoned building, Siik clambered down the side and entered through a window. "He's coming, get ready," he squeaked, then climbed up a pile of boxes so he would have a safe view of the upcoming bloodbath. Siik was useless in a fight himself, but the others tolerated him because he was such a good informant. After this, they would love him.

The other gang members crouched down in the darkness. All except their leader, Zerfust, a stocky Vhelran with yellow scales and three nostrils. He threw the door open wide just as Bloodstone walked past.

"What's the hurry, dome-head? Come rest a minute." Bloodstone ignored him at first. "Hey! I'm talking to you! This is a toll street. All persons passin' through got to pay me." The green glow of a luminous knife was now visible in

Zerfust's hand.

Siik heard modulated laughter from outside the door. From his angle, he could just see the bounty hunter over the boss man's shoulder. Bloodstone started to reach for a pistol, but appeared to change his mind. Then he pulled his own AON knife from his boot instead. At first it appeared to be a normal steel knife, but once activated, the blade began to glow a bright red. Bloodstone's voice echoed through the doorway. "I don't have time for this. You're in over your head. I'll give you one chance to back out. If you continue this foolishness, it won't turn out well for you."

"Come on, sissy huntsman, I can take you." Zerfust sounded anxious but not nervous.

Bloodstone sighed, like this encounter was beneath him. He set down his bag of supplies, then stepped through the doorway and into the building. While it was dark inside, Bloodstone didn't appear to have any trouble seeing. The bounty hunter faced not one, but nearly twenty well-armed adversaries of various species. If he'd thought it was a simple mugging before, he now knew it was a set-up.

"We heard you was going to take the Sarr job," Zerfust said, pointing the glowing blade at Bloodstone. "We can't let you do that unless we get a piece of the prize."

"I work alone," Bloodstone answered. "I don't need help, I don't split the rewards, and I don't do charity. If you guys think you can find her first, you can go ahead and try. But if you just want to shorten your life spans we can do that right here."

"I'm sorry you feel that way… Nah, I'm not sorry. We've always wanted to do this." Zerfust lunged forward, knife thrust ahead. Bloodstone swiftly dodged the attack and grabbed the man's sleeve. Turning around, he redirected Zerfust's forward motion and slammed him into the wall. The gang leader fell, his knife flying out of his hand. Bloodstone caught the knife as the rest of the aggressors swarmed toward him. Doubly armed, he cut two enemies at once, catching them right across their chests. Then he threw the green knife at another assailant, penetrating their shoulder.

He stabbed another man in the side with the red knife as he drew his pistol with his other hand. Ducking a large creature's fist, he sliced the brute's knee while firing energy blasts at three others. Four attackers drew their energy rifles, but only one had the chance to fire before being cut down by Bloodstone's pistol fire. Bloodstone delivered a roundhouse kick to a reptilian when three energy blasts just missed his head. Another blast glanced off his chest armor and he returned fire, hitting a heavily armed mercenary in the face.

Duck, shoot, stab. Punch, slash, kick. Bloodstone became a machine, taking out his attackers quickly and efficiently. Siik got the impression that he wasn't even using a tenth of his skills. In fact, his motions were so robotic, he looked almost... bored. Soon it was all over. Bloodstone stood alone. Siik's allies were strewn about the room, too wounded to fight. Most of them would live, but they wouldn't try this again.

Bloodstone looked directly at Siik, despite the informant's concealed location. "Don't follow me again," he said, and left the building. Grabbing his bag, he resumed his walk toward the parking garage.

On the outskirts of town, several small, nondescript homes littered the landscape. Each was built for function over form, mostly used by people who didn't want to be found. Each of these square, steel domiciles sat next to a landing pad. On one particular pad sat a sleek, black spaceship with red markings.

A shadowy figure watched as Bloodstone made small trips back and forth, from the home to the spaceship. *Is this really where he lives? Surely a bounty hunter of his renown could afford something grander.* Bounty hunting wasn't always a lucrative career – it certainly hadn't been for Whisper – but the big names could negotiate big fees. Many of the most famous hunters lived in luxury.

Whisper waited until Bloodstone was inside the house, then sneaked closer. For such a tiny place, the security was insane, bordering on paranoid. She had already stepped over several detection lasers, as well as some old-school tripwires and pressure plates. But avoiding detection was her specialty. She would never be famous like Bloodstone, even if she were to somehow match his success rate, because her entire shtick was avoiding notice. Not that she'd ever wanted fame. She valued her anonymity, especially right now.

She reached the house and hid around the corner, watching as Bloodstone performed equipment checks and loaded several items onto the ship. The next time Bloodstone went back inside, she quickly slipped aboard the ship.

This was stupid. Of all the people with whom she could hitch a ride, Bloodstone was undoubtedly the most dangerous. But he was also the most likely to be going where she needed to go. While other hunters pursued false leads, Bloodstone wouldn't move without evidence.

There were several storage lockers on the back wall of the cockpit, and luckily, one of them was nearly empty. She hid in the narrow compartment, watching the cockpit through several small vents. After a few minutes, Bloodstone entered the cockpit and sat down at the controls. She could see the queries he made on his computer, but only understood half of them.

It looked like Bloodstone had his own monitoring satellites scattered around the most popular space travel routes. As far as Whisper could tell from her vantage point, his satellites had managed to track Alterra much farther than anyone else had. On another screen, he was hacking into the travel grid, viewing unauthorized data from all the nearest warp gates. Even the unregistered ones, which Whisper wouldn't have thought was possible.

Eventually, he found his target. "Computer," Bloodstone said, "Set a course for Warp Gate U-3112."

Whisper relaxed, leaning against the back wall of the locker, and accidentally knocked a wrench off the wall behind her. Bloodstone immediately stood up and drew his gun. "Who's there?" he asked. He walked over to the storage locker next to Whisper's, pulled it open, then slammed it shut. Then he opened Whisper's locker and immediately slammed it shut as well. He searched two more lockers on the other side of the cockpit door, then sat back down, mumbling something about nerves.

Whisper – extra quietly – sighed in relief. Her abilities had saved her once again. It was a close call, and she still wasn't sure this was a safe place to be, but it was too late to back out. Bloodstone finished making pre-flight checks, and the ship blasted off into space.

01.04 *Journey*

ED.02500.01.01

Somewhere in the vastness of space, a tiny ship carrying two scientists raced towards Valos. Raven's eyes were transfixed on a tablet, where she was already designing upgrades for her bodysuit. She now wore a long black trenchcoat, which completely obscured her metal limbs, as well as a pair of sunglasses to disguise her white eyes.

I hope you've thought this thing through, Trenyn thought aloud, but they couldn't be sure Raven was paying attention. That was the nature of the telepathic abilities of Trenyn's species. Navorans could transmit mental signals to any being that would listen, but they were unable to actually "read" minds. They were, however, extremely receptive to the thought transmissions of other psychic races, which was the only reason Trenyn could hear Raven's weak signals at all.

Trenyn wasn't completely adept with all of their mental abilities; on their homeworld they were considered handicapped. While Trenyn could communicate with ease, they were very poor at using the telekinetic abilities that were common to their people. The highly advanced Navoran telekinesis had resulted in the evolution of a race of beings that rarely used their hands. They used their minds to open doors, to operate machinery, and even to control their vehicles. As a result, computers and other machinery had no external buttons, levers, or handles. It was not a world for someone like Trenyn, who couldn't even open doors on Navor. This is why they had gone to Earth.

They looked down at their four hands and sighed. It seemed ironic that Navorans had so many hands and yet so rarely used them. Navorans had two arms, but each arm split at the elbow to become two forearms. Each hand had two fingers and two thumbs, on opposite sides of the fingers. This configuration of digits made them much more dexterous than other species, and it angered Trenyn that their society squandered this advantage.

"Of course I've thought it through." Trenyn jumped when Raven finally answered. They'd been so lost in thought that they'd forgotten their original statement. "I've thought of nothing else since he did this to me," Raven continued, "and I've been waiting for this chance for too long to back out now." Raven's father had been responsible for everything that had gone wrong in her life. Now that resolution seemed so near, she was becoming anxious.

Raven's father was Teykor Vermon, supreme ruler of the Planet Valos, one of the wealthiest and most splendorous planets in the galaxy. He was also, though it had never been proven, the leader of the largest criminal organization in this galaxy. Raven stared off into space, reliving the day she'd learned the extent of her father's cruelty.

Six years earlier, Raven was fifteen years old and living on Earth. It had been seven years since her mother had taken her from Valos. Raven's mother, Shalia, worked hard to provide her daughter with a good life. They lived in a mansion that had been bought with Vermon hush money. Shalia had long since told her daughter about Teykor's dark business, but Raven still had trouble believing it. Despite repeated threats from her ex-husband, Shalia continued to try to prove his guilt to both Raven and the galaxy.

Late one afternoon, Raven was at her terminal writing a program for school when the front door beeped. Half-turning as her mother answered the door, Raven recognized the visitors as men who worked for her father. Raven had decided it was none of her business and resumed typing when her mother screamed. Raven turned back around just in time to see her mother fall down, covered in blood. One of the men was holding an energy pistol. The other man pointed toward Raven.

"We were told to punish the daughter," he said. "Give her a taste of what will happen to her if she talks."

"Heh, heh," the larger of the two men said, approaching Raven, "she's a pretty little thing. This'll be a pleasure."

Raven's stomach churned. She tried to run past the two hitmen but they knocked her to the floor. "Don't do that," warned the bigger thug, "Now... what have you got for me?" He reached for her.

"You're sick," the smaller man said. "She's just a kid."

"She's old enough..."

"Touch her that way and Vermon will skin us both. He gave me very specific instructions on how to deal with her."

Raven had almost completely blocked out the beating that followed. It was a painful blur, all she could remember was wishing that they would kill her and get it over with. Twenty minutes later – but it felt like hours - Raven lay battered and bruised, unable to move. One of the men pulled a knife from its sheath, and it started to glow a bright white. Raven was frightened, but also slightly hopeful. *Just finish it*, she thought, as he brought the blade closer. She could join her mother and be free from the pain.

She couldn't remember what it was like to enjoy life as she had just one hour before. The knife represented a release to her, and she welcomed it. She knew that these AON knives were hot enough to melt skin and bone on contact. The knife would enter her chest like she was pudding, and then she could rest. But... he was aiming higher than her heart. *Just as well,* she thought. He could cut off her head, then. Unconsciousness would be immediate, and she would never even bleed. But no, the blade was moving towards her shoulder. And as it touched her skin...

Raven snapped back to the present. Trenyn was trying to tell her something. *You shouldn't let bad memories cloud your mind. Instead, you could be thinking about what we're going to do once we get to Valos. They don't let just anyone land there. We need clearance codes...*

"My father will see me," Raven interrupted. "When they hear it's me on the shuttle, my father will give us clearance. He might be surprised that I have limbs now, but I think I can convince him that we're on the same side. Then, once I have his trust, I'll kill him."

'Convince him that we're on the same side?' Trenyn thought loudly, *What about those eyes of his? He can read minds... even control them!*

"I don't think so. Don't forget, I inherited some of his abilities. I can sense things about people when I look into their eyes, but it doesn't work on you. Maybe his power won't work on you either. Or on me."

That's a lot of maybes, Trenyn replied, looking skeptical.

Suddenly the ship shook violently. Raven called up a damage report while Trenyn turned on the viewscreen. They were being attacked by a large red ship with inverted wings.

That's a pirate ship! Trenyn reported.

Raven looked skeptical. "Pirates in space? Like with eye patches and peg legs and all that?" As intelligent as she was, Raven had spent most of her life with her nose buried in a science book. She could build a spaceship from scratch, but had no idea what sort of people you would run into in space. As always, she found people far more complex than machines. She would be the first to admit that she lacked certain "street smarts" associated with space travel. Still, this sounded like a bad joke.

Get that silly image out of your head, Trenyn ordered. *Real space pirates are highly intelligent criminals who make a living by capturing smaller spacecraft. If we don't get away, they'll strip our ship for parts, take any valuables and weapons they can find, hold us for ransom...*

"Ransom? Who would pay for us? Besides, it may be too late." Raven pointed to a sensor. Their vessel was already being restrained by the pirate ship's Levatech emitters. "Our ship has no weapons. How can we fight back?"

Okay, we'll wait for an opportunity. Be ready for anything.

The tiny white ship was grappled by the larger craft's magnetic cables, guiding it into place so that the two ships' airlocks lined up. Their computer's comm system beeped, and Trenyn accepted the call.

A man with an eye patch appeared on the viewscreen. "Ahoy, mateys," he said. "Prepare to be boarded, you scallywags! Surrender now or we'll send ya to Davey Jones' locker."

Raven and Trenyn just stared at each other.

"Just kidding," the pirate said, removing his eye patch and laughing. "Can you imagine if we were really like that? Nah, we hacked into your comms system five minutes ago, and after hearing that last comment about pirates, I couldn't resist."

"So you're not here to rob us?" Raven asked hopefully.

"Oh no, we totally are. But there's no reason we can't have fun with it. Listen, here's what's going to happen. We're going to board your ship. You're going to come with us and we'll put you in a nice cell. We'll tear your ship apart looking for valuables, then have one of our crew pilot your ship to the nearest planet to sell it. If you two are wearing any expensive jewelry, we'll take it. If you're famous or rich, we'll hold you for ransom. Otherwise, we'll drop you on the next planet to fend for yourselves. But if you fight us on any of this, we'll just throw you into space. Cool?"

The airlock doors opened, and three rifle-wielding men pointed their weapons at their new prisoners. The pirates were dressed in normal civilian attire. Cheap, threadbare clothing, but hardly pirate-themed.

Trenyn stared at one of their rifles. As they concentrated, the weapon began to vibrate. The pirate was startled. "What's this?"

No! Raven mentally shouted to Trenyn. *Let's go peacefully. We'll look for a better opportunity later.*

Bloodstone's ship drew close to a warp gate. Whisper watched him from inside the locker. The bounty hunter had stopped the ship, and seemed to be pondering his next move. Then he tapped a few keys. Suddenly all the lights started flashing red, and a klaxon sounded. A computer voice shouted, "Self-destruct activated. You have one minute to reach minimum safe distance."

Whisper tried to open the locker door, but it was locked. She kicked and pounded on the door, but the lock was too strong, and she was too cramped to get much leverage. She was so busy looking for some sort of tool that she didn't even notice that Bloodstone continued calmly sitting at the bridge. As the computer counted down the final ten seconds, Whisper shouted for help.

"Just kidding," Bloodstone said, turning the alarm off. He stood up and strode over to the locker, then unlocked it.

The door opened. "So you did see me," Whisper said sheepishly.

"Whatever concealment device you're using made it look unnaturally dark in there," Bloodstone said. "But it was still impressive. I wouldn't mind a look at the tech later."

"No tech, it's just me," she said.

Bloodstone returned to the controls. "I was just sitting here trying to decide whether to toss you out the airlock now, or after the warp gate. You know they charge by total mass."

"I'll pay you for the ride," Whisper offered. "Just let me off at the next inhabited planet."

"As you wish," Bloodstone said. "But as long as you're here, I'll need your help at the warp gate."

"Where are we warping to?"

Bloodstone sighed. "I'm not completely sure yet. Part of the problem is that they don't even know where Alterra's transmission came from. She wasn't on the station when it exploded. She had to be on a nearby ship, so she could make a getaway, right? Except they were able to estimate the general area where the transmission originated, and they found no record of any ships."

"So… where did the transmission come from?"

"A satellite," Bloodstone said. "Alterra beamed a direct transmission to the satellite, which rebroadcast to the space station. When the station exploded, the satellite self-destructed as well, leaving no evidence. Alterra's ship, already at a safe distance, was able to flee at its leisure."

"How did you…" Whisper began.

"I have data tracking satellites of my own. Her transmission came from a Venaran C112 Cruiser. It was encrypted to look like white noise, but I know how to hack Venaran encryptions. I also tracked the ship's most likely destination: an unlicensed warp gate just a few hours from Earth."

"Isn't that still a dead end? Private gates don't usually keep destination logs. Anonymity is the only reason people use them. They charge more, they're not as safe…" Whisper ticked off the reasons on her fingers.

Bloodstone interrupted. "No, they don't actively keep records. But the software they use tracks destinations if you know how to look for it."

"But that data would be encrypted!"

Bloodstone stared at her. She imagined she could see the smugness through his visor.

* * *

They reached the warp gate in just under three hours. It wasn't exactly a pretty structure. This rectangular space station had exactly one purpose – to transport any ship to any other unlicensed gate in the galaxy, no questions asked. The official gates may have been safer to use, but safety is a relative term to a fugitive. The hanger door slowly slid open as their ship approached, and they entered the giant bay. A notification popped up on the ship's viewscreen: "Incoming Transmission." Before accepting the call, Bloodstone said, "Keep him talking while I hack their database. It won't take but a minute. Flirt or something."

"I don't know how to fl—" Whisper started to complain, but then the caller popped up on the screen.

A bored-looking man with mauve skin stared at them, waiting for them to speak first. When Whisper didn't say anything, he spoke in a thick Venusian accent. "Please transmit your destination request."

Whisper didn't know what to say. "Um… hold on, I've got it around here somewhere…" She pretended to search the console, while Bloodstone transmitted the decryption virus.

"Surely you know where you are going?" the irritated gatekeeper asked.

"The system, sure, but the specific gate I need is… around here somewhere… Say, you have nice eye stalks…" Whisper stammered.

Bloodstone groaned as he examined the data from his virus. This gate didn't get a lot of traffic, and he found Alterra's ship almost instantly. He started to send over the coordinates, then a thought occurred to him. Changing his mind, he sent across a different set of coordinates.

"Don't waste my time. If you can't—" Just then his notification dinged, and he nodded. "Very well, gate G-231, Grunthar System. Transfer the payment and power down all systems for transport."

Bloodstone transferred the payment and began powering

down the systems. As the lights dimmed, Whisper asked, "Why would Alterra go to Grunthar?"

"She didn't. She went to Valos."

Something changed in Whisper's stance when she heard that. "Vermon. I should have known. Wait, then why are we going to…"

"Does it matter? I'm dropping you off on Grunthar."

"Look, I can help you," Whisper pleaded.

"You know, I remember you," Bloodstone said. "You're that carrion hunter who stole the Glymm bounty from me."

"That was a misunderstanding," Whisper said. "I didn't know…"

"I caught him," Bloodstone interrupted. "I tied him up. I only left him so I could nab his accomplice."

"Well, he wasn't tied up when I found him," Whisper said.

"So you say," Bloodstone replied. "I looked you up after that. You tend to pick your hunts based on the crime, not the reward. You keep your head low. You've been a hunter for at least three years, but you're still an unknown. You stowed away on my ship, so I assume you must also be after Alterra Sarr. I just wouldn't picture you on such a high-profile hunt. Why are you here?"

"She killed a lot of good people, and should be brought to justice. If we work together, I'll donate my half to the victims. Can we do that, or are you going to toss me out the airlock?" There was no fear in her voice, and Bloodstone knew it wouldn't be easy to force her off the ship.

Bloodstone sighed. "Not many people get the best of me. I respect your skills. But I work alone. Period. Next time we land, we go our separate ways. I intend to be the one to collect this reward. Don't expect to steal another one from me."

"That's fair," Whisper relented. "We'll split up once we reach Grunthar."

"Actually," Bloodstone said, "I have an idea. You're just

going to drop me off on Grunthar. From there I'm going to hitch a ride to Valos, and you're going to take this ship back to Chirminon."

"If I have this ship, what's to stop me from taking it straight to Valos and catching Alterra myself?"

"The same reason I don't. The Valos defense systems would blow this ship out of the sky as soon as it got close. They know me there, and they'd know why I was there. Besides, I plan to lock the controls so you can only choose from the destinations I allow."

Whisper nodded in agreement. Of course she was hoping to find a way to override Bloodstone's lockout, but she also knew Bloodstone wouldn't even consider handing the ship over if it would be that easy.

The ship warped to gate G-231 and set a course to Grunthar.

01.05 *Transport*

ED.02500.01.01

The cell didn't look like something you would see on a spaceship. There was no high-tech force field or laser grid. An ordinary wall of iron bars separated the cell from the rest of the room. While the cell door did feature an electronic keypad instead of a keyhole, it wasn't enough to offset the rustic feel of this room. This cell could have been on any backwater planet, instead of flying through space.

There were no beds or benches, so the prisoners sat with their backs against the wall. Of course in her new body, Raven was no less comfortable standing than sitting, but since Trenyn was sitting, it felt more natural to sit next to them.

Trenyn stared intently through the bars, concentrating on a computer terminal across the room. They were trying to operate the computer with their mind. *It's no good,* they said telepathically. *Even if I could move the keys, it requires a password.*

"Well... what about me? This body you built for me seems pretty strong. Want me to try..."

Maybe later, Trenyn replied. *Someone's coming.*

A door slid open on the other side of the room. A disheveled young woman entered and timidly approached the bars. It was difficult to tell her age because of her emaciated condition and general filthiness, but Raven estimated her to be in her early twenties. Her blonde hair was cut haphazardly, and her clothing was obviously just some discarded cloth that had been stitched into a wearable shape. All in all, she looked like a living afterthought.

She held a tray of questionable food and a pitcher of grayish water. She set both down just outside the bars, then quickly stepped backward out of arm's reach. Raven and Trenyn eyed the tray, both losing their appetites at the sight of the stale, rotten mess it held.

As the servant turned to leave, Raven spoke up. "Excuse me, can we talk a minute?" The woman turned around and cocked her head questioningly. Raven wasn't sure what she wanted to say. The servant looked timid, and Raven didn't want to scare her off. She studied the woman for a minute. Raven hadn't noticed at first, but the woman sported several large bruises and wore a tight metal collar around her neck. "Listen," Raven said, "We can help you. What's your name?" Raven tried to sound soothing and reassuring, but she was out of practice.

After a moment, the servant carefully answered, "Yna."

"Ee-na? Your name is Yna?" Raven asked, not sure if the servant was answering her question or speaking an alien language.

"Yes, Yna," she confirmed. Yna had an unusual accent, one Raven had never heard before. "I'm not supposed to talk to the prisoners," she continued, and started to turn away again.

"Wait! We can help each other. Help us escape, and I promise we'll take you with us." Yna paused, unsure. "I know they don't treat you well," Raven continued. "They'll do even worse to us. But together, maybe we can get out of here. They won't be able to hurt you ever again."

Yna turned back toward the cell. "I can't leave the ship," she said, pointing at her collar. "This will kill me."

Some sort of tracking collar? Trenyn's telepathic voice caused Yna to jump.

"Probably wired to explode if she moves too far from the control room," Raven said.

...or electrocute her, or there could be some sort of poison injection system... Trenyn continued the thought. *I wonder if we could deactivate it. Yna, can you come closer?*

Yna shook her head and glanced toward a panel on the wall. "They're watching us. I have to go now." She ran out the door without listening to another word.

A small craft was entering the atmosphere of Grunthar.

"Now be on your guard. The Grunthians are a brutish, warlike species." Bloodstone spoke with a lecturing tone that Whisper didn't fully appreciate.

"Seriously?" she snapped back, "You've been watching too many bad sci-fi holos. There's no such thing as a 'warlike species.' Every society has aggressive members and peaceful ones. No species can have one universal attitude! You can't just..."

A harsh voice crackled in on the transmission speakers, interrupting her. It was in a guttural language, but the computer translated automatically. "Attention! You are violating Grunthian airspace. You are hereby sentenced to fifty years of hard labor, after which you will be tortured, mutilated, and killed. Surrender now or your punishment will be more severe. You will follow our courier ships to the docking station."

"You think you're so smart, don't you," Whisper mumbled.

Bloodstone shrugged, then said in a determined voice, "Well, kipa will fly before I let them catch me. Strap in!" Bloodstone pressed a customized button labeled "evasive maneuvers." This pre-programmed function caused the ship to detect and avoid anything moving toward it, including energy blasts and cannon fire, all the while flying at high speed in whichever direction they steered. This function saved them for about four seconds, at which point the overwhelming volleys of cannon fire rocked the ship incessantly.

"We can't take much more! Quick! Get in there!" Whisper could barely hear Bloodstone over the sounds of the ship's instruments exploding.

On the surface of Grunthar, several large, brutish creatures applauded as they watched the tiny ship erupt into a bright ball of flaming debris.

A small IGP patrol ship jetted through space, far from its normal patrol range. Special agent Vik Lambert was following a lead. Actually, it was more of a hunch. He called up some data on his computer. A list of Alterra Sarr's initial demands appeared on the screen. The list included several prisoners whom she had asked to be released. He then cross-referenced their names to see how they might be connected. They were all believed to be members of the Inner Eye, a major criminal group. Though it had never been proven, it was thought that the leader of the Inner Eye was Teykor Vermon. Vik changed his heading to Valos. If Sarr worked for Vermon, she might be there.

Vik felt very fortunate to have this chance. Doctor Eshton had softened up a bit at the last minute and helped him requisition this ship. Eshton convinced his superiors it was for a "field test," and that was pretty close to the truth. Vik was given one week of freedom, after which he would return, whether he found Sarr or not.

He wasn't going to squander this opportunity. Fueled more by anger than a sense of justice, Vik pushed the engines to their limits.

A few kilometers from the Grunthian defense towers, several large pieces of debris slowly sank into a murky pond. One particularly large chunk of detritus suddenly opened up to reveal a tight, human-sized compartment, from which emerged a human, of all things. Bloodstone swam to land and scanned the area for threats. No Grunthians in sight. No Whisper either. But the sound of approaching vehicles echoed in the distance. The bounty hunter was gone by the time they arrived.

Bloodstone arrived at the shipyard a few hours later. It was guarded by a pair of huge soldiers, but they were easy enough to evade. Once inside the fence, no more guards were seen. There were cameras, of course, but Bloodstone had already hacked them. In war, Grunthians were a force to reckon with. But their cybersecurity was a joke.

The freighter wasn't pretty. It looked like it had been pieced together from at least three unrelated vehicles. The cargo bay took up two-thirds of the ship and was obviously of Grunthian design. It was basically a large box with no thought put into the aesthetics. The rest of the ship was a bit sleeker, though it had seen better days. The middle section was a large sphere connecting the cargo bay to the command section. There was a docking port on each side of the sphere, where smaller ships could attach. The front section was more triangular, angling down from the roof and coming to a snub nose.

It was fairly large and would make a big scene exiting Grunthian airspace. Bloodstone had a plan for that, too. Making his way aboard the ship, he crept down the halls, constantly scanning for any occupants. So far it was empty. Finally, he reached the bridge. There was a large command chair in front of the main computer. It was the only thing on the bridge designed for a Grunthian's size. Bloodstone raised a gun and approached the chair.

The chair turned around at his approach. "Shotgun," Whisper said, sitting cross-legged in the oversized chair.

Bloodstone had a reputation for being unshakable, but he had to take a couple of deep breaths before speaking. "We had a deal... when we reached the surface, we would separate."

"We did separate. I got here first, so this is my ship."

"But it was my plan," Bloodstone growled.

"My ship."

"My plan."

"My ship."

"My plan."

Whisper had a knack for reading body language. It was part of her upbringing, and the basis of her fighting style. But she didn't need her skills to see that she was really getting under Bloodstone's skin. The bounty hunter was visibly shaking. "You know, I could have just taken off before you got here," she offered.

"But... hold it. Why did you wait—" Bloodstone was interrupted as a rhino-skinned pilot lumbered into the room. It was more than two meters tall, with natural armor plating. It had four eyes and four arms, two of which were the size of a gorilla's. It was as if nature had dressed this creature for combat. With its larger arms, it clenched its basketball-sized fists and shouted at the bounty hunters. Although it yelled in Grunthian, the meaning was clear.

Bloodstone drew his pistol and fired before the pilot could react. It took three shots to fell the giant, who landed with a thud that shook the room. The creature was still breathing, but out like a light.

"I think he's unconscious," Bloodstone said.

"It might be a she," Whisper said.

"Whatever, let's get out of here." Bloodstone looked over the controls, which were labeled in Grunthian.

"Now you know why I waited for you," Whisper said softly under her breath.

"Your helmet doesn't do real-time text translation?"

"Can't afford the plug-in yet," Whisper said. Working together, they managed to launch the ship. The ugly metal behemoth burst from the dock. Within minutes they had escaped the atmosphere and were on their way.

01.06 Cargo

ED.02500.01.01

Vik's ship was on autopilot. He thumbed through the photos on his comm, pausing on one of them together. They were a high contrast couple – his pasty human face, her pastel feline features. It had been a big shock to his parents. "If you wanted a cat, you could have gone to the pound," his father had said. Racist bastard. Vik wondered if Zhari's parents had said similar things to her. He'd only met them a few times, and they seemed to like him, but who knows what they said behind his back? Of course, they'd be at Zhari's funeral, but Vik wouldn't. He had other plans.

Vik was the most stereotypical cop one could imagine. Human, late twenties, square jaw, pale skin, brown hair, crew cut. Everything about him was peak human, but exceptionally generic - no scars, no blemishes, he could have been pressed from a mold. He and Zhari looked like they were from different worlds, which was technically true, though she'd lived most of her life on Earth. Vik usually only dated humans, but something about Zhari had really stood out. Okay, so it may have started when he found out that humans couldn't get Galeans pregnant, but their affection grew much deeper than their lust. At least, hers did. Vik was never sure if what he felt was actually love, or if he only felt it because he thought he was supposed to feel it. But now, today, knowing that Zhari was lost to him forever, he knew what he felt. Anger. Loss. Rage. Hatred.

His friends, his coworkers, the love-at-least-I-think-it's-love of his life. They had all been taken from him. He had been robbed, and he intended to get even.

...But it was a long flight, and even with his single-minded fury, there was only so long he could watch the blackness of space through his viewscreen.

Well, Vik thought, *As long as I'm out here, let's see what's happening in the area.* He called up some data on local ship activity, hoping someone had seen Sarr's ship. Scanning a screen full of irrelevant data about cargo ships and such, his eyes came to halt at the word "pirates." The computer said that several pirate raids had occurred recently in the area. Vik was excited. Maybe he would have a chance to try out his new abilities sooner than he'd expected.

"Doesn't this crate move any faster?" Whisper stood behind Bloodstone's chair, playing backseat driver. They had just gone through the warp gate to the Valos system, but the planet was still several hours away.

"It wasn't built for speed. If you're so anxious, see if there's a faster ship in the cargo bay."

"I already looked. It's nearly empty, there's just a few large boxes."

Bloodstone visibly relaxed. "Good. Maybe the Grunthians won't chase us. A nearly empty cargo ship probably isn't worth the trouble. It's not like it's in the best of condition or anything."

"But our cargo must have some value if it's being sent to Valos. What do you suppose we're carrying? Surely not just weapons."

"I don't know. Let's go see." Bloodstone engaged the autopilot and stood up.

They strode through the corridors, side by side.

Whisper's footsteps were a silent contradiction to Bloodstone's clumping footfalls against the metal floor. She only seemed to be heard when she wanted to be.

They reached the cargo area, which was large enough to hold two landing shuttles and a good deal of cargo. However, as Whisper had said, it was nearly empty. Just one large metal crate and a few smaller boxes. Bloodstone walked over to the crate and searched the sides for writing. He found a shipping manifest, written in Grunthian.

"It just says 'Gift for Lord Vermon' on it."

"Wait," Whisper said. "How did you know this ship would be going to Valos?"

"Grunthians run weapons back and forth from Valos all the time. I've had this idea in mind long before Alterra, just in case I ever needed a way to get to Valos." He turned back to the crate. "Shall we open it?" He was already drawing his red-bladed AON knife.

"But you don't know what's inside!"

"Exactly. Hence, the reason I'm opening it. Glad you were paying attention." He carefully cut along one edge of the hovercar-sized box.

"There could be a weapon or something inside that might go off." Whisper wasn't actually afraid, she just enjoyed the argument.

"If there's one thing I can handle, it's a weapon." Bloodstone almost had the crate open.

"What if it's a bomb? Maybe the Grunthians were trying to blow up Valos. It could be set to go off when opened!"

"At least that would shut you up. Voilà!" The side of the crate fell to the floor, and they saw a large device inside that they couldn't immediately identify. Bloodstone dismantled the rest of the crate so they could get a better look.

The device was a two-meter long cylinder resting horizontally on a large base with many instruments and gauges on the side. "Maybe it really is a bomb," Bloodstone said in quiet astonishment.

"No, I think it's a cryo tube." Whisper went to the side and flipped a few switches. With a loud hiss, the tube began to open.

"Wait!" shouted Bloodstone. "It could be another Grunthian!" Smoke or steam was escaping from the tube.

"Too late," Whisper replied. "Besides, I think the two of us can handle whatever's in there."

The smoke cleared, revealing a beautiful human woman. She had long red hair and was completely nude. Her eyes opened and she sat up. She looked past Whisper and her eyes settled on Bloodstone. She climbed out of the cryo tube and stood up. Still staring at Bloodstone, she spoke. "You must be Lord Vermon. I am Dervish. You may do with me as you please." Then she embraced him.

"Yeah, I think we can handle it," Bloodstone squeaked.

As she watched the nubile young woman run her hands down Bloodstone's back and kiss his helmet, Whisper felt a twinge of... was that jealousy? Seriously? Whisper was stunned by the emotion. *Back burner,* she told herself. *You have bigger problems right now.* At least Bloodstone didn't appear to be reciprocating the woman's advances.

Bloodstone stepped away from the woman. "Wait a minute! I'm not—"

"You don't like me?" the nymph pouted. "Maybe you would prefer something in a blond?" Dervish's hair suddenly lightened from red to a golden yellow. Even the style changed slightly.

"No, that's not it. Nice trick, though," Bloodstone said. While Whisper couldn't see Bloodstone's eyes, she got the impression he was having trouble keeping his gaze at eye level.

"Then it's her, isn't it," Dervish turned toward Whisper. "She's trying to take you away from me!" She began to change. Her soft pink flesh became coarse green scales and her fingers became claws. She was now a chetal, a type of reptilian cat. Whisper drew her whip as Dervish prepared to pounce.

"No! Stop!" Bloodstone yelled, and Dervish immediately reverted to her redheaded human form.

"Yes, master? How may I serve you?"

"I'm not your master. My name is Bloodstone."

"You aren't Lord Vermon? Then where is he?"

"We'll take you to him. We're headed that way anyway. Come with us and we'll explain." He gestured to Whisper and the three of them began the hike back to the bridge.

Whisper looked Dervish over. "Shouldn't we get her some clothing?"

Dervish answered, "Clothing? If you wish." Her skin changed color, shape, and texture until she looked to be wearing an aqua-colored bodysuit. "Of course, it's still really my skin, but at least I don't look naked. Oh! I'm sorry, I'm talking too much."

Whisper felt immediate compassion towards her. "You're a slave, aren't you? A peace offering from the Grunthian government." Such an arrangement was not uncommon, especially in this part of the galaxy.

"I'm not a slave, I'm a gift. I've been trained since birth to be a companion for Teykor Vermon. I will be his protector, his lover, whatever he needs."

"Do you really want to do this? We could help you, set you free."

"Whisper..." Bloodstone began, not wanting to join her crusade against injustice. It just wasn't the time.

Dervish took this as a cue to speak more quietly. She said softly, "I love Teykor Vermon."

"You've never met him," Whisper insisted. Pointing her thumb at Bloodstone, she added, "A minute ago you thought this dope was Vermon." Bloodstone shot her a look but didn't say anything.

"I love Teykor Vermon," Dervish repeated.

"But what if you could do something else with your life?" Whisper asked.

"Whisper," Bloodstone said, "She's been groomed. The Grunthians brainwashed her to make her more servile. She's been taught since birth that she only has one purpose. This is who she is now."

Still talking to Dervish, Whisper said, "But do you *want* to do this? Do you want to spend your life as a harem girl?"

Dervish faltered. "It's... my job. Does anybody really enjoy their job?"

"I do," said Bloodstone.

"But with your shapeshifting ability," Whisper added, "you could achieve whatever you wish. You can be whoever you want to be. In your case, literally."

"I'll... think it over," Dervish said, though she wasn't sure if she actually would. This discussion made her feel uncomfortable. She'd been taught not to argue, but she'd also been taught not to question her destiny. This was her first real conversation with someone who wasn't a handler, and she found herself unable to pick a position without breaking one of those two rules.

They reached the bridge. Bloodstone was about to sit down at the flight controls when the alarms started going off.

"We're being hacked," Bloodstone said, pointing to some lights on the control panel. "We're losing air in the cargo bay."

Whisper looked at the indicators. The oxygen wasn't leaking out into space, it was just very quickly being sucked into reservoirs designed for this purpose. The hangar functioned as a giant airlock, so that fighters could be launched while still in space.

"And now the hangar bay door is opening by itself," Bloodstone said.

"Can't you counter hack it? I thought you were good at that sort of thing."

"If I had more time, maybe. These people have obviously hacked Grunthian ships before. They're actually using the fighter deployment subroutines against us."

As they watched the viewscreen, a battle-worn ship roughly half the size of the hangar bay floated in. Landing legs extended and magnetized to the floor. The bay door closed again, and the room started refilling with oxygen. A surprisingly pleasant voice came over the ship's speakers. "Greetings, friends! We have control of your ship. If you remain on the bridge, we'll simply take your cargo then be on our way. If you challenge us, we will blast you to pieces."

"Does that actually work on the Grunthians?" Whisper wondered aloud. "They seem like the 'death before dishonor' types."

"Doesn't matter," Bloodstone replied. "I know these pirates. They don't like witnesses. They'll claim they're going to leave peacefully, but they'll hack the ship's life support before they go. Maybe I can bluff them." Into the speaker, Bloodstone said in a gruff voice, "This freighter is en route to Valos, to deliver important cargo to Lord Teykor Vermon, supreme leader of the Inner Eye. You do not want to make an enemy of him."

They heard laughter over the speaker. "You don't sound Grunthian, and I don't believe your Valos story either. I don't care how you came to be in possession of this vessel, but consider yourselves lucky we only want the cargo. Just stay where you are, we'll be done soon."

Bloodstone sighed. "Even if he's telling the truth, they'll change their mind when they see there's no cargo. They'll refuse to leave empty-handed. Get ready for a fight."

Raven and Trenyn felt the pirate ship land. Outside their cell, the outer door opened, and Yna burst into the room. She ran straight up to the bars. "They've targeted another ship. No one is watching us right now, they'll be getting ready to board the other ship."

"This is our chance," Raven said. "Yna, can you get us out of here?"

"I don't have the code," she said. "But I can do this..." She held up her left hand. Her eyes clenched with concentration, and the hand started to glow a bright blue. She touched it to one of the bars, and the metal started to melt.

Raven and Trenyn stood with their mouths open. As Yna worked on the bars, Trenyn asked, *If you can do that, can't you remove the collar?*

Yna had finished melting a gap through the bottom of the bar, and was working on another part towards the top. She looked to be in extreme pain. "The collar is a different kind of metal. I can't melt it."

Yna finished melting off the second bar, leaving a gap large enough for Raven and Trenyn to fit through. Her hand returned to normal, but her skin looked badly sunburned. Her fingernails were gone, and spots of blood were bubbling up to the surface. As she shoved her hand into the folds of her tunic, she noticed Raven's concerned expression. "You get used to it," Yna said, grimacing.

Now freed from the cell, Trenyn examined Yna's collar. *I don't see any obvious electronics... I wonder if I could...* They tugged on the collar experimentally. *Yna, would it detonate if I were to remove it, or only if the collar goes too far from the ship?*

"I don't know," she answered. "I think it's just distance. They never told me not to take it off, because they knew I couldn't."

So odd... I see no clasp, no lock, no mechanisms... I'm not even sure how they put it on you. But this metal is extremely resilient. They looked at Raven. *You want to try?*

Raven gripped one edge of the collar, and tried to bend the metal. She could hear the gears grinding in her metal fingers. "Not going to happen," she said. "Try your telekinesis."

I suppose it's worth a... Before Trenyn could finish the thought, the collar snapped in half, the two pieces flying across the room. Telekinetically manipulating the collar had been so unexpectedly effortless, it was like trying to bash down a steel door that turns out to be made of gelatin. *What in the name of...* they exclaimed, and made the pieces fly into their hand. *This metal... its molecular density is so high that I have no trouble manipulating it. Also...* They examined the collar more closely. *...there are no mechanisms, electronics, or explosives in this at all. The pirates lied to you, Yna. They knew you wouldn't risk running if you thought the collar was deadly.*

Yna looked embarrassed for a moment, then perked up. "Then I'm finally free!"

"Don't celebrate yet," Raven said. "We still have to get out of here. You said they're about to raid another ship? Then I see two options. We can either wait until the pirates have boarded the other ship, then take off in this one..."

Of course they'll leave a few crew members behind, Trenyn interrupted. *We'll have to do something about them.*

"Or," Raven continued, "we wait until the raid is fully underway, sneak onto the other ship after them, hide, and stay hidden until after they leave."

Trenyn looked thoughtful. *Also quite risky. They might take the ship in tow. They might detonate it as they leave. They might raid all the fuel, leaving us dead in space. Yna, what do you know about their modus operandi?*

Yna stared at them blankly.

Have you been with them on a raid? Do you know what they take, and what they leave behind? What do you think would be the safer course of action?

Yna brightened. No one had ever asked her opinion on anything. "Yes, they've taken me on several raids, when they needed me to melt something."

"Will they detonate the ship when they leave?" Raven asked.

"...maybe?" Yna said, shrugging. "I'm always back on this ship by then."

Raven sighed. "You know what? We're taking risks either way. And I doubt we're getting out of here without a fight. I say we head to the bridge, and try to take off."

"Um... there's one other stop we need to make," Yna said. "I have a friend I can't leave behind."

"You're sure it won't attack us?" Raven asked. They were now in another detention room across the hall.

"He hates the pirates. They use shockprods on him," Yna answered. "But I bring him food, and he lets me pet him."

"If you're sure," Raven said skeptically, and Yna melted the bars. She had to remove more bars than last time, to accommodate the occupant's bulk. The beast didn't attack them, but nuzzled up against Yna's side.

"Okay, now I have to do my thing," Yna said. "I hate this part. I only go 'all over' for emergencies." Yna took a deep breath, and Raven could sense that she was not looking forward to this. Yna let her arms go limp. She raised her head and closed her eyes, all the while taking slow, deep breaths. Then she began to shine. Her skin quickly became a bright light blue, and energy traveled in waves across her body.

Her clothing instantly burned off, actually disintegrating into ash. Her feet gently left the floor, leaving a blackened spot where she'd been standing. She was now a creature of pure energy, floating a few centimeters off the ground. Her blue-white skin was difficult to look at without squinting, and she was surrounded by a slight corona of energy. She still retained a human shape, but she no longer had any facial features.

"To the bridge," Raven said.

01.07 *Convergence*

ED.02500.01.01

While the majority of the pirates remained in the cargo bay looking for anything valuable, a boarding party was sent to take control of the ship. Fifteen pirates made their way down the hall toward the freighter's main bridge. Then the pirate in front stopped, noticing movement up ahead in the darkened hallway. "Slow up a second. You see something?"

Another pirate squinted and suddenly dropped his weapon. The lead pirate turned to watch him run in the opposite direction. "What in bloody—" he murmured, turning back to the hallway. He blinked. Coming down the hall, straight towards them, was something strange. All the pirate could make out was a large number of arms and legs converging on a central body. The lead pirate nearly fainted but decided to run instead.

The creature had six arms and four legs that spread out in every direction from its body. Some of the appendages grabbed the floor, the walls, and even the ceiling as the monster swiftly climbed its way through the hall. Its demonic head stared at them with an evil glare, its tooth-filled mouth looking famished. If the pirates had been more educated or less horrified, they might have recognized the creature as a wirze, a cave-dwelling carnivore found on many planets throughout the galaxy. This wirze was smaller than the norm, but it was still more than adequate to scare off the pirates.

The pirates scrambled back in horror. One of them tripped and screamed as the creature came upon him. As a last-ditch effort, he hurled his rifle at the terrifying animal. The gun hit it in the side of the head, and the creature immediately crashed to the floor. Then it reverted to its natural state, that of a scarlet-haired woman with a bruise now forming on her left cheek.

"We've been duped, boys!" the fallen pirate called, climbing to his feet. His retreating comrades stopped and turned back. "Now lookee here, what 'ave we got..." Dervish raised her head nervously as the pirates approached her.

Then four small explosions sounded, and six of the pirates were ripped to shreds. Bloodstone stood at the end of the hall, one hand on a Grunthian mini-cannon mounted on a tripod.

The nine remaining invaders gasped and dove to the floor. One of them grabbed the still-weak Dervish by the neck with one hand and drew his gun with the other. "Try and shoot now!" he yelled, using Dervish as a shield.

"No problem," Bloodstone responded, swiveling the cannon.

"Bloodstone, don't you dare!" a voice cried out, and Whisper appeared from a darkened corner behind the pirate. With a quick THWIK she slashed her whip and it wrapped around the pirate's neck.

Bloodstone sighed. "You ruined my bluff," he said, releasing the cannon.

Whisper's captive released Dervish and tried to raise his weapon. Whisper quickly squeezed part of the whip's handle. The whip glowed yellow for a split second, and the pirate was electrocuted. He fell to the floor, whimpering and smelling of burnt flesh. Realizing that Bloodstone wouldn't fire, the other eight pirates closed in on Whisper.

One pirate lunged at Whisper only to be met with a kick to the ribs. Whisper ducked another pirate's punch, grabbing him and using his own force to propel him into one of his teammates. Another pirate tried to draw his pistol, but another kick sent the gun sailing. After ducking another punch and foot-sweeping a pirate, Whisper jumped high into the air and kicked one of her attackers in the face.

Whisper's fighting style had a dance-like rhythm to it, as if it had been choreographed. Whisper saw the fight as a high-speed puzzle in which she had to find the perfect counter-move for every move. Her ability to read body language meant that she knew what attack was coming before it even started.

Bloodstone started to come help, but then stood still and watched the fight, as if in awe. All eight pirates lay immobile, still breathing but badly hurt. "Not bad..." Bloodstone began.

"Can the sarcasm. There's more of them in the landing bay." Whisper's mind was still in "battle mode," and she was far down the hall before Bloodstone could react.

"Wait for me!" he called after her, and followed at a quick pace.

Dervish sat on the floor, holding her hand to her cheek. She could change her shape, color, texture, even her size to a small extent, but not her strength. The scare tactic had almost worked, but she didn't know if she was going to be of any real help to them. And after her near execution by Bloodstone, she didn't know if she even wanted to help them.

No, she thought, *he has the right*. She was just a slave girl, after all. It was her job to follow orders, not to have opinions. Right now the closest thing she had to a master was Bloodstone, and Whisper was the closest thing she had to a friend. And they were about to be in danger. It was her job to protect them. She stood up and followed them towards the cargo bay.

* * *

In the landing bay, a few dozen pirates stood ready in case the first team needed backup. Some were exploring the nearly-empty room, looking for any valuable loot. They had already discovered the cryo tube but found no use for it.

Aboard the pirate ship, two weapons officers stared at a display screen. It showed the door that led from the cargo bay to the main hallway. "Now," one explained, "We have our guns aimed at the door, see. If anything comes through there that ain't one of us, we blast 'im."

As if on cue, the doors on the screen opened, revealing the two bounty hunters. Immediately the pirates outside the ship reacted, firing their weapons at the doorway. Bloodstone and Whisper ducked back into the hallway, taking cover behind the edges of the open doorway. Occasionally Bloodstone fired a few shots back at the pirate crowd. The two weapons officers aboard the craft prepared to fire. "This'll hit 'em," he remarked, knowing that it would take out the entire wall, bounty hunters and all. He powered up the cannon.

Before he could fire, however, there was a loud noise behind him. The two pirates turned to face Yna, two ex-prisoners, and a black cat the size of a lion. Yna flew forward and put her hand on one pirate's face. In seconds his face was one big third-degree burn, and he fell to his knees gurgling, his face smoking. The other pirate was so shocked that he didn't even have time to void his bladder before the enormous cat sliced his face to ribbons.

"Tell me again," Raven said, "why you needed our help." She wasn't actually expecting an answer. She knew that Yna couldn't speak in her current form.

Another pirate entered the room. "Why aren't you firing at—" He stopped when he saw the situation, and drew his pistol. He fired two shots at Yna, but they were simply absorbed into her form. Raven was closest to the pirate, and she grabbed him by the arm. Her metal body moved much more quickly than she expected. She threw the man across the room, and he hit the wall so hard that it shattered his skull. Raven was surprised by the power of her suit.

The amount of emotion you put into your movements makes a difference, Trenyn thought to her. *Be careful.*

Yna changed back to her human form and collapsed on the floor. As the last bit of smoke wisped from her skin, Raven saw that Yna no longer had any hair and was bleeding from her fingers and toes. Yna managed to pull herself up to her hands and knees and then threw up on the floor. "I'll be... Hurgh... okay in a minute..." she rasped, and then regurgitated more blood and bile.

The large feline rubbed up against Yna, trying to comfort her. It made a confused trilling sound.

"The transformation takes a lot out of her," Raven said plainly, fascinated.

Looks like it burns off anything on her that isn't living, Trenyn added. *Hair, fingernails, clothing, eyelashes... probably her stomach lining, judging by the nausea..."*

Raven took off her overcoat and put it on Yna. Upon seeing Raven's body for the first time, Yna's eyes grew wide. "You're a robot?" she asked.

"No, actually, this is just..." Raven trailed off. "Later. Obviously we've all got a lot more explaining to do about who and what we are. But right now I think we'd best try to get this ship moving before any pirates come back aboard."

"Right, right," Yna said softly. She sat down at a flight terminal. "Blazes. It requires a password."

Trenyn sat down next to her. *Give me a few minutes, I think I can break it,* they thought to everyone.

Bloodstone was fighting a losing battle. Crouched behind the door frame, he managed to pick off any pirate who ventured closer, but the overwhelming energy fire coming through the doorway meant that he couldn't keep this up forever. Whisper was gone, she had vanished into the shadows a few minutes earlier, surely to pop up again when she felt the time was right. Dervish was huddled beside him, obviously scared. She wasn't used to battle, and it showed in the way she shivered.

Dervish felt disgusted with herself, and was sure Bloodstone must hate her. Here she was, having just sworn to protect this man with her life, and now she was too frightened to move. She was the one being protected, the exact opposite of her job.

Bloodstone was considering crawling through a maintenance shaft when all the gunfire stopped. Confused, Bloodstone experimentally held his gun out in the doorway to see if anyone shot at him. "This is it," Bloodstone muttered, "Whisper has gone out there and defeated the entire army by herself, and now I have to kill her, because I hate other people being better than me."

The ship lurched a little. "Docking initiated," an automated voice said in Grunthian. There was a sound of a hatch opening in the distance.

"Another one?" Bloodstone mused. He heard footsteps, but not from the cargo bay. A police officer came running down the hall from Bloodstone's right. They both seemed surprised to see each other.

"Aren't you that bounty hunter?" Vik asked. "I thought this ship was under attack by pirates."

"That way," Bloodstone said, pointing toward the cargo hold.

Aboard the pirate craft, Trenyn had just found the access code when the computer alerted them to police presence. "Docking where? I don't see anything," Raven said, looking out the side windows of the pirate craft.

Perhaps this ship has multiple landing bays, Trenyn guessed. *Or external docking ports.*

"What's going on?" Yna asked, buttoning up the shirt she'd taken from one of the dead weapons officers.

Raven, now back in her overcoat, filled her in. "The computer says an IGP craft has docked nearby."

Through the viewport, they watched as Vik stepped into the cargo bay.

Though he was ridiculously outnumbered, Vik stood confidently and held up his badge. He spoke into his comm unit, using it as an amplifier. "Attention pirates! You are under arrest for attempting to capture a Grunthian freighter. Throw down your weapons and surrender now!"

Technically, the planet Grunthar wasn't a member of the Galactic Nations, and therefore wasn't covered by the IGP Protection Act. And the Valos system was well out of IGP jurisdiction. But Vik hoped the pirates would be intimidated enough to surrender anyway.

They were not. The pirates in the cargo hold looked at each other, looked back at Vik, raised their weapons, and opened fire.

"Is he really all by himself?" Raven asked.

Let's go help him, Trenyn sighed.

"Won't the police arrest me too?" Yna asked.

"Not if we show him we're on his side," Raven said. "Let's go."

Raven's eyes lingered on the three dead pirates scattered about the bridge, particularly the one she'd killed. This wasn't her. She had devoted her life to helping people. But what did she think was going to happen when she finally got her hands on her father?

I know what you're thinking, Trenyn thought to her. *Come to terms with it later. Right now someone needs our help.*

For all the firepower the pirates had aimed at the lone IGP officer standing in the doorway, they were expecting to see an unrecognizable charred corpse when the smoke cleared. Instead, there was nothing where the cop had been, not even a pile of ashes.

Vik dropped down from the ceiling, firing three shots with his stun gun, two of them hitting pirates. The pirates opened fire again, once again missing their mark. Vik leaped straight up, fully avoiding the barrage. This time he did not come down.

As the smoke cleared, the pirates squinted to locate the officer. Vik was upside down, on the ceiling, standing just as if he were on the ground. To any upside-down observer, he would have appeared perfectly normal.

The pirates were stunned once again, giving Vik time to fire three shots with his pistol before they recovered. All three shots found their targets, and three pirates collapsed as the rest of the group returned fire.

Vik stayed one step ahead of the blasts. Using the power of his Levatech implants as well as his own gymnastic skills to the best of his ability, he leaped from ceiling to wall to floor and back to wall again. Doctor Eshton would have been proud. Actually, Doctor Eshton would have been panicking. Ricocheting from wall to wall and periodically firing back, Vik hoped he could keep this up. It would only take one lucky shot, and this game would be over.

"Look at him fight!" Yna said, as she and her friends exited the pirate craft. She was awestruck by Vik's amazing feats.

"Let's do this," Raven said, and ran down the ramp and into the crowd. Grabbing one pirate from behind, she swung him like a club, knocking two others high into the air. Yna once again transformed into her alternate form and joined the battle.

Bloodstone could see that the cavalry had arrived, even if he didn't know them. Now that the odds were in his favor, he rushed headlong into battle. Dervish soon followed, overcoming her fears and changing her form to that of a grotesque monster. Whisper finally emerged from a shadowed corner to participate in the fracas.

The pirates still outnumbered their foes, but not for long at this rate. While those opposing the pirates didn't know each other, they fought together well. Bloodstone, Whisper, and Dervish worked their way into the center of the crowd, using fighting finesse and surprise tactics to thin out the small army. Raven, Trenyn, Yna, and the cat worked at the outer edges of the pirate mass, and all the while Vik drew the pirates' attention with his airborne attacks.

The pirates soon realized the tide had turned. "Retreat!" one shouted, and the survivors swarmed back into their ship. Once again, the cargo bay started losing air as the hatch prepared to open. Only this time, the pirates didn't have the patience to wait for the air pressure to equalize. Unconcerned about the fates of those in the cargo bay, they overrode the freighter's safety protocols and commanded the hatch to open immediately.

As the rear hatch inched upwards, the air started blowing out of the room. Pirate corpses slid across the floor. "Everyone to the hallway!" Whisper shouted, but it was easier said than done.

Vik stretched his hand toward the doorway and used his Levatech implants to pull himself toward the hall. Once through the doorway, he held onto the wall with one hand, and stretched out his other hand toward the rest of the people still in the cargo bay. First, he pulled a very confused Dervish to him.

It was windy in the hallway as well, and Dervish had to hold onto a pipe running down the wall. She reformed her left hand into a tentacle, wrapping it around the pipe so she wouldn't be blown back into the cargo bay. Then she transformed her right hand into another tentacle, making it as long as she could manage, and reached out for the others.

Once Trenyn was in the hallway, they attempted to use their telekinesis to help Vik and Dervish save the others. They were hoping that their mental powers would improve in a crisis. But it was to no avail. Instead, they had to slip into the side hallway and hold on.

As the rushing air buffeted Yna, her power faded. This left her so weak she could barely stand, much less fight the airflow. An unconscious pirate blew past her, his arm tripping her as he slid past. Yna fell forward, but rather than hit the floor, she found herself in Vik's gravitational pull. Once she was in the hallway, Dervish helped her get into the side hall, where Trenyn held onto her tight.

And so it went with the others – Raven, Whisper, and the cat each made it out of the cargo bay with the help of their new allies. The last holdout was Bloodstone, who crouched against the cryo tube. It was the only object in the cargo bay not getting blown out into space. Either it was just too heavy, or it had a magnetic base.

Bloodstone held on tight, air rushing past him. The outer hatch was almost completely open, and Bloodstone watched as the pirate ship flew out of the cargo bay. He was too far for Dervish to reach, but Vik pulled at the lone bounty hunter. For a second, Bloodstone resisted Vik's pull, holding on to the cryo tube even more tightly. It was tough for the hunter to trust others, and the thought of getting rescued by someone else was loathsome.

But that was no reason to die. Bloodstone finally let go of the cryo tube and trusted in the officer's strange power. Once everyone was in the hallway, they closed the hatch to the cargo bay. Everyone breathed a sigh of relief.

"Not very good safety protocols," Raven noted.

"We were hacked, they probably overrode those systems," Whisper said.

Vik turned to Bloodstone. "Is this your ship?" he asked.

"It is now," Bloodstone said. His disdain for authority figures came across in his body language.

"This is a Grunthian ship. If you stole it..." Vik knew who Bloodstone was by reputation, and he wasn't fond of bounty hunters. Even if he wasn't obligated to help the

Grunthians, he wanted to see justice done.

"If I stole it, then it's mine now. And if you want it..." Bloodstone reached for his holster. Vik did the same.

Whisper stepped between them. "To your corners a sec, guys. Vi—" Whisper interrupted herself. She recognized Vik, but he wouldn't know her. "Officer," she continued, "Bloodstone can help you out. He can find Alterra Sarr."

"I don't need help from the likes of him," Vik protested.

"And I work alone," Bloodstone added.

At this point, Raven, whose party had been watching the escalating disagreement, broke in. "Excuse me," she said, "If you could just drop us off at your next stop..."

Bloodstone only spared her a second's glance. "This ship isn't stopping until we reach Valos."

Raven and Vik both snapped to attention. "Valos?" they both asked simultaneously.

Perhaps, Trenyn projected, startling nearly everyone with a telepathic interjection, *we should find a more comfortable place to discuss this.*

01.08 *Alliance*

ED.02500.01.01

The group reached the bridge, with multiple conversations going on at once. "Everyone, this is what we're going to do." Bloodstone kept trying to exercise some sort of control over these interlopers. "This is my ship. Now, I'll be happy to drop you off at the nearest..."

"It's not your ship, though," Vik said. "It's a Grunthian ship."

"They owe me a ship, after they destroyed the Bloodhawk."

"What's the Bloodhawk?" Dervish asked.

"The ship Whisper and I took to Grunthar. Now I don't..."

"You called it the Bloodhawk?" Whisper asked. "Please tell me you don't own a car called the Bloodmobile."

"No," Bloodstone sighed. Then he mumbled, "Not anymore..."

"You have no more right to this ship than..." Vik started to say. The ship suddenly rocked violently. Alarm klaxons sounded, and red lights flashed. "...the pirates," Vik finished.

"They're firing at us," Whisper said, running to a viewscreen.

Turning to Trenyn, Raven asked, "What about that surprise you left them?"

Any minute now, Trenyn replied.

The ship rocked a few more times. "What's the damage?" Whisper asked.

Bloodstone's fingers flew over the controls. "Superficial so far, but we can't take too many more hits like that."

Then the attack stopped. Everyone held in a breath as they waited for another explosion, but none came. Bloodstone checked the scanners. The pirate ship was floating dead in space.

"There it goes," Raven said.

I left a virus in their mainframe, Trenyn explained. *Should take out everything – propulsion, weapons, all of it. They're going to be too busy restoring life support to get their other systems online any time soon.*

"Nice work," Bloodstone said appreciatively. It was rare for the bounty hunter to compliment anyone. "But," he continued, "I still want all of you off of my ship. There's a police cruiser currently docked on the starboard docking port. You can all use that."

"A police cruiser won't make it anywhere near Valos," Whisper said. "It's out of IGP jurisdiction. They'll blast it to pieces the minute it gets close."

"I was planning to mask the IGP signature when I got closer," Vik said. "It has an undercover mode that prevents it from being..."

"I don't care," Bloodstone interrupted. "Take the cruiser and go wherever you want, just stay out of my way. I'm not your chauffeur."

"I'm afraid you are, for now," Raven said, studying the damage report on the computer viewscreen. "The police cruiser was destroyed in that last attack."

Bloodstone pushed Raven aside and examined the screen. "Damn," he said. "Okay, new plan. I'll take the lot of you to Valos, but once we get there, you're on your own. We all go our separate ways, I don't want to know you, and I definitely won't help you. Alterra Sarr is my prize, and no way am I going along on any vendetta against Vermon."

Everyone murmured in agreement.

Whisper added, "It will be a few hours before we reach Valos. I don't know about the rest of you, but I haven't slept since... before EarthStation 1 exploded." Her shoulders fell a bit, mentioning the explosion out loud. "If anybody wants to rest up, there's some crew quarters a few decks down."

All disputes having been settled, or at least postponed, the band dispersed. Bloodstone remained behind, claiming he wanted to monitor any other pirate activity in the area. Whisper suspected that the actual reason he stayed at the controls was to make sure no one else did. Or possibly to keep from getting to know the others better. No sense forming attachments.

Three decks down, the rest of the group explored the hallways to find suitable temporary living quarters. By now they had introduced themselves to each other, and were now making small talk.

Vik fell into pace beside Raven and Trenyn. Yna was currently wearing Raven's trenchcoat, and the sight of Raven's metal body piqued Vik's curiosity. "So, Raven, are you some kind of cyborg?" he asked.

Raven, in mild annoyance, gave him the quick version of her life story. "I lost my limbs a few years ago, and Trenyn built me a robotic body."

"Sounds like you've been through a lot. Want to sit down sometime and talk about it?"

Raven was only partially successful in masking her disgust at Vik's invitation. "I've thought about it enough," was all she said.

Vik was hurt by her tone of voice. Then Trenyn mentally told him, *She doesn't like men.*

"Trenyn!" Raven exclaimed indignantly.

Vik's eyes widened. Then, to Trenyn, he asked, "But she likes you?"

I am not male, they replied. *My species only has one sex.*

"So…" Vik asked cautiously, "do I call you he or she?"

I tend to use they/them pronouns for my species, but you may use whatever makes you comfortable.

Looking confused, Vik asked, "Yeah, but… I mean… what have you got, you know, down there?" He made a vague gesture toward his crotch.

We have…

"Don't answer that," Raven interrupted.

I'm not offended. Knowledge is —

"He doesn't care about knowledge," Raven said. "In his mind there are two boxes, and he wants to know which to put you in."

"Hey, that's not fair," Vik said. "I'm open minded. I've even dated a Galean. You don't know me at all."

Raven sighed. She lifted her sunglasses and looked into Vik's eyes. Then she shook her head. "You're right. I don't know you. But I know your type. And I don't plan on knowing you long enough to explain all the reasons I don't want to know you better."

Vik looked confused, then angry. He stuck his tongue out. Trenyn's face flashed yellow with shock. Navorans didn't have a lot of social taboos, but that was one of them.

Vik fell behind the pair and found himself walking beside Yna and her giant cat. Vik had seen her change back to her human form in the cargo bay, and asked her a few questions about it.

"I don't know how I became like this," Yna said. "Maybe I'm a crossbreed. Maybe there's a race of energy beings out there, and one mated with a human."

"That doesn't seem likely. At least not without an outside source of genetic engineering," Vik said thoughtfully. He was reminded of Doctor Eshton, who would have loved this conversation. "What's the deal with the cat?"

"I call him Panther. The pirates picked him up on a planet somewhere. He's very smart." She didn't know what else to say, so she asked, "What about you, Vik? How do you jump so high?"

"I have complete control over my gravity. It's part of an experiment the IGP was doing. They gave me these implants, using the same technology as tractor beams and artificial gravity, like on this ship. It's sort of a 'push and pull' thing. I can will myself to push away from one surface and pull myself to another. It was originally designed so that the IGP could have all-purpose soldiers who could fight on any planet or moon. But so far, I'm the only recipient who was one hundred percent successful." He spoke proudly, hoping to impress her.

"What about the other... uh... recipients?" Yna asked, not entirely sure she wanted to know the answer.

"Most of them had to have the implants removed. A few died, and a couple still have the implants but can't use them. Another was paralyzed, and one guy just disappeared."

"Disappeared?" Yna asked.

"Yeah. He was a strange guy, a Glorkan, I think," Vik remembered. Noticing her vacant expression, he explained, "Glorkans are a species of people with a single large eye on a stalk instead of a head. Anyway, this guy, his name was Analon, came through all the surgery just fine. Then, when they tried to test his implants, he just vanished. He was just sort of... sucked into thin air. There was this noise, like a pop, and everything in the room was pulled toward the spot where he had been, like... as if he had created a vacuum. He still hasn't been found."

"Why did you go through this if it's so dangerous?" Yna was beginning to show concern for the police agent.

"It's part of being a cop," Vik answered, his ego boosted by Yna's fascination.

Raven and Trenyn picked a room to share. Vik entered another room, and Yna and Panther entered another together. Last in line, Whisper and Dervish had been having a conversation of their own.

"So, you can turn into anything you can imagine?" Whisper was asking her.

"Kinda. I can't really change my size much, it's always still the same amount of 'me' here, no matter what I turn into."

"So your mass always remains constant," Whisper clarified.

"...Right," she said, though she didn't sound sure. "So if I change into something smaller, like a chetal, or something larger, like a wirze, I'm still just as heavy."

"Your molecules must just change their density when you change size."

"Sure," Dervish said, not really understanding some of those words. "But when I change my shape, it's still me. I mean, I look different, but... well, for instance, I could turn into a dragon, but I couldn't breathe fire."

"So you only change your size, shape, texture, and color," Whisper concluded, "but not your chemical composition."

"I guess..." This conversation was way over her head. Whisper could expect nothing more from her. Dervish's entire education had been based around pleasing Lord Vermon. Whisper wouldn't hold it against her or let it stand in the way of a possible friendship.

Dervish found a room that suited her and they separated.

Yna looked around her room. It wasn't much, but compared to her accommodations on the pirate ship, it was luxurious. The bed was soft, and there were clean clothes in the locker. She took off Raven's trenchcoat and tried on a plain gray jumpsuit. It was a little loose, but it would do. Still dizzy from the fighting and her transformations, she lay down on the bed and was out like a light.

The bed wasn't big enough for Panther too, but at least the floor was clean. He curled up beside the bed and napped.

Once in her room, Raven relaxed and opened the chest of her

artificial body. Then her metal arms reached in and pulled her real body from the cybernetic one. Though she was no longer in the robotic form, she still had complete control over it. It was harder to control the suit from this angle. She'd gotten used to thinking of the suit's limbs as her limbs, so holding herself outside of it was a bit disorienting. It was a bit like trying to apply makeup with a funhouse mirror. Not that she ever went to funhouses. Or wore makeup.

She willed the machine to carry her limbless body into the restroom. As she urinated, she mentally designed three different versions of a waste system for a future suit upgrade. It was how she saw the universe. No matter how good something was, there was always room for improvement.

She considered the shower, and mentally projected a question to the next room. *Yes, it's waterproof*, Trenyn answered. Raven had the robot body assist her in a quick shower before returning to the main room.

The body set her down on the bed next to Trenyn, who helped tuck her in. Its tasks finished, the body stood in the corner, becoming a rigid, headless statue.

As Raven attempted to take a nap, her thoughts turned to the earlier conversation with Vik. More specifically, she thought of Trenyn's statement, that she disliked men. She had never given it much thought, but looking back, she recalled many instances over the years since the attack in which she displayed more hostility towards males than females. Trenyn must have picked up on this, even if Raven herself had not.

But then, she felt she had every right to her opinion. She had never known men to be anything but brutish backstabbers. Her father and his henchmen were responsible for her mother's death, as well as Raven's dismemberment.

She was just now realizing how this had affected her. She didn't indiscriminately hate all males, but she did find that she was much more comfortable in the company of women than with men. She wasn't particularly attracted to women, but she wasn't attracted to men, either. Masculinity now disgusted her.

This was why she felt comfortable with Trenyn. They had met in college, a few years after her attack. Both were science majors, and Trenyn reminded her more of a mobile brain than an actual man or woman. Trenyn was just effeminate enough to make Raven feel safe. Their personalities meshed so well that it seemed their friendship was meant to be. As lab partners, they worked together smoothly. Trenyn was slightly smarter and much more analytical, while Raven was more creative and saw new possibilities more readily.

They had no physical attraction toward each other, though they had experimented with dating in the past. In any event, their bodies would have proven incompatible if their relationship had progressed to that point. Raven was glad that they were just friends.

But now it dawned on her that she'd ruled out both men and women as candidates for potential relationships. She hadn't done so intentionally, but now that she thought about it, she just couldn't imagine herself with a romantic partner. It had never bothered her before, but the realization that it would never happen still felt like a punch to the gut. Was she missing out? Would she regret it later in life?

Even though Trenyn was lying right next to her, Raven suddenly felt very alone.

Whisper entered her room and locked the door. The room didn't look like it had been used in a long time. It was obviously not of Grunthian design. There was a bed, a small table with two chairs, a desk, and a clothes locker, all sized for a human. But Whisper was too preoccupied to think about the history of this ship. She went straight to the restroom, removed her helmet, and looked in the mirror.

Ice blue eyes stared back at her. Short, black hair framed the pale skin of her face. It was a young face, considered conventionally attractive by the standards of most humanoid species. It could have been the face of a model, but for now it was the face of a fugitive.

Alterra Sarr was born on Auroris. The Aurorans were a xenophobic people, who hid their society underground to avoid being discovered by outsiders. As a dutiful citizen, Alterra learned all the Auro-Chi traditions. She mastered their dance-like fighting style, she followed their moral code, and she even got engaged to bring two families together.

But she always wanted more. Her planet was so limited, its citizens so close-minded. She didn't want to get married to a near stranger, just to raise the next generation of conformists, another cog in the wheel of tradition. She wanted to see the universe. She wanted to know what her elders were afraid of.

So when a ship of explorers using experimental warp tech stumbled upon her planet, she helped them escape. The elders would have executed the visitors to prevent the planet's location from being known, if not for Alterra. Still loyal to her people, she convinced the astronauts to wipe the location of Auroris from their ship's flight records. At this moment, even Alterra wasn't sure where her home planet was.

The explorers took her to Earth, where she experienced a huge amount of culture shock. There was so much to see, do, and learn. So many interesting people to meet. But there were a lot of bad people as well, more than she thought there would be. Why was evil so prevalent? Her culture didn't use money, so the lengths people would go to acquire it astounded her. The thought of actually killing someone for something as worthless as money... it just didn't make sense, and the thought made her sick. But so did the thought of killing someone just to keep the location of her planet a secret.

She joined the IGP in the hopes of helping people. She found their training a useful complement to her own martial arts skills, but the actual job was a bit of a letdown. She saved a few lives, but the limits of the law often prevented her from going after the true villains. So she cut her IGP hours to part-time, and started moonlighting as a bounty hunter. Unlike most hunters, she wasn't in it for the money, so she only took jobs that aligned with her moral compass.

The more vile the target, the more she wanted to take the case. About a year ago, she became aware of Teykor Vermon, ruler of Valos, and rumored to be the leader of a crime syndicate known as the Inner Eye. Alterra wanted nothing more than to take him down. She tried on many occasions, both as an officer and as a bounty hunter. But he was resourceful, and always had ways of covering his tracks. In her zeal to catch him, she'd gotten a bit reckless, and apparently Vermon had noticed her. At one point he even offered her a job, but she turned him down.

She felt a tremendous amount of guilt over EarthStation 1. All those lives lost… It had to be Vermon's doing, he was the only one powerful enough to pull that off. Did he really kill all those people just to frame her? So she would have to go on the run, and stop going after him? The thought brought tears to her eyes. *If I had just left him alone…*

No! You can't think like that, Alterra thought. *It's not all about you. Destroying the station left the IGP in chaos, which has to be a boon for the Inner Eye. He was probably planning to destroy the station anyway, then saw the opportunity to frame you. You can't blame yourself for his actions.*

She wiped her eyes. *So where do I go from here?* It had been five Earth years since she'd left Auroris. Would she go back if she could? She stared into her own eyes, looking for answers. She was on the run, falsely accused of a terrible crime, and part of her did miss the safety of her homeworld. But no. Even a short life of freedom was preferable to bonds of Auroran tradition.

Her only option was to go to Valos. Somehow get proof that she was framed, and that Vermon was responsible. But even so, was hitching a ride with Bloodstone the safest way to get there? If anyone was capable of figuring out she was Alterra, it was Bloodstone. But safety was relative. Right now, the entire galaxy was looking for her, and she was in danger no matter where she was.

But there was something she could do about that. In addition to being able to absorb sound and manipulate shadow, Aurorans had another genetic trick up their sleeves. She watched her face in the mirror and concentrated. Gray splotches appeared on her cheeks, spreading across her face. All over her body, her peach tones lost their hue, until her skin was a dark gray. Then she concentrated on her eyes, the blue giving way to a deep purple.

She couldn't do anything about her facial features, and would have to keep wearing masks. Facial reconstruction was right out. There wasn't a plastic surgeon in the galaxy who didn't know her face right now, and allowing one to use anesthesia on her was a bad idea. But at least this change of skin tone would give her an extra layer of protection. Maybe she could get away with a mask that only showed her eyes. Even if she were unmasked, people would have to look twice to recognize her.

She hoped.

01.09 *Arrival*

ED.02500.01.02

The Grunthian freighter now neared its destination. As Valos grew larger and larger on the viewscreen, the cargo ship slowed until it finally stopped. The freighter sent out a signal to announce its arrival, a customary but unnecessary action. The detection stations surrounding Valos had been well aware of their impending arrival for quite some time. So far all was going well, according to Bloodstone's plan.

A large ship approached. The closer it came, the more colossal it seemed, less of a ship and more of a mobile space station. When it finally halted, it dwarfed the Grunthian vessel. This perimeter ship was easily a hundred times the size of the freighter.

"Just stick with the plan," Bloodstone said, and he and six others left the control room.

"Lord Vermon! It's the freighter from Grunthar. It has finally arrived."

"That freighter was reported stolen. I received the transmission myself," spoke a dignified but harsh voice.

"But Lord, why would anyone steal a cargo ship and still deliver the cargo?"

"Just put it on my viewscreen, you imbecile."

The screen, which had previously displayed an image of the freighter, now showed the ship's main bridge. A single Grunthian pilot sat in the command chair.

"Lord Vermon of Valos," the Grunthian said, "we present you with a gift from our leader, the Grag Prime Arak... no, Arathnon."

"I was told your ship was stolen," Vermon said.

"Yes, Lord Vermon. But we have regained control and have punished those involved," the Grunthian replied quickly.

"You have clearance. Please link to our docking beacon," Vermon said politely and succinctly. Then he had his comm officer end the transmission.

"Speaks terribly good English for a Grunthian," Vermon remarked.

With the transmission now finished, the Grunthian pilot changed form to that of a red-haired human woman. Dervish's shipmates re-entered the room. "He's making us land in that ship," she told them.

"I heard," stated Bloodstone. "Not exactly what I planned, but it's a start. If Sarr works for Vermon, she could be on that ship. Let's take her in."

The freighter slowly approached the immense docking bays of Vermon's mothership.

Once the freighter was within range to do so, the mothership took over its controls and guided it into one of the landing bays. This was a precaution Vermon took with all arriving ships, not just suspicious Grunthian freighters that had previously been reported stolen. With this ship, however, Vermon went a step further. After the freighter landed, and the outer hatch sealed shut, the mothership filled the freighter with sleeping gas. Aboard the cargo ship, all but two of the passengers fell unconscious.

Lord Teykor Vermon entered the landing bay. He was a

tall, regal man, with long gray hair and a commanding stature. His black emperor's garb and bone-white eyes only added to the intimidating air he gave off naturally. He appeared distinguished, well-groomed, and very evil.

Vermon began giving orders to a small army of blank-faced android lackeys. "Explore every inch of the ship. Anything living I want disarmed and confined to a cell. I want the cargo taken to my personal quarters." Then he walked off, leaving the androids to carry out his orders.

Raven awoke to find herself in a large unfurnished cell. A few other prisoners stood around, inspecting every inch of the wall for some sort of egress. *Are you awake?* Trenyn asked.

"What did they hit me with, anyway?" asked Raven, as she climbed to her feet.

"Standard knockout gas," said Vik, "fed into our ship's ventilation system. Pretty old trick."

Raven looked around the room. Yna was trying to burn open the door with one glowing hand. Vik was helping Dervish, who was just waking up herself. Panther still slept, curled up on the floor. Also, a Grunthian slumped in one corner.

"Who's that?" Raven asked, indicating the Grunthian.

"He was on the freighter," Dervish said, coming over to them. "Bloodstone and Whisper had knocked him out and stuffed him in a supply closet. They had me look at him so I could copy his appearance."

"Speaking of Bloodstone and Whisper..." Raven looked around the room, not seeing them anywhere.

No idea, Trenyn answered.

"There were some pirates here too, when we first woke up," Dervish said. "Leftovers from the fight, I guess. Must have still been hiding in the halls."

"What happened to them?" Raven asked.

"They started a fight with Yna, and some guards took

them to another cell."

Raven looked at the door, where Yna was having no luck damaging the exotic metal. "Maybe if I tried punching through..." Raven began.

No. Trenyn interrupted her. *If Yna can't burn through it, I doubt you're strong enough. You would probably damage your hand.*

"Keep thinking. There has to be a way out of here," Raven said, though her hope was waning. Her father was a very careful man, and the upper hand was his.

"Sir, we've identified some of the prisoners..." said one of the android lackeys, whose face – if you could call it a face – appeared on a viewscreen in Vermon's quarters.

"Later," Vermon answered, turning off the screen as he did so. "I've got a present to unwrap."

Turning around, Lord Vermon looked at the package. It was a long cylindrical tube on a huge metallic base. "Within this cryovault lies the newest addition to our family. I will love her as I do all of my wives. Vraxx, do the honors."

Vraxx was a dragon-like humanoid with purple skin. As Vermon's right-hand "man" and bodyguard, it was his job to make certain the cryo-vault wasn't booby-trapped. "The sensors detect no explosives or poisonous gasses. There are no signs of tampering. The cryotube contains one humanoid-sized living being."

"Very good. Open it."

Vraxx did as his master commanded. The vault opened with a hiss, and for a moment they could see nothing but mist. Then a shadowy figure sprang from the vault, knocking Vermon across the room with a jump kick to the face.

"Vraxx!" he shouted, as he rose to his feet to face his enemy.

Whisper stood before him, whip in hand and battle-ready. "You bastard... you killed all those officers... framed me..." Whisper seethed with hatred so fiery that she couldn't speak clearly.

Vermon was much calmer. "That I did. And I won't stop there. I'm going to make your life hell, Alterra. You're going to wish you had simply turned yourself in."

"You're not going to get away with this. I'll make you confess! I'll..." Whisper raised her whip. She was about to slash Vermon when something grabbed her wrist. Whisper turned around and could barely comprehend what she saw. A large purple mass of tentacles grabbed at her, wrapping its tendrils around her arms and legs. Then she was jerked sideways, causing her to drop the whip. The tentacles pulled her over to a wall, to which she was manacled and chained. Unable to move her arms or legs, Whisper watched as the tentacles reverted to their true form, the shapeshifter Vraxx.

"Recognize my friend, here?" Vermon asked, indicating his monstrous bodyguard. "You've been working with him for quite a while." As Vermon spoke, Vraxx changed shape until he resembled one of Alterra's former IGP partners. "Of course," Vermon continued, "you might recognize this form even better." Vermon nodded to Vraxx, who then changed once again to resemble Whisper's alter ego, Alterra Sarr.

Whisper couldn't restrain herself from trying to lunge at her two captors. Unfortunately, the manacles restrained her just fine.

Somewhere deep within Vermon's station, a lone bounty hunter crept through the corridors, taking every precaution to avoid being seen. After many near misses, he finally found an empty security room. Actually, it was occupied when he found it, but after a few quick shots, it was vacant. Pushing aside the unconscious body of a security officer, Bloodstone sat down at a monitoring station and began his search.

Navigating his way through menus and sub-menus on the security computer, he finally managed to release the computer's control over the Grunthian freighter. Then he began scanning security images taken from the countless cameras throughout the giant station. After a short search, he found the feeds from the command-level crew quarters, and after a bit of code-cracking, he managed to call up a view of Vermon's quarters.

Bloodstone blinked. The screen displayed the image of Whisper, clamped to a wall. Before her stood Lord Teykor Vermon himself, and alongside him stood Bloodstone's intended prey, Alterra Sarr.

"You just couldn't stay away, could you? It's not as if you didn't have any other options. You could have simply assumed a new identity, and lived out your life peacefully, having learned your lesson well enough to let me be." Whisper only half listened to Vermon's tirade. In reality, she scanned the room for any sort of tool to help her escape. Vermon continued, "Even if you had turned yourself in to the IGP, your punishment would have been much less severe than the pain I will inflict upon you. My Alterra has much more work to do."

Whisper didn't waste her energy with anger this time. She continued to stand quietly, trying without luck to think of a way to release herself from the manacles which held her.

"Vraxx, your ship is on deck eleven. Your flight coordinates are already set. Proceed to your destination and await further orders."

"It will be done, Lord," said Vraxx, in Sarr's form. Then the shapeshifter left for the docking bay.

Vermon turned back to Whisper. "If you think your reputation is bad now," he said, "wait until you see what Vraxx does next. Very soon, you'll wish I had simply decided to kill you."

Bloodstone watched the silent video as Vermon appeared to

give Alterra Sarr an order. He used the cameras to track her as she left the room. Sarr walked down the hall and stepped onto a transport cart. The cart was a small floating platform with a handrail, often used in ships this size when walking would take too long. Bloodstone hacked into the command codes for the transport carts to find out Sarr's destination.

Seeing that Alterra was headed for the hangar, Bloodstone started to follow. No way was Alterra going to escape again. But then he looked at the viewscreen again. Whisper was still in danger. He looked back and forth between two screens, one showing Alterra, the other Whisper and Vermon.

"Damn it," Bloodstone said, leaving the security room.

Leaving Whisper to her thoughts, Vermon went on to other business. He wasn't worried about the possibility of Whisper trying to escape; she was clamped down well. She couldn't have broken those bonds even if she had a bazooka tucked up her sleeves. And knowing the Auroran aversion to firearms, that was not a likely possibility.

Vermon used his terminal to call Hantrix, the android in charge of the detention center. "Hantrix, report. Who are my prisoners?"

"We've ID'ed most of them, my Lord. But you should know first, one of them is your daughter!"

"Which daughter?"

"The one whose mother you had killed."

"Could you narrow that down a little more?"

"The one whose limbs were cut off!"

"Ah, Raven. The daughter of my twelfth wife." Vermon remembered that marriage well, and bristled with anger at his wife's betrayal. *Why must all my relationships return to haunt me?* "Very well. I will be there shortly to see my daughter."

01.10 Confrontation

ED.02500.01.02

Back in the cell, the prisoners still tried to find a way to escape. The Grunthian was now awake, helping Raven push against the door. The Grunthian seemed confused and angry, and none of them could communicate with him. But he recognized a prison cell when he saw one, so his anger was directed at his captors rather than his cellmates.

Even with the Grunthian's gorilla strength, the door wouldn't budge.

Dervish offered a timid suggestion. "Maybe if I turned into something that could fit into the air vents..."

"You can change your size?" Vik asked.

"Only a little, but if I turned into something really long and skinny, like a snake or something, my..." she tried to remember the word Whisper had used. "...My *mass* would remain the same." Dervish was reasonably bright, she just didn't know the right words.

The air ducts are sealed by filters, Trenyn told her, looking through one of the ducts. *You could try it, but I don't think you'll get far.*

Raven asked, "Yna, are you solid when in your energy form?"

"Afraid so," Yna replied.

"Rats. Well then," Raven said, "Trenyn, did you try to use telekinesis?"

Not yet, they answered, *but I doubt it would do much good. My abilities aren't usually good enough to open unlocked doors, much less...*

"Just try, please," Raven insisted.

Trenyn concentrated on the door. At first, there was nothing but a slight tremble. Then, suddenly, the door burst from the wall and flew across the room, making a huge commotion as it slammed against the back wall. Trenyn's eyes went wide, and their skin flashed yellow.

Raven's mouth hung open. "Is that the same metal as the collar?"

Before they could answer, blank-faced android guards came running from the halls and filled the doorway, weapons drawn. Everyone stood battle ready, each prepared to take out as many guards as they could or die trying. Before a single shot was fired, however, the small force of guards was smashed to pieces by a flying door.

The ex-prisoners began arming themselves with the weapons of their fallen enemies. *I believe the door is made of virtrinium,* Trenyn explained, still holding it in the air with their mind.

"Incredible," Raven said.

I should really take some of this back with me. The dense molecular structure is almost effortless to manipulate. Clearly I will have to do many experiments once we—

"Guys," Vik said, "Later."

They left the detention area, taking out any adversaries they encountered on the way, and searched for a way off the prison level. Finally they discovered an access elevator that took them to the main deck. They used a computer at one of the management stations to find out where Vermon's private office was located. "This way," Raven said, leading them down a hallway, "I know where to find Vermon!"

Turning a corner, they came to a screeching halt as they

entered a large, heavily occupied foyer. They now faced a battalion of androids, in the center of which stood Lord Vermon himself. "...And he knows where to find you," he said, smiling.

In Vermon's quarters, Whisper witnessed the action from her position manacled to the wall. She hung directly across from Vermon's computer, which displayed several of the station's areas on its many screens. She saw her friends facing Vermon and his legions. She wished she could be there to help them. In the short period of time since Vermon had left her, Whisper had tried every trick at her disposal to escape from her bonds, without any success. Her hands and feet were bound too tightly to allow for any movement, and even if she could free a weapon, the metallic shackles would have been too strong to open. Still, as long as she was alive, she had to keep trying, even if she had to rip off her own hands. Visually scanning the room for some kind of inspiration, she saw herself on a viewscreen. Not actually herself, but a reasonable facsimile of her alter ego was now getting closer to the landing bay.

On another screen, she saw Bloodstone sneaking through the hallways. Since he wasn't with the others, he'd probably abandoned his new friends to capture Alterra. *Well, there goes one hope*, she thought. She was disappointed, but she had expected no more from him. Whisper continued to struggle in her bonds.

"Raven, my lovely daughter, to what do I owe this pleasant visit?" Vermon spoke with the same polite highbrow inflections that had been used by the classier supervillains for centuries. "You and your group have shown some impressive skills. I could use people like you on my payroll. I would be willing to forgive your entire intrusion upon this station if you would assist me in my efforts."

"Your efforts?" Raven made no attempt to disguise her

hostility. "Your efforts to rule the galaxy? To enslave mankind? To eliminate anyone who disagrees with you? Is that why you killed my mother? So you could control the universe? Or was it just so that she wouldn't leak the word out about what kind of jerk you really are?"

"Actually, it was a little bit of both. But I digress. Obviously you don't wish to be a part of my plans, so therefore you are of no use to me." Turning to his minions, he said, "You may kill them."

Scores upon scores of androids converged on the group. Vik immediately jumped straight up to the ceiling, to get a better vantage from which to fire at his enemies. Several villains piled upon Yna, who then changed her form and melted them. Raven smashed many of them with her brute strength. Panther also used his raw power to dismember his opponents. Dervish used form after form to confuse her enemy. The Grunthian pilot tore many androids apart with his bare hands.

Even with all their abilities, Vermon's army was just too overwhelming. One of the androids managed to hit Yna dead on with a CO2 cannon, bringing her to the ground. She lay helpless on the floor, now human again, naked and bleeding. Vik jumped down from his safe perch and carried Yna to safety.

The Grunthian appeared to be having the time of his life. This was what he lived for. He threw androids at each other, knocking down several at once like bowling pins. But he couldn't keep up with the sheer number of enemies, and the swarms of androids finally brought him down. Every time he tried to stand back up, more and more opponents pulled him back down.

A dozen of Vermon's troopers dragged Panther to the floor and began beating him mercilessly. Dervish tried to help him, becoming a snake to slither through the legs of her opponents. Upon reaching Panther, she became a zondarg, a humanoid creature with sharp claws and horns. Dervish grabbed several androids and smashed them into each other, throwing their pieces at other approaching enemies.

Although strength was not one of the attributes that Dervish was usually able to control in her transformations, she now discovered that if she concentrated her muscular density to certain parts of her body, she could become stronger. In this case, the creature she had become was smaller than her natural form, meaning her cells were denser since her mass was constant. She would never have been able to explain in words exactly how she was doing it, but the effect was that she did have some control over her strength. She couldn't wait to talk to the others about it... assuming they got out of this alive.

Two androids grabbed Raven's left arm and ripped it off. Raven had a sudden flash of her original dismemberment, but put it out of her mind. She looked around and saw that fewer of her comrades were still standing. Wondering if Trenyn had been injured, Raven suddenly realized that she hadn't seen them for the entire fight. She was about to call them telepathically when several more attackers knocked her to the ground. They yanked her chest doors open and pulled her from her metallic body. One of the androids held her helplessly as another raised an energy weapon towards her head.

Then both androids fell over, dropping Raven to the floor. Unable to see much from her position, Raven craned her neck and saw the robots falling down all over the room. She mentally called to her own robotic body, which came to her and helped her reposition herself inside. It was more difficult with one arm, but she managed it. She could now see that all the enemies had fallen, except for a very confused-looking Teykor Vermon. Then a door opened on one side of the room, and Trenyn stepped out, that flying door still hovering behind them. Everyone heard them think, *It took some cracking, but I managed to turn off the androids using one of the security computers.*

Vermon just stood there, seething. Then, calmly, he said, "Then I'll simply have to take care of you myself."

Raven pointed at her father with her one remaining hand. "Get him!" The group all ran towards Vermon, except for Yna, who was unconscious on the floor. Then Vermon's eyes started to glow. They gleamed an eerie black, as ludicrous as that sounded. This black aura clouded the brains of his attackers, and all but Raven and Trenyn stopped short. Panther, Vik, and Dervish were now frozen like statues.

"Now," Vermon growled at his thralls, "*You* get *them*." The three suddenly came alive again, this time attacking Raven and Trenyn. Vik pushed Raven to the ground and pounded at her, while Dervish imitated Panther, both trying to pounce on a fleeing Trenyn. Trenyn used their door to knock their attackers away, before turning on Vermon. Using all the mental force they could muster, they launched the door at a very high speed straight towards Vermon's head. Just before it hit him, however, it stopped dead in midair.

"You underestimate my abilities," Vermon said, and sent the door right back toward Trenyn. The two battled it out mentally for a little while, and the door flew back and forth between them, giving way to whoever had the greater mental faculties at the moment. Trenyn's face had turned a dark shade of turquoise, as they strained to gain control.

Tiring of the game, Vermon glared at the door intently and sent a huge wave of psychic energy into it. The door exploded into thousands of virtrinium shards, which would have skewered everyone in the room if Trenyn hadn't mentally halted them. Momentarily drained, Vermon had to take a breath before continuing.

Trenyn used this brief respite to deal a final blow. They took control of all the virtrinium shards in the room, and sent them straight back at Vermon. With no time to react, Vermon was hit from every direction simultaneously. Shards stuck out all over his body, and he screamed in pain. With his last ounce of strength, he expelled the shards, which flew out in every direction. Once again Trenyn shielded their friends with their telekinesis. Vermon then fell to the floor in a bloody heap.

Vermon's thralls now regained their senses, blinking in confusion. The Grunthian pilot groaned and emerged from under a pile of deactivated androids. As the others recovered from the battle, Trenyn and Raven ran over to Vermon. *His life signs are weakening*, Trenyn told her.

"I know," Raven said without much pity, "I can feel it. So, Father, do you have any last words?"

"Yes..." Vermon said weakly, "Computer, activate self-destruct sequence, authorization Titus-One-Nine-Eight-Eight." Then his eyes closed.

"Uh oh," said Raven.

Vik picked up and carried Yna, and the group ran in the direction of the landing bay.

Whisper, still in her restraints, heard the computer announce, "Attention. Station will self-destruct in ten minutes."

Oh, this is good, she thought sarcastically, *Looks like I get to die here. At least Vermon bought it first.* Then the door opened.

Bloodstone rushed into the room and immediately went to a control panel. Opening her manacles, he asked, "Ready to get out of here?"

"Bloodstone? You came for me?"

"Well, you and one other thing," Bloodstone said. He spent about thirty seconds furiously typing on Vermon's computer, and then they ran out the door together.

As soon as the fleeing bounty hunters were out of sight, Vermon stood up and brushed himself off. His wounds were not nearly as bad as he had led them to believe. "Idiots," he said, not that anyone was around to hear him. "As if I would destroy all of this just to swat a few flies. Computer: Cancel self-destruct."

A monotone female voice answered. "Voice commands not accepted."

Vermon blinked. "…What? Why not?"

"User Teykor Vermon is locked out."

"Override!" he barked angrily. "Authorization Tyverm-One-One-Six-Zero!"

"Authorization not recognized."

"I order you to override!"

"Authorization not recognized."

Vermon cursed and rushed back towards his quarters.

The groups converged in the landing bay. When the Grunthian pilot spotted Bloodstone and Whisper, he became very angry. However, more androids followed them, as well as spider-shaped robots and security drones. Rather than attack the bounty hunters, the Grunthian spotted the freighter and ran towards it. Unfortunately, he was the largest target in the group, and he was hit by several blasts from the pursuing androids. The Grunthian used the last of his strength to grab an android and break it in half. Then he slumped to the floor, dead.

While the rest of the group boarded the ramp to the freighter, Bloodstone turned around to give his allies some cover fire. He destroyed three androids as the rest of his group ran past him, Raven taking up the rear. Bloodstone backed up the ramp, then suddenly cried out in pain. A powerful energy blast had hit him in the side, and he crumpled onto the ramp. Trenyn and Raven pulled him the rest of the way into the ship as the ramp raised.

Vermon reached his quarters. He was incensed to discover that Whisper had escaped her manacles, but that wasn't important at the moment. "Station will explode in two minutes," a computer voice said.

Vermon's personal computer could override any command on the ship. He pressed a button, but the computer was locked. He typed his login ID and password, only to find that he was locked out.

Vermon was getting desperate. "Prepare escape pod!"

"Escape pods offline."

"Get them online!"

"Authorization not recognized."

Vermon's eyes narrowed. "Computer. List current system administrators."

"Administrator privileges currently registered to Detanna Taush."

"Who the hell is Detanna Taush? Get IT on the comm! Reboot the system! Disconnect power from the... self-destruct... things!"

"Commands not recognized."

Vermon looked at the security monitors and saw his former prisoners boarding the freighter. "Damn them all..." he muttered, but then his eyes fell on an object on the other side of the room. *Hmm.*

Vik sat in the pilot's seat of the freighter, franticly powering up the flight systems. Whisper stood nearby, torn between trying to help Vik and seeing what the commotion was in the hallway. "How are we going to open the air hatch?" she asked.

Vik read the control panel. "We... we have access. Somehow. Bloodstone must have done something."

Air rushed past the freighter as the mothership's outer hatch opened. Androids continued firing at the ship, even as they were blown out into space. The freighter shook and shuddered, but it held together, hurtling out of the landing bay just in time. Vermon's mothership filled with fire and blew itself apart, in a sight very similar to the demise of the IGP's EarthStation 1. "I suppose that's justice," Whisper said quietly, watching the destruction on a viewscreen.

"Help me get his armor off!" Raven shouted from down the hall. Whisper, Dervish, and Yna stepped into the hallway, their eyes widening at Bloodstone's injuries. "I don't think he's breathing! How do you get this stupid helmet off?" Whisper leaped to Raven's side, quickly locating the helmet's hidden latches and pulling it off Bloodstone's head. She jumped back at the face she saw.

Bloodstone was a woman. A tall, muscular woman, but very obviously female. She had brown skin, and her short hair was dyed purple. Her face looked very calm, like she was already dead.

Always professional, Raven didn't skip a beat. She went straight to work, giving orders and delegating responsibilities. Bloodstone was breathing, but the breaths were very shallow. The armor came off, and they managed to stabilize her enough to move her to the medical bay. Then Raven and Trenyn ordered the others to leave and let them work.

The ship was now on autopilot, headed towards a warp gate. The crew, however, wasn't quite sure what to do when they got there. Dervish, Vik, Whisper, and Yna relaxed around the bridge, making light conversation.

"Do you think she'll make it?" Yna asked. She sat in the pilot's seat, her legs pulled up against her chest. Dervish sat beside her, the Grunthian-sized chair easily wide enough for the two of them. Panther lay curled on the floor beside them.

"She's strong," Whisper answered. "I'm sure she's survived worse injuries than this." Whisper leaned against the wall, idly swinging her whip back and forth.

"I still can't believe it," Vik said, taking his eyes off the instrument panel for a second. "The great Bloodstone, a woman?"

"Something wrong with that?" Whisper asked, genuinely curious. After the day she'd had, she didn't have the energy to feel indignant.

"No, no, of course not. It's just a shock is all. Why would she hide it? There's female bounty hunters."

"I'm aware of that," Whisper said with a touch of

sarcasm. "And I don't know, some cultures are still pretty sexist. If I had to guess, she wanted an identity that would garner respect and inspire fear."

"What's scarier than a woman?" Vik asked jokingly.

Whisper ignored him. "I mean, look how well it's worked for her. But you know what? That's her business," she concluded. She wanted to change the subject. Something didn't add up, and she felt uncomfortable speculating about it with someone like Vik. "Now, where do we go from here?"

"Not back to Earth," Vik answered. "Not until I find Alterra. She has a lot to answer for."

"I don't have anywhere to go," Dervish added.

"Same," said Yna, meekly raising her hand.

Whisper nodded. Dervish and Yna were a lot alike, bred for obedience by harsh masters, to the point that even their imaginations were stunted. The idea of freedom had to be overwhelming to them. Where does one even start, when one has no idea what's outside their cage? "Don't worry," she told them. "Whatever the group decides, I'm not going to abandon you. When you know what you want to do with your lives, I'll help you make it happen." She looked back and forth from Dervish to Yna, both of whom smiled with relief. Whisper hoped she wasn't lying to them. She wanted to help them however she could, but her own life was such a mess right now.

"…and Vik," Whisper continued, "You might want to stick around until Bloodstone wakes up. She has a lot of resources, and may have some ideas about finding Alterra." She didn't actually care whether Vik stayed around or not, but she didn't like the idea of someone with such a grudge against her running around the universe unchecked. Not that he was the only cop who had it in for her, but she couldn't do anything about that. If she could find a way to convince Vik of her innocence, he might be able to help her clear her name. But it was too risky to consider that right now. The truth was, she didn't know what she wanted to do about Vik, but she definitely wanted more time to think.

"Like Bloodstone would share that information," Vik said. "All she cares about is collecting the bounty. We should both be on our guard. She might decide to kill off her competition when she's feeling better."

Whisper just nodded. She didn't know what to believe. Bloodstone had a widespread reputation for being ruthless and cold-blooded. But then, the galaxy also believed Bloodstone to be male, so reputations weren't always accurate. Whisper would remain cautious regardless, but a small part of her hoped that there was more to Bloodstone than her public persona.

Detanna Taush slipped in and out of consciousness. Dreamlike images and random memories mixed with Raven's emotionless voice. Unable to hear Trenyn's side of the conversation, Detanna's mind filled in the blanks by casting her mother in the role of nurse.

"...need to seal the wound. Can you hold this? I can't do it with one arm. Yes, right there. As still as you can."

"He drove his father off, did he tell you? Then he ran away from home, leaving me all alone."

"Is there any A-Bac salve in there? Or spray?"

"Doesn't matter. The only medicine he cares about is his hormones."

"Check that cabinet. Yes, that should work. The green one."

"Stop coddling him. He doesn't deserve it. I gave birth to a beautiful son, but he threw it away."

"Okay, hold her still while I apply this."

"He was a pirate, you know, did he tell you that? He left the family to become a pirate, just like his father. And when he couldn't hack it there, he became a bounty hunter. Hiding his face beneath that ridiculous helmet, so no one would see him transition... You couldn't trust him then, you can't trust him now..."

There were dreams now, very vivid dreams comprised of

guilt-ridden memories. Detanna saw herself as a pirate, still presenting as male. She had to – female pirates were usually treated as concubines, and rarely got a cut of the stolen goods. In the dream state, she looked like a historical sea pirate, in an exaggerated costume including peg leg, eye patch, and parrot. Joining the pirate crew wasn't the best decision she'd made, but it got her off the planet. Unfortunately, she soon found that her cut of the loot was never enough to save up. Pirates at her rank were paid barely enough to buy food. She'd have to do a lot of unpalatable things to rise in the ranks. She'd never achieve her transition goals at this rate.

So, she left them. She put on a suit and mask so they'd never recognize her, and became the galaxy's greatest bounty hunter. She still presented as male because she was early in her transition. Her wide shoulders and tall frame made it difficult to look female in that outfit. She turned out to be pretty good at this job. But she'd never have the respect of her family. No amount of fame or fortune would allow her to buy her way back home.

It felt like some time had passed when she started to hear Raven's voice again. There were strange sensations from various parts of her body, but she couldn't pin down what aches were coming from where. Occasionally it seemed like something hot was repeatedly slamming into her, and she envisioned various scenarios like being hit by a flaming hovercar, or side tackled by a giant porcupine. Now and then Detanna could hear a woman moaning in pain. It sounded like her own voice, but off in the distance.

"Damn these Grunthians. The brutes don't even stock pain meds."

"*Good. A little pain will finally make a man out of him.*" Apparently, dad had taken over mom's shift at the hospital.

"This might numb it a bit. I have to be conservative with the dosage… It was designed for Grunthian physiology."

"What's the worst that can happen? One less sissy in the universe."

"It's working. I think she's stabilizing."

"Just toss him out the airlock. He's not worth the effort."

"May still need a transfusion…"

"I wouldn't waste a drop of blood on that ungrateful bastard. I tried so hard to give him the perfect childhood, but all he wanted to do was embarrass me by wearing dresses and playing with dolls. I will never call him 'daughter.' Either he goes or I go. I will never…"

The words faded away as Detanna fell into a deep sleep.

Detanna moaned. Her eyes fluttered partly open. Her hand went to her face, and upon realizing her helmet was off, her eyes opened wide. Raven was standing next to the bed, reading something on a tablet.

"Did… we… catch Alterra?"

Raven set down her tablet and looked at her. "No, the trail is cold."

"I'll be the judge of that," Detanna said, struggling to get out of bed. She winced in pain, and Raven held up her hand.

"Take it easy, please. You still need time to recover. I can bring you anything you need."

Detanna lifted the thin blanket and looked down at her nude body. There was a huge patch of gauze starting just beneath her right breast, that went down to her hip. It went around her side to the middle of her back. When she saw the catheter leading into her penis, something occurred to her. "The others, do they know —"

"They just saw your face," Raven said. "They know you're a woman. Only Trenyn and I know the rest. As medical professionals, we would never share your private information without your consent. Your secret is safe with us, Bloodstone."

"You can call me Detanna."

A few hours later, Detanna was dressed and up and about.

Raven didn't like her rushing it, but Detanna had always been headstrong. She gathered the crew into the galley, and addressed them while sipping a cup of soup.

Detanna sighed. "Where do I even begin?"

"You could start with the fact that you're a woman," Vik said. "Why did you hide that?"

"That's my business," Detanna said. "The important thing is, I spent years creating this identity, and I would appreciate it if you don't let this get out."

"So..." Whisper asked, "Do we still call you Bloodstone?"

"If my helmet is on, please stay in the habit of calling me Bloodstone, and referring to me as male. Think of it as a character I play. If we're in private, and the helmet's off, you can call me Detanna."

"So what happens now?" Dervish asked.

Detanna looked to each of them in turn. Dervish, Vik, Raven, Trenyn, Yna, Panther. Her eyes finally settled on Whisper. "You're the only people in the galaxy who know my real name, and have seen my face. I don't like that knowledge being out there, and I want to keep an eye on you. If I were the kind of person the galaxy thinks I am, I'd make sure none of you left here alive. But instead, I want to make an offer. Why don't we stay together? Form our own bounty hunting team. I'll train you to be the best hunters in the galaxy, and you'll make the credits you need to work on your own goals. I'll assign you contracts based on your skills, and we'll all split the profits."

She looked around at their reactions before continuing. "More importantly, working together we have a greater chance of finding Alterra Sarr, and bringing her to justice. What do you think?"

Some of them had to sleep on it, but in the end, all of them agreed to stay on. For Dervish and Yna, this group was the closest thing to family they had ever known. Raven and Trenyn saw it as a way to fund their scientific pursuits, including designing more lifelike bodysuits for Raven.

Vik decided that staying close to Bloodstone put him on the most direct path to catching Alterra Sarr, allowing him to have his revenge. He made arrangements with the IGP, placing him on extended leave. It was either that or quit, and the IGP didn't want to cut ties with such a valuable asset if they could avoid it. So they gave him some leeway. While working with the bounty hunters, Vik would also act as their liaison with the IGP when necessary.

Whisper told them she was staying for similar reasons, that staying with this group would make it easier for her to bring this dangerous fugitive to justice. In truth, she wasn't sure why she wanted to stay. It still seemed dangerous to be so close to Bloodstone. He… no, *she*, Whisper corrected herself… may not be as uncompromising as Whisper had previously thought, but Detanna was still a professional. She would still turn Alterra in without considering whether she was actually guilty. And yet, it seemed like this was the best place to be if she was going to prove her innocence to the galaxy. Detanna believed there was a connection between Alterra Sarr and Teykor Vermon, and her pursuits stood the best chance of shaking out the truth.

Was that all, though? Was there another reason she felt the need to stay close to Detanna? Hopefully not, but she refused to acknowledge that her inexplicable attraction might be a factor.

After the meeting, Raven somehow managed to convince Detanna to take it easy while they ran a few more tests. Detanna insisted they do it in her own quarters. She didn't like the medbay; it reminded her that she wasn't perfect. The door beeped, and Detanna waved it open. Whisper entered. Instead of her usual helmet, she was wearing a light jacket with a large hood. The shadow cast by the hood somehow enveloped everything below it, so that her entire face was lost in darkness. She also muted the timbre of her voice, which made her sound like a completely different person.

"Can I talk to you, Detanna?" She glanced at Raven. "Alone?"

Raven nodded, walking towards the door. "I have to run this blood test in the medbay anyway. I'll be back in twenty minutes."

When they were alone, Whisper sat at the foot of Detanna's bed. "Are you doing okay?"

Detanna leaned forward, then winced in pain. "I've had worse injuries. Honestly, my pride hurts more than my body. I don't like people seeing me helpless."

"I understand," Whisper answered. "But I think you can trust these people. I think you'll find us to be a worthy crew."

Detanna chuckled. "Let's hope. Now let me ask you something. You're the only one on the ship whose face I haven't seen. If I'm to truly trust you, I'd like to know who I'm dealing with. I showed you mine, care to show me yours?" She winked as she said it.

"I'm sorry," Whisper answered. "It's a cultural thing. My religion requires that I hide my face from everyone but my life partner." It wasn't a huge lie; the followers of Auria did have such a rule. But modern Aurorans typically only observed it on holy days. Aurorans were so xenophobic, that it wasn't likely any non-Aurorans would know this.

"But," Whisper continued, "I will go this far." She pulled back her hood. Beneath it, she wore a cloth mask, which didn't reveal much more than her eyes and the bridge of her nose. Her skin tone was gray, much darker than Alterra's pale complexion. Her eyes were purple, while Alterra's were known to be blue. Whisper held her breath for a moment. Just how good was Bloodstone's attention to detail? Would she recognize Alterra by the shape of her eyes?

But there was no look of recognition on Detanna's face. "It'll do for now," she said. Noting Whisper's gray skin, Detanna asked, "Where are you from, anyway?"

"Around," Whisper answered.

"Same," Detanna said.

A thought occurred to Whisper. "Can I ask you a personal question? Why are you hiding your sex? There's plenty of female bounty hunters out there, it's not like it's something to be ashamed of."

Detanna sighed. Whisper was the closest thing she had to a friend on this ship. Detanna was a private person by necessity, but the solitary lifestyle had been weighing on her lately. "Branding," she said. "As I said earlier, I've been using the Bloodstone persona for a long time, and I've earned a lot of respect. I don't let the public see me bleed. I don't even use public restrooms because I don't want people to know that I pee."

"Oh my god..." Whisper said. "For the galaxy's most feared bounty hunter, you're kind of neurotic."

Detanna sighed. "The persona has served me well. People pay me the highest rates. Fugitives sometimes surrender to me as soon as they know I'm on their planet. Sometimes people I'm not even looking for run up to me and surrender. Some people think I'm a robot or some some genetically enhanced creature designed for hunting. If I were to reveal my true identity now, it would make me look weak. People might not even believe I'm the same Bloodstone."

"Okay, sure, but why did you start using a male persona in the first place? Why didn't you just start out as a female Bloodstone?"

"It's a long story," she said. Then she paused, conflicted. Privacy was important to her, but it had been years since she'd had an actual friend.

Finally, she decided to tell Whisper everything.

Part 2

02.00   Assignments

ED.02500.02.05

The moons of Rabinaar were just becoming visible when the Great Valla Chorno prepared to address his people. Tens of thousands of citizens, nearly every soul in Charta, looked toward their highest of leaders as he spoke against a backdrop of the setting sun. He used no microphone – their society was aware of advanced technology, but shunned it. Nevertheless, the immense outdoor stadium was acoustically sound, and the audience understood every word of his speech.

"Citizens of Charta, today is a day of great triumph. Though it cost the lives of many brave men, our spies have returned from the land of our hated enemies, the Gorvanans. And with them, they brought... this!"

The Great Valla Chorno lifted a small green gem high above his head. The stone glittered brightly in what little sunlight was left.

"This... is the Eye of Norgalla. It is the holy symbol of the Gorvanans' false god. But the fact that we were able to abduct it so easily only proves that there can be only one god... our god... the great Ris Kiree!" He gestured toward a large stone statue of their god, which had a humanoid body and two serpent heads.

The audience cheered and began chanting "Kiree! Kiree!" When it quieted down again, the Valla continued.

"Until the day Ris Kiree invites my soul unto his holy realm, I shall wear this gem around my neck as a symbol of the superiority of our god!" The audience cheered even louder.

"Now return to your homes, and sleep secure in the knowledge that our god, the one true god, Ris Kiree, watches over you and protects you. Good night to you all." The crowd applauded for several minutes and finally dispersed.

The Great Valla Chorno walked the halls of his grand palace, followed closely by three strong bodyguards. As he neared his quarters, he was approached by his head servant, Savno. "Is there anything I may do for you sire, before you retire for the night?"

"Yes. Tomorrow will be a very hectic day for me. The Gorvanans may be preparing their forces for war at this very moment. I must insure that Charta's defenses are prepared. I fear that I should need something to keep my mind occupied tonight. A stress reliever, if you will, to lull me to sleep."

"Naturally, sire. And whose company do you wish to have tonight?"

"Oh, how about Nisa."

"Very good, sire. Expect her shortly."

The guards took their place outside Chorno's door as he entered his room. The Valla removed his shoes and made himself comfortable. After a short period of time, there was a knock at the door.

"Come in," said Chorno, now reclining on a large soft bed.

The door opened, and a timid harem girl entered the room. "You wanted me?" she asked.

"Your company would be most welcome," he replied. He

gestured for her to come to him, which she did. Slowly, seductively, she began removing his clothing. Then she tried to remove his necklace, from which dangled the Eye of Norgalla. "No," he objected. "That I wish to wear always."

"But, would you not be more comfortable without it? Just for a little while?" Once again she tugged at the neckchain.

"No," he replied, holding her hands. "It is a symbol of devotion to our highest of masters. I wear it out of respect for Ris Kiree."

"As you wish." Nisa massaged his neck. "Now, about that stress relief you requested." Her hands wandered over his body, softly kneading his flesh in ways even more pleasurable than usual.

"You've gotten better at this. Have you been taking lessons?"

"Only from you," she replied pleasantly.

Chorno allowed himself to relax. He closed his eyes and enjoyed the moment. Her touches were so soft and soothing, as she massaged his chest, his shoulders, and especially his neck.

"Keep your eyes closed, lover, I have a special treat for you," said Nisa's seductive voice.

But something about the way she'd said it felt wrong. Chorno opened his eyes just in time to see Nisa tucking the Eye of Norgalla into her pocket.

Chorno shouted, "Thief!" and backhanded her across the face, knocking her to the floor. "That stone is the property of Ris Kiree!" Two guards burst into the room and approached Nisa.

"You fool," the harem girl laughed as she rose. "Do you not know your own lord when he stands before you?"

Her body changed its shape before their very eyes. Her head split like an amoeba and became elongated and serpentine. Her body became larger and masculine. Chorno recognized her final form as the great Ris Kiree himself. The guards backed away, dumbstruck.

Chorno immediately assumed a more penitent position. "Forgive me my lord, I did not know!"

"Silence! How dare you presume to 'honor' me by wearing the symbol of my greatest rival close to your heart!" His voice was like that of a wirze gargling gravel.

"I apologize, my master, I did not think—"

"I will take this jewel to my realm, where it will serve my purposes." The snake-headed god hung the gem about one of his necks.

"Whatever you wish, my master! Of course! Of course!" Chorno had always dreamed of speaking to his god in person, but now he could only stammer with fear.

Ris Kiree's body changed to match his head. He was now a giant two-headed snake. The Eye of Norgalla still dangled from one neck. "You are forgiven. If such a thing happens again, our next meeting will not be so pleasant." Ris Kiree slithered out the window and was gone.

When the guards could finally stop shaking, they began to revive Chorno, who had fainted. If they had glanced out the window at that moment, they might have seen a scarlet-haired woman running toward the forest on the outskirts of the city. A few minutes later a small spacecraft shot out from the treetops and into the black sky.

The Grunthian freighter – now renamed the Bloodwind - was full of activity. The crew had been together for about a month, during which time they had taken on six successful bounties. Raven and Trenyn had finished modifying the freighter so that the controls were in English, and had replaced most of the Grunthian-sized furniture with more comfortable pieces.

During the upgrade, they did some research on the ship's history. They found it had been stolen at least three times before the Grunthians got their hands on it, and parts of it originally belonged to three separate ships. Any guilt feelings they may have had for stealing it from the

Grunthians were now gone.

In the newly-added training hall, Whisper and Vik stood facing each other, each posed in a fighting stance. Whisper wore a cloth mask and a workout jumpsuit, and Vik was in his IGP training tracksuit.

"I'm going to show you some moves you haven't seen before," Whisper said. "This form is called Auro-Chi-Vau. All your movements should flow, like water. Rely less on brute force and more on fluidity of motion. It's less important to hit your opponent and more about using their own kinetic energy against them."

"Less talk, more fight," Vik said, and lunged forward. Whisper avoided him easily, locking elbows with him as he passed and twirling him to the floor.

Detanna, watching from off to the side, just laughed. "You said 'Auro-Chi-Vau?' Never heard of it, but that looked a lot like Aikido."

"My clan believes that many martial arts were inspired by ancient alien visitors. It's possible the two styles share a common origin."

"Interesting theory," Detanna said. Then she asked, "Care for a real challenge?"

Whisper looked her over and said, "You? Detanna, my fighting prowess is more than you could ever handle."

"I'm an expert in more than thirty forms of martial arts," Detanna boasted, "I think I can take you."

"I have no need to prove myself," Whisper said, "but I'm always willing to teach others a lesson."

The two women stood face-to-face, about two meters apart, sizing each other up. Vik watched with anticipation, anxious to see which bounty hunter would prevail. Just then Yna came running into the room. "Dervish is back," she announced. The four of them went to the landing bay to greet her.

There were now two shuttles in the landing bay, and two more latched onto the Bloodwind's side ports. The landing shuttles had been brought in from one of Bloodstone's planetside bases. As they entered the bay, the door of one of the shuttles opened, and Dervish stepped out. "Here you go," she said, and handed a beautiful jewel to Detanna.

"Excellent work, Dervish," she said, "The Gorvanan government will pay well to have their holy symbol back."

"How much did they offer?" Vik asked.

"Offer?" Detanna replied, "They haven't even hired us... yet. I just heard that the Chartans had stolen the gem, and we happened to be in the area..."

Whisper gasped. "They don't even know you have it? It's like you're holding it for ransom!" Ever since learning of Bloodstone's true identity, Whisper had found that a lot of the bounty hunter's reputation was exaggerated. Detanna wasn't nearly as cutthroat as people believed her alter ego to be. But she was still a serious bounty hunter, and some of her tactics rubbed Whisper the wrong way.

"This is how you do business," Detanna said. "You see a need, you fill it. Now I'm going to go planetside and offer my services to the Gorvanans. Once hired, I will disappear for a while, and return with the jewel."

Whisper shook her head. "I want to have a talk with you when you get back."

A few hours later, Whisper and Detanna sat across from each other at the small table in Whisper's quarters. They often had talks like this. They were the only two experienced bounty hunters on the ship, and this gave them some shared experiences on which to build a friendship.

"I still don't approve of what you did on Rabinaar," Whisper said.

"I never asked for your approval," Detanna answered cheerfully.

"For the sake of argument, how do you know that Charna's god isn't the one true god?" Whisper asked. "My people believe that many planets, and many cultures on those planets, worship the same god. It may be that the prayers of any monotheistic religion go to the same supreme being, whether his name is Jehovah or Ris Kiree."

Detanna snorted. "If there is a supreme being controlling the universe, and that's a pretty big if, it's not Ris Kiree. Non-terrestrial historians have extensively documented the history of Rabinaar's culture. Less than a thousand years ago, the Chartans and the Gorvanans were one culture, worshiping the same god. At one point they were split between two continents, and over time they evolved into two distinct societies, each with its own religion. The idiots are constantly at war, and they don't even realize that they worship the same guy."

"Well, in a way, that proves my point," Whisper said. "Their original god could very well have been the same one I worship. So what if the people of Rabinaar got a little confused?"

"I'll take my chances," Detanna answered. "Is that really what you wanted to talk about?"

"No," Whisper said. "It's about Dervish. You sent her on her first solo mission, and it was a seduction mission?"

"It's what she's best at," Detanna replied. "Pleasing men comes naturally to her."

"Yes, because she was raised by monsters who groomed her to be a sex object."

"Exactly," Detanna replied. "She was designed to be a concubine. Why shouldn't I let her exercise her strengths? You don't hire the world's greatest archeball pitcher and then stick them on sixth base."

The sports metaphor was lost on Whisper, but she got the meaning. "We owe it to her to help her grow as a person. Let her know that there's more to her than that. When she's a more complete being, if she still enjoys playing the seductress, that will be her choice."

Detanna thought it over and sighed. "You're right," she said, surprising Whisper. "I wasn't thinking about how this might affect her emotional growth. Besides, I ought to be concentrating on her combat skills. Someone who can grow fangs and claws on demand could be a real asset if she knew when to use them…" Detanna trailed off, muttering something about a training schedule.

Close enough, Whisper decided. Aurorans didn't have the sexual hangups that plagued many cultures, but Whisper still felt it was exploitative to send Dervish out on such missions. Dervish may have been an adult, but that didn't mean she was mature. The Grunthian conditioning had set her back by years. Her mind had to catch up with her body.

A few hundred years ago, the Grunthians had been a slave race. They'd been genetically designed to be soldiers and bodyguards, by a species of vulnerable geniuses called the Ythorl. It didn't take a genius to see the flaw in that plan, but the Ythorl were conceited and believed their ideas above reproach.

While they were initially bred to follow orders and never to think for themselves, some Grunthians were given more complex duties, and therefore needed to be more intelligent. The more intelligent Grunthians soon found themselves wondering why they should take orders from the Ythorl, and within ten years the Grunthians ruled the planet. With the Ythorl wiped out, the Grunthians began breeding their own slave race. Keeping their own history in mind, the Grunthians were much more careful to give these creatures subservient personalities.

Hence the Marae. Shape-shifting creatures with minds as malleable as their bodies. When properly educated and allowed to mature on their own, Marae could be just as independent as any other sapient race. But they were only bred on Grunthar, where their development was strictly controlled.

"Judging by that long silence, I'm going to assume we're done here," Detanna said, standing up. "Thank you for voicing your concerns. Now, if you'll excuse me, I have some missions to distribute among the crew. Meeting in fifteen minutes."

The crew all met in the galley, ready to give Bloodstone their full attention. Except for Vik, who, as usual, was more interested in his personal vendetta.

"Any new Sarr sightings?" Vik asked, the second Bloodstone walked through the door. He already knew the answer, as he'd been obsessively watching the tip lines all morning. But Bloodstone had access to informants Vik didn't, so it was always worth asking.

"No," Bloodstone said. "But I have several other assignments…"

"I don't like the idea of being off ship if we get a lead on Sarr."

"Vik," Bloodstone said. "I earned my reputation. I know what I'm doing."

"But—" Vik began.

"But nothing," Bloodstone said. "You know you have a better chance of finding her if you stick with us. But you can only stay on this ship if you earn your keep. Every fugitive on our roster is dangerous and deserves to be behind bars. At least one of us will stay on the Bloodwind at all times to monitor the tip lines. If there are any leads, I promise you I'll let you know immediately, wherever you are at the time. Got it?"

Vik nodded, but he didn't look happy.

"As I was saying," Bloodstone continued, "Here are your assignments…"

02.01   *The Chauffeur*

ED.02500.02.10

Sigran "Siggy" Trihannen leaned against the inside wall of the trash bin, trying to catch his breath. Had he lost his pursuer? He thought so. He hadn't seen any sign of him for three blocks. Still, this wasn't just any old bounty hunter he was fleeing. Siggy put his ear up to the side of the bin, listening for footsteps. Nothing. He waited another five minutes before daring to push up on the lid for a peek at his surroundings.

The lid wouldn't open. That was interesting. He pushed a bit harder, but it didn't give. Siggy hadn't always been claustrophobic, but the past few months in prison had changed him. Now that he might be trapped, the oxygen seemed thinner in a way it hadn't just a minute ago. Were these things airtight? He didn't think so, but that was the type of trivia he'd rather look up online than test in person. Slogging through trash juice, he pushed his way to the other side of the bin and tried the lid there. It didn't give a bit.

"Not good," he murmured. He pushed harder and harder, until finally he banged on the inside of the lid, his fear of suffocation drowning out his desire to stay hidden. "Hey!" he shouted. Something on top of the lid shifted, then slid off onto the ground. Siggy gave one final push, throwing the lid back, only to find an energy blaster pointed at his face.

"Don't try anything," an electronically-enhanced voice said. Siggy saw his own horrified face reflected in the blood-red domed helmet of his captor. Oh well, at least there was no shame in getting caught by Bloodstone.

It was a long drive back to the prison. Siggy sat in the back of a sleek black hovercar. There were no buttons or switches back here, no way to open the doors. A sheet of unbreakable glass separated him from his captor-slash-chauffer. Siggy looked out the windows. It was the mother of all traffic jams. The freeway was four lanes wide and three lanes high, and every lane was at a standstill. Siggy wondered if his escape had had anything to do with the traffic. He'd caused a few explosions earlier to distract the police; that kind of thing tended to affect the local traffic.

Well, this is it, he thought. *The last car ride I'll ever get.* His escape hadn't been planned. He actually took advantage of another prisoner's attempt to escape, running off while the cops were busy catching the first guy. The other prisoner had been planning his escape for three months, but it took Siggy less than a second to plot his own. Not that his escape had been successful, but he sure made it farther than the other guy. Siggy had a knack for making the most of an opportunity, and he started to wonder if this traffic jam might be another one.

"Look, can we talk?" Siggy said to the driver.

"No," the bounty hunter said.

Siggy sighed. "Any chance you could stop by a restroom? I really need to go."

"I doubt that," Bloodstone answered. "You already wet yourself when I caught you."

Siggy looked down and realized the bounty hunter was correct. With all the trash juice on his legs, he hadn't even noticed. The combination of smells in the backseat was starting to make his eyes water. "I just want to clean up a little. Can you at least crack a window back here?"

"No." But Bloodstone did press a button on the dashboard, increasing the air circulation in the back seat. Clean air blew in, stale air was sucked out, and the stench became a bit more bearable.

Hmmm, Siggy thought. So the bounty hunter did have a heart after all. Or maybe he just didn't want his captive getting sick all over this nice car. Siggy went back to studying his surroundings. He knew better than to try smashing the windows. Not only would they be unbreakable, but he wanted to stay on Bloodstone's good side, such as it was. There were no other potential exits – double-sealing doors, no control panels, no hatches in the roof or floor, no behind-the-seat passage to the trunk. It was a custom-built vehicle, and the backseat was specifically designed to be a mobile prison cell.

But there was always psychology. Siggy believed things happened for a reason. His execution was supposed to be tomorrow; why would he be presented with an opportunity to escape, if he wasn't meant to take it? And this traffic jam was obviously another gift from fate, he just had to figure out how he was meant to use it. Maybe he could talk his captor into helping him. It was a long shot, but he'd always been good at long shots.

"You know I'm sentenced to death, right? And that my execution is tomorrow?"

"Yes." It was like talking to a computer.

"So by turning me back in, you're basically killing me."

No response. Siggy was pretty good at reading body language, but Bloodstone just kept both hands on the wheel with no change in posture.

"I was framed, you know. You're killing an innocent person."

Bloodstone appeared to take a deep breath before answering. "That's for the courts to decide. And they did. You are guilty of murder, and you will be punished by the authorities. My only job is to bring you in."

Siggy hadn't expected to get so many words out of the stoic bounty hunter. This was good. Maybe he could coax out a few more. Get him talking, get a dialogue going, and he would see Siggy as more than just a job. Maybe even see him as a victim.

"I understand," Siggy said. "We all have our roles in life, why try to break the mold?"

No answer, not even a twitch.

"But the truth will come out after I'm gone. And you'll have to live with that on your conscience forever."

Bloodstone appeared to sigh at this. Siggy wasn't sure if he was getting through, or just irritating his captor. Probably the latter.

"Well, I'm just going to talk, okay? After this, they're going to push the execution through as quickly as possible, so this is my last chance to tell anyone the true story. If you don't want to listen, that's fine, but I have to get this off my chest."

Bloodstone nodded, almost imperceptibly.

"I never wanted to be a criminal. I don't like hurting people. But I had to steal to survive, living on the streets. I had to join a gang for the shelter and protection they offered. I was only a kid when my parents kicked me out."

"Why?" Bloodstone's head was cocked slightly.

What was this? Actual interest? Was this a shared experience? Siggy wasn't going to waste it, though.

"Well, the first thing you have to know is that I was born a girl. I'm transgender."

Bloodstone only nodded, but body language told Siggy that this was new information to the bounty hunter. The local judicial system had its flaws, but they were impeccable when it came to privacy. Siggy could tell Bloodstone was trying hard not to react. For whatever reason, he had the hunter's full interest.

"I got lucky. Really lucky. It turns out my gang's leader had a sister who was trans. The sister had killed herself.

They were very understanding."

Bloodstone nodded slowly, and sat up a little straighter.

Siggy sensed a connection. He was good at that. Much like the mythical Aurorans, his species had a knack for body language. The Knarvans came from a planet with a thin atmosphere, where sound didn't travel particularly well. His people used hand signals and body language for most communication. While Aurorans supposedly used this skill to develop their unique martial arts, the Knarvans mostly used their skill for socialization. They made great negotiators, politicians, and con artists.

Siggy had gleaned more intel from the position of Bloodstone's shoulders than from anything the bounty hunter had actually said. He didn't know what the connection might be, but something was definitely there. Had Bloodstone also grown up on the streets? Or maybe he had a family member who was transgender? Siggy knew better than to ask. If he did, Bloodstone would retreat into his shell and become a brick wall for the rest of the ride.

"My parents came to this planet when I was just a baby," Siggy continued. "They weren't rich, but they made good money. They weren't abusive, but they were strict. They weren't ethical, but they had traditional values. I have eight identical sisters. That's how my people are born – in litters, usually about eight to twelve. But I always knew I was different. I knew before I could even walk."

Siggy intentionally paused a few seconds longer than he normally would have. When he finally saw Bloodstone's head turn a bit to the side, he knew the bounty hunter was invested, waiting for Siggy to continue. Good.

"It was like... It was like I was wearing a costume. I was wearing a girl suit, and the zipper was stuck. And I didn't hate the costume. It was a nice costume. But whenever I looked in the mirror, I didn't see me, I saw the costume. And the older I got, the more uncomfortable the costume got. The worse it felt that I never saw my own face in the mirror. The more frustrating it was that everyone recognized me by my costume, but didn't know the real me."

Bloodstone nodded, and Siggy kept talking. "I confided in my sisters, hoping for a shared experience, hoping to find someone to talk to. But none of them felt the same way. Weird, isn't it? All of us are identical, and yet..." he trailed off. "Anyway, one of my sisters outed me to our parents, and I was out on the street."

"That is unfortunate," Bloodstone said.

"So yeah, I joined the gang to survive, and stole so I could eat and buy hormones. And to hopefully save up for my transition. This went on for years. I kept saving and saving, but crime just doesn't pay much. With every big score there was a setback. At the rate I was going, I would be ancient by the time I could afford any operations. And then one day… an opportunity presented itself."

"The Valmer Estate," Bloodstone said.

Excellent, Siggy thought. *We've gone from mild interest to full-on interaction. By the time we're out of this traffic jam, Bloodstone will be begging to set me free.*

"Yes," the captive confirmed. "It was my sister Sephra who tipped me off. She'd been working for the Valmers as a maid. She knew all their security passwords, and when they'd be on vacation."

"But I thought your family was estranged?" Bloodstone asked.

"She sought me out. She said she wanted to be a family again, despite our parents' wishes. And of course, she knew I had thieving skills. I was so starved for family that I didn't question it."

"So she offered to give you all the information you needed to rob the place, in return for which you'd split the money," Bloodstone said.

"Exactly! So, I waited until the Valmers were on vacation, wrote down all their security codes and procedures, and went to work. Only…"

"Only they weren't on vacation after all."

"Yeah… I thought the house was empty, but they were just asleep. I heard footsteps, saw Mr. Valmer, he shouted something, and I ran. That's it. I didn't kill them, I swear. I've never killed anyone."

"Your hand was found at the crime scene," Bloodstone said. "Sliced off by Mrs. Valmer's AON knife."

"I've never lost a hand in my life," Siggy answered, holding up both hands in protest.

"Except your species can regenerate limbs," Bloodstone said. "A fact you tried to hide at your trial."

They were out of the traffic jam now, on the final stretch of road to the prison. Siggy didn't have much time left. "Yeah, my lawyer's an idiot," he lamented. "He didn't think the prosecutor would come across that bit of trivia. He said when I showed up with two hands, it was going to be an open-and-shut case. But when the prosecutor spouted that little fact, it just made me look that much guiltier. But that wasn't my hand they found, I swear!"

Bloodstone sighed. "The hand was a one hundred percent match with your DNA." The exasperated I'm-tired-of-your-lies tone said it all. The experienced hunter had probably had similar conversations with hundreds of captives over the years.

"I told you, I have identical sisters."

The hovercar slowed down a little.

"Sephra… betrayed me. Her plan, right from the start, was to kill her employers, steal what she could, and blame me. She chose me as her patsy because I had a criminal record, and because she hates trans people."

The car pulled over to the side of the road. Siggy trembled with anticipation. Had he gotten through to the hunter?

"Why didn't you mention this at the trial?" Bloodstone asked.

"At that point, I knew I was being framed, but I didn't know it was by her," Siggy answered. "I couldn't believe she would do that to me, and I didn't want to do anything that might place the blame on her. It wasn't until later, when she visited me in prison, that she made her transphobic attitude clear."

Bloodstone pushed a button on the car's center console. Much to the captive's disappointment, it wasn't the button to open the back doors. A holo screen blinked on, hovering a few centimeters in front of the center console. "Computer," Bloodstone said. "Hack into Sigran Trihannen's case documents."

A loading bar briefly crossed the screen, and a computer voice announced, "Documents found."

Bloodstone tapped the air, swiping through several pieces of evidence on the holographic screen, finally enlarging one. It was a chemical breakdown of the hand that had been left at the crime scene. "Includes traces of artificial testosterone," Bloodstone read aloud.

Uh oh. "Well, see, Sephra is also transgender..."

"You just said she was transphobic. And you keep calling her 'she.' A trans person would never misgender someone that way."

"Okay, maybe it wasn't Sephra. I have seven identical sisters..."

"Eight."

"Yes! I meant I'm one of eight. Look..." The story was falling apart. "Listen, I have money stashed away. Whatever they're paying you to bring me in, I can double it. Triple it!"

Bloodstone made a disgusted sound, pulling the car back onto the road. "Are you even actually trans?"

"Yeah," Siggy said. "That part was true." They didn't speak again for the rest of the ride.

The final stretch of road was a long bridge over the rough, choppy waters of Lake Maligna. It was an artificial lake created specifically for the island prison, full of sharp rocks, toxic water, and genetically-modified piranha. The lake's rotten egg odor made Siggy's stomach lurch, even from this height with the windows sealed. It made his own trash-and-urine-soaked pants smell mild by comparison. The bounty hunter in the front seat appeared to be unaffected, probably because of that fancy helmet's filtering system.

Siggy grew more anxious the closer they got. "Look," he said, panic raising his voice half an octave. "I'm sorry I lied before, but it's death we're talking about. You'd do the same if it was your neck." No reaction. Time was short, so he started talking faster. "Just hear me out. Yes, I'm guilty. As per this planet's privacy laws, they kept my gender out of the news during the trial. Court evidence remains encrypted for a hundred years, by which time I'll be long forgotten. They sent me to a unisex prison with a private cell. Even the warden doesn't know I was born female. As far as the world is concerned, I've always been a guy. But after my death, the coroner isn't bound by the same laws as the judicial system. My birth sex will be made public, and I will become a joke. All I'm asking is for a chance to die with dignity, as a man. Don't let them make me into a joke."

They finished crossing the bridge, and parked the hovercar in the outer courtyard near the gatehouse. Bloodstone got out and took in the scenery. A stone monolith stood in the center of the courtyard, engraved with the words: JUSTICE IS RARELY KIN TO MERCY. – ZURA CHIPRYSS III. There was a picnic area here for who-knows-what reason, and a spectacular panoramic view of the planet's ugliest lake. Beyond the gatehouse, an electrified fence, and a laser grid, the prison itself was a featureless black box that stretched way too far up in the sky. It reminded Bloodstone of a giant anvil, partially buried and abandoned by a long-extinct race of titans.

Two guards and a processing agent came out of the gatehouse to greet the bounty hunter. Bloodstone opened the back door and grabbed Siggy roughly by the wrist. As he was being pulled from the car, Siggy felt something being shoved into his hand. He clenched his fist, not knowing what he was holding but determined to keep whatever it was. Then he was handed off to the guards. Bloodstone spoke to the agent while the guards led Siggy away. As the officer marked the bounty complete on his datapad, authorizing the payment, there was a commotion in the distance. Bloodstone and the agent turned their heads just in time to see a flash of light and some smoke.

The two guards were on the ground, looking confused and dizzy. Siggy ran towards the edge of the grounds. "Stop him!" the processing agent shouted, and Bloodstone patted an empty holster. It was too late to catch Siggy, who reached the outer guardrail and hurled himself over the side. Everyone ran to the edge and studied the waters far down below. There was already a foamy mass of activity as the mutant piranha skeletonized their victim. Within seconds, there would be nothing left to identify.

Sirens blared overhead, and more guards appeared. Too little, too late. The prison's reputation for being inescapable had made the staff arrogant, and their reflexes were slow. There would be a major inquiry after this, and a lot of retraining.

"I apologize," Bloodstone said to the processing agent. "I left my sidearm in the car. Your guards should have done a better job of checking him for weapons. Good thing it was just a flash grenade, it could have been a lot worse."

With the job completed and payment received, the bounty hunter got back into the hovercar. As the vehicle sped back over the bridge, the guards continued watching the bubbling waters down below, mouths wide open, wondering how they'd dropped the ball so badly.

Alterra Sarr was meditating in her room when there was a beep at the door. She reached over and grabbed her mask, pulling it over her head. "Come in," she said. At this voice command, the door automatically unlocked and opened.

As Bloodstone entered the room, Whisper immediately

thought, *Tension*. Even through all that body armor, Whisper could read her body language. Apparently, Bloodstone hadn't had a good day.

"I could come back later if you're..." Bloodstone began, indicating Whisper's state of dress.

Whisper looked down, realizing she was in her underwear. When the door chimed, clothing hadn't seemed nearly as important as disguising her face. Not that it was a big deal for her. Aurorans weren't typically shy about their bodies.

"No, you're fine," Whisper said, reaching for a robe. "Please sit down."

While other members of the crew had redecorated their rooms to feel more like home, Whisper's room remained spartan. Unsure of how long she could risk sticking around, and not really being into creature comforts, she kept it simple. Her room had a bed, a meditation mat on the floor, and a small table with two chairs. Bloodstone sat down on one of the chairs.

"Bad day?" Whisper asked, tying her robe shut.

Bloodstone took off her helmet, and her whole demeanor changed. She subconsciously put on her Bloodstone persona whenever the mask was on, and it affected everything from her body language to her speech patterns. Unmasked, she was no longer Bloodstone, but Detanna Taush. Still tough, still dangerous, but a bit more relatable.

"I..." Detanna said, then paused. Taking a deep breath, she said, "Today I helped a trans person kill himself."

Whisper's eyes widened. Seeing Detanna's expression, Whisper could feel the woman's turmoil. Detanna really wasn't the stone-hearted creature she portrayed when she put the mask on.

"He was a murderer," Detanna continued, "and he was going to die either way, but still..."

Whisper stood up, walked over to Detanna, and gave her a hug. "I understand. Do you want to talk about it?"

They sat and talked for several hours.

02.02 *Gravity*

ED.02500.03.12

Whisper lay on her back, unable to move. The gravity distortion was overwhelming. Although she couldn't lift her head, she could just barely see the tower as it pulsed with bright blue lights. The field affected everything around it. What little vegetation existed on this desolate world was pulled to the ground. A few flying reptiles crashed hard into the cracked, dry soil. Dust rained from above. The ground dampened as even water vapor was pulled from the sky.

Whisper could barely breathe. The very air itself seemed to be crushing her. Out of the corner of her eye, she saw the tower pulse more rapidly. There was a hum in the air that was almost deafening. It increased in pitch until it became an ear-splitting whine. Whisper knew that she couldn't take much more of the crushing force. She could no longer fill her lungs with oxygen. Her own arm, lying across her chest, threatened to flatten her body.

And then it all stopped.

The shaking ground came to rest. The air immediately felt lighter. All sound ceased to exist. Exhausted, Whisper rolled over and pushed herself off of the ground. She gazed upwards at the tower. It had gone dark. Whisper continued to stare at the tower, wondering what would happen next.

She didn't have to wait long. The tower lit up again, this time in pulsating green. A different sort of hum assaulted her ears. The ground once again shook, and the air was pushed away from the ground, nearly taking Whisper with it. As quickly as she could, Whisper ran towards the tower, trying to reach it before gravity gave out completely. With about ten meters to go, she leaped toward the tower with all her might.

With the aid of the dissipating gravity, she hit the tower at over a hundred meters off the ground. She nearly bounced right back off, but at the last second she managed to grab onto an outcrop of electronic sensors. Using electromagnetic pads in her gloves, Whisper secured her position and held on tight. The tower was strangely cool, considering the amount of power flowing through it. It vibrated rhythmically, increasing in magnitude until suddenly a burst of blinding light erupted from the top of the tower.

For that's what the tower was. This cold, dark, thousand-meter-tall structure, the only artificial construct on this nearly barren planet, was actually just the barrel of a monstrous weapon rooted many kilometers under the planet's desolate surface. It was designed by the galaxy's most intelligent scientists, and was now in the hands of the galaxy's most destructive warriors. Simply put, it was the largest Levatech beam ever built. First developed only a hundred years before, Levatech was the innovation that allowed for the invention of artificial gravity, tractor beams, repulsor rays, and even defensive shielding. It was a wonderful discovery that revolutionized everyday lives, and now existed in thousands of machines, performing various functions. But never before had it been used in a device of this scale. This immense weapon was designed to gather all of a planet's gravitational power, and focus it into an incredibly powerful beam.

Holding onto the tower with all her might, Whisper tried not to think about what was probably happening at this very moment to the recipient of the gravity beam. Whatever the outcome, she blamed herself. Bloodstone had asked her not to go on this mission. It wasn't a very high-paying job; it was practically charity. But when Whisper heard about the destructive power this weapon possessed, she'd had to take the case.

She had been hired to apprehend the Grag Prime Arathnon, leader of the planet Grunthar, and to destroy his gravity weapon. She had hoped to stop the beam before it ever had a chance to fire. But she had failed. And somewhere, right now, an entire planet was probably paying the price.

Self-pity won't get you anywhere, Whisper told herself, as she climbed the tower, looking for an access door. Even if she had botched her prime objective, she could still stop the man responsible, and prevent any further misuse of this monstrous device. Climbing the barrel was slow business. The device continued to shake, there were very few handholds, and her electromagnetic gloves weren't nearly as powerful as the strong winds that threatened to knock her off. On the plus side, there was very little gravity at this moment, so she wasn't afraid of falling to her death. With all the gravitational fluctuations, she was actually more afraid of somehow being blasted off into space, where she would float helplessly until her suit's oxygen reserves ran out.

But that wasn't going to happen. The gravitational blast finally ceased. The tower's lights once again faded out, and the shaking finally stopped. The planet's gravity returned to normal. Whisper was almost knocked off the tower as air rushed past her. She was becoming disoriented. The fluctuations of gravity and air pressure were playing hell on her equilibrium. But she'd been trained in the arts of the Auro-Chi, and she knew how to focus her mind and body to accomplish the task at hand. She closed her eyes, took a few deep breaths, popped her ears, and continued the climb.

After another twenty meters, she found what she had been looking for. It was a securely locked maintenance panel, large enough for a Grunthian to climb into. Using a tiny AON welder from her wrist pack, Whisper opened the panel and climbed inside, closing the panel door behind her. It was pitch black, but her already excellent night vision was enhanced further by her helmet. She wasn't sure where she needed to go, but she was fairly certain the main control room would be downwards, deep under the planet's surface. The problem was, this access port didn't provide a direct route downwards. It was merely a small hallway, meant to provide a way of repairing components on this level only. She followed the hallway for about fifteen meters and opened the door at the other end. As she expected, the door opened to the inside of the barrel of the cannon. Leaning over the edge of the doorway, she stared downwards into the barrel. It was a long, smooth tunnel, probably twenty meters across. She couldn't see the bottom. It seemed to go all the way to the center of the planet. It was positively frightening.

It was also her only way down. Taking a deep breath, she climbed through the door and began her descent. There were absolutely no handholds this time, but there also weren't any vibrations or winds, so her gloves worked just fine. Even so, it was a long trip. She couldn't afford to hurry. One slip and her mission would be over for good. She proceeded slowly and carefully, ever mindful that she could be discovered at any time. After descending for quite some time, she found a small ledge. It jutted out from the wall only a few centimeters, but it was enough to rest her toes. Whisper managed to turn her feet sideways and stand on the tiny ledge. She took a short break to rest her arms and collect her thoughts. She had to be below the surface level by now. How much deeper could this possibly go?

Soon she continued her downward climb. But she had only gone a few meters when she heard a noise. It began as a low hum, but increased to a whine. "Oh, great," Whisper said aloud. Some panels on the inside of the barrel began to light up. They were dim at first, but soon they were a bright blue that illuminated the entire tunnel. Whisper could feel the electricity in the air. Gravity was beginning to increase again. *What the hell are they doing?* thought Whisper. *Why would they be firing again so soon? What kind of target could have survived that first blast?* Whisper started descending faster, which wasn't difficult with the increased gravity.

Soon she wasn't even climbing. She was merely using the gloves to hold her to the wall, while the gravitational forces slid her downwards. She looked all around for some way out of this tunnel. She just missed another access panel, sliding by too fast to do anything about it. This continued for quite some time... and then the lights dimmed, and gravity returned to normal.

This was not good. Whisper knew what would happen next. Hanging against the smooth barrel wall, she looked around frantically for any other access panels. And then she saw it. About fifteen meters down, nearly on the opposite side of the barrel, there was a round access port with a circular handle. There was no time to climb down to it. With all her strength, Whisper pushed herself from the wall. As she fell, she grabbed her whip hilt off of her wrist. She pressed the release button, and the whip, made of a super-strong but very compactible synthetic nylon, burst from its hilt. Whisper quickly whipped at the hatch's handle, and luckily it caught. She swung into the far wall, knocking the breath out of her. But she couldn't be slowed. Like the last time, gravity began to lighten and the lights started glowing green.

With all her strength, Whisper climbed the whip up to the door. It was difficult turning the handle, but she managed it. With no time to spare, she opened the access door and climbed through, quickly closing it and locking it behind her.

Almost immediately the tower shook violently and a deafening whine permeated the structure. Whisper got dizzy and fell against the wall. Despite all her Auro-Chi heritage and training, this time it was all too much for her.

She surrendered her mind to the blackness.

Whisper didn't know how long she'd been unconscious. It was impossible to tell the passage of time in this place. She did have a chronometer on her wrist, but the gravity distortions had caused it to reset. Whisper shakily stood up, and carefully explored the room she was in. There were a few status lights on the wall, some pipes and wires, but no actual control panels. There was, however, a hatch on the floor. Whisper opened the hatch and found a tunnel leading downwards. There was a ladder on the wall, and several signs written in an alien language. Whisper descended the ladder for more than fifty meters until she finally reached the control level. Then she began to explore.

The Grag Prime Arathnon was a powerful creature. He was much larger than most Grunthians, but then, that was to be expected. The entire Grunthian chain of command was based on the concept of "might equals right." But he was also highly intelligent for a Grunthian. While he was no scientist, he had one of the most brilliant strategic minds in the galaxy. At this moment his strategic mind was contemplating how he could most effectively use his new toy to rule the galaxy. After all, there was only so much you could do with the ability to destroy a planet. An act of genocide might be fun, and in some ways even therapeutic, but it was also a surefire way to exterminate the very beings you intended to enslave.

No, the threat of using the weapon was a much better tool than the actual weapon itself. And that was the purpose of these tests. Not only to see if it worked, but to prove to anyone watching that yes, indeed, the Grunthians had the power to eliminate anyone who stood in their way. The first shot had blown away an uninhabited world about the same size as Earth. The next shot had destroyed an ancient gas giant, in a spectacularly colorful explosion. Now Arathnon had only to contact Earth and reveal the threat of his weapon. And if they did not immediately submit to Grunthian rule, he would destroy one of Earth's less-populated sister planets, such as Venus or Mars.

The Grunthian leader pondered on this. How badly would the destruction of Mars affect Earth? Would its proximity cause Earth to break from her orbit, dooming all her inhabitants? He knew he could probably look up the answer in some scientific journal, but research wasn't the Grunthian way. It would be much more entertaining to try it and find out. But wait, once again we were dangerously close to exterminating a species he wished to rule. No, first he would destroy something farther away, less likely to affect Earth, but close enough to cause panic. Like Saturn, maybe. And then if they still did not yield, he would destroy Venus, then Mars, and finally the Earth's moon. It was possible that any one of these demonstrations of power would destroy Earth as well, but it was a risk the Grag would make. Besides, he didn't think it would get that far. If Earth didn't surrender immediately after the first threat, then they would surrender after he destroyed Venus. And that's all there was to it.

"Lord?"

"What!" Arathnon snapped. He didn't appreciate having his fantasies interrupted.

The Grunthian underling cringed but continued his report. "My Lord, we've detected an intruder."

"What? Where?" Arathnon also didn't appreciate intruders.

The underling swallowed. "I don't know, Lord. We detected... something in one of the crawlspaces, but it disappeared. We thought it was a sensor glitch. Then we picked it up again, a few levels lower, but only briefly. And one more time, just now, just a few levels above us."

"I should have been notified immediately. Very well. We will flush this spy out, and punish him."

* * *

Whisper watched all of this from an air vent above the control room. She saw the Grunthian leader speaking to his underling, but she couldn't hear anything they were saying. Not that it would have helped her to hear them. They were speaking in Grunthian, which Whisper had yet to learn. Now the leader was gesturing wildly, and pointing to a control panel. What could they be up to? Surely they weren't going to fire again. As she watched, the underling spoke into a speaker, and a loud message resounded through the structure. It sounded rather important, but it was still in Grunthian. Then Arathnon and his underling both reached for some electronic devices, which they put on over their ears. Arathnon gave another order, and his henchman pressed a few buttons on a control panel.

There was a low humming. In the air duct, Whisper wondered what was going on. It wasn't the same sort of hum as when they fired the weapon. This hum was lower, and it sent rapid vibrations through all the walls and floors. Just what were they doing?

The hum increased in pitch. It became higher and higher. And louder, much louder than the noise from the cannon. The noise made Whisper's ears ache, and threw off her equilibrium. Late, too late, Whisper realized that the dizziness was not a side effect of noise, but rather, the point. The Grunthians were trying to flush her out. Fighting to stay conscious, Whisper started to crawl, but she didn't get very far. Her vision spun, her head pounded, and her arms and legs gave out beneath her. She made one last effort to raise her head, and then all went black.

Slowly she regained consciousness. It was bright. Too bright. This wasn't the air duct. As objects came into focus, Whisper realized that she was in a very sterile room. She was lying on a hard steel "bed" with no mattress, pillow, or sheets of any sort. The only other piece of furniture was a waste receptacle against the opposite wall. There were no windows and only one door. The door didn't have any sort of latch on this side.

Whisper also became aware that she was completely nude. *I guess those Grunthians don't leave anything to chance*, she thought, lamenting the loss of the plethora of hidden weapons contained in her stolen clothing. *Well, no use crying over it now,* she decided, and looked around the room. Closer inspection revealed very little else. The door was one of those that slid into the wall, and there was no way to open it from the inside. The air ducts were just small holes in the wall, none of which were large enough for her hand, much less her entire body. There were some drainage holes in the floor, no bigger around than her little finger. The toilet was simply a cylindrical stool about half a meter tall, welded to the floor. The hole in the seat wasn't wide enough for Whisper's head... not that she would want to escape that way. There was no water at the bottom, and it appeared to use an energy grid to dispose of wastes. There were no buttons on the waste device. There was some sort of shower nozzle hanging from the ceiling above the toilet, but Whisper couldn't tell how one was supposed to turn it on.

As long as I'm here... Whisper thought, and she sat on the device and voided her bladder. She could hear an electric crackle coming from deep within the tube, as the energy grid did its work. When she was done, she stood up. Immediately the shower came on, drenching her with a high-pressure blast of water. The water burned slightly, as it seemed to be mixed with some sort of disinfectant. Then the shower cut off, and the water quickly drained into the holes in the floor. *Yeesh*, Whisper thought.

Probably alerted by her activity, the Grag Prime Arathnon entered the room just a few seconds later. He was flanked by two well-armed guards, who took position on each side of the door as it slid back shut. Arathnon, wielding a huge energy weapon, immediately stepped up to Whisper and boomed in perfect English, "All right, spill it. Who are you?"

Whisper was naked, cold, and dripping wet. She felt very

vulnerable, but tried not to let it show. She didn't so much as tremble as Arathnon barked in her face. She stood tall and straight, and while she was dwarfed by the Grunthian leader, she was still imposing in her own right. She looked him right back in the eyes, and told him, "You're under arrest."

The hulking Grunthian squinted slightly with all four eyes. Then he burst out laughing. He held out his two smaller arms, wrists out, and said in mock derision, "You've got me. Here, cuff me!"

Whisper didn't laugh with him. "You are in violation of IGP galactic peace treaty. No weapons capable of genocide are allowed to be used during peacetime."

Arathnon smiled. "I don't recognize the IGP here. They can pass all the stupid laws they want, but they don't apply to me. And what makes you think this is peacetime? We are always in a state of war. Just because we aren't currently in battle doesn't mean we are at peace. And you still have not answered my question. Just who are you?"

Whisper was privately grateful that he didn't recognize her. If he knew that she was Alterra Sarr, the outlaw cop sought for the death of thousands of IGP officers, it could complicate her position. For one thing, Arathnon could use her as a bargaining chip with the IGP, who would pay dearly for the chance to get her back. Or he could offer her to Vermon's home planet Valos in trade for god-knows-what. But then, both of those scenarios could be moot if she couldn't find a way to destroy the cannon.

Actually, it wasn't that surprising that he didn't know who she was. The Alterra Sarr incident was human news, and beyond the Grunthian's spectrum of concern. The huge bounty would have meant nothing to someone as wealthy as Arathnon. And besides, humans probably all looked alike to him.

Whisper decided to come clean, to a point. "I'm a bounty hunter. I was hired by the IGP to find this weapon and disarm it. If I don't make it out of here alive, the IGP will send a fleet to destroy the weapon."

"Let them come," said the Grunthian. "I will destroy anyone who gets near. But first, I will take care of you."

"Of course you will," Whisper taunted. "Because, really, how hard can it be? I'm standing here at your mercy, unarmed and unarmored, naked as the day I was born. Is that really how you want it? Where's the sport?"

The Grunthian leader reached out with one of his two larger arms. He gripped her around the waist, and his fingers actually touched around her back. He squeezed slightly, but to Whisper it felt like he was going to break her back. "You are stalling," he said. "Hoping to weasel your way out of here. You won't succeed."

"I'll admit that. Of course I want to prolong my life. But surely you're not such a wimp that you'd just shoot me dead point-blank? You're a race of hunters. So I challenge you to a hunt."

Arathnon growled, deep in his throat. "You are just a slight human female. You are not worthy to challenge me. It would be over too quickly. As you say, where's the sport in that?"

Whisper took a proud stance, looking more confident than she felt. "It won't be over that quickly. Let me prove it to you."

Arathnon turned to one of his guards and shouted something in his native tongue. The guard gently set down his weapons, and assumed a fighting stance. Lifting one of his two larger arms, he threw a powerful punch in Whisper's direction. It never connected. Before the fist was even halfway to its target, Whisper was in the air, having launched herself up and over the Grunthian's head. As she landed, she threw a hard punch to the base of the monster's spine, causing him to growl in pain. As he turned to face her, his large flat nose was greeted by the heel of Whisper's foot. Her attacker momentarily stunned, Whisper took this opportunity to throw one final punch. Using every last ounce of her strength, she drove her fist at his face, once again targeting his nose. This time the flesh burst upon contact, bones were shattered, and her opponent crashed to the floor.

Whisper stood straight and defiant, even though Arathnon and his surviving guard now had their weapons drawn on her. Pointing at Arathnon, she bravely announced, "I am an Auro-Chi warrior, and I challenge you. That is, if you are brave enough to face me."

The Grunthian leader smiled coldly. "You are full of surprises. Auro-Chi? I thought they were extinct. Very well, then. I could never pass up such an opportunity." Then the Grunthians left, taking the fallen guard with them.

The following morning Whisper woke up in a different cell. She knew that she'd been drugged at some point. They could never have moved her without waking her, and besides, she had a strange groggy feeling that those of her species seldom experienced. She sat up and looked around the cell. This one was smaller than the previous cell. There was a small table next to the door. On the table was a plate of food, a plain shirt and pants, a cloth belt, and a small knife.

Whisper's first instinct was to grab the knife and hide it, but logic told her that it wasn't going anywhere. Instead, she calmly got to her feet, used the crude toilet, put on the clothing, and ate the bland food. Only when she was ready for action did she grab the knife and tuck it in her belt.

She turned to the door, which had a handle this time. Whisper turned the handle and the door opened easily. She looked cautiously out the door and saw only a huge empty room. There was an exit at the far end of the room, several hundred meters away. She stepped out of the cell and the door swung shut behind her. Then, from some hidden speaker, a voice loudly proclaimed, "The hunt has begun."

In seconds, everything changed. Walls slid upward from

various niches in the floor, creating a maze of hallways and corridors. The lights dimmed, and fog filled the room. Whisper, whose feet were still bare, jumped as a jolt of electricity ran through the floor tile she'd been standing on. There was a now-familiar humming sound, and the gravity in the room started to get lighter. There was a high-pitched whine which gave her a headache and made her dizzy.

Why did they even build this? Whisper thought. But it wasn't too surprising, knowing the Grunthians. Before this site was chosen for the gravity cannon experiment, it had probably been home to a training facility. Most Grunthian-owned planets ended up housing military bases sooner or later.

For a short while she stood there, trying to adjust herself to these attacks on her senses. Then she entered the maze. She had heard of these Grunthian death hunts. Somewhere in this maze, Arathnon was trying to find her. He would probably be armed the same as she was, with only a simple knife. Also, somewhere in the maze there was an exit, the same exit she saw before the walls went up, only now it was obscured by the maze. If she could make it to the exit, she would live. Maybe they would let her go free, or maybe they would keep her captive until they found a way to profit from her. But at least she would survive the day.

On the other hand, if Arathnon found her, it was even money. Maybe she would defeat him, and maybe she wouldn't. The Grunthian guard had been an easy kill, but Whisper knew that Arathnon was a much greater opponent. Grunthian leaders were chosen based on their strength and fighting skills. Whisper, like all those of her species, could size up an opponent simply by the way they moved. She had known from the moment she saw Arathnon that he was a highly skilled warrior. It would be a difficult fight. Arathnon was obviously stronger, but Whisper had the advantage when it came to speed.

The environment was also a factor. Arathnon had probably completed many hunts in mazes such as this, so he had the home court advantage. If it weren't for the noises throwing off her balance and making it difficult to think, Whisper could probably have just closed her eyes and used her other senses to find her way to the exit. But instead, she had to try to mentally block out the noises and rely on her excellent night vision to guide her.

Whisper continued down the hallways, dodging electrified tiles, avoiding pits that would sometimes open up under her feet, and ducking under the occasional flame jet that erupted from holes in the walls. Gravity fluctuated from corridor to corridor, and some of the walls were covered with tiny sharp blades. It was slow going at best, but Whisper managed to make some headway. She had a great sense of direction, and even with all the maze's distractions, she did a reasonably good job at choosing corridors that took her closer to her goal.

As she turned one corner, she was thrown off her feet by a huge burst of wind. Some sort of concussion cannon, protruding only slightly from the ceiling, had blasted her. She was knocked roughly across the hallway, barely missing a row of spikes protruding from the wall. She was still seeing stars when she heard a loud roar. She couldn't tell which direction the noise was coming from. She had no time to react as a huge bellowing figure came running down the hall, reaching for her.

The Grag Prime Arathnon grabbed the still-stunned bounty hunter around her waist with one huge hand and threw her across the corridor. In mid-flight, Whisper twisted and turned with cat-like grace, and landed in a battle-ready crouch. As the Grunthian leader ran toward her, wielding a large hunting knife, a dozen fighting strategies ran through Whisper's mind. She considered tossing her much-smaller knife straight for his jugular, but she didn't want to part with her only weapon. If he were to block or dodge the throw, she would have to face this monster completely unarmed.

When Arathnon finally reached her, Whisper vaulted backward, rebounding off the wall and over the

Grunthian's head. As she landed on the other side, she narrowly avoided her opponent's huge fist. He had anticipated her move and had already turned to face her. Whisper watched her opponent closely, for any sign of what he might do next. A twitch of his upper right shoulder told her to expect another blow. Immediately she dodged his upcoming punch...

...And she was knocked senseless by a kick to the ribs. Arathnon was smart, and he knew who he was facing. This experienced warlord knew how to avoid telegraphing his moves. Still, Whisper was faster, and she managed to roll into a defensive crouch before shooting down a side hallway. When Arathnon came around the corner, Whisper wasn't there. Using her stealth abilities to blend in with the shadows, she watched as the Grunthian slowly walked by her, looking every which way. He came within inches of her but finally moved on. When his back was finally to her, Whisper slowly raised her knife and prepared for the killing strike.

And then he turned back around. He walked back towards her again, stopped, and looked around the room with a puzzled look on his face. He started to turn away again...

And without warning, moving impossibly fast, Arathnon whirled towards Whisper and swung his knife at her head. She quickly thrust herself backward but still received a gash across her forehead. She hit the floor, rolled towards her opponent, and sprung through his legs and out of harm's way. Arathnon turned to face her, but she was gone. He looked all around the room, but she was nowhere to be found.

Whisper then dropped from the ceiling and landed on the Grunthian's back. She wrapped one arm across Arathnon's head, covering his eyes. In her other hand she still held her knife, which she used to fend off her enemy's four groping hands. Whisper knew that she could win it all right here. From this position, if she moved quickly enough, she could easily give the Grunthian a lethal laceration in one of a dozen vital areas.

But what would that get her? Once she won the battle, the other Grunthians would simply gas the maze, and she would wake up in another cell. No, if she was going to get out of here, and destroy the gravity cannon as well, she would have to play this one another way. But how? She had to make a decision quickly. The time to strike was now. If she didn't use her advantage, Arathnon would soon grab her and kill her.

Whisper gave one last stab at Arathnon's grasping fingers, and then she brought her knife down, hard and deep, into the Grunthian's shoulder. He bellowed in pain and crashed to the floor. Whisper didn't know much about Grunthian physiology, but she knew a lot about humanoid anatomy in general, and she was good at extrapolation. She had pierced Arathnon in a very important nerve, one which controlled a lot of his motor functions. The Grunthian was paralyzed from the neck down.

"Imbecile," Arathnon said. "You should have killed me. What do you hope to gain by keeping me alive?"

"You're my ticket out of here," Whisper replied.

"You obviously know very little of our culture. Do you honestly think any of my followers will care if I die? They're probably already fighting amongst themselves over who will take my place. And now that they've seen me in such a state of weakness, I will never hold such a high office again. I will probably be executed."

"Then help me," Whisper offered. "In exchange, I will restore your status."

"What do you have in mind?"

"Can they hear us?" Whisper asked.

"No. There are cameras but no microphones," Arathnon answered.

"All right," Whisper said. "First off, I should tell you, you're not paralyzed for life. It was a very precise cut. It didn't sever the nerve, it only grazed it. If I remove the knife, you should be able to walk within a few minutes, and you'll be completely healed in a few days. But I'm sure that won't make any difference to your followers here. They'll take advantage of your temporary weakness to finish you off. But if we destroy this complex, with everyone in it, then no one on your homeworld will ever know you were wounded. You can report back to Grunthar that the weapon self-destructed due to some malfunction, or you can even claim that it was a saboteur whom you later found and killed. This would even give you an alibi for the time it takes you to return to your home planet... time which you will actually spend recovering from this wound."

"Destroy the cannon? That device cost me a lot," Arathnon growled.

"If you don't accept my offer, you will lose your command and die. It's not up for negotiation."

Arathnon fumed. "Agreed," he finally said. Whisper removed the knife. Using cloth from Arathnon's shirt, she dressed the wound.

"Can you stand yet?" Whisper asked.

"No," Arathnon replied. "And time is running out. My guards have probably already entered the maze. We need to get out of here before they reach us."

"I should be able to handle them," Whisper began. "How many—"

"No," Arathnon interrupted. "If the operators in the control room see you defeat the guards, they'll release poison gas into the maze. But I have an escape route. There is a small device clipped to my belt..." Whisper found the device and looked at it. It was some sort of remote control. "Show it to me. Good. Now press the third button from the left, in the second row." Whisper pressed the button, and several doors closed throughout the maze. "That should buy us some time," Arathnon said.

A few minutes later Arathnon was able to walk, and they

started to move. He continued to give Whisper orders, and she continued to use the remote to open various doors and guide them through the maze. Eventually they came to a final secret passage that took them out of the maze. They took several other secret hallways until they reached the control room. Before entering, they scoped out the situation. Three armed guards stood against the walls, and two operators sat at computers.

By this time, Arathnon was able to use his arms, but he was still very weak. Whisper was going to have to take care of this room herself. "Stay here," Whisper said. Arathnon nodded. He watched from a small vent as Whisper sneaked into the room. Using her stealth abilities, she slid along the shadows until she was behind one of the guards. Suddenly she burst from a corner, slitting one guard's throat with Arathnon's knife. The other two guards immediately turned on her and fired, but Whisper rolled under their shots and back into the shadows. They kept aiming at where she'd been, ready to fire when she emerged, but she surprised them yet again by emerging from the shadows behind them.

She disarmed the next guard before he even knew she was there. Now holding the guard's weapon, she used it as a club and knocked him hard in the face. She then tossed the energy weapon aside and jumped at the next guard with her knife. Still watching from the secret passage, Arathnon thought this a curious move. If you have the gun, why throw it away in favor of a knife? Hers was a strange species indeed.

Now all three guards were down, and Whisper easily took out the computer operators, who weren't used to combat situations. Arathnon came out of hiding and sat down at a computer terminal. First he sealed off all the doors in the complex. Then he reconfigured the settings on the gravity cannon. "This should take care of everything," he said. "This will cause the cannon to draw in power, the same as it does before it fires. Only this time it will do it continuously, until it finally crushes this planet and everything on it. Now let us depart, we haven't got much time."

Gravity was already starting increase in the room. The unlikely pair ran through the complex, Arathnon using his remote to open doors as they came to them. Soon they made it to the landing bay, where they went their separate ways. The two escape ships blasted off from the collapsing planet. At first it was hard to break orbit, because of the power of the device. Both ships were almost pulled back to the surface. But then the complex caved in, destroying the device's power source, and gravity burst forth from the planet. Both ships were snapped away from the planet as if they had been launched by rubber bands. The planet burst apart until it was just a cloud of cosmic dust.

Whisper's ship fought its way through the turbulence created by the planet's explosion. It was almost clear when it was struck by a large chunk of rock. Whisper held the controls tight, fighting desperately to keep control of the ship. She was just congratulating herself for her maneuvers when all the lights went out. It was pitch black for a few seconds, until the backup power supply kicked in and a few dim lights came back on.

Whisper played around with the controls. No luck. She was floating dead in space. She went to the back of the ship to survey the damage. She opened a large panel on the back wall, and found that several power glanges had overloaded. *Thank goodness*, Whisper thought. At least that was something she could fix. However, it would take a good while, especially without replacement glanges. She would have to remove each glange individually, take them apart, reposition the turblexes, recalibrate the zikk valves, reset the klop fuses, put the glanges back together, and hope they would still hold a charge.

And until then, she was vulnerable. The ship couldn't move or fire weapons. She might be able to send a message, but only at sublight frequencies. It would take days if not weeks for the Bloodwind to receive whatever message she sent. By then it would be a moot point - either her repairs would already be done, or she would be dead.

Something caught Whisper's attention, out of the corner of her eye. She turned and looked out the window. Arathnon's ship sat there in space, facing her. A light blinked on her communications panel. She only had enough power for audio, but she knew Arathnon's voice immediately. "So, once again I find you at my mercy."

"I'm a little busy at the moment," Whisper said back, desperately trying to disassemble a glange without the benefit of tools.

"I can see that," Arathnon's voice continued. "I've run a diagnostic scan on your ship. You are completely helpless."

"Yes, and what a fine trophy I would make," Whisper spat back, banging a glange against the wall in a futile attempt to get it open.

"You will find a set of replacement glanges behind the panel under the fire suppression system. There should also be a toolkit there as well."

Whisper looked and found that he was correct. "Thank you," she said.

"Something you should know," Arathnon said. "The cannon you destroyed today was the second such cannon built. The first was demolished before it was even finished. I doubt my people will attempt to build another. We don't repeat failures. But the Grunthians are not the only ones to have acquired the technology. The Inner Eye also has a copy of the blueprints. Keep your eyes open."

"Thanks again," Whisper said. "But why tell me?"

"You are a brave fighter," Arathnon answered. "I look forward to facing you in battle again someday." Then the communicator went silent. Outside the window, Whisper saw the other escape shuttle turn and blast away in the other direction.

For a while, Whisper just stood there, staring off into empty space. "See ya," she finally said, to no one in particular. Then she finished her repairs and went on her way.

Having lost her equipment during the mission, Whisper had to improvise an outfit before she returned to the Bloodwind. Luckily there was some spare clothing in a locker on the escape ship. It was Grunthian sized, but Whisper was able to fashion a mask with some of the material.

Later, back on the freighter, she sat with Detanna at the little table in her room, just talking, as had become a habit for them lately.

"You actually managed to defeat Arathnon in hand-to-hand combat?" Detanna asked incredulously.

"I'm not bragging or anything," Whisper said. "You did ask for a full report. But don't tell anyone. I promised the Grag Prime I wouldn't let anyone know of his defeat."

"Who would believe me?" Detanna said. "But I have to know something. You keep referring to your clan, but you're very vague about the specifics. I analyzed your fighting style, but it's not in my database. Not to mention your ability to absorb light and sound. Who exactly are your people?"

"I'm not allowed to say," Whisper answered.

"You're from Auroris," Detanna said.

"What?" Whisper was always surprised when someone knew about her planet.

"You called your fighting style 'Auro-Chi-Vau.' Aren't the Auro-Chi those mystic martial artists from a forgotten planet?"

"That's cryptozoology," Whisper answered. "The Auro-Chi are a myth."

"They're not. I met one a couple of years ago. He called himself Crossbones. He had gray skin like yours."

Whisper's eyes sparked with recognition, but she didn't say anything.

"I knew it," Detanna said. "See? You can't hide anything

from me. Crossbones had a similar fighting style. You guys don't get out much, do you?"

"We have good reason to be xenophobic," Whisper admitted. "We have abilities that some people want to exploit. Your friend and I are probably the only ones to have left our homeworld in a century."

"I wouldn't call him a friend. He was a pirate. Come to think of it, I never saw his face, either," Detanna recalled.

Good, Whisper thought. That made her lie about masks more plausible. She'd heard of Crossbones, the the so-called "pirate ninja." She even had a sneaky suspicion as to his true identity. If she was right, she wasn't surprised that Crossbones always kept his mask on. He was a true believer.

"Your fighting style is impressive," Detanna offered. "It's both beautiful and effective. Like a deadly… ballet."

"What about you?" Whisper asked. "I've watched you fight as well. Once I identified fourteen different martial arts moves in a ten-minute fight. Your reflexes are superhuman. Not to mention your weapon skills. Have you been training since birth or what?"

"It's a secret," Bloodstone said. "Ask me again later, when I know I can trust you. Maybe by then, you'll trust me with your face."

On a remote area of the planet Mars, far from any settlements, a privately owned patch of land was barren except for a large crater. Measuring approximately seventy-five kilometers on each side, this property was owned by a mining company called Mervon Incorporated. The edges of the property were blocked off by high electric fences, decorated with large signs proclaiming "Private Property! Danger! Keep Out! High Risk of Toxic Exposure!" in multiple languages. They needn't have bothered, as no actual roads led to this property. A few buildings surrounded the crater, but little movement was ever seen on the surface.

In the center of the crater, there was a huge round hatch, which was almost always sealed shut. Despite being owned by a mining company, the crater did not, in fact, lead to any caves full of precious metals. But if one were to find a way through the center hatch, they would discover a huge underground complex, alive with activity. All manner of automated construction equipment worked day and night, while eight-legged androids labored tirelessly around their project. In the center of it all, a giant cylindrical cannon pointed towards the hatch.

Standing on a walkway, a striking young woman surveyed the progress. She was dressed in bright crimson, from her tight leather jacket down to her dangerously-inappropriate-for-a-construction-environment heels. She looked over various reports with her white eyes, ticked off electronic checklists with razor-sharp nails, and studied holographic star charts. The planets would align in approximately two years, giving her a perfect line of sight to Earth. Her bright red lips curled into a truly frightening smile. The cannon would be ready by then, no question.

02.03   *Science Experiments*

ED.02500.04.21

Raven sat in a chair in the lab, unarmored and limbless, as one headless robot performed the final tweaks on another headless robot. When the fine-tuning was done, she commanded model v01 to stand in the recharging station in the corner, and transferred her mental control to model v02.

The sculptor, Raven's long-time best friend Trenyn, had done their job well. It was a perfect human body. It now had soft flesh-colored "skin" - actually a synthetic polymer - covering muscles that actually flexed when the body moved. The body was sexy and feminine, soft to the touch and perfectly proportioned. It wasn't anatomically correct in the intimate areas, but so what? Anyone who got that close to her would probably already know the body wasn't real. And nobody ever got that close to her.

Raven, though having no arms of her own, thought about putting her hands on her hips. The new body immediately did so. This entertained Raven, so she had the body do a little dance. It was a little clumsy, but it looked okay. Then Raven thought of finishing up the dance with a nice little spin, and the robot complied - knocking Raven off of the chair in the process.

Raven was glad that no one had seen her do that. She had

never been one for frivolity, not even when she was alone. However, after so many years of having been confined to a chair, these new bodies occasionally made her feel a bit euphoric. But that was enough for now. At Raven's mental command, the robot picked her up off of the floor. The robot's chest opened up, and Raven was placed inside the chest cavity. The chest closed again, and Raven looked in the mirror.

She looked almost like a perfect human woman. Sure, her head looked slightly small compared to her body, and the skin tones didn't match exactly, but it wasn't noticeable. At the neckline it was very obvious that it was a suit, but a high-collared shirt or even a well-placed necklace could fix that, if it was thick enough. With the right ensemble, this body was perfect. She could now fit into a crowd quite easily, and she could live a more normal life.

Except she couldn't feel. She could touch an object, but she couldn't tell its texture, its temperature, or even its weight. She could lie on a bed of satin, and she wouldn't be able to tell it from broken glass. And she could caress a lover's body... but she would never know the warmth of his skin, the roughness of his unshaven face, or the soft downy feel of his chest hair. Not that this was important to her. Raven cared little for men; they had only caused her pain in her life. She much preferred intellectual pursuits now.

Still, she'd been having these dreams lately. She could never really remember them, but she always awoke feeling... unfulfilled.

Raven shook her head. This wasn't the kind of thing she wanted to think about. Her mother was dead, killed by two male thugs, hired by her own father. Her mother had been a great woman. Her father had been an evil monster. Both parents had been true to their gender; it was as simple as that.

Stop that, she thought, once again catching herself in unhealthy thoughts. She definitely believed that, on the whole, men had contributed more evil to the universe than women. But blanket statements didn't help anyone. It was an opinion born from emotion, and she preferred facts over feelings.

Raven left the lab and returned to her room. She put on a pair of boots and pulled on some gloves. Then she pulled her trenchcoat out of the closet and slipped it on. Now she looked perfectly human.

Except, of course, for her eyes. A genetic gift from her father, Raven's eyes had no pigment. In public she usually wore sunglasses, but here, on board this ship, she didn't bother. Everyone here knew who and what she was. Raven left the room and headed for the ship's main control room.

The woman in the picture was tall and fair-skinned. She was strikingly beautiful, but she also had a toughness about her, a determination that showed through in her facial expressions. This was a woman who was unaccustomed to failure.

"Her name," Bloodstone said, "is Doctor Veloria Keen. Reports say that she has invented a new energy source that could revolutionize space travel. But only if she survives long enough to finish her research. Someone is trying to kill her, we're not sure who. Probably a seller of alternative fuels, not wanting her invention to edge them out of business." Bloodstone turned off the video screen and pointed to Raven.

"Your job is just to keep her safe," Bloodstone explained, "while the rest of us track down her assassins. We'll also be playing decoy - her hitmen will believe that she is on this ship; meanwhile, you and Keen will be planetside together."

Raven nodded. "What if the assassins show up?"

"They won't," Bloodstone answered. "Even if they figure out that Veloria's not here, they still won't know where to find you. But... just in case... I'll see to it that you're well armed."

* * *

Ten hours later, Veloria Keen and Raven Vermon found themselves in a well-stocked office, nearly two hundred stories above street level. They had rented some office space and turned it into temporary living quarters, with a couple of cots and some suitcases full of clothes. There weren't a lot of creature comforts, but neither of them were creatures of comfort.

They were, of course, talking science. Raven expounded on every single feature of her new robot body, and Veloria spent hours explaining her discovery to a somewhat skeptical Raven. But while Raven had trouble believing Veloria's theories, overall she found the scientist to be a rather engaging conversationalist.

"Doctor Keen," Raven said, "how can you possibly be so sure about the efficiency of your power source if you haven't even built one yet?"

"Please call me Veloria. Or Vel. And I may not have had the opportunity to build an actual battery yet, but I've done hundreds of computer simulations," Keen answered.

"Computer simulations are often wrong," Raven said. "Did the simulations account for real-world variations, such as mag—"

"—netic fluctuations? Of course. I've tried it at all tolerances, and in all environments. On the last test, the margin for error was less than point zero two percent. This is legit."

Raven looked back over the doctor's work. It was impressive. Some of it was way over even Raven's head. She doubted Trenyn would make much sense of it either. "And the only reason you haven't built one is—"

Keen took a step toward Raven. "I can't get my hands on the materials. For it to work, I'll need pure urallian ore. It's not easy to come by, but only because no one's had any use for it until now. When this battery tests successfully, the urallian mining process will be refined until it's commonplace."

"Vel, I want to believe you," Raven said after a pause. "I hope you're correct."

"I am," Veloria answered. "You'll see."

They were awakened that night by a loud banging. The entire skyscraper shook as if hit by a meteor. Raven quickly got into her robot body and ran to Veloria's room. Vel was already halfway dressed. Raven ran past her and looked out the window. Two large ships flew around the building, firing missiles at the structure. Local police ships were fighting back, but they were clearly outclassed.

"If they're here for you," Raven said, "they only know that you're in this building. Not which floor. That should buy us some time."

"Not if they destroy the entire building," Veloria answered. "And they will." As if to punctuate her statement, the building rocked violently as it took another powerful hit.

"Dammit!" Raven said. "Grab a shirt. We're getting out of here."

Instead of finding a shirt, Vel started shoving papers into her satchel. "What are we going to do?" she asked. "We'll never make it all the way down in time."

The building shuddered again. Outside the window, the police ships were winning. The attackers were huge, but they were outnumbered by the swarm of IGP ships. But the attackers had one more card to play. In unison, both enemy ships changed their course and headed straight for the tower. As Raven watched in horror, they collided, probably fifty stories below, with enough force to break the building in half.

"Come on!" Raven shouted, grabbing Vel by the arm. With her other hand Raven smashed the window. Now holding Vel around the waist, Raven jumped out the window. After several seconds of freefall, Raven activated one of her suit's more interesting features. Two small propulsion devices popped out of her hips, and two more emerged from her ankles. They were Levatech jets - not powerful enough to actually grant flight, but enough to slow down a fall, like an electronic parachute.

They fell for what seemed like hours. Actually, it was about six minutes, all told. On the way down, they had a good view of the destruction that had been caused. The building had been cleaved in two. The top half had fallen sideways, toppling several nearby buildings like giant dominoes. The lower half, with the remains of the two ships burning on top, slowly crumbled. Fires occasionally erupted throughout the building, and every few seconds a window or two would burst with flame.

The ships had been highly explosive, that was obvious. This had been their plan all along. Maybe the ships had been empty, remotely piloted from somewhere far away. Or maybe this was the work of someone very dedicated to what they were doing.

Raven and Vel continued falling, putting as much distance as possible between themselves and the building. This was going to cause a chain reaction of destruction that would affect several city blocks, and there might be further attacks. They needed to get out of town.

They set down on the South side of town, many blocks from the chaos. Once they landed, they found an abandoned hovercar. The engine was still running. The owner had probably stepped out to find a place to hide. Raven and Vel jumped into the car and sped out of the city. They weren't the only ones with this idea. A lot of citizens were trying to flee. But Raven was a good driver and she managed to avoid the other cars as she floored her way out of town.

Several hours later, Raven and Veloria hid in the basement of an empty house. No one seemed to be home, but they decided to stay in the basement just the same. It would have been ironic to survive a collapsing building and then get shot as burglars. Veloria, wearing pants and a bra but no shirt, looked through her satchel, making sure she still had all her notes. Raven tended to some of her "wounds," actually places where her suit's artificial skin had been torn or otherwise damaged. She used a polymer resin, which she kept in a first aid kit inside her leg, to mend these areas.

"Thank you for saving my life," Veloria said. Satisfied by what she had found, Vel closed up the satchel and set it aside.

"It's why you hired me," Raven answered. "But I probably would have done it anyway. I would hate to see such a fine scientific mind get extinguished. I'm just sorry so many innocent people had to die."

Vel stood up and walked over to Raven. She stood close, closer than Raven usually got to people. She put her hands on each of Raven's shoulders, looking her in the eyes. Though Raven couldn't feel Vel's touch, she felt an odd tingle anyway.

"If it makes you feel any better," Vel said, "Downtown is empty on the weekends. There are no events, no shopping, and nothing's open. The loss of life was probably minimal." They were almost touching noses. "But," Vel added, "It's good that you care."

Vel leaned in and kissed Raven on the lips. Raven was surprised at first, and almost pulled away. But then she gave in and started kissing back, if only to satisfy her scientific curiosity.

Finally, they separated. Vel smiled until she noticed Raven's odd expression. "What's wrong?" she asked.

"...Huh," Raven said, uncharacteristically at a loss for words.

"What?" Vel asked.

"Well," Raven said, "That was... not unpleasant. But... I am most definitely not a lesbian."

"Oh," Vel said, disappointed.

"...Sorry? I wasn't trying to lead you on or anything..."

"No, no, it's fine," Vel said, blushing. "I just thought I picked up on a vibe."

Raven sighed. "You're not... wrong. I just... I always wondered about my sexuality. I wasn't into men, and I assumed that if it wasn't men, it must be women. But... apparently not. Sorry."

"It's fine," Vel repeated, patting Raven on the shoulder. "This... experiment failed. But we both derived knowledge from it, and that knowledge will strengthen our friendship in the future."

Raven half-smiled at the labored metaphor, then changed the subject. "I don't get it," she said. "The assassins are so bent on killing you, they destroyed half a city. If it's a rival fuel company, it seems like they'd at least want to steal your research first, and see if it's viable for them to manufacture. They wouldn't destroy the entire building you're in, research and all. And how did they find you, anyway?"

"I swear I don't know," Vel said.

They waited a bit more, then risked going upstairs. The house was still unoccupied. They found a shirt for Vel, and some plain clothing Raven could wear over her robot body. She also managed to scrounge up a pair of sunglasses.

"Maybe we shouldn't stay in one place for too long," Raven suggested. "They found you once... are you sure there aren't any tracking devices on you?"

"Good question," Vel said. Raven flipped open a panel on the back of her left hand. She tapped a few keys on a tiny viewscreen, then pointed at Vel with her index finger. A built-in scanner analyzed Vel and her satchel, looking for anything that might be giving off a signal. Nothing.

"I left a whole suitcase back at the skyscraper," Vel offered. "Maybe there was a tracker in there."

"Even so," Raven said. "I'd feel better if we weren't just waiting around for my teammates to find your assassins. What if we sent your papers to the media?"

"Then I might not get credit," Vel said. "Once the data leaves my person, anybody could claim they discovered it first."

"But they'll stop trying to kill you," Raven said. "And your invention will still make the galaxy a better place. Isn't that enough?"

"This is my life's work," Vel said indignantly. "I lived on noodles and water for a decade, putting every extra credit into this research. I'm not asking to be rich, but I've put in my hours. I deserve to be recognized, and to live comfortably."

Raven couldn't argue with that. While she'd had her tragedies, she'd also been privileged enough not to live hand-to-mouth. While money and fame had never been Raven's motivation, she couldn't fault Vel for wanting the break she'd earned.

"But," Vel offered, "I have an idea. Back at my lab, I have notes on all the stages of the experiment. I have data going back years. If I can get my hands on that, I can prove that the tech is mine. We can release the notes to the media, and I'll have backup proof that I was the one who developed the process."

Raven shook her head. "We can't go back to your lab. The assassins will be watching it."

"Not this lab," Vel said. "I have a second, secret lab, that no one knows about."

Raven looked skeptical, but she agreed.

They left through the back door. A creek ran along behind the house's backyard. They followed the creek into a wooded area, and eventually came out in a park. The park was nearly empty, due to the disaster downtown. It would probably be a few weeks before people felt safe in public spaces again.

But the park wasn't completely unoccupied. As Raven and Vel walked past the playground area, they heard the whine of a cheap energy pistol warming up. *Great,* Raven thought, turning around.

But it wasn't a professional assassin. It was just some guy. He wore a brown overcoat and looked like he hadn't shaved in four days. He pointed his pistol at the two women, moving it back and forth between them. "Fancy a ride, ladies?" he said, gesturing toward the parking lot with his chin.

"No thank you," Vel said, eyeing the gun nervously.

"Leave us alone," Raven said, much more calmly.

"Oh, would that I could, my lovelies, but you've stolen my heart. How could I possibly—"

"I'm bored with this," Raven said, quickly snatching the weapon from the man's hands. "Now," she said, turning the weapon back on him, "You said you have a car?"

Half an hour later, Raven and Vel pulled into the parking lot of a small office building. "Trevill's Chemical Supply?" Raven asked, reading the sign above the door.

"Side business. Trevill's my lab assistant," Vel said. "Don't worry, he's out of town. The lab is in the basement."

"But you said no one else knew about this lab," Raven said.

"No one but him. But he wouldn't try to kill me," Vel said.

They walked around to the back of the building. The back door was securely locked, with an electronic keypad above the handle. "Shoot," Vel said. "I had the code in my suitcase back at the skyscraper..."

Raven held up her right index finger, and a small data interface connector protruded from the tip. She inserted it into a dataport on the side of the keypad. Within a few seconds, she'd hacked the code. The door popped open, and no alarms sounded. They went through the door and down some stairs.

It was a lab, all right. Several tables were full of microscopes and beakers, alongside more high-tech devices.

A glowing energy cell sat on one table. "There it is," Vel said, grabbing the battery. "My one working prototype."

Raven looked confused. "I thought you hadn't built one yet?" she asked.

"Trevill must have finished it in my absence. Now if you'll help me hack into this computer, I can download the rest of my notes." She indicated a large monitor with a keyboard in front of it.

"Don't you remember any of your passwords?" Raven asked.

Vel laughed. "I know, right? Typical 'absent-minded professor' syndrome. I can unlock the secrets to unlimited energy, but I can't set the clock in my hovercar."

Raven managed to access the computer, and Vel pushed her aside. "Just give me a few minutes and I'll have everything I need," Vel said, transferring files to a data stick.

As Vel worked, Raven looked around the lab. There were several plaques on the wall, awards recognizing the brilliance of one Doctor Arvan Trevill. There was a photo of Doctor Trevill receiving a diploma from the Vhelra Science Academy. There was nothing commemorating Vel. "So…" Raven began, then paused. "Earlier you tried to explain the science of your invention to me, but I really didn't get it. Could you dumb it down for me?"

Vel was more than eager to show off her genius. She explained how the power source worked, as best as she could, but it involved so many new theories and extrapolations that Raven still wasn't sure how it came together. The first time they'd spoken about it, back in the skyscraper, Raven had just assumed that Vel's mind was so vast that she had difficulty communicating her thoughts clearly. Raven had met scientists like that. Sometimes Trenyn was like that.

But this time, it felt different. Vel definitely had a brilliant mind, no question. She knew just the right gibberish to say to make it sound like her science was viable, if beyond the understanding of most people. But it was, in fact, gibberish.

"Shoot, I forgot," Raven said, interrupting Vel's lecture. "I need to check in with my teammates. They need to know where I am." Raven pulled out her comm unit.

"There's no need for that," Vel said. "We're almost done here. You can call them from the car."

Raven shook her head. "I'm overdue. They'll worry."

"Okay, but first…" Vel stood up and gave Raven a hug. Raven froze. It didn't seem like a huggable moment, but how would Raven know? "Thank you so much for helping me today," Vel said.

"You're… welcome?" Raven said uncertainly.

Vel pulled away. "And thank you for telling me so much about your suit," she said, holding up a small rectangular object. Raven recognized it immediately. It was the battery pack that powered her body. Vel had taken it out during the hug. Raven tried to grab it back, but she couldn't move. She was trapped in her own body, a living statue.

Raven sighed. "Trevill isn't actually your lab partner, is he?"

"Nope," Vel answered with a wink.

"The invention is Trevill's. You stole his notes, and now you're stealing the rest of his research."

"And I couldn't have done it without you," Vel said, tossing the battery pack over her shoulder. "It turns out knowledge really is power."

Maybe I can keep her talking, Raven thought. She hadn't told Vel about her backup battery. Unfortunately, it would take about two minutes to come online. She had the sneaky suspicion Vel didn't intend to let Raven live that long.

The downloads had finished, and Vel pulled her data stick out of the computer. She put it in her pocket, then held a gun at Raven's head. It was the mugger's gun, from the park. She popped out the gun's universal power cell, and replaced it with Trevill's prototype battery.

"I'm sorry it had to end this way," she said, walking

backward toward the stairs, all the while keeping the weapon aimed at Raven. "But at least you can help me test this new energy source." Unsure of how powerful the blast would be, Vel waited until she was halfway up the stairs before she pulled the trigger.

The gun exploded in a flash of green light. The stairs collapsed beneath Vel, and chunks of the ceiling fell on top of her. "Help me, please," Vel moaned.

Raven was unharmed. Her backup battery came online a few seconds later. Always the professional, she unburied Vel and gave her prompt medical attention.

Doctor Veloria Keen lost both hands and one eye in the explosion. She ended up in prison for conspiracy and fraud. Raven chose not to press charges for attempted murder, and she even wrote to her in prison. Stuck within the walls of the penitentiary, Vel was no longer distracted by greed or the promise of fame. She moved on to other research, motivated by her passion for science for the first time in years. For her, it was like being in college again, and she loved it. A few months into her sentence, Raven visited her and gifted her with new prosthetic hands and an eye.

For his role in the destruction of downtown, Doctor Arvan Trevill was charged with terrorism and multiple murders. Instead of prison, he was sent to a maximum security mental health facility. It turned out that working with urallian ore had some nasty side effects, at least for Vhelrans like Doctor Trevill. Long-term contact caused the user to completely lose control of their emotions. This is why Trevill resorted to such overkill in his attempt to get revenge on Vel, instead of just going to the police like a rational person.

Vel had seen that Trevill was losing his mind, and had jumped on the opportunity to take over his research. From Vel's point of view, if Trevill was losing his faculties anyway, he had no use for fame and fortune. And why deprive the universe of a new energy source?

Unfortunately, after all the fighting over who got credit, Doctor Trevill's discovery didn't pan out. This new energy source proved too unstable to be used reliably. It wasn't entirely for nothing, though. His research was released to the general public, and the data helped scientists across the galaxy avoid pursuing the same dead end. One college student changed her major because of it, switched to medical science instead, and went on to cure a disease that once killed millions.

Sometimes one failure can do more good than a thousand successes.

02.04 *Safeguards*

ED.02500.05.07

The Navoran language is difficult for outsiders to understand. Being a purely telepathic race, their language incorporates pictures more than words. When communicating with each other, they often exchange relevant memories rather than construct sentences. While they do have a written language, it uses more pictograms than letters, making them one of the few modern cultures to use emojis in formal writing. When dealing with emotional topics, they are often prone to exaggerated metaphors, using images that convey how they feel rather than literal descriptions of events.

So when Trenyn visualized a black bird flying off with their right arm, what they really meant was that they missed Raven. The two had been inseparable for years, and the truth was, she was the only non-Navoran that Trenyn really trusted. Most cultures were so prone to secrecy that they always seemed like they were hiding something. Humans were so embarrassed by perfectly normal things, like bodily functions. But not Raven. She never kept secrets from Trenyn. She was as open as the people on Trenyn's own planet, and interacting with her made them feel at home. Of course, they had observed Raven being less forthcoming with other humans. She called it "propriety," but Trenyn never really understood the concept. The subjects humans found humiliating just seemed so random.

Trenyn should have been at her side, helping her with her mission. But no, someone had to watch the ship. They were currently docked at StarDock M113, having the Bloodwind's hull recoated while the crew was off on various missions.

Trenyn had caught up on their duties, and their personal research projects were currently at a stage where the computers had to process data without their input. Bored, they decided to look through the crew's computer usage history. Trenyn wasn't sure if this would be considered a breach of privacy, but it wasn't like they were hacking into encrypted files, they were just seeing what types of public media their friends had been viewing. Knowing their interests would make future interactions easier.

Bloodstone's data was mostly encrypted. She was a very secretive person and didn't like others to know her too well. Her non-encrypted history mostly consisted of news streams related to wanted fugitives. She also had an interest in emerging technologies. That was good to know; it might make a decent conversational topic later. When she was in the mood for entertainment, she often watched martial arts films. She had also watched a couple of makeup tutorials. Humans were weird.

Whisper's media history was almost empty. She had watched a few streams regarding sightings of Alterra Sarr, the terrorist-at-large who had inadvertently brought this group together. But beyond that, she didn't seem to consume media for personal enjoyment. Trenyn knew she spent a lot of time in the gym practicing her martial arts, and she had also mentioned a love of meditation. So perhaps entertainment media just wasn't for her.

Yna and Dervish were both new to movies, and they were hooked. They spent a lot of time watching media together, mostly animated programs about winged horses. Apart, Yna tended to watch a lot of action movies, and

Dervish had a thing for sappy love stories.

Vik's history was the most interesting of all. He seemed to be doing a lot of research into human sexual reproduction. Approximately ninety percent of his viewing history was of people performing sexual acts, in a wide variety of positions. Oddly, he only ever seemed to watch the conception stage of reproduction, never the gestation or childbirth.

Trenyn was also fascinated by human reproduction, and couldn't wait to ask Vik about his thoughts on the subject. It would make an excellent dinner topic.

Navoran reproduction was very different. They only had one sex, but it took three Navorans to conceive a child. When they had sexual intercourse for pleasure, they copulated in pairs to avoid pregnancy. They weren't aroused by nudity or by watching others have intercourse, so they had no need for pornography. While they looked forward to their sexual activity, they didn't spend nearly as much time thinking about sex as humans did.

Trenyn was intrigued by how much sex pervaded human society. It was used to sell products, it was regulated by the government, and it was even a motive for murder. Gender roles probably confused them most of all. Raven was the most capable human being they had ever met, and yet some human males would consider her their lesser, simply because she was female. It didn't make sense.

Why did Bloodstone want to be female? What did the distinction actually mean to her? Trenyn had no problem accepting her identity and calling her by her preferred pronouns, but it confused them as to why it was so important to her. Trenyn tended to use they/them pronouns for Navorans, but most humans assumed Trenyn was male because of their body shape. Trenyn was often called "he" and "him" by people they didn't know, and it didn't bother them one bit. Their native language didn't even have pronouns.

Perhaps more importantly, why did some humans have a problem with Bloodstone's transition? It didn't affect them, it's not like she was forcing them to get surgery. Roughly half of Earth's population was female, nearly half was male, and neither half seemed to care who was born which. But try to change from one to the other, and people made up all sorts of moral reasons to find it objectionable. Reasons that didn't even appear in the religious documents they claimed to use as a source.

As Trenyn pondered the inconsistent ways humans approached gender, they heard a strange whirring sound. From somewhere above them, there came a light thumping. Trenyn tapped at a computer screen, requesting a security scan, but found that a scan was already in progress. *Huh?* They hadn't started a scan, and they weren't aware of any autoscans scheduled for this time of day. The tapping moved along the ceiling, headed in the direction of the hallway. Trenyn started to follow the sound, but stopped when another message flashed on the computer screen. This one was in Grunthian, but the translation software they'd installed instantly converted it into: "THREATS DETECTED. EXTERMINATION PROTOCOL INITIATED."

Well, that sounded ominous. Trenyn wondered if it sounded any friendlier in the original Grunthian. Another tapping sound started, from a spot further down the room. Again, it moved towards the hallway. Trenyn stepped into the hallway, where they could hear several more tappings moving up and down the ceiling. Something was walking around above them. Several somethings. Trenyn considered the ship's layout. There was at least a meter between this deck and the next, but these things sounded just on the other side of the ceiling. There was a maintenance level between decks, but they'd yet to have a reason to explore it. Had today's maintenance somehow activated a dormant Grunthian security system?

They heard an access hatch open around the corner. Trenyn ran down the hall, and stopped when they saw something emerge from the sliding panel. It was a metal sphere, about the size of a bowling ball. It rested on a metal ring, from which six tiny metal legs carried it across the floor making tik-tik-tik sounds. As Trenyn watched, the sphere opened like a mouth, the edges lined with jagged metal teeth. Inside the mouth was a small tube topped by a red light. Trenyn guessed that the tube was the barrel of some sort of weapon. They didn't stick around long enough to find out if they were right. Trenyn ran back the way they had come, hearing more hatches open and more tik-tik-tik sounds from every direction.

They rushed back into the lab, closing the door and manually locking it. They looked around the lab, searching for anything that could be used as a weapon. Their virtrinium blades were back in their quarters, and they couldn't call them from this distance. By now there were probably dozens of sphere bots between Trenyn and their quarters. Surely the lab contained something they could use as a weapon. They heard a clang against the door.

There had to be something... they'd been working on weaponizing Raven's robotic arms, maybe they could – *Yes!* They found a tiny rocket launcher designed to fit in a spring-loaded compartment on Raven's forearm. Of course, the actual rockets were in the armory three doors down. Trenyn heard a sizzling sound. An acrid scent attacked their nasal passages, reminding them of vinegar. Holes were starting to appear in the door. As they watched in horror, one of the holes grew large enough for a bot to crawl through. Others began to follow. Trenyn backed up towards the wall, trying their hardest to pick up the bots with their mind. But no, they were not made of virtrinium.

The lead bot stood squarely in front of Trenyn. The tube inside its mouth repositioned until it had its prey perfectly targeted. It fired, covering Trenyn in acidic goop. Believing its foe neutralized, the bot took several steps back.

Another fun fact about Navorans: At some point in their evolutionary history, their planet was plagued with acid rain. Most of the creatures on their planet evolved to be immune to acids. A Navoran's skin is clammy and slightly viscous like a frog's, due to an outer coating secreted from their pores. This layer of sweat acts as a base that protects them from the acid.

Maybe I was afraid for nothing, Trenyn thought. They grabbed a prototype robotic arm from a shelf and swung it at the nearest bot. The bot immediately swiveled in the direction of the arm, its jaws clamping down hard and biting the arm in half. Then it swiveled back towards Trenyn, jaws snapping open and shut repeatedly.

The wall behind Trenyn hissed and bubbled. The floor was covered in a rubbery finish that seemed immune to the acid, but Trenyn's clothing was not. Now nearly nude, Trenyn banged on the wall behind them with all four hands. A large piece fell away, making a hole large enough to climb through. As Trenyn squeezed into the next room, they briefly worried about the bots getting acid on the outer walls of the ship, and blowing them out into space. Then they remembered they were in spacedock. That might actually be a good strategy – if they could trick the bots into making a hole in the hull, Trenyn could flee the ship and get the station's security to help them. Their mind reeled with possibilities.

Trenyn looked around. They were in a small access room with a high ceiling. Several large pipes took up most of the room. They could hear the Grunthian security bots climbing towards the hole behind them, and the door beside them was already sizzling from another bot's acid.

Trenyn considered opening the door and trying their luck at running past all the bots in the hallway. However, a quick glimpse at the rapidly growing hole in the door changed their mind. There was a sea of these bots in the hallway. They would skeletonize Trenyn like piranha if they even got close. The bots came crawling through the door and the wall at the same time. Trenyn started climbing the pipes. Their four hands made them an excellent climber, and they had sticky pads on their fingertips to aid them further. They quickly reached the top of the pipe, which disappeared into the ceiling. Trenyn desperately searched for an access hatch or something to escape this room.

The bots swarmed below Trenyn, waiting for them to fall. Some started climbing the walls. None of them tried firing their acid weapons – apparently they shared a hive mind, and had already learned that Trenyn was immune. Backed against the ceiling, with doom climbing ever closer, Trenyn tried the only thing they could reach – a water release valve. While their left arm gripped the pipe for dear life, their right hands turned the valve wheel. With a loud squeak the pipe opened, flooding the room with cold water. Water gushed out with incredible force, causing Trenyn to fall to the floor. The bots were too busy getting swept away to bite them.

Despite the water flowing out through the holes in the door and the wall, the room rapidly filled up. Trenyn did some calculations in their head. This room… the lab… the hallway. The hallway was T-shaped but sealed at each of the three ends by airtight doors. The bots had come through access hatches, but those probably closed behind the bots. Did the ship even store enough water to flood that entire area? Once again they remembered they were in spacedock. During maintenance, the ship's water and electricity were hooked up to the station's. The water could pretty much flow all day.

Trenyn swam towards the ceiling. The bots worked their tiny legs trying to grip something, but they were helpless. One by one their lights started blinking out. Their circuitry wasn't designed for total submersion. Soon the bots were rendered inactive. Both rooms and the hallway were now completely submerged, so Trenyn closed the valve. They took their time, wanting to make sure all the bots had been deactivated. After all, they had all the time in the world. Navorans were an amphibious species.

"Why is everything wet?" Raven asked. Not "Hello," not

"How was your day," she always got straight to the point, and Trenyn loved that about her. "And why are there holes in the door? And… why are you naked?"

Trenyn was hunched over a deactivated bot, studying its circuitry. They turned around and hugged her tight. While she couldn't actually feel the hug through her robotic body, the close contact still made her feel uncomfortable. She'd never been much of a hugger, and just recently a hug had nearly gotten her killed. They released her and telepathically told her, *I have an interesting story for you. But first, I had a new idea for your suit's embedded weaponry. Have you considered an acid cannon?*

02.05 *Paradise*

ED.02500.06.24

The beaches of Sandhaven were some of the most beautiful in the galaxy. The water was always crystal clear, and the dunes of multicolored sand were natural works of art. Enormous waterfalls flowed over cliffs of glistening colored glass. Exotic flora and fauna made this paradise truly unique.

In an effort to keep Sandhaven beautiful, few people were allowed to actually live there. Park rangers pulled triple duty as security officers, medical personnel, and merchants to the planet's small number of visitors. Tourism was limited to the super-rich, celebrities, and in this case, those who could impersonate celebrities.

Toola Vandersmith, the worlds-famous supermodel, descended the ramp, accompanied by a photographer and a suitcase-laden assistant. She wore a sparkling red ball gown that looked out of place in this tropical environment. As her ship's ramp closed behind her, Toola stepped up to the automated security checkpoint. A facial scanner confirmed her identity, and a wooden gate lifted. A park ranger hurried up to greet her, then led her to her cabin.

Fifteen minutes later, the ship's ramp opened again. Toola Vandersmith, the worlds-famous supermodel, descended the ramp, this time alone. She wore a sparkling red ball gown that looked out of place in this tropical environment. As the ramp closed behind her, she surveyed her surroundings. The landing area was enclosed by a tall wooden fence. Toola briefly considered climbing over the fence, but she knew there would be cameras everywhere.

Instead, she walked confidently up to the facial scanner. Seconds later, the gate opened, and she proceeded to the path that led to the resort cabins. She passed a park ranger, who looked at her quizzically. "Didn't you just—" he began.

"Forgot my purse," Toola answered, holding up her designer bag. The ranger nodded and went back to his business. As soon as he was out of sight, Toola ducked behind a refreshment stand. Her body began to lose its color and shape, turning gray for just a moment before redefining into a new shape – that of the park ranger. He was now six inches taller, had tanned skin, and wore a khaki uniform. And he still carried a designer purse that probably cost more than a park ranger made in a year. He tossed the purse into a waste receptacle as he proceeded down the path toward the ranger station.

Once the station was in view, he hid behind some purple palm trees and waited. He'd seen Toola's itinerary, and he knew that the facilities were lightly staffed. At sunset, Toola was scheduled for a photoshoot on the beach, followed by dinner on the resort's yacht. The ranger station would be empty while all available employees tended to her every need.

As the sun went down, the station emptied, and the shapeshifter sneaked into the small building. It wasn't even locked. The planet was so careful about who was allowed to land, that they had little use for security on the planet's surface. Nearly everyone who came here was already rich, and even if they weren't, what was there to steal in a ranger station?

The shapeshifter changed again, this time to a female ranger. She was now identical to the last employee she'd seen leave the building. If anyone did catch her in here, hopefully she could come up with a believable excuse as to why she was here instead of pampering the supermodel.

Dervish smiled. She was enjoying this. She felt like she was an intergalactic super spy like in those bad movies Yna was always watching. Sneaking on board Toola's ship had been child's play. The ship's security program had easily recognized her face; it didn't care if she'd boarded twice. Then all she'd had to do was hide in a storage room for the entire trip. Not every Marae was good enough to fool facial scanners, but Dervish had always had a knack for faces.

So far the hardest part had been emulating that ridiculous sparkly dress. Reflective materials were hard, and she doubted she'd pulled off the effect. But the ranger didn't seem to have noticed anything unusual.

She was still a little nervous, though. They didn't allow guns on this planet, so she wasn't concerned about the rangers using deadly force. But she didn't want to find out what the penalty was for coming here uninvited. She quickly searched the ranger computers for the data she needed. Again, they didn't even password-protect their computers. They'd probably never had a need to.

Bingo. Her target was at a different resort, but it wasn't too far. She'd have to lift a hoverjeep, but judging by what she'd seen so far, she doubted the garage was locked. Best to get moving if she wanted to take advantage of the lack of staff.

It was well after dark when she approached the other resort. Luckily the jeep didn't need headlights – the rangers didn't like to disturb the local animals. Instead, the jeep's windshield was basically a computer monitor, the full-screen HUD displaying the road ahead as if it were daytime. Dervish was also glad the hovering vehicle didn't make much noise, though it did tend to leave a cloud of sand in its wake.

She didn't know her target's itinerary, or where this resort's rangers might currently be stationed. Rather than let them wonder why they were getting a visit from another resort's ranger, Dervish parked on the side of the road about a kilometer from the second resort. Hopefully she'd be off-planet by the time the jeep was discovered.

Dervish had better night vision than humans did, but she was still thankful for the nearly full moon. She heard leaves rustling on the side of the road, and some strange chittering noises. Everything she'd read about this planet had said that the local animals were harmless, but she was still afraid of what might be watching her.

It took her about half an hour to reach the resort. She would have made the trip faster, but she kept jumping at shadows and hiding behind rocks whenever she thought she'd heard someone approaching. At one point she'd disguised herself as a rather unconvincing tree, in a poorly thought out attempt to hide from what turned out to be an anteater-like mammal. She'd tried to stand perfectly still, making jazz hands with her bark-covered fingers. The blue-furred creature had moseyed straight up to her, sniffed her leg, and peed on her before walking away.

But now she could see her target's cabin. There was a light on in the window. Dervish found a good hiding spot and watched from a distance, pondering her next move.

The target's name was Chesner Guildman III. He wasn't an actor or a CEO, he was just one of those "famous for being rich" celebrities. Born into wealth, he had never done an honest day's work, and he didn't care who he hurt to keep it that way. Recently it was discovered that he had ties to the Inner Eye, and he was doing his best to lay low until he could buy his way out of trouble.

He had information the IGP wanted. But the IGP had no jurisdiction on Sandhaven. Of course, even Guildman's bank account had limits – there was only so long he'd be able to stay on this extravagant planet. But the longer he remained, the more time he had to eliminate evidence. He was probably on an encrypted line right now, ordering various contacts to erase incriminating records.

Rumor had it that the Inner Eye was also putting pressure on Guildman, waiting to see whether or not he needed to be permanently silenced before the IGP got to him. The IGP and the Inner Eye both probably had ships in orbit around Sandhaven, waiting for Guildman to leave, each wanting to place him in their own version of protective custody.

It was a complicated situation, and Dervish didn't have a head for details. The important part was that there was no legal extradition from Sandhaven. Guildman had to leave the planet willingly, or the IGP would be caught up in a huge legal snarl. Also, they needed him alive, or there was no reward. This meant getting him to the IGP before any Inner Eye assassins caught him.

Dervish had no idea how she was going to accomplish any of that. How was she even going to approach him? Her first idea was to seduce him, tangle him up in a whirlwind romance, and see if his lust was stronger than his common sense. What sort of woman would appeal to him? Was there any supermodel or actress who could convince him to cut his ties to organized crime? Potentially losing some of his income and even putting his life at risk?

But no. Just once, she wanted to accomplish a mission without resorting to seduction. Raven and Whisper had both told her that she was capable of so much more, and while Dervish didn't agree with their moral judgments, she did want to prove to herself that she wasn't just a pretty face. She would convince Guildman to leave the planet and assist the IGP, and she would do it without using feminine wiles.

Somehow.

What if she were to convince him that he was in more

trouble than he was in? If he thought the Inner Eye had already run out of patience, and assassins were on their way, then he'd have no choice but to accept the IGP's protection. Dervish wondered what an Inner Eye assassin might look like. She settled on a generic ninja-style outfit, and shifted to match that mental image.

Inside the cabin, Chesner Guildman III cursed at his comm. He was trying to reach his financial advisor, to have him do some quick creative accounting. First, he'd had trouble getting an encrypted connection. He was using the fanciest, most expensive comm available, and subscribed to a communications plan that guaranteed the clearest planet-to-planet calls in the galaxy. But he was also using unbreakable encryption software, and this meant connections took longer.

It didn't help that his contact was probably asleep right now. Even when the connection went through, nobody picked up on the other end. It just beeped and beeped until the connection was lost. This infuriated Guildman. People were supposed to be at his beck and call at all hours, and he wasn't used to having to wait on anything. This betrayal would not go unpunished.

Guildman jumped as there was a knock at the door. He stuck his eye to the peephole but saw nothing. He opened the door and looked around. As he turned to go back in, Dervish dropped on him from above. He threw her off of him and ran inside, but Dervish followed. They now stood face to face.

"Chesner Guildman III, you have betrayed the Inner Eye," Dervish said in her scariest voice. For a shapeshifter, she wasn't much of an actor. "Prepare to die!" Her plan was to botch the assassination attempt, then return disguised as a park ranger, and convince him to turn himself in to the IGP for protection.

Guildman dropped to his knees in terror, and there was a

loud crash as a window shattered behind him. An arrow whizzed straight through where Guildman's head had been a moment before. Dervish's eyes widened as the arrow thunked into the wall behind her. *There really is an assassin!* Thinking quickly, Dervish slammed the panel next to the door, turning off the lights. Guildman crawled towards the bathroom, whimpering. *Good,* Dervish thought. *You hide.*

Outside, the Inner Eye assassin circled the cabin. It hadn't been easy to get access to this planet, but he'd managed to hack their personnel records and sneak in as a ranger. Since their weapon detectors were top-notch, he'd had to craft a bow and some arrows after landing. He was only supposed to watch Guildman, looking for signs he might go to the IGP. And then this other figure showed up, dressed like a ninja from a cheesy action movie.

He didn't know who this person was, but he couldn't take a chance. He knew it wasn't anyone from the Inner Eye, but it could be an undercover IGP agent in the guise of an Inner Eye contact, tricking Guildman into giving out information. Whatever was going on, this could be their last chance to silence Guildman. So he'd fired.

Unfortunately, he wasn't sure if he'd hit or not. As he approached the front of the cabin, he got his answer. Guildman burst out the door, heading for the treeline. The assassin followed, easily catching up to the out-of-shape trillionaire. The assassin tackled Guildman, and the two wrestled in the sand.

The assassin didn't have any weapons on him, other than the bow, which wouldn't help in a hand-to-hand fight. But he liked his chances. He tried to get Guildman into a chokehold, but somehow he kept wriggling out of the assassin's grip. He sure was flexible. The assassin finally had his victim pinned, when Guildman's arms started bending and twisting in unnatural ways. They were no longer like arms, and more like tentacles. One of these appendages wrapped around the assassin's neck, squeezing with all its might.

Unable to free himself of the tentacles, the assassin lost consciousness. Dervish, disguised as Guildman, stood over the assassin, wondering what to do next. She wasn't sure how long he'd be out, and it wasn't in her to kill someone in their sleep, even if they were a killer. She needed to check on the real Guildman, but not while in this form. She didn't want to scare him any further.

She considered changing into an IGP officer. Guildman would be easy to convince now, but she was afraid to leave the planet in Guildman's ship. The Inner Eye would be looking for it, and it might get attacked as soon as it left Sandhaven's atmosphere. Then she had an idea.

Guildman peeked his head out of the closet just in time to see Toola Vandersmith, the worlds-famous supermodel, dragging an unconscious assassin into the cabin. "Help me lock him in the closet!" she ordered. Guildman was very confused, but he helped her anyway. As they worked, she explained. "I'm an undercover agent for the IGP. The Inner Eye is trying to kill you, but we can protect you if you come with me."

She still wasn't a great actor, but Guildman's head was reeling, and he probably would have believed anything at this point. "You're a secret agent *and* a supermodel?"

She nodded. "Sure, why not. Will you submit to police protection?"

"Yes, anything, just get me to safety!"

She led him to the hoverjeep and drove him to Toola's ship. It wasn't quite dawn yet, and they managed to escape notice. The security checkpoint and the ship still recognized Toola's face, and unrecognized guests were not a problem as long as they were accompanied by Toola.

As soon as they left the atmosphere, she contacted Vik, who had been waiting nearby in one of the Bloodwind's small shuttles. Vik contacted the nearest IGP vessel and explained the situation. Chesner Guildman III was put in police custody, where he was happy to divulge everything he knew. He would need to increase his personal security for a while, but he could afford it. The information he provided led to the arrest of two political officials and prevented a terrorist attack on one of Jupiter's moons.

Dervish collected the reward money, though a much-need confidence boost was the greater reward. The assassin wasn't found, but this event led to greater security measures on Sandhaven. Toola's ship was returned to her, and Vik gave Dervish a ride back to the Bloodwind.

Dervish slept well that night, feeling more useful than she had in a long time.

02.06 POP

ED.02500.07.09

Vik was taken aback by the variety of species and cultures surrounding him. At first, he'd been grateful to get this mission, anything to get off the ship for a while. He respected his fellow teammates, but sometimes he found their open-mindedness a bit much. Vik had been raised with a specific set of beliefs. His parents had taught him a recipe for living well, and it had never steered him wrong. Family first, then country and planet. He didn't think of himself as prejudiced, though others had accused him of such once or twice. But how could he be? His last girlfriend had been Galean.

It still hurt to think about her. His parents had been cold at first, but eventually they'd warmed up to her. He'd finally convinced them that Zhari was one of the good ones. He'd been ready to marry that girl. He still wasn't sure if he'd loved her, or if he understood what love actually felt like. But he knew he wanted a stable relationship of his own. Most of his friends were already married, and some even had children. It was normal, and that's all he wanted – a normal life.

Here, now, at this shopping bazaar on the planet Jetsam, things felt far from his idea of normal. The street was lined with stalls promoting all manner of items that would be illegal on Earth – chemical-based handguns, mind-expanding narcotics, and even exotic pets. Vik noted one booth where a cannibalistic butcher sold cuts of his own species.

But the wares were nothing compared to the clientèle. Shoppers of every species lined the streets. Religious cultists walked side-by-side with sapient androids. Marae sex workers mimicked the species of each passerby. Some patrons wore head-to-toe armor that obscured every centimeter of their bodies, while some shoppers wore nothing at all.

Culture shock was an understatement. Eight years of IGP training caused his instincts to go crazy. He counted over a hundred people he could have arrested on the spot. If this had been Earth. And if he'd still been on active duty. But it wasn't and he wasn't, and he forced himself to ignore the debauchery and concentrated on finding his target. Despite being such a diverse crowd, people still eyed him with suspicion. Even though Bloodstone had helped him with his outfit, Vik still looked like an undercover cop trying to look casual. His face was too clean, his body language was too uncomfortable.

A young Vhelran girl approached him, and Vik knew it was a scam before she even got close. She said something about her mother being sick, and she tried to sell Vik a soda. When he ignored her, she burst into tears and hugged Vik, all the while attempting to pick his pocket. Vik grabbed her hand and pushed her away. Then she got angry and pulled out an AON dagger. Vik quickly disarmed her and threw her weapon across the street. She ran off after it, and Vik continued pushing through the mass of shoppers.

In the distance, in the swarm of oddly-shaped heads, he saw a single eyestalk moving through the crowd. Vik did a double-take. That couldn't possibly be… It didn't matter; he was on a mission, and that was not his target. He was looking for an Ezarran, not a Glorkan. Still, there was no reason he couldn't look for the Ezarran in the direction of that eyestalk. He shouldered his way through the crowd.

By the time he reached the place where he'd seen the Glorkan, they were gone. Vik looked around but didn't see the eyestalk anywhere. It didn't matter. It couldn't have been who he thought it was. It's not like there was only one Glorkan in the universe, and besides, Analon Leebo was dead. And yet... the Glorkan species was blessed with a wide variety of skin and eye colors. Seeing an eyestalk with that exact combination – light blue skin and yellow eye – and factoring in the rarity of seeing such a xenophobic species away from their home planet... it was an odd coincidence, that's all.

Vik thought back to the experiments. So many participants had suffered injuries, that the project was on the verge of cancellation. One officer, Ferrik Vinders, showed promise. His body had taken to the Levatech implants rather well, with no signs of infection or rejection. Then came his first test. An iron ball was placed in front of him, and he was to stretch out his hand and repel the object. Ferrik stretched out his hand, flexed his fingers, and promptly blew his entire hand across the room. Similar cases plagued the project. Those who got past the implant stage couldn't successfully use their powers. It finally came down to Vik and Leebo.

By this time the project was all but canceled, merely awaiting a few signatures to make it official. But their implants were in, so there was no reason not to test the outcomes. Vik and Leebo had been given the same test as Vinders. Vik cleared his mind, stretched out his hand, and pushed the ball away. Then he called it back, catching it perfectly in his palm. He felt no strain, no threat of being pulled apart. It felt perfectly natural to him. Many, many further tests would follow, of course, but for now, it looked like a success. Then they gave the same test to Leebo. Pushing the object went just fine, but then he tried to pull the ball back to him. It pained Vik to remember what happened next.

Something about Glorkan physiology must have had unpredictable results with the Levatech. Of course, it was impossible to know what went wrong, because there was no body to examine. It was as if every cell of Leebo's body was pulled towards a central singularity. Sitting across the room, Vik could even feel himself ever so slightly being pulled toward Leebo. Then, in a split second that felt like years, Leebo was just gone. No blood, no scraps of clothing, all he left behind was an empty chair.

"Excuse me, sir?" Vik blinked and looked up. A four-eyed shopkeeper gawked at him. "You've been staring off into space for a very long time. Are you going to buy anything?" Vik realized he was blocking the man's booth and made to move out of the way, when he saw a flash of yellow feathers out of the corner of his eye. Someone had seen him, then turned and ran. Someone of the Ezarran persuasion. As Vik began his pursuit, it occurred to him that this might have been Bloodstone's plan all along. Dress Vik up like an undercover cop, he gets seen by the criminal, who makes themselves extra noticeable when they flee... *Damn that Bloodstone*, Vik thought. She didn't trust him to have a strategy of his own. She treated him like he was a tool.

The crowd was thick, but many of the shoppers made room for Vik as he barreled through them. They were used to the cat-and-mouse games of cops, robbers, and bounty hunters, and none of them wanted to get caught in the crossfire if it came to that. Vik was gaining on his prey, finding himself closer every time he caught sight of the yellow-feathered fugitive. He reached an open area where the crowd was much thinner, and Vik judged that the Ezarran was close enough to end this. Vik outstretched his hand and willed the Ezarran to be pulled towards him. The fugitive stopped in his tracks, digging in his heels as Vik's power started to pull him inexorably backward. But before he got very far, Vik was tackled from the side. Something blue grasped him hard, holding his arms to his sides. A large yellow eyeball stared him in the face.

"Leebo?" Vik tried to ask, but his lungs were constricted by the Glorkan's python-like arms. Then the entire world seemed to collapse in on itself. All the colors streaked towards Vik and his captor, followed by black lines converging into a point just to Vik's right. For a split second everything was black, then all the colors burst back out again with a loud POP. Except this time all the colors were shades of purple, the hues of Jetsam's sky. There was no ground beneath his feet. He felt the arms release him, as the Glorkan vanished in collapsing streaks of color. POP. Vik was alone and the ground was coming up fast. He didn't panic; his training had taught him to use his powers like a parachute. As he approached the ground, he willed himself to slow his descent. He landed dramatically on one knee like he'd seen his heroes do in the movies.

POP. Arms grabbed him again. POP. Now Vik and the Glorkan were standing face to face, on top of a building. Vik reached for his gun, but suddenly he felt an uncontrollable wave of dizziness. He went to his knees, nausea taking over. His opponent stepped back as Vik emptied the contents of his stomach. "Leebo?" he managed to ask, wiping the vomit from his lips.

"I'm going to say this once," the Glorkan answered. His species only spoke in clicks and whirrs, which emanated from a slit on his neck. A small box mounted on Leebo's collar translated. "Leave me alone. I'm not going back."

"I'm… not… here for you," Vik gasped, still trying to catch his breath. Glorkans didn't have facial expressions, but looking up into that cantaloupe-sized eyeball, Vik was pretty sure that Leebo didn't believe him.

"Get off this planet and never come back," Leebo said. "If I see you again, I'll leave you in the limbo."

Leebo blinked out of existence again, leaving a confused Vik to recover.

* * *

Jeke Skeeper, known as "Berdawg" to his friends, was grateful to be free. He didn't know how that cop had known he'd be here, but it looked like he'd given up the chase. Berdawg leaned against a building, catching his breath. How did he get into these situations? Not three days ago, he'd been on the hunt himself, looking for one of Jetsam's most elusive criminals. But now he was the one being hunted. He'd been framed for the very crimes he'd tried to solve. The way he saw it, he had two choices: Try to get off planet, or keep looking for the actual culprit. He didn't want to spend the rest of his life as a suspect, so he opted for the latter.

Unfortunately, he had trouble blending in with the crowd, even a diverse crowd like this one. With his canine snout and bright yellow feathers, his unique appearance made him an obvious target. His people didn't get out much – he'd never even met another Ezarran – so it wasn't like he could claim to be someone else.

If he was going to get through this, he'd need a better disguise. He pulled his hood down farther over his face, and once again merged with the crowd. He was still panting, but he couldn't afford to rest too long. As he hustled through the swarm of people, he looked around for clothing merchants that might have something to cover his face. As he eyed one booth's selection, he felt something tugging on his overcoat. Before he could react, his entire body was pulled through the air.

He landed roughly on top of a building, face-to-face with a human male. The man was dressed like a local, but it was an obvious disguise. He looked like a cop. He even smelled like a cop. "Jeke Skeeper?" the man said, holding a gun at him.

"I'm innocent, I swear! I came here to find the vault robber, just like you!" The officer wasn't even listening. Berdawg considered running or fighting back, but decided that would just make him look guiltier. He kept talking at rapid speed as the cop pulled out some restraints. "I'm a bounty hunter! I was on the trail of the actual robber, but he framed me. It was a Glorkan!"

At that final word, his captor stopped. "Did you say Glorkan?"

Vik and Berdawg sat in a crowded café, sipping on some of the worst coffee either had ever tasted. Vik listened intently as Berdawg let the entire story spill out. There had been a chain of bank robberies. In each case, the money had disappeared from the vaults overnight. The vault cameras were somehow disabled right before the crime occurred. Footage showed static shortly before they blinked out, causing investigators to believe an EMP device was used.

Berdawg was a master of scents. He had visited each bank that had been robbed, and picked up a scent he'd never smelled before. It smelled like body odor, but of a species he'd never encountered. Then he'd scoured the town, trying to pick up the scent again. He finally found it, in a basement beneath an abandoned restaurant. Someone had been sleeping there, and Berdawg turned the place upside down looking for clues. Unfortunately, that's when the robber had returned. With a loud POP, the Glorkan had appeared in the middle of the room, and they fought. It wasn't a long fight. Once the Glorkan had managed to catch Berdawg in a body hug, it was over. POP. Berdawg had found himself in a locked bank vault. POP. Alone. He'd escaped, but not without being seen, and now Berdawg was the number one suspect for the vault robberies.

"While you were rooting through his hideout," Vik asked, "did you find anything that might tell you which bank he's going to hit next?"

"Actually… yes."

The Upper Redgrove branch of Happy Friendship Bank didn't look like a bank. It was in a building that obviously used to be something else, probably a fast food restaurant.

The new owners had done a pretty good job of modifying the building when they bought it, but there was still a brightly colored playground out front, and the drive-thru had you guiding your vehicle through a giant clown's mouth. A sign on the window proudly proclaimed, "We make banking fun! Ask about our low-interest mortgage rates!"

From the shadows across the street, Vik watched intently through a pair of night vision binoculars. Berdawg kept sniffing the air. "How do we know he hasn't already popped in and out?" Vik asked.

"I smelled him at the other locations, and that was days later. There's no way he can get in and out without me smelling him." Berdawg gave the air another sniff. "Nothing yet. How far do you think he can teleport from?"

"I don't know," Vik answered. "He took me pretty far up in the air. But I would bet he's more careful when he can't see his destination. He wouldn't want to appear halfway through a wall. He could—"

At that moment, they both heard Leebo's signature POP off in the distance. "I don't see him," Berdawg said, his nostrils working overtime. "…and the wind's blowing the wrong way to…"

Another POP, much louder this time. Leebo's thin but powerful arms wrapped around Vik and Berdawg. "I told you to leave me alone," came the electronically translated voice, as the world drained of color and they both found themselves high in the air. Plummeting toward the ground, Vik reached for Berdawg, but they were too far apart. Vik used his power to pull his companion toward him, then slowed their descent once Berdawg was safely in his arms.

They had barely touched the ground when Leebo appeared again, wrapped his snakelike arms around Berdawg, and vanished. Vik watched the sky, waiting for them to reappear. Five seconds… ten seconds…thirty… He finally heard another POP and quickly turned around.

Leebo released Berdawg, who collapsed to the ground. Some of his feathers had fallen out, and he was panting heavily. The colors drained from the sky as Leebo started to disappear again.

Vik held out his hand and pulled at Leebo with all his will. Those odd streaks of color started veering towards Vik. He could feel Leebo pulling back, and for several seconds they were evenly matched. Leebo put all his energy into trying to teleport. Vik wanted to reach for his gun, but it took every ounce of concentration he had to keep Leebo from teleporting. The stalemate would last until one of them passed out.

Then Leebo cried out in pain. Berdawg had his jaws around the Glorkan's ankle. Having lost his concentration, the streaks of light dissipated. Vik nearly fell backward, but recovered quickly. He drew his gun and fired three stun blasts at his enemy. Leebo collapsed. Vik walked over to check on Berdawg, who had released his hold on Leebo's ankle. "There's so many worlds in there..." he said, with a crazed look in his eye. Then he passed out. Vik sat on the ground, exhausted.

It may have been a small bank, but its security was excellent. Cameras had caught the fight from every angle, and Vik had no trouble convincing the police that Analon Leebo was the real vault robber. Vik and Berdawg split the bounty, and Leebo was taken into custody. Vik warned them of Leebo's abilities, and the officers agreed to keep the Glorkan sedated until they could come up with a way to contain him.

Vik and Berdawg parted ways, exchanging contact codes just in case. That night, after enduring a rant from Bloodstone for only bringing back half a reward, Vik relaxed and watched the news. Curious, he searched for Jetsam's local news streams. Yep, just as he thought. Leebo had already escaped.

Well, he thought. *I guess I'll have to deal with that someday.* In a strange way, having an arch enemy felt validating somehow. He turned out the lights and closed his eyes. It had been a good day.

02.07 Adrift

ED.02500.08.15

Space is cold. You wouldn't think that was a controversial opinion, but if you were to phrase it that way in front of Raven or Trenyn, you might find yourself the target of a mini-lecture about the nature of temperature. After all, temperature is the measurement of the kinetic energy of molecules, and in space there are no molecules to measure. Therefore, it's more accurate to say space has no temperature, though it does tend to make things in it cold. Any heat transfer you might experience is actually the temperature of cosmic radiation, which... and this is the point where most listeners zone out, vowing to keep their mouths shut around science geeks.

But if, instead of asking a scientist, you were to ask Yna, who currently floated in the empty blackness without the benefit of a spaceship... She would inform you that yes, space is indeed very cold. Especially when you're naked. As Yna floated helplessly, protected from the vacuum by her mysterious energy form, she wondered how she could still be alive. Or was she? Could this be the afterlife? Floating in nothingness for eternity?

I must be alive, she thought. *I have to pee.*

So apparently her energy form gave her the ability to

survive in the void of space. This was an amazing realization. If she could survive here, she could survive anywhere. Well, except for underwater, of course. Water had a tendency to short-circuit her power. Still, the scientific implications were staggering. She had always assumed that her energy form consumed oxygen, like fire. Obviously, it did not. The practical possibilities were pretty impressive as well. In a pinch, she might be able to exit a spacecraft to do emergency welding on the outer hull.

But as quickly as all these thoughts went through her head, they were pushed aside by more urgent considerations. She was in space. She was light-years from anyone who knew her. No one knew exactly where she was. She had no way to send a message. While she could propel herself to some degree, it would take her a million years to reach the nearest planet, even if she knew which way to go.

And worse yet, she knew she couldn't stay in her energy form for too long. She always got sick when she reverted to human form, and experience had taught her that the longer she was energized, the sicker she would be when human again. The longest she had ever managed to stay energized was just over two hours. And that time she had paid for it, by coughing up blood for hours and nursing a harsh sunburn for a week. Being energized also made her very tired. Sooner or later she would lose consciousness, at which time her body would automatically revert to human form. And when that happened here, trapped in the infinite emptiness, she would die.

She was screwed.

Even if it was futile, there had to be something she could do. She tried sending out a telepathic message. Of course, she wasn't telepathic, but there was little point piddling over the small details now. Some species could read the minds of non-telepaths. Maybe one was listening now.

Okay, probably not, but it was pointless to just float here waiting for death. She had to think... The research station! That would be the closest object to her in space. Of course it would still take many lifetimes for her to reach it, but at least it gave her a direction. But... what direction was that? Yna was good at starmapping, and had learned a bit about stellar navigation when she'd been a pirate. But that was in a cartographer's study, with maps and pens and other instruments at her fingertips. Floating here, in an unfamiliar area of space, it was a lot different.

However. She'd been heading towards the research station when her ship had exploded. She had just come from Vikara Prime, and she knew that the station was towards the outer rim of the solar system. Yna rotated around, taking in all the stars, until she centered herself on Vikara's sun. She considered. Would Vikara Prime be closer? Yna doubted it. Her ship had flown for a good while before it exploded. Besides, both Vikara Prime and the research station were both impossibly far away, so she was as good as dead whichever way she went. With that cheery thought, Yna turned herself directly away from the sun and propelled herself forward. Rationally she knew that she would never reach it before she died, but it was nice to have a destination. As she flew through space, she recalled the events that had brought her here.

Bloodstone had sent her on a mission, to apprehend a rather cunning villain named Asdith. He was wanted for murder on twelve planets. There were at least four bounties on his head, from various sources. Bloodstone wasn't even sure which bounty they would collect. They would probably just sell Asdith to the highest bidder.

Yna found and caught Asdith quickly and easily. Too easily. She should have been more suspicious, but she was excited about having done such a good job. So excited that she nearly forgot her secondary mission. On her way back to the Bloodwind, she was to stop off at Vortal Station, a large research vessel that studied Marae. The Marae were a species of shapeshifters, like Yna's crewmate Dervish. Until recently, Marae had only been found on one of Grunthar's moons. The Grunthians even claimed to have engineered the species. But now a few had been discovered in the asteroid belt outside the Vikara system.

One Marae, Vraxx, had worked for Lord Vermon of Valos. Whisper believed that Vraxx framed IGP Officer Alterra Sarr for the destruction of the IGP Space Station. So Yna was asked to stop by Vortal Station and just see if they had more information on the species. Maybe Vraxx had visited the asteroid belt. Maybe the scientists had developed ways to track Marae. It was probably a pointless stop, but it never hurt to ask.

A few hours after Yna set a course for the station, she went to the back of her vessel to check on her prisoner. But what she found was a trap. Her "prisoner" was actually an android, an artificial duplicate of Asdith meant to throw bounty hunters off the scent. *And doing a damn good job,* Yna thought. Yna was just about to turn the ship back around, but the android had one more nasty surprise for her.

When the android exploded, Yna reflexively changed to her energy form. The explosion ruptured Yna's tiny ship, causing several smaller blasts throughout the vessel, and blowing Yna out into space. Which was a lucky deal, because otherwise she would still have been inside the ship when the engines finally joined the bandwagon and blew apart, all but vaporizing the ship.

And that's how Yna came to be here, in the cold blackness, on a doomed course towards Vortal Station. She was moving pretty quickly, actually, but distances in space were something on the vast side, so she knew she would only get so far. After about an hour, Yna started to get tired. She looked behind her. Vikara's sun didn't look any farther away than it had when she started. Not that she expected it to. There weren't a lot of options available to her at the moment, so Yna kept on going.

Another hour. Probably. Yna was exhausted. All she

wanted was to turn off her power and go to sleep. And she was very tempted to do so. She could still see no sign of any space station, and she was starting to get dizzy. She was just contemplating taking a short break when something hit her. Something big. And then there was nothing.

Blackness. Alarms blaring in the distance. Mechanical whirring. Dull pain, followed by cool wind. A whoosh, a metallic clang - a door closing? Skin burning, then cooling. More mechanical whirring. Electronic beeping. Pinpricks. Blackness.

Yna dreamed of nothing. She slowly regained consciousness, one sense at a time. For several minutes she lay there, eyes closed, listening. A steady beep. A heart monitor, chiming at a calm rate. She wondered if it was hers. She opened her eyes slowly, dreading the light. Fortunately the room was dim. She was in some sort of... medical facility? Was this Vortal Station? She sat up and looked down at her body. She was naked, except for some wires and sensors stuck to her in various places. She was expecting third-degree burns, but her skin was fair and healthy.

Odd.

Yna looked around the room. No one else was present. She removed the wires from her body and tossed her legs over the side of the bed. Shakily she put her feet on the floor and tried to stand. She was a little weak, but overall she felt okay. She looked at her surroundings. There were fourteen beds. All of them were empty but one. The occupant of the last bed was covered by a bloodstained sheet. Yna nervously walked over to the bed.

Obviously the patient was dead. They wouldn't just leave a bloody sheet draped over the body of a live patient, not over the head like that. And there wasn't any monitoring equipment around this patient. Nothing scary, nothing to worry about. People die, even on space stations. But all the blood... Well, it was a research vessel after all, and they do sometimes have accidents in the name of science. Could have been a chemical explosion or something.

But why was the body still just lying in the medical bay like this? Even if it was an autopsy, they should have rolled the body back into the freezer when they were done. Wouldn't want him releasing any microbes and viruses and whatnot around live patients.

And where were all the doctors?

Yna cautiously put her hand on the sheet. One quick look, just out of curiosity. It's not disrespectful. She didn't mean any harm. She just had to know. Yna took a deep breath and pulled back the sheet. And then she screamed.

It was a human woman. Or most of one. Her body had been ripped open from the base of the throat to her navel. But it wasn't the surgical precision one would expect from an autopsy. The edges of her skin were jagged and ripped, like torn fabric. Several organs had been removed from her chest cavity, but not by a doctor - that much was obvious. Most of her ribs had been broken off, her heart and one lung were missing, her remaining lung was only half there, her stomach had been punctured, and her intestines were torn.

The woman had other wounds as well. She was missing an eye and an ear. She had several tears on her face, arms, neck, and chest. In some places shredded muscle hung out from the wounds, morbidly reminding Yna of pulled pork. Her left arm was badly broken, with splintered bone protruding from the skin. One of her legs was gone. It was missing from about mid-thigh. It looked as if it had been gnawed off.

Yna had seen a lot of death in her lifetime. At times she had even been the one doing the killing. She had seen people shot, stabbed, blown up, and even ripped in half. She had always been able to distance herself from disturbing imagery, to disassociate herself from the horrors of reality and look at things rationally and calmly. But this woman -

her one eye staring off into space, her bloody mouth open in an expression of horror - this woman chilled Yna to the bone, and made her sick to her stomach. Yna turned away, fell to her knees, and regurgitated.

Once she recovered, Yna stood up and explored a bit. She found a gown and put it on. The doorway was unlocked, but she didn't want to leave this room just yet. Shouldn't the doctors be back soon to check up on her? In hopes of learning something useful, Yna approached one of the nearby computers and browsed the system. The first thing she did was confirm what she already suspected - this was Vortal Station, the research vessel. A little more poking around and she found a map of the ship. She was indeed in the medical bay, which was adjacent to the main cargo airlock. Not the most popular configuration, but in this case it made sense - they were searching the asteroids for Marae, and the medbay would be the first stop for any they brought aboard.

The main bridge was three levels up and on the other end of the ship - really about as far from her as it could be. Yna tried to call the bridge, but the intercom didn't work. Then she tried using the computer to locate the crew, but the search found nothing. Either the computer was broken or everyone else had evacuated.

That was a chilling thought. Why would they evacuate? Well, obviously it had something to do with whatever killed her buddy over there. So, why not just stay in this room, and send a message? No good. All outside communications had to be done from the bridge. This kept the scientists from sharing - and selling - their discoveries behind their colleagues' backs. So... to the bridge then. Or not. Yna was reluctant to leave this room without knowing what might be out there. She explored the computer further, stumbling across the ship's logs.

First, she read the computer's daily autolog. As she had guessed, she had been rescued by one of the station's automatic probes. The probes were designed to scan the asteroids for anything unusual, especially life signs. Yna had been hit by an asteroid and knocked for a loop. A nearby probe then used its Levatech beam to pull her inside. Luckily she hadn't reverted to her human form until she was inside the probe. Once inside the station, the medical droids must have gone to work on her.

How long had she been out? According to the computer, that had been two days ago. Well, this was all interesting, but it didn't tell her what she needed to know. Yna began reading the message logs.

Message To Command 12453:

We have set up our station near this asteroid field. This belt of debris was formed as the result of an exploded moon. The moon must have been the home to a community of Marae shapeshifters. A few Marae survived the explosion and continued to live on the asteroids. They are a hardy species - they require very little food and can breathe a variety of gases. Some have survived by burrowing into the rock and living off of the various chemical compounds.

The Marae are not easily found in the galaxy. This is only the second discovery of the species. The only other existing community of Marae is on the second moon of Grunthar, which houses their slave breeding labs. The Grunthians exercise absolute control over their Marae resources, and therefore this is the first time humans have had a chance to study this species.

And it is a fascinating species. Their ability to change shape is unequaled in the galaxy. We look forward to studying this species as much as possible in the coming months.

So far, every specimen we've rescued has died in our lab a few hours later.

Message To Command 13422:

We have acquired another specimen today. Due to the

radioactivity of the asteroid belt, Marae 427 has lost most of his shapeshifting ability. When we found him, he had degenerated into a mass of tentacles without the ability to maintain cohesion. Wild Marae are often non-sapient, surviving on instinct and achieving self-awareness only after encountering other cultures. This Marae, however, appears to be rather intelligent, and has even tried to communicate with us.

Message to Command 13512:

Marae 427 has given himself a name. "Xox" has picked up our language quite easily and now has perfectly normal conversations with us. We have constructed an outfit for him which allows him to walk freely about the ship, despite his lack of cohesion.

Message to Command 13515:

Xox has escaped. Sometime during the night he disabled our security programs and stole a shuttle. The irony is that we were working on a treatment that might have eventually cured his shapeshifting disability.

While Yna found the story interesting, it didn't tell her what was going on right now. She skipped ahead a few months and continued.

Message to Command 13624:

We found another live one. Marae 521 is much larger than other Marae we've encountered. He is also more malleable: his shapeshifting ability is the greatest we've seen so far. However, the time spent in space and the radiation from the asteroid have rendered him insane. At first, we thought that he was simply having trouble achieving sapience, but we soon discovered he possesses a cunning intelligence. His violent sociopathic behavior has forced us to keep him confined to a cell.

* * *

Message to Command 13628:

Please send help. It's loose. I'm the only one left. Please sen

AUTOSAVED.

MESSAGE TIMED OUT.

"Blazes," Yna said, and stood back from the computer. She held her hand out in front of her and tried to ignite it with energy. Nope. Just as she suspected, she couldn't change into her other form just yet. Her body needed to recuperate first. If she was going to make it to the bridge alive, she would need a weapon. There wasn't much in this room. Yna rummaged through the medical instruments. Finally, she found an AON scalpel. It was a decent weapon; the superheated blade was designed both to cut and to cauterize. It wasn't very large, but holding it made Yna feel less vulnerable.

She tried to find a better weapon, but apparently someone else had already picked out the best stuff. Yna thought for a minute. She had been in the medical bay for two days. If the Marae was still on board, it obviously would have had time to get to her by now. So either it didn't know she was here, or it couldn't get into the medical lab. That was promising. The final message log had been written five days ago. According to the computer, the author had written it from the bridge. Which made sense, because that was the only place you could send a message. That wasn't good.

Okay, but that was five days ago. There was no reason to believe the Marae was still up there. It could be anywhere in the vessel, returning to its previous kills for further nourishment. It wasn't a pleasant thought, but it might be Yna's only chance for survival. Yna used the computer to call up a map of the ship. She studied all the routes, committing them to memory as best as she could. She considered the most direct route and all alternate routes.

Would the maintenance tunnels be safer? Maybe that would be less conspicuous. Then again, she knew nothing about this creature. It might have made those tunnels its home. At least in the hallways she would have room to move around. Okay then. Direct route it was. Yna approached the entrance to the medlab. She took a deep breath and opened the hatchway.

The hallway was deserted. Yna's footsteps, while nearly silent for lack of footwear, still made an echoing rhythmic thud that resounded through the hallway. At least they sounded that way to Yna, whose senses were heightened with fear. After a few minutes, she became aware of a loud breathing sound. She almost panicked before she realized that it was her own.

She made it to the lift without incident. If this creature was still alive and on board, it wasn't on this level. Yna entered the lift and pressed the button for the bridge. The doors slid closed, and the lift hummed as it started towards its destination. Then it stopped, much too early, with a shuddering thud. Yna gasped. She pushed the buttons, but there was no response. She tried to pry the doors open, but they wouldn't budge.

Only one thing to do. Yna opened the top hatch and climbed through. Something was stuck in the elevator's track, preventing it from moving further. There was very little light, so Yna used the AON scalpel to illuminate the track. She found a foreign object wedged in the track, and moved closer to investigate. Yna nearly shrieked. It was a human head.

Yna looked around and listened, but she was still alone. Still, knowing that it had been here, that it could still be here, in the shadows, gave Yna chills. But she knew she couldn't stay here, or hide in the lift.

Or could she? That was one possibility. She could go back into the lift, seal the hatch, and wait there until she was rested enough to change to her other form. Once she could use her energy form, she would be a much more formidable opponent.

But that wouldn't work, for obvious reasons. First off, she had no idea how long it would be before she would be able to change forms again. She could starve to death first. Second, there was no reason to believe that this creature wouldn't be able to break into the lift. And third, until she sent some sort of distress call from the bridge, there was no reason to believe help was coming. She was alone. She had to get a move on, and soon.

Yna couldn't fix the lift. She didn't want to spend any more time in the elevator shaft than necessary, but it looked like the only way to get any farther would be to climb. Small rungs lined the sides of the shaft, which she now used. Before she even got underway, however, something stopped her. A noise, from above. Some sort of groaning, which echoed down the shaft.

Oh, crap, thought Yna. She pulled out her AON scalpel and ignited the blade. Warily she looked upwards, for some sign of movement. And then she saw it. Only it wasn't a monster she saw, but rather the bottom of another lift. It was shaking. Something was inside it, moving around. The lift began to move downwards, towards Yna. If it reached her, it would crush her. Yna had to get out of the shaft, and now. Yna was just a few meters below the door to the second level of the ship. She climbed the rungs until she was next to the hatchway, and looked for a way to open it.

Above, the elevator shook noisily. Something snapped, and a wheel plummeted down the shaft, clanging its way from wall to wall, just passing Yna on its way down. The lift above lurched and squealed, and then moved towards Yna at high velocity. Yna quickly found the door override switch, and the entry door swooshed open. At the last possible second, she threw herself into the hallway, the elevator just missing her as it fell down the shaft. There was an explosive crash as it collided with the other lift. Smoke filled the hallway.

Yna looked back at the elevator shaft. It was now

completely blocked. She stood there, scalpel ready, expecting a shapeshifting monster to burst from the rubble at any moment. Had the Marae been in the elevator above when it fell? Yna knew she had heard something moving around in it, but that could have just been the beginning of its fall, combined with her nervous imagination. And if the creature had been inside, was it dead now?

She would have to find another way to the next level. Remembering the map, Yna knew that there was another elevator at the other end of the ship. Alternatively, she could take the maintenance tunnels to a higher place in the elevator shaft. But she still didn't like that idea. Nope, she would have to go the long way. The upside to this was that by taking the hallway she might find some supplies or an armory or something.

Yna proceeded down the hallway. It was very quiet. Yna's heartbeat pounded loudly in her ears. She was about to turn a corner, but she stopped. There was a smell... it wasn't a good smell. And... movement? No... the lights were flickering in that direction. Yna had seen a similar short in the lights on the lower level. Yna stood, her back to the wall, wondering if she should turn the corner. On the one hand, if the creature had been in the elevator, then it was behind her now. Or still on the upper level, where the second lift had originated. Either way, the Marae would not be in this hallway.

On the other hand, the movement in the elevator might have been her imagination. And she really had no idea what she was dealing with. Yna pondered this, but not for too long. She couldn't keep second-guessing herself. She could keep going back and forth between routes forever, but the only way out of this was to make a decision and proceed. Yna mustered all her energy and turned the corner.

There was a man on the floor. Or at least most of one. The corpse, bloated and mangled, lay in a large puddle of blood. Flesh had been gouged out from numerous locations. Much like the body in the medlab, this one had been cut open, and many of its organs were gone. And from his mouth protruded a strange bumpy cable. This thick gray cord extended from the man's face, up the side of the wall, and into the air ducts. And it was moving. Pulsating. The dead man's jaw opened and closed as the tentacle convulsed.

Shocked, Yna dropped the scalpel. The gray vine reacted instantly, withdrawing itself from the corpse's mouth and facing Yna. The end of the tentacle sported a mouth of its own, filled with many needle-like teeth. Yna could only stare, wide-eyed and open-mouthed. The tentacle bubbled, and from the left side, one bump split open to reveal a bloodshot eyeball. One which centered on Yna. The rest of the creature's gray mass began to pour from the air duct. As it hit the floor, it started to re-form itself.

Yna didn't stick around to see what this form would be. She was off like a shot, running at top speed in the other direction. She picked a door at random and went inside, shutting and locking the door behind her. Yna looked around for some sort of weapon. She was in a laundry room. Nothing of use in here, unless this creature was allergic to chlorine bleach. Yna doubted it. She stood there for a minute, listening. She heard something moving in the hallway. A sort of half-step, half-slither. The sound passed by her without stopping.

Yna, now feeling very helpless, went through the laundry until she found some actual clothing. She found a blue jumpsuit and hastily put it on. Then she looked around the room for other exits. The laundry chute. She was on the second level now; the chute would lead up to the crew deck. A definite improvement, it would get her both closer to the bridge and farther from the monster.

The laundry chute was a little tight, but Yna managed to squeeze into it. It was a difficult climb, as the chute was mostly vertical, but she made it. As she pulled herself out of the top of the chute, she thought she heard some noises from down in the laundry room. She listened carefully but heard nothing further. Hopefully, it was just her imagination. She closed the chute behind her and started down the hallway.

She wasn't that far from the elevator shaft. Running as fast as she could, Yna reached the shaft, opened the doors, and climbed up the next level. But when she reached the hatchway to the bridge, the doors wouldn't open. She tried hitting the override switch, but they wouldn't budge. Severely disappointed, Yna climbed back down the shaft, arriving once again on the crew deck.

Yna explored a few rooms, looking for one with a working computer. The first room she entered was a crew quarters, with all the amenities, including another mangled corpse and a smashed computer. The next room she tried was more promising: no corpse, and a working computer. Yna sat down and searched the logs for information pertaining to the bridge. It turned out that the door wouldn't open because the bridge wasn't safe to enter. Apparently, there had been a hull breach, and the bridge was now completely without oxygen.

Yna thought through this for a while. She could try to find a pressure suit, and then attempt to enter the bridge from the outside... probably not a good idea. The computers up there probably didn't even work anymore. Which meant, once again, that Yna was screwed.

Yna poked around some more, looking for anything that might help her. The crewman who had once occupied this room kept an encrypted journal. Yna looked around the room for clues to the password. She took a couple of guesses, then got locked out. A pop-up prompted her to reset the password, and she clicked OK. She pulled up the crewman's e-mail, which was already logged in, and had just received a "password reset" message. Within a few moments, Yna had access to the journals.

Dr. Morvik Personal Journal 13626:

I hate working with fools. The other scientists don't realize the military applications these creatures could have.

They're so short-sighted. They should realize that it's not about research, it's about profit. The government's not going to fund their projects if they're not pulling in money.

The Grunthians make a tidy sum by selling their bodyguards and harem girls, but with my experimental Marae steroid, the Grunthians can build an army of powerful shapeshifting soldiers. And so what if they use their new army to conquer other planets? Even if they conquer Earth, I don't care. I'll be retired and living on Valos by then.

Dr. Morvik Personal Journal 13627:

It's done. The Marae is loose. It will be another week before I can leave, but I should be safe in this room. The door is reinforced, and the air vent isn't connected to the main ventilation system. If the Marae does try to break in here, I have built a sonic transmitter that will calm him. One more week and my Grunthian transport will arrive, taking me to a new life of luxury.

Yna kept reading Morvik's logs. Interesting. So it wasn't radiation that had caused this Marae's mutation after all. This Doctor Morvik had been planning to betray them all along. He was planning to escape on a Grunthian ship. Yna quickly pulled up the ship's security cameras on the computer. And there it was, pulling into the landing bay. "The rendezvous ship!" Yna said aloud, and stood up. She turned, ready to head out the door...

...And found herself facing the business end of an energy pistol. The wielder was a short, balding man with a sneer on his face. "Doctor Morvik, I presume," Yna said, putting her hands in the air.

"Who are you?" he asked nervously. "How much do you know?"

He must think I'm law enforcement, Yna thought. "Okay, you caught me," Yna said. "I was just the first scout. The IGP is on its way. But if you'll let me go, and help me get off this ship, I won't tell them what I've found."

Morvik considered this proposal. "You're lying," he finally decided. He raised his weapon, aiming it at Yna's head.

Yna didn't flinch. Her expression remained neutral. Calmly, she explained, "If you kill me, the IGP will definitely show up and arrest you. However, if you take me to a transmitter, I'll call them and tell them not to come."

Morvik shook his head. "You're no cop. And even if you are, I'll be long gone by the time they get here. And this vessel won't be here either. It's on a collision course for the asteroid field." He held the gun up again, ready to pull the trigger. Suddenly there was a loud pounding at the door. Morvik instinctively turned his head. In that brief moment of distraction, Yna lunged at the scientist and grabbed for the gun. She gripped his wrist tightly, preventing him from aiming at her.

Morvik punched her in the face with his free hand, but he wasn't very fit and Yna recovered quickly. She kneed him in the stomach, still holding tight to his gun hand. As she fought for control of the weapon, Yna's fingers began to burn.

Yna's left hand, now clasped around Morvik's gun and fingers, glowed a bright blue. There was a quick, intense blast of heat, and Morvik's hand was melted to the gun. The scientist screamed in pain and cradled his misshapen hand. Yna jumped backward, considering her next course of action. She couldn't waste any more time fighting this man. Yna put her back to the wall, next to the door. She pressed the button to leave. As the door slid open, the angry Marae burst into the room, headed right past Yna. Yna quickly jumped into the hallway and closed the door behind her.

As she ran down the hall, she wondered if this was the last she would see of Morvik. If he managed to reach his sonic transmitter, he would survive. But if he was still preoccupied with his mangled hand, the creature would devour him before he could stop it. Either way, Yna had to get to the landing bay as soon as possible.

The landing bay was back on the lowest level, and it took several minutes of exploration to find it. Yna sneaked into the large landing area, staying in the shadows. The ship sat in the bay, and two armed Grunthians stood outside the doors, waiting. Yna would have to sneak aboard the ship and hide. Whether Morvik showed up or not, the Grunthians would have to leave before the research vessel hit the asteroid field. But sneaking aboard could be difficult.

Yna was an experienced pirate. Stowing away was her specialty. The ship's door stood wide open, so all she really needed to do was distract the guards. But how to do that?

Then an echoing scream came from down the hall. Both Grunthians approached the noise, weapons raised. Yna swiftly sneaked behind them, and went through the door. Once inside, she found a storage locker large enough to fit in. It was pitch black, but she could still hear weapons fire and screaming.

Three sets of footsteps ran into the ship, and the door closed. There was a lot of shaking from outside the small craft. The ship lifted off and blasted away from the science vessel. Once things had calmed down, Yna listened carefully to the occupants of the ship.

"Whew, thanks. I thought I was dead back there," said Morvik.

"Where is the formula for the Marae steroid?" said a Grunthian voice.

"In due time," Morvik said.

"Now. Or you will die."

"I don't have it written down," Morvik replied. "It's all in my head. I will tell it only to your scientists, and only when we reach the Grunthian moon."

The Grunthian growled in disappointment. It was clear

that they had been planning to kill him once they received the steroid. Morvik must have had experience in dealing with such unsavory types. Yna wondered what Morvik's plan was once he got to Grunthar. Well, it wasn't her problem. All Yna had to do was hope she remained undiscovered, and then steal this ship once it was empty.

It was a promising plan, and it might have worked if Morvik hadn't needed medical supplies for his hand. When the supply locker opened, Yna once again found herself face-to-face with the mad doctor. "You!" he shouted. Both Grunthians, weapons drawn, stood up and regarded the stowaway. Morvik ordered them to kill her, and they were more than willing to comply. They aimed their weapons...

And once more Yna was rescued by events beyond her control. The ship shook violently, knocking all the occupants from wall to wall. All eyes turned to the front of the ship, where they beheld a terrifying sight. The forward window, usually offering a panoramic view of the stars, was completely covered by a shapeless gray mass. One large pseudopod hammered relentlessly at the window, finally cracking it.

Yna wondered, *It can survive the vacuum of space?* Then, *Well, duh, that's where they found it.* The ship's four passengers looked on in horror, unable to prevent what was about to happen. One final punch and the window shattered. Everything that wasn't welded down got blown out the window. The Marae used one leathery tentacle to latch onto the pilot's seat. As the ship's occupants flew past it, the Marae grabbed Dr. Morvik with another appendage and bit his head off.

Yna's survival instincts took over, and once again she found herself in her energy form, floating helplessly in space. One of the dead Grunthians floated past her, and Yna grabbed him. His flesh sizzled from her touch, but she held on tight and searched his outfit for anything she could use, like a communicator. Of course, there were all kinds of reasons she wouldn't have been able to use a communicator even if she had found one, but she was in a hopeless situation and therefore grasping at straws.

It was pitch black in space, especially at this time of night. But Yna's energy form gave off a blue glow which helped her search the Grunthian's corpse. She found nothing but his sidearm, which wasn't going to be of much use to her. Yna clung to the corpse, parts of which gradually burned away from her touch. The vacuum of space prevented the corpse from actually catching on fire. Instead, it just slowly melted in the spots she touched.

For the seventh time this mission, Yna knew that this was the end. She wouldn't be able to stay in her energy form for as long this time, she was still too weak. She simply had no options.

In the distance, Yna could just make out the lights of the decompressed Grunthian ship from which she had been expelled. There was no longer anyone at the helm, but apparently the autopilot mode was still working. It would continue on its original course until it was recovered by the Grunthians or someone else.

If the Marae was still in it, they might be able to extract the steroid from its system. Or even if not, they might be able to use the Marae itself to breed a more powerful type of warrior. Either way, it was giving the Grunthians more power than Yna wanted them to have. Yna considered. If she was going to die in space anyway, she might as well do something productive with her time.

Yna drew the dead Grunthian's weapon. She aimed carefully, using the long-range scope, and fired several shots at the escaping ship. Her third shot hit its mark, piercing the ship's engines and causing a bright but quickly extinguished explosion. If the Marae was still inside, it would be toast. That done, Yna released the weapon and corpse, allowing them to float free into eternity. She watched them coast casually away, the gun still bright white from where she had gripped it. It was soon just a pinprick of light in the distance, lost among the other tiny pinpricks of light.

Yna realized that one of the pinpricks was moving closer. *What the hell?* Was the gun coming back? She squinted, but she couldn't make out any details. All she could tell was that a light was moving towards her. Yna was anxious, not wanting to get her hopes up, but still bristling with curiosity.

When it finally got near, Yna saw that it was a glowing ship of strange design. It was round, with no engine or jetstream or any of the features you would expect from a ship. Yna wasn't even sure how she knew it was a ship, except that something in the back of her memory told her it was. It had no windows, but the entire vessel had a transparent quality to it.

Inside the ship, she saw several people watching her. They were human-shaped, but featureless, with bright glowing skin. Yna felt an immediate kinship with them. The ship got closer, and she could feel herself being pulled toward it. Soon, all she could see was the bright light emanating from the ship.

Light... and then darkness.

Yna woke in a medical bay, covered with a thin turquoise blanket. A medical technician saw her stir and came over to check up on her.

"Where am I?"

"You're safe. You're on Outpost Station 4132. You had some burns when you arrived, but they're almost gone. Is there someone you would like us to contact?"

"How... how did I get here?"

"We've been wondering that ourselves. You were dropped off, we think."

"By who?"

"We don't know," the med tech said. "Our computers went glitchy, then alerted us that an airlock had been activated. You were inside, unconscious, nude, and covered in burns. What happened to you?"

Yna stared off into space. "I think... I think it was a family reunion."

Far away, a large chunk of metal debris floated through space. It had once been the hull of a small Grunthian craft, but now it was just a tangle of twisted junk. Clinging to this useless scrap of machinery, however, was something decidedly nonmetallic. This "something" was gray, shapeless, grotesque... and moving.

<h2 style="text-align:center">02.08   Identity Politics</h2>

ED.02500.09.27

Focus, Bloodstone told herself. She couldn't get the previous night out of her head. She wasn't usually so emotional, especially when the armor was on. But today, Detanna just couldn't get into what she called "Bloodstone Mode." She looked down below, at the sleeping gang members. She'd tracked them to this abandoned factory, which they had been using as their home base. They were sleeping on bare mattresses, fully dressed.

She only needed one of them. Zak, the leader of the East Side Daggers. The other fifteen thugs could just stay asleep for all Bloodstone cared. Zak had the information she needed. She had already welded the doors shut from the outside, in case he made a run for it. Then she came in through the large skylight that ran the length of the building. Now she squatted on a catwalk, sizing up her target.

This should be easy. Her visor allowed her to see in total darkness, while the gang members would be stumbling in the dark. With any luck, she'd grab Zak and get out without waking any of the others. She considered using sleeping gas on the entire group, but she didn't want to have to wait for it to wear off before interrogating Zak. A young woman's life was at stake, and time was of the essence.

Charlotte Lisbon had actually been missing for over a year, and the police had stopped looking for her months ago. That is, until this morning, when her property had turned up in Zak's apartment. The police had raided his place hoping to tie him to a gang-related homicide. When they got there, it looked like he hadn't been home for months. They didn't find the evidence they needed, but they did find Charlotte's purse, including her identity cards.

The Lisbons didn't want to waste another minute working with the police, who had been so ineffectual in the past year. They wanted the best, and the best was Bloodstone.

Bloodstone did one last mental checklist. She tugged on the cable that would carry her to the ground floor. It was stable, and more than strong enough to pull two people up once she grabbed Zak. She checked the gag she planned to slap over Zak's mouth before he could wake the others. She checked her gas grenades, one of which she planned to drop behind her as the cable pulled them up.

She thought about how to get Zak to talk. She thought about what questions to ask, and what questions might trick him into revealing more than he wanted to reveal. She thought about Whisper. Her beautiful violet eyes, her smell, the touch of her skin. She thought about last night and… she shook herself back to the present. She was getting distracted again.

She drew no weapons. She didn't want any violence on this mission, just information. And she would need both hands free to subdue Zak. She gave the cable one last tug, made sure it was securely attached to her harness, and she jumped to the floor. The cable's retractor unit slowed her fall just enough so that she landed silently on the floor. She carefully stepped over to Zak, squatted beside him, and pulled out the gag.

And then there was a loud crash from up above. Glass

rained down from the skylight, and more than twenty armored invaders – or possibly humanoid robots – descended from the ceiling. "Mom!" Zak shouted, apparently awakened from an intense dream. He immediately recognized the danger and tried to get to his feet. The East Side Daggers had good reflexes. More than half of them had the presence of mind to roll over, dragging their mattresses on top of themselves, as protection from the falling glass.

Bloodstone grabbed Zak from behind in a bear hug. He fought back, but she held on tight. She pulled him back just in time to prevent a large shard of glass from slicing him in half. The androids – they moved too efficiently to be armored humans – landed one by one among the startled gang members.

Bloodstone wasn't sure what to do. She wasn't sure who the good guys were here. These robots didn't sport any logos or markings that would indicate a connection to the police department. And besides, Bloodstone knew the local police didn't have the budget for androids. The androids started firing gas out of their fingers.

Hey, that was my idea, Bloodstone thought. She activated her cable, which swiftly pulled her up to the catwalk, still holding Zak. As they landed on the platform, Zak wrestled his way out of her arms and turned to face her. He hesitated when he saw she wasn't an android. "You're not with them?"

The scene down below was chaos. Gang members covered their mouths and ran in random directions, unable to see through the gas. They pounded on the doors, but couldn't open them thanks to Bloodstone's earlier sabotage. A few of the androids had started climbing the stairs, intent on chasing Zak and Bloodstone. Apparently, they couldn't actually fly, but had used Levatech gravity dampeners for a softer landing.

"Let's get you out of here," Bloodstone said, and Zak agreed. Bloodstone drew her energy pistol and fired at a few of the pursuing androids, really hoping they actually were enemies. The good news was that it didn't take a lot of hits to put them down. A well-aimed shot to the waist caused their batteries to short out. But more kept coming. One fired a blast that grazed Bloodstone's side, leaving a hole in her flightsuit and a nasty burn on her skin.

Bloodstone handed Zak a stun gun. She didn't trust him with anything lethal, but hopefully the harmless weapon would at least slow the androids down. Zak turned out to be a pretty good shot as well.

"I can't leave my friends," Zak shouted, but Bloodstone grabbed him by the wrist and pulled him along. Whatever this mess was, it wasn't Bloodstone's fight. She just needed Zak's intel. Besides, they could both see it was a losing battle down below. Bloodstone had gotten lucky with the few androids that pursued them, but Zak's information was too important to risk by staying around here.

"Take me somewhere we can talk," Bloodstone said. "If you help me, I'll help you."

Zak nodded. They found an emergency exit and ran down the fire escape. Bloodstone still had to fire back at a couple of pursuers, but eventually the androids lost their trail. Zak led Bloodstone through several alleys, down into a storm sewer, up to another alley, and finally to the basement of a closed-down diner. "Nobody knows about this hideout but me," Zak said, locking the door behind them.

Bloodstone looked around the room, her helmet scanning for any threats. "Good," she finally said. "Now, why don't we ARGH!" She felt a sharp pain in her side, then started to get dizzy. As everything went black, she saw Zak holding the stun gun. Then she lost consciousness and had dreams about Whisper.

Twelve hours earlier, Detanna and Whisper sat at the small table in Detanna's room, discussing a recent job.

"...and that's when I realized he was telling the truth,"

Detanna said.

"So he was innocent?" Whisper asked. "What did you do?"

"What do you think? I turned him in, and collected the money."

"Detanna!"

"If I didn't turn him in, someone else would have," Detanna said. "The reward was dead or alive. Another hunter might have killed him. At least now he's safe behind bars."

"But his crime has the death penalty!"

"I know," Detanna said. "I'm going to wait until the payment is completely processed, then I'm going to anonymously send them some evidence I found that implicates the real killer. With any luck, I can collect a bounty on that guy too."

Whisper nodded. "Sounds like you."

"Hey, I did the work. I deserve to get paid," Detanna said.

"No judgment here," Whisper said. "It sounds like you did the right thing. If not necessarily for the right reasons."

Detanna ignored the last part. "It wasn't easy, either. I had to fight off two carrion hunters. They jumped me from behind."

"Did you get hurt?"

"Not a scratch," Detanna said. She paused, then continued. "A few months ago, you asked me about my fighting style. The truth is, I'm a sham. Yes, I study martial arts, and I practice them daily. But my greatest skill is programming. My suit constantly scans the environment for threats. My helmet has a HUD that points out where attacks are coming from, and analyzes the weak points in my opponents. I don't have to think, I just have to punch where it tells me to punch."

"You're not a sham. Designing that system took a lot of skill. And you're still the one doing the punching."

"Thanks," Detanna said.

"No, thank you for sharing that," Whisper said. "I know you don't like to feel vulnerable. I promise not to tell anyone."

Detanna looked deeply into Whisper's eyes. "And I promise not to tell anyone whatever you're hiding, either." She tentatively reached for Whisper's mask. "May I?"

Whisper raised her palm, shaking her head. "I'm sorry. I just can't."

"I understand," Detanna said. "Well, I don't really understand. But I will respect your boundaries. I'm going to go, now. I have paperwork to do." She stood and turned toward the door.

"Wait," Whisper said, her heart torn by the rejected look on Detanna's face. She grabbed Detanna's arm and turned her back around. "Lights," Whisper said, and the room went pitch black. Whisper pulled off her mask, then pulled Detanna in for a deep kiss.

"Oh," Detanna said, and they kissed again.

For a moment it felt like things would go further, but Whisper pulled away. She pulled her mask back on. "Lights," she said again. They looked into each other's eyes again. "I wish things were different," Whisper finally said.

"If there's anything I can do..." Detanna began.

Whisper shook her head. "I just have to work this out for myself. But if anything changes, I promise you'll be the first to know."

Detanna left Whisper's quarters with an uncharacteristic lightness in her step.

"Yerma frilly loadstone..." Bloodstone heard, as the basement faded into view.

"Whu?" she asked. Her helmet was off, and she was tied to a brick column.

"I said, you're not really Bloodstone. He's a man. Or maybe a robot. Definitely not some chick."

"You're right," Detanna lied, seizing the opportunity. "I'm

not Bloodstone. I thought if I wore this costume, you'd be intimidated, and more likely to answer some questions."

"Well, I got no place to be, thanks to you. What questions?"

"I was going to ask if you knew where I could find Charlotte Lisbon. But now I have a bonus question. When the flek did this backwater planet get android cops?"

Zak sighed. "The Lisbon's hired you? To look for Charlotte?"

Detanna nodded.

"You… idiot!" Zak said. "Why won't she just leave me alone?"

"Talk to me," Detanna said. "Maybe I can help."

Zak moved close to Detanna until their faces were just centimeters apart. "Look at my face," Zak said. "Really look at it."

Detanna studied his features. Come to think of it, there was a resemblance to… was he Charlotte's brother? Then the truth dawned on her, hitting her like a ton of bricks. "You're… I mean, you used to be… Charlotte?"

"That's why I ran away," he said. "Mom couldn't accept me for who I really was."

"So you joined a gang," Detanna said.

"We're not really a gang," Zak said. "Just a bunch of runaways, doing whatever we can to survive. We all have our reasons for leaving home. Good reasons, too, we're not just 'lashing out at authority' or whatever. Most of us would rather die on the street than have to relive the abuse our parents put us through."

Detanna nodded. "And the androids?"

"Those are Mom's. She owns the company that makes them. Sells them to criminals because the money's better and she doesn't have to follow government regulations." Now that she thought about it, Detanna remembered having seen similar androids on Vermon's space station. Zak cursed. "The androids probably followed you to our hideout. You led them to us, and now my friends are gone."

"I'm sorry," Detanna said. "If I'd known the truth, I wouldn't have accepted the job. If there's anything I can do to help…"

"First let's see what's left," Zak said. He started to untie her, only to find she'd already managed to cut through her ropes. "When did you—"

Detanna shrugged and stood up. "About five minutes ago. But I wanted to hear what you had to say." She grabbed her helmet and put it on. "Let's go help your friends."

The factory was empty. There were a few bloodstains on the floor, but no bodies. "Is there anywhere they would go?" Bloodstone asked. "A secondary hideout they might use if this one wasn't available?"

Zak led her to another abandoned business, a pizza restaurant this time. He was greeted at the door by several friends. "Hugo! Vex! You're alive!" he exclaimed.

"Those robots left right after you did," Vex explained. She had blue hair and wore a leather jacket. "I think they were only looking for you, man."

"Did everybody make it?" Zak asked.

"Yeah, but some are in really bad shape. They'll be out of it for a while," she said.

"Let me see if I can help anyone," Bloodstone offered, and they led her inside. Six of the East Side Daggers lay on cots, their wounds bandaged with scraps of torn clothing. They had some nasty cuts and bruises, and a couple suffered from burns, but they would live. Bloodstone pulled a first aid kit out of one of her side pouches and proceeded to do what she could. She handed a tube of salve to Vex, instructing her to apply it to any burns.

"What are we going to do now?" Zak asked. "Mom's just going to keep coming after me…"

"I have a thought," Bloodstone said. "Come with me, I need to make a quick trip back to my ship. I may need your help carrying some things."

Zak's mother, Sandara Lisbon, was having her evening tea when her earpiece beeped. "Yes?"

"Ms. Lisbon? This is Bloodstone."

"Have you found my sweet Charlotte?"

"I did, but I lost her. I'm sorry, it's been a strange twenty-four hours. I thought I had her last night, but then I was attacked by a bunch of robots and I lost track of her."

"I'm afraid that's not my problem, dear. Surely in your profession, you're used to the occasional fracas."

"Yes ma'am. But I have a tip on where she is right now. Apparently she's at 1245 Market Street, in the old munitions factory. Unfortunately, I'm an hour away, and the police could probably get there faster. I'm afraid she might leave before I get there. Would you mind calling the police for me and telling them where to find her?"

"Of course dear. You were right to call me first. I'll make sure they get the call."

Bloodstone, Zak, and nine of the East Side Daggers waited outside, watching the factory from an otherwise empty skate park. All of them were armed with weapons Bloodstone had retrieved from her shuttle. Of course, the police did not show up. Instead, they saw an aircraft fly overhead, and dozens of androids rained out, dropping onto the factory roof.

"Now? Now?" Zak asked.

"Wait for it..." Bloodstone said, watching as the robots cut holes in the roof and jumped down into the factory. When the final robot was inside, Bloodstone nodded and said, "Now."

Zak pressed a button on a remote he was holding. There was a loud boom, and fire erupted from the factory's windows. Smoke billowed out of the broken windows, and flames flickered from the fresh holes in the roof.

"You think that got them all?" Zak asked, but his question was immediately answered. A handful of partially damaged androids began climbing out of the windows. Bloodstone fired her pistol, hitting one square in the face despite the extreme distance.

"You really are Bloodstone, aren't you?" Zak asked, and she nodded. "Don't worry," Zak said, leaning in close. "I won't tell anyone you're a girl. Why hide it, though?"

"Now's not the time," Bloodstone said, gesturing toward the factory with her gun. The androids had noted their location and were starting to advance. "Don't fire until you see the lights in their eyes," Bloodstone quipped.

Only a few of the surviving androids could still run, and the others limped or dragged themselves toward the skate park. As each one got close, Bloodstone and the East Side Daggers fired at them. None of them reached the skate park. Shortly after the last one was destroyed, they heard sirens in the distance. "Time to go," Bloodstone said.

Sandara Lisbon was just sitting down to dinner when her earpiece beeped again. Rolling her eyes, she said, "Yes?"

"Ms. Lisbon, it's Bloodstone again."

"Oh, did you find her?"

"There was an explosion at the factory. I'm sorry to have to tell you this, but I believe your daughter was killed in the fire. They haven't found a body yet, but witnesses say she was in the building at the time of the explosion."

"Oh... dear, I'm sorry to hear that," Ms. Lisbon said. Bloodstone didn't think she sounded very sincere, but everyone grieved in their own way.

"I'm very sorry for your loss," Bloodstone said. "Of course, I won't be charging you for my services."

"That's kind of you, dear," Lisbon answered. "If that's all..."

"There is just one more thing," Bloodstone said.

"Hmmm?"

"They found the remains of several androids at the scene. The police think they might have been involved in your daughter's murder. The bots didn't have any serial numbers, which is both unusual and illegal. The police were stumped at first, but I helped them out. I wouldn't be doing my job if I left your daughter's murder unsolved, right? A deep scan of one of their circuit boards revealed a digital signature that matches the ones manufactured by your company. Odd coincidence, right?"

"Right… erm…" There was a loud chime as someone rang Ms. Lisbon's doorbell. Through her window, she could see flashing blue lights.

"Well, I know you're a busy lady, so I'll let you go."

The police did eventually find a body in the factory. It was too badly burned to get a DNA sample, but since witnesses put Charlotte at the factory at the time of the explosion, it was taken as fact that the body was hers. Only a few people knew that the body was actually a Jane Doe that had been stolen from the county morgue, and none of them were going to tell.

There wasn't enough evidence to pin any specific crimes on Sandara Lisbon, but the incident did cause the police to keep a closer eye on her business dealings. This constant surveillance tainted her reputation and cost her some of her bigger clients, who preferred more anonymity.

Bloodstone helped Zak get off-planet, along with Vex and three other members of the East Side Daggers who wanted to start new lives elsewhere. She even helped them find jobs. Zak decided that he was going to follow in Bloodstone's footsteps, and become a bounty hunter. Bloodstone wasn't sure she wanted to encourage it, but she gave him a few tips and promised to put in a good word for him if and when he applied to the Bounty Hunter Registry.

Bloodstone had made no money for this job, and yet she'd found it more fulfilling than most jobs lately. Helping these kids made her feel the way bounty hunting used to make her feel, back before it became such a grind. She used to feel a sense of pride after every successful catch, knowing that she'd made the universe a little bit safer by taking a dangerous criminal off the streets. But lately, it was all about saving up for that operation.

Zak's question kept bouncing through her mind. "Why hide it, though?" The question was getting harder and harder to answer. This was the second time this year one of her targets turned out to be trans. Was the universe trying to tell her that it was time to come out?

Not that she believed in that sort of thing. If there were any sort of Great Power controlling the fates, it was a cruel being and Detanna wanted nothing to do with it. No benevolent power would allow all the atrocities that permeated the galaxy. Innocent deaths. Disease, famine, war. Terrorist acts like the destruction of EarthStation 1. People being born the wrong sex, to bigoted parents who would toss them out on the street.

Still... Apparently, Bloodstone had a knack for finding these jobs. Perhaps she was picking them subconsciously, her intuition guiding her to people with similar problems. Was her subconscious trying to tell her something? *I already know about my issues, but should I be helping others? Is it time to shed the mask, and tell the world my story?* She shook her head. This didn't feel like the right time.

She had to keep her reputation up, at least for now, at least until Alterra Sarr was caught. Then she'd have the money she needed, she could get the operation, and she could even retire from bounty hunting if that's what she wanted.

And then her life could truly begin.

02.09 *Mindwipe*

ED.02500.10.04

It was not a sanctioned mission. As far as Bloodstone and the others knew, Whisper was following up on some leads, gathering information about some Alterra Sarr sightings. In reality, she was trying to solve a mystery that only she could solve.

Over the past few months, eight female celebrities had gone missing. Three of them had since turned up, but with no memory of where they'd been. One had been missing a week, another three weeks, and one showed up six weeks after her initial disappearance. But regardless of how long they'd been missing, each one's last memory had been a day or two before their disappearance.

While all the women were famous and attractive, that was about all they had in common. The victims were a mix of movie stars, athletes, musicians, and models. When they turned up, they weren't injured or malnourished. They were wearing the same clothing they'd been wearing when they'd disappeared. None of them could tell the investigators where they had been abducted from. They just remembered going to bed one night, then waking up in a garbage bin in an alley, with no memories in between.

To get this far, Whisper had to look into details IGP didn't notice. She retraced each victim's steps the day before they were kidnapped. The IGP had already gone over their bank records to see where they might have spent money on the day of the kidnapping. The only charge they had in common was "StarStruck Coffee," which was such a common purchase that no one would question it.

But Whisper knew something the IGP didn't. During her brief time in the IGP, she had put a lot of effort into investigating the Inner Eye. One of their tricks was to disguise purchases as other purchases. She knew where to start.

The Red Star was a super-secret nightclub, located on a space station near Valos. Customers were sworn to absolute secrecy, on penalty of death. The IGP wasn't allowed there. Bounty hunters weren't allowed there. It was invitation only, and those invitations were only given to criminals, celebrities, and the super-rich. It was one of the few places a wanted criminal could walk around without worrying about being arrested.

For this mission, she didn't need her martial arts skills or her Auroran abilities. She needed her fame.

With Whisper's skills, it was easy enough to sneak in. The problem was not getting kicked out once she was there. She entered disguised as a kitchen worker, and later emerged from the bathroom in a stunning black dress. Alterra Sarr turned a lot of heads as she confidently strode through the crowd.

It was crowded. People danced and drank. Strobe lights flashed in shades of red, while the music thump thump thumped with a deep bass that she could feel in her gut. She recognized a few celebrities here and there.

And a few people recognized her. Some looked angry, others were awed. A couple of people took pictures of her. Alterra didn't like that, but there wasn't much she could do about it. At least this club had a "no extradition" policy. She might have to find a clever way to leave at the end of the night, but no one was going to drag her out and turn her in.

Her instincts told her to duck, but she was too slow. A champagne glass hit her in the back of the head, smashing the glass and getting her hair wet. Alterra turned. A red-faced woman pointed at her, screaming, "You killed my cousin!" as security escorted her away. When the woman was gone, a well-dressed man appeared and handed Alterra a fine linen towel.

The concierge was an older gentleman, with graying hair and blue-green skin. "Alterra Sarr," he said. "I apologize for the incident. I will make sure that the offending patron is never allowed to return. However, while we are honored that you're here, I don't recall seeing your name on tonight's invitation list."

"I'm sure it was lost in the mail," Alterra said, toweling her hair. "After all, I'm on the run. Where would you have sent it?"

"There is that," he replied. "Still, my manager would like to have a word with you. It will only take a minute. Would you follow me?"

Alterra's instincts told her to run, but she also felt like she might be on to something. She followed the concierge over to the bar, where a small hallway led to an office. "Please wait in here," the concierge said, opening the door for her. Then he left.

Almost immediately, the door opened again. A man wearing a black mask entered. The mask covered everything but his eyes, which had white irises. "Does anyone know you're here?" he asked. His eyes flickered as he asked the question, in a way Whisper had seen before.

Alterra found herself unable to lie. It didn't feel like she was being forced to tell the truth, it was more like nothing existed but the truth. All other possible answers had been erased from her mind. "No one knows I'm here," she answered robotically.

"Come with me," he said, turning around.

"Yes sir," Alterra said, and followed him. Again, it was as if no other course of action made sense. Of course she should follow him, what else was there?

"You will forget the route we took here," he said. It felt like some time had passed since he'd told her to follow him, but Alterra didn't know how much. The last thing she remembered was following him out of the office, and then suddenly she was here, in what looked like someone's kitchen. And a rustic kitchen at that, with wallpaper and wooden floors. There was no way they were still on the space station.

"It's time you met the others," the man said. He opened a door, and wooden stairs led down to a basement. "Walk down the stairs, open the cell door, enter the cell, and close the door behind you. I will be along shortly."

She did as told. When she reached the bottom of the stairs, she saw the layout of the room. It was a large basement, with concrete floors and brick walls. Halfway across the room, a series of metal bars divided the room in half, like a prison cell. There was a barred door in the center of the bars. On this side of the bars, there were several boxes stacked against the wall, and some video monitors mounted from the ceiling.

On the other side of the bars, she could see eight cots, a toilet, and a sink. Five women stood inside the cell, watching her. Alterra recognized all of them. First, there was Katrice Velt, who recently won a "Best Actress" award for her role in "Watercress Nation." Then there was Amber Nuvon, the comedian-slash-actress from the popular sitcom, "Slums of Jupiter." Behind her stood Zinfany Nanders, the tennis player. Next to her stood Vanella Kreem, the pop star. And finally there was Ellena Van Dart, who was pretty much famous for being famous.

They seemed to recognize Alterra as well, if their shocked

and angry expressions were anything to go by. Alterra walked up to the barred door, opened it, entered, and closed the door behind her.

She looked at the other prisoners. "Why are we here?" she asked.

"You're the only one who deserves to be here," Zinfany Nanders spat, glaring at her.

"Better just let him tell you," Ellena Van Dart said. "He'll be in here soon to brief you. We've all heard his speech several times now."

"But who is he?" Alterra asked.

"My name is Mindwipe," a male voice said, coming down the stairs. After sending Alterra downstairs, he had changed into a more ridiculous outfit. He looked like some sort of Zorro-wannabe with a black suit and cape. He held a cane with a head that looked like an eyeball.

"I am the master of mind manipulation," he said with a flourish. "You are my prisoner until it is time to let you go. Rule one: You will not attempt to escape. Rule two: You will not try to hurt me."

"Why are we here?" Alterra asked.

"Getting to that," he said. "You can stay here as long as you choose. I will take good care of you. When you are ready to earn your freedom, you will *willingly* spend the night with me. After that, I will wipe your memory of your time here, and set you free."

"So this is all about having sex with celebrities?" Alterra asked.

"You make it sound so vulgar," Mindwipe said.

"If you have the power to make us do what you want, why wait until we decide to submit willingly?"

"Because I am not a rapist!" he shouted.

You're delusional, Alterra thought, but didn't say it out loud. She wanted to tell him off, but she also wanted more information, and making him mad might not be the way to go. "How do we know you'll let us go if we submit?"

"Surely you've seen the news," he said. "Three of my honeys have already been returned unharmed. Three more notches on my bedpost. Actresses, supermodels, and now you, Alterra Sarr. You're the first serial killer we've had in here."

"I'm not a serial killer," she said.

"Fine, mass murderer. Big difference."

"I didn't do it," Alterra said.

Mindwipe groaned. "Come here," he said, pointing to a spot on the floor in front of the bars. "Look at me."

She stood where he indicated, facing him. They were less than a meter apart, separated by the barred wall. Alterra stared into his eyes. She couldn't find the will to turn away.

"Why did you destroy EarthStation 1? Were you working for Lord Vermon?"

"I did not destroy EarthStation 1," Alterra said, robotically.

"You're really innocent?" he asked.

"I am." The other women in the room gasped at the revelation.

"You're telling the truth," Mindwipe said. It wasn't a question, he was confident in his abilities.

"I am," Alterra replied honestly.

"Huh," Mindwipe said. "Well, sucks to be you. Now I must bid you farewell. I will be back down later to bring you ladies dinner. If any of you are ready to get out of here, you can tell me then." He went back up the stairs.

"You didn't blow up the station?" Zinfany asked, and Alterra shook her head. "I'm sorry, I didn't know."

Alterra looked at the barred door. "Have any of you tried to pick the lock? Or force the door open?"

"It's not locked," Katrice said. "Seriously, try it."

Alterra reached for the door, but changed her mind just before touching it. She could get her hand within a centimeter of the door, but then she just sort of lost interest until she pulled her hand away. "Interesting," she said.

If Raven were here, she'd be able to resist the mind tricks. Alterra wondered if she might be able to overcome Mindwipe's power if she concentrated enough. But right now, she had more questions.

She turned to the others. "How did you learn about The Red Star?"

Vanella Kreem answered first. "I got an invitation in my e-mail. It said it was only good for the next night. It claimed it was a great honor, only a select few are invited, and I would get an award. It specifically said not to tell anyone, so it would be a surprise when the award show was broadcast."

Alterra thought it through. "So he invites celebrities, but makes sure they show up shortly after they receive the invitation. So that when he wipes their memory later, he only has to erase through the day they receive the e-mail. How does he know you won't tell anyone where you're going?"

"Mindwipe met me at the door," Vanella answered. "He looked into my eyes and asked if I'd told anyone where I was going. I couldn't lie. I don't go anywhere without my personal assistant, but he's the only one I told. But now my assistant is on the news, saying he has no idea where I am, so Mindwipe must have wiped his memory."

Alterra fumed. Seriously, who did this guy think he was? She had a pretty good idea of who his father was, but even Lord Vermon hadn't been so brazen.

"I can get us out of here," Alterra said. "We stand together. Nobody agree to sleep with him until I come up with a plan."

Amber looked away. "I don't know... I want to go home. Is it really so bad if I'm not going to remember it?"

Alterra put her hand on Amber's shoulder. "I know you miss your loved ones. But I also know I can get us out of this. Just give me a little time."

* * *

At dinner time, Mindwipe came down with several trays of vegetables. "Nothing but healthy food for my honeys," he said. "Wouldn't want you to get fat. After dinner, is anyone ready to spend some time with me?"

"We're standing together!" Ellena said.

"Huh?" Mindwipe asked.

"She means you're sleeping alone tonight," Zinfany said. "We don't care how long you keep us here, none of us are ever going to sleep with you."

"Be honest, how do you really feel?" Mindwipe said, looking at each of them in turn. Amber flinched. "Yes, Amber?"

"I... I'm wavering," she said. "I really want to see my family. If you aren't stopped in another week, I might give in."

He turned to Alterra. "What about you?"

"I'm staying until I find a way to stop you." There was no hesitation in her voice.

"Good luck with that," he said, and went back upstairs.

Alterra meditated all night. She was sure that if she explored her own mind thoroughly enough, she could unlock the mental blocks Mindwipe had placed on her. Every once in a while she got up and tried to open the cell door, but still found herself unable to do so.

The next morning Mindwipe brought them breakfast – more veggie trays – and left without saying a word. The prisoners spent the next few hours discussing possible escape plans. Everyone had strange mental blocks. A plan might be making good headway until they reached a certain point, then all of them would simultaneously say, "I don't want to do that."

Maybe it was just a matter of framing the escape in a way that didn't violate the rules Mindwipe had imposed. But the first rule, "You will not attempt to escape," was a pretty big one to get around.

A few hours later, the viewscreens came on by themselves. "They always do this when there's news about his kidnappings," Katrice explained.

"Feeds his ego," Zinfany added. "He likes us to see what he's gotten away with."

All of their hearts sank when they saw the news. Tiffina Zeet, a thirteen-year-old starlet who had most recently starred in the movie "Red Candy," had gone missing.

"He wouldn't," Alterra said.

"I wouldn't put it past him," Ellena said.

A few hours later, Tiffina came down the stairs, followed by Mindwipe. The prisoners were beyond livid, but couldn't do anything about it.

"Surely you're not this low," Alterra said, as Tiffina entered the cell.

"Do you really think so little of me?" Mindwipe said. "No, I'm not into that."

"Then why did you take her?" Alterra asked.

"Insurance. What happens to Tiffina depends on you," he said. "After last night's rejection, I thought it was time to update the rules."

How much worse can this get? Alterra thought.

"Tonight, after dinner, one of you will willingly come upstairs with me. If no one volunteers, then Tiffina will come upstairs with me."

Alterra wanted to murder him right then and there. She rushed forward, ready to throttle him through the bars, but came to a standstill half a meter short. "You sure have an odd definition of 'willingly,'" she said.

"No one resists me for long," he replied, and went back upstairs.

Alterra meditated until close to dinner time. She was sure she could break his hold if she could just concentrate. A few minutes before Mindwipe came down, she addressed the rest of the prisoners. "I'm going to go with him. I think I can break his hold on me."

"You won't," Amber said. "I believe you're strong, but nobody's that strong."

"It's our only chance," Alterra said. "I won't let him touch Tiffina."

After dinner, Mindwipe came downstairs to retrieve the empty trays. "Well," he asked, "Any volunteers?"

Alterra stood up. "I will come with you," she said.

"Excellent!" he said. "Follow me."

Mindwipe's bedroom was disgusting. There were posters of nude celebrities on the walls, the trash can was overflowing with wadded-up tissues, and the floor hadn't been vacuumed in years. The sheets on his bed were covered in crusty stains that Alterra didn't want to think about. In one corner, a camera stood on a tripod.

"You record yourself with the celebrities?" Alterra asked, suddenly even more nauseous.

"Every time," he said, turning on the camera. "Now, before we begin, look at me."

Alterra looked into his eyes.

"You will not attempt to escape. You will not try to hurt me."

"I will not attempt to escape. I will not try to hurt you," she repeated.

"Now take off your clothes," he said. She could feel a difference in the tone. The request was not pushed by his mind control powers. She was to do so willingly. The only unbreakable orders currently affecting her were rules one and two. Somehow it made it worse, knowing that she was undressing willingly, rather than being controlled.

As Alterra began to undress, so did Mindwipe. He took off his mask, and Alterra saw his full face for the first time. He was in his late teens or early twenties, with bad acne and a poorly-grown mustache.

Now shirtless, Alterra reached over and stroked Mindwipe's face. "You're really handsome," she said. She wasn't sure if he believed her.

He leaned in for a kiss, and Alterra jabbed her fingers into his eyes. She heard a sickening pop as her fingernails punctured his eyeballs. He screamed.

Alterra immediately felt something unlock in her mind. She now had full autonomy. She kneed him in the crotch and threw him against the wall.

He sat on the floor, whimpering, his hands over his eyes. "You said... you said you wouldn't try to hurt me," he said.

"I never 'try' anything," Alterra answered, wiping her hands on a fresh tissue.

All the celebrities went home that night, and Mindwipe was arrested. Alterra made her way back to her shuttle, and eventually returned to the Bloodwind.

She found the crew watching the news. Reporters were interviewing pop sensation Vanella Kreem, who described her ordeal. "Oh, and Alterra Sarr was there. She saved us! The hypnotist guy – Mindwipe – He looked her right in the eyes and asked her if she was innocent, and she said she was. We couldn't lie when he did that, none of us could!"

Whisper turned to Detanna. "What do you think?"

Detanna thought a minute before answering. "I think Alterra has a very strong mind. I wouldn't be surprised if she could resist that sort of mind control. It's probably how she managed to defeat Mindwipe."

Whisper tried not to lose her temper. "What sort of evidence would it take..."

Detanna interrupted, "Whisper, I know you want to believe the best in people. But I'm a bounty hunter, not a judge. If Alterra would willingly turn herself in and face trial, I'd be a lot more likely to believe her."

"I understand," Whisper said. And she really did. She had

often considered doing just that – turning herself in and letting the courts decide. But it was too risky for now. She had to get some sort of evidence first. Otherwise she would be going straight to her death.

She pushed those thoughts away. Today she had earned a minor victory. Not only had she saved some kidnap victims and put a rapist in jail, but word of her innocence was spreading across the news. Of course it wasn't enough to prove anything, but it put some doubt out there in the universe. Maybe by the time she did turn herself in, she would have some public support.

Maybe.

02.10 Brimstone

ED.02500.11.28

It was often said that planet Korrigan looked like a tribute to 1950s America. Full of small towns with a friendly "everyone knows everyone" attitude, it was a place where people felt safe. Kids played ball in the streets, police stations only had three officers, and the smell of apple pie wafted from every open window.

It still had its nightlife, with dance clubs and bars, but people respected each other and altercations rarely happened. They had a decent economy that insured that everyone had food and shelter, so the crime rate was relatively low. In short, it was a quiet society.

On the outskirts of a town called Autumn Grove, a couple parked their "Model T"-style hovercar in the woods, and walked along the river for about a kilometer. When they reached their destination, they stared judgmentally at the abomination before them. It was a riverside nightclub called "Rainbow Dreams." They watched as people went in and out of the club's doors, smiling and hanging on each other. All kinds of couples frequented the establishment. Every combination of sex, race, and species.

The couple shook their heads. They hugged each other, then prayed. The man then stretched his arms wide, raising his face to the sky. His prayer was immediately answered, as fire rained down from the heavens. Survivors panicked and fled in all directions as the club was pulverized by the onslaught of flame.

"That's enough," the woman said, and the man nodded. The woman raised her arms, and heavy storm clouds gathered over the remains of the club. There was a sudden downpour centered over the wreckage, rain pounding the ground like a giant fire hose. It caused a flash flood that washed the debris into the river, along with the parked hovercars, and many of the fleeing patrons.

The rain stopped as abruptly as it began. The entire scene had taken less than ten minutes. The police hadn't even been alerted yet. Satisfied that enough sins had been washed away, the couple walked back to their old-fashioned hovercar and drove away.

So what's the story? Trenyn asked.

"Serial arsonist," Bloodstone said. "The targets appear to be religiously motivated. LGBTQ+ night clubs and bars, abortion clinics, and churches."

Raven raised an eyebrow. "Churches?"

"Yes, but only for Vorsheim," Bloodstone added. "It's one of the planet's lesser followed religions. I believe the arsonist worships Hysuun. It's the most popular religion on this planet. Generally, it's a peaceful religion, but the extremists can be a bit... entitled."

So why are they outsourcing this one to bounty hunters? Trenyn asked.

"The police force on Korrigan is laughable. They're not used to this level of violence. Plus, some of them are worried that... well... that this all might be a sign from Hysuun."

Raven scoffed.

"Look, I don't believe in Hysuun either," Bloodstone continued, "but the police will be less cooperative if you mock their religion. You will show them respect while you're there."

"Of course," Raven said. "When do we leave?"

A few hours later, Raven and Trenyn sat at a table in a homey kitchen, speaking to a friendly man in uniform.

"Sheriff," Raven began.

"Please, call me Donald," he said with a genuine smile. Sheriff Donald Mayfair was human, or at least appeared to be. He had large ears and a kindly face that made you want to sit a spell and talk about the weather. Which was, technically speaking, why the bounty hunters were here.

"Donald," Raven continued, "I appreciate your hospitality, but why didn't you want to talk at the police station?"

"Because it's Restday," the sheriff answered, as if that explained everything.

Raven let it go. "So what do you know?" she asked. She did most of the talking because Trenyn's telepathy tended to make some people uncomfortable.

Donald was suddenly all business. "Not enough. Very few survivors, most of whom are still too hurt to answer any questions. A suspicious pair shows up in a couple of surveillance videos, but they're wearing hoods. We think one's male and one's female. No accelerants were found at the fire. One minute a building is fine, the next it's burning so hot that even the bricks melt. Some witnesses claim they saw, and I quote, 'fire and brimstone rain from the sky.' After just a few minutes of burning, it starts raining. An absolute gusher, localized specifically over the fire. And then it all just stops."

"We'd like a list of witnesses, and any survivors who are well enough to interview," Raven said. "Also, any employees of these establishments who weren't working the nights the attacks happened. And I'll need to see that surveillance footage."

"I'll get right on it," Donald obliged. "But first, would you like some apple pie?"

The witnesses and survivors weren't much help. Those who saw what happened all said the same thing. Balls of fire, then heavy rainfall, like something out of The Books of Hysuun. The surveillance footage wasn't much better. The mysterious couple wore dark clothing and hoods, completely out of season for this warm summer weather. Their body language did seem to indicate that they'd caused the disasters, but "how" was still up in the air.

Next they met with Elgeron Smyth, the owner of Rainbow Dreams. His eyes were red, and he looked like he hadn't slept since the fire two nights ago. His boyfriend had been tending bar when it happened.

Raven wasn't particularly good at touchy-feely, but she put a reassuring hand on top of his and spoke in the most comforting voice she could manage. "Have there been any religious objections to your business?"

"Only all the time. Ever since we opened, we've been getting flyers taped to our door, vandalism, windows broken… You know, I picked this planet for my bar because it had a reputation for kindness, but the smallest groups of bigots are always the loudest."

"Anything recent that stands out?"

Elgeron thought a moment. "There's this one couple that's been coming by a lot this last month. They kept passing pamphlets under the door. Said things like, 'The end is coming soon' and 'You will be judged.' Nothing I haven't seen before, but I guess it is strange timing. Come to think of it, I got one of the pamphlets the day of the bombing. I was on the way out the door when I saw it. I threw it away, kissed Griff goodbye, and went home for the night. If I'd known it would be the last time I'd see him…"

"Did you get a good look at the couple?"

"No, they wore hooded jackets, and kept their faces down."

"Do you have one of their pamphlets?"

"No, sorry, I always just threw them away."

Raven turned to Trenyn. "We need to get our hands on one of those pamphlets."

By the end of the day, they had made three more interviews. They spoke to a Vorsheimic priest, who was home in bed when his mosque burned down. Next, they spoke to a nurse from a planned parenthood clinic, who'd had the good fortune of being out with the flu when her place of employment was hit. Finally, they spoke to a bartender from a tavern called "Love Wins." The bar had been destroyed on her night off. She still had one of the pamphlets.

"I don't even know why I kept it," she said, handing it over. "I just... I don't know how anybody who claims to come from a religion of peace can be so.... so...." She broke down in tears before she could finish the sentence.

Raven studied the pamphlet. It showed flames in the background, with text that read:

SINNERS!
The End is Coming!

Attention all:
Homosexuals!
Fornicators!
Prostitutes!
Feminists!
AlcoHolics!
Drug abusers!
Thieves!
Liars!
Science Lovers!
baby Killers!
Masturbators!

Adulterers!
Dancers!

You Will be Judged! Is your soul Prepared? You will End up in fire!
Get right with Hysuun, Get right with yourself.

"Science lovers? Really?" Raven asked.

I think the random capitalization really helps drive the message home, Trenyn remarked.

"There's no net address, no mention of a specific church," Raven said, thinking out loud.

No mention of a specific doctrine at all, Trenyn added. *If I wanted people to join my cult, I'd at least give them an address.*

"Maybe they don't have one yet. Maybe they're just testing the waters, waiting to see how people react to the attacks. If it drives the 'fear of god' into some of them, they'll be more likely to join a new church that pops up."

So we wait around to see if any new churches pop up?

"I'd rather catch them before anyone else dies," Raven said. "That last sentence, though… 'Get right with Hysuun, Get right with yourself.' That sounds like a motto or something."

It's a start, Trenyn replied, already typing on their tablet.

Raven and Trenyn took a hovercab back to "Hope's Bed & Breakfast," where they currently shared a room. They ate dinner silently, both staring at their tablets, trying to find leads. There were six churches of Hysuun in town, and four of them posted their sermons online. But none had posted the phrase, "Get right with Hysuun, Get right with yourself" anywhere on their site.

They expanded their search to nearby towns. All the attacks so far had been in Autumn Grove, or at least on the town's outskirts, but that didn't mean the terrorists lived there. In fact, it made sense that they would practice these attacks on a nearby town rather than risk burning down or flooding their own.

They got back to their room and showered. Rather than have Raven struggle with her robot bodysuit, Trenyn held her limbless body while they showered together. It was an arrangement they'd utilized many times before, and nothing was enticing about it for either of them. It was simply efficient hygiene. They used this time to discuss what they'd learned so far, and brainstormed on what to do next.

When they were done in the shower, they got right back on their tablets. After picking each other's brains, they each had new search parameters in mind. After about ten minutes, they experienced simultaneous eureka moments. They looked up at each other.

You go first, Trenyn offered.

Raven held up her tablet. "It wasn't on a church website, but someone's personal blog. This young woman - she goes by 'TrulySaved2525' – posts mostly 'daily affirmations' and other religious musings. Apparently, she frequents a variety of churches and reviews their sermons the way some people review restaurants. In one blog, she talks about attending a sermon where the phrase 'Get right with Hysuun, Get right with yourself' came up multiple times. She says it's one of the few times she felt creeped out by a sermon."

Trenyn asked, *Where's the church?*

"In the next town North of here, in Oak Hollow. It's called the 'One Mind Church.' Sounds charming."

Want to head there now?

"It might save a few lives if we did. But what was your thing?"

Trenyn wasn't even holding a tablet. Instead, they were carefully rubbing the pamphlet between two of their fingers. They held it up. *There's something in here. Embedded inside the paper. It feels like an extremely thin microchip. I think they might be tracking the pamphlets.*

"Why would they do that? Most of them are going to end

up in the trash," Raven said.

I don't know, Trenyn answered. *Maybe to see who doesn't throw them away, to find potential followers. Let's head to Oak Hollow.*

It was too late to catch a hovercab in this sleepy town, but it was only a fifteen-minute walk to the shuttleport where their landing shuttle was parked. They flew over to Oak Hollow and landed at that town's shuttleport, where it would be another twenty-minute walk to the church. On the way, Raven looked up more information about One Mind Church.

"Apparently the church is run by a man and his daughter. Fyran Brimstone and Helen Highwater."

Please tell me those are aliases.

"Yes," Raven said. "Fyran was born Fargus Kludge, and Helen was born Helga Kludge."

Yikes. I think I'd change my name too. Criminal record?

"You called it," Raven replied. "Fargus has a long history of vandalism and was once arrested for inciting a riot. And this is interesting, Helga has been arrested for hacking."

Hacking what?

"It looks like she was trying to erase her father's criminal record. She also tried to hack the local fire station's computer for some reason. And then – oh yuck!"

Whoa, what? It wasn't often Raven was so expressive.

Raven composed herself and continued. "When her parents divorced, Fargus lost custody of Helga because of 'suspected inappropriate relationship between father and daughter.' The minute she turned twenty – that's the legal age of adulthood for this planet - she left her mother and went straight back to Fargus. That was three years ago. They've been preaching together ever since, and who knows what else. Incest between consenting adults is perfectly legal on this planet, but still… Ew. I know I just showered but I already feel like I need another one."

Trenyn still had issues grasping human sexuality and the cultural taboos surrounding it. *If she's legally an adult, it's her choice…*

Raven interrupted. "Only after her father spent her childhood brainwashing her into thinking it was normal."

Trenyn still didn't really understand. Wasn't Raven likewise brainwashed by society into believing incest was "icky?" And why was sex treated with more respect than other biological functions? You didn't see people get so worked up about eating. Unhealthy foods were worse for your body than sex, but you never saw people try to ban bacon from being shown in movies.

Trenyn knew Navorans were an anomaly, but recognizing that didn't help. It was so much simpler on Trenyn's planet. On Navor, sex was how friends bonded. Since it took three Navorans to conceive a child, there were no unwanted pregnancies. They didn't have all these hang-ups over incest or nudity or who was cheating on who.

They also didn't have erotica, fetishes, or rape. One-on-one sex was just for fun and had no more psychological weight than other pastimes, such as playing board games or watching a movie. Why weren't more worlds like this?

But Trenyn respected Raven's opinions. She was the most intelligent being they had ever met, and if she believed something, you could bet she had a good reason. So Trenyn dropped the subject, resolving to ask additional questions at a more appropriate time. For now, it was back to business. *It sounds like we're on the right track, in any event. Should we call the police?*

"And wake up Donald? Let's just see what evidence we can find first."

They reached the One Mind church. It was dark, but they both wore eyewear with night vision modes. Staying in the shadows, they approached the back of the building and found a stairway leading to the basement.

That's an expensive-looking lock, Trenyn noted.

"If we're wrong, I'll buy them a new one," Raven said, as she broke the lock and opened the door.

They waited a few seconds, listening for any alarms, then went inside. It didn't take long to find what they needed; the basement was full of incriminating evidence. There were boxes and boxes of those pamphlets. A calendar on the wall showed the dates of the bombings, with the locations written on each day. There was one scheduled for tomorrow night, with the exact time and place written in red ink.

Before they could look at much more, they heard a man's voice. "Who's down there?" Raven and Trenyn looked at each other. Would this man destroy his own church to keep from being caught? This was not the time to find out. The duo ran up the stairs and into the night, but someone wasn't far behind.

"Come back or face the wrath of Hysuun!" they heard the voice shout. They kept running.

In the lot behind the church, they came to an old barn. *Should we hide in here?* Trenyn asked.

"Sounds like a good... wait, do you still have that pamphlet?" Trenyn handed her the pamphlet, and she threw it into the barn's open window. They had now lost sight of their pursuer, so they ran a bit further until they found an embankment to hide behind. They watched the barn from a distance.

The figure of a man stood outside the barn. "I know you're in there," he said. "This is your last chance." He folded his hands as if in prayer, then raised his arms wide. Several bright objects fell from the sky, destroying the barn in a fiery explosion. Satisfied that the trespassers had paid for their sins, the man walked back towards the church.

"Did that look like fire and brimstone to you?" Raven asked.

If I was superstitious, maybe. But what I saw looked more technological.

"Let's get back to the B&B," Raven said. "I have a thought. We'll need to wake Donald."

The following night, two hooded figures approached a library. In their eyes, it was a place of debauchery, that encouraged people to open their minds to new ideas. Fargus and Helga turned to each other and nodded. They folded their hands and prayed for the salvation of those inside. Then Fargus held his arms open wide, summoning Hysuun's fire of judgment. And he waited. And waited. Suddenly six police officers – a joint task force of Autumn Grove's and Oak Hollow's finest - burst from nearby unmarked vehicles and arrested them.

"You'll all burn! You'll burn! You'll see!" Helga shouted as they shoved her into the back of a hovercar. Fargus just kept his mouth shut. There was no point in wasting his breath on those who couldn't understand. They would face judgment when it was their time.

"Thank you so much," Donald said, shaking Raven's and Trenyn's hands. "How did you figure it out?"

"It was really quite simple," Raven explained. "When I saw Helga had been arrested for hacking, I put two and two together pretty quickly. She had hacked one of the planet's defense satellites, which holds a battery of air-to-surface missiles. And then of course there was the forest fire suppression drone system. Put enough of those drones in one spot, and you can drown a city. The tracking chips embedded in the pamphlets enhanced the satellite's targeting systems, so they wouldn't accidentally hit any surrounding buildings."

Donald was in awe. This was a lot of technical information to process at once, and way above his pay grade.

Raven continued. "Once we managed to hack the same systems Helga had, we were able to break her control of the satellite and drones. Which reminds me, I'm going to have to make a couple of calls to your planet's defense department. They're in need of an upgrade."

In the end, Raven and Trenyn made more money from upgrading Korrigan's security than they did for catching the criminals. Fargus and Helga were charged with multiple counts of terrorism, murder, destruction of property, and a few dozen smaller charges. To his credit, Fargus accepted all the responsibility he could, claiming that Helga was his unwitting pawn.

They were sent to prisons on different planets and were prevented from having any contact with each other. While Fargus would most likely never see freedom again, Helga at least had some hope. She would receive intensive counseling, and if she made enough progress, she might earn her freedom after a decade or two. Only time would tell if it would be possible for her to live a normal life.

The following week, a memorial / ice cream social was held in Autumn Grove. While Raven didn't care for ice cream, or anything labeled "social" for that matter, she and Trenyn put in an appearance and accepted an award. Each received a small gilded trophy in the shape of a Grove Apple Pie, the town's claim to fame. Each trophy was engraved with the recipient's name and the words "Hero of Autumn Grove."

And while Raven didn't care for sentiment any more than she cared for ice cream, that trophy found a prominent place on her desk in the Bloodwind's medbay. The monetary reward had been nice, but this cheap statue was a reminder of the lives she'd saved. In the end, that was far more valuable than credits.

02.11 Blackmail

ED.002500.12.15

It was Christmas season, but Vik was the only one on board who celebrated the holiday. The rest of the crew either weren't from Earth or just didn't seem to believe in fun. Vik was planning to go home for Christmas to visit some friends and family, but before he left, he was determined to bring a little Christmas spirit to the Bloodwind crew. He resolved to buy a small gift for each of them, and he set up a Christmas tree in the galley. Yna and Dervish helped him decorate the ship. Neither of them knew much about Christmas or any other holiday, but it was a fun diversion for them.

"Wow, they're really going all out," Whisper said, looking at the garlands hanging around the medbay. She knew Raven wouldn't have put them up, and Trenyn probably didn't celebrate Christmas.

"As long as they take it all down before January," Raven said. She ran a handheld x-ray device up and down her patient's arm. Whisper had broken it a couple of weeks earlier, but it was mending nicely. "Any pain when I do this?"

"Yow! Sweet mother of kittens!" Whisper cursed, wincing.

"I'll take that as a yes," Raven said, making a note on her

tablet. "I'd say you're ready for duty again. You're going to be tender for a while, so just try not to get hit in the right forearm."

"I generally try not to get hit at all," Whisper said.

"And we see how that worked out," Raven said.

Whisper was still kicking herself for that one. It had been a relatively successful hunt until that point. She'd cornered the guy, fought off his minions, fended off swords, lead pipes, and some nut wielding a double-bladed chainsaw… and then one of them got in a cheap shot with a bowling pin. Why did they even have a bowling pin?

The door to the medbay opened, and Detanna entered. "Sorry to bother you in the middle of an examination, but I'm handing out assignments and the medbay was on my way." Then she turned to Whisper and said, "How's your arm? Ready for a job?"

Before Whisper could answer, Vik popped his head in. "Detanna, can I see you a moment?"

Detanna followed Vik out into the hallway. "So, I was browsing the bounty postings, and I came across this entry, posted by the Grunthian government." Vik pointed to a line on his tablet.

WANTED – BLOODSTONE – GRAND THEFT

Detanna didn't look surprised. "I'm on there at least once a month, ever since I stole the freighter. They only post on the unofficial sites, though. The Bounty Hunter Registry doesn't accept listings from Grunthar."

"Does anyone ever come after you?" Vik asked.

"Not really," Detanna answered. "Usually I hack the boards and remove the listings as soon as they're posted. But even when I don't, they don't get many bites. They only tend to offer five, maybe ten thousand credits, and that's just not tempting enough to risk what I'd do to anyone who tries to bring me in."

"Umm… you might want to look closer this time," Vik said, expanding the listing.

WANTED – BLOODSTONE – GRAND THEFT
REWARD: 247,101.26 CREDITS
LIVE ONLY – NO REWARD IF DECEASED

"Set a course for the nearest warp gate," Detanna ordered.

The crew all met on the bridge. It now had enough seating for everyone, and none of the chairs were oversized. Even Panther had a large cat bed in one corner, and he reclined on it now.

"It's weird," Vik said. "They could buy a new freighter for that. One in much better condition than this junker."

"Maybe there's something on the ship we haven't found," Yna suggested. "Something that makes it valuable."

"There could be diamonds hidden between the floors," Dervish added.

Except they aren't asking for the ship back, Trenyn replied. *They only seem to care about acquiring Bloodstone.*

"They want you alive," Whisper said. "At least that's something."

"Still, that's a lot of money," Vik said. "People are going to try to collect this time."

"I've already hacked the board and removed the listing," Raven said. "But who knows how many bounty hunters already saw it. Does anybody else think the reward amount is oddly specific? Does that number mean anything to you?"

"Yes," Detanna replied. "It's my birthdate." Everyone stared at her.

"That's… not listed in public records, is it?" Whisper asked.

"No," Detanna said. "Not even the BHR has that information. If the Grunthians know my birthdate, then they know my real name. The listing is a message, directed at me. A threat. If I don't turn myself in, they'll expose my identity."

"So, what do we do?" Vik said.

"Get ready for a fight," Bloodstone said.

Bloodstone, now fully suited up, was triple-checking her equipment when the door beeped. "Come in," she said.

Whisper stepped through the door into Bloodstone's quarters. She was also fully decked out, with her whip, protective vest, and mirror-faced helmet. "Are you worried?" she asked.

"I've faced worse," Bloodstone said.

"The last time we went to Grunthar, they blew your ship out of the sky," Whisper said.

"Good times," Bloodstone recalled.

Whisper hesitated before asking her next question. "Would it... would it be so bad if your identity was exposed? I know you're afraid of looking weak or whatever, but I swear you'd still be respected."

Bloodstone sighed. "Sit down," she said, also sitting down herself. "I've been thinking about that a lot lately. I've always enjoyed the mystique, people wondering if I'm some sort of cyborg or genetically enhanced mutant. It's seriously helped my career over the years. But you're right. Most of my clients would still respect Bloodstone regardless of her species, sex, or gender orientation."

"If a few idiots don't want to hire you anymore, that's their loss," Whisper added. "I'm sure you'll still find more work than you could possibly handle on your own."

Bloodstone nodded. "But that's not the point. When and if I decide to come out to the universe, it will be on my terms. This secret is not theirs to spread. I may have stolen their ship, but they're trying to steal something much bigger. They want to steal my right to control my own life, my right to present myself as I see fit. And I don't intend to let them get away with it."

Whisper stood up. "Whatever you need, I'm right beside you."

The full crew was present on the bridge, each at their stations. After taking the warp gate to the Grunthar system, they set a course for the planet itself. They didn't get far before the ship's alarms went off.

"Three different ships are attempting to hack us," Raven said.

"Can you fight them off?" Bloodstone asked.

They're not getting through our firewalls, Trenyn replied, their skin flashing purple.

"They're hailing us," Dervish said, sitting at communications.

"Which one?" Bloodstone asked.

"All of them. There's five ships out there now."

"I'm not having the same conversation five times," Bloodstone said. "Transmit this to all of them, now."

Dervish pressed a few keys, then gave Bloodstone a thumbs up.

"Attention rival hunters. This is Bloodstone. I am turning myself in for the reward. I have already made the Grunthians aware of this. If you attempt to capture me before I reach Grunthar, then you will not only face my wrath, but that of the Grunthians as well."

"Think they'll buy it?" Vik asked.

"Wait until I turn off the comm before saying things like that," Dervish said, cutting the transmission.

I'm not sure it matters at this point, Trenyn told them. *Long-range sensors detect a massive ship, headed in our direction.*

On the main viewscreen, they watched the ship approach. The five small bounty hunter crafts scattered and fled. The new arrival was moon-sized, and obviously of Grunthian design. It was rectangular, well-armed, and unconscionably ugly. As the Bloodwind approached, a large hatch opened on the front. It was clear that the freighter was meant to dock.

"Their systems are attempting to override our controls," Raven reported.

"Let them," Bloodstone said.

The freighter landed in the bay and the hatch closed. A Grunthian's face appeared on the viewscreen. In English, it said, "The Grag Prime Krithhelm wishes to speak to Bloodstone alone." The screen immediately blinked out.

"Krithhelm? I wonder what happened to Arathnon," Whisper said.

"No one rules Grunthar for long," Bloodstone said, leaving the bridge.

Vik stood up and grabbed Bloodstone by the shoulder. "You're really going out there alone?"

"We're at their mercy," Bloodstone said. "If I don't make it back, do whatever you have to do. Whisper, you're in charge."

Bloodstone was escorted to a hovering platform, which took her through many long hallways before arriving at the Grag Prime's throne room. It was the only room Bloodstone had seen so far with any sense of style, but it still wasn't pretty. Dark crimson curtains adorned the walls, with matching carpet down below. There was a mural on the ceiling, an explicit depiction of a bloody battle. The heads of former Grag Primes, encased in acrylic cubes, sat on pedestals behind the throne. The only light in the room came from four ax-shaped torches.

The throne itself was the least comfortable-looking piece of furniture Bloodstone had ever seen. Instead of cushions, it featured blunt metal spikes all over the seat and the back. They weren't sharp enough to hurt someone, but they sure didn't look relaxing. It was probably meant to be a reminder that power is fleeting, so leaders shouldn't get too comfortable in their position. Or perhaps it was to show that the burdens of leadership are heavier than those of the common soldier. But it may have just been a macho "look how much pain I can withstand" kind of thing.

Twenty Grunthian soldiers stood at attention at regular intervals around the room. The soldiers were identical, right down to the number of spikes on their shoulders. Most Grunthian soldiers were clones, though each battalion used different source donors. There was a huge variety between battalions, but not within a battalion itself.

Some Grunthians had rough, rhino-like skin, while others had thick body hair. Some had armor plating like an armadillo, while others had horns, spikes, or quills. Grunthians were bred to be powerful, and only the strongest had their DNA harvested for cloning. But the various cloners had their own ideas about which bodily features made the strongest soldiers.

The Grag Prime that currently sat on the throne was nearly three meters tall, with broad, spiked shoulders, and the horns of a ram. Their larger set of arms rested on the throne's spiked armrests, while they kept their smaller arms crossed across their chest. Because the light was dim, they kept their lower eyes closed, and they used their upper eyes to size up Bloodstone.

Bloodstone wasn't sure how to properly address a Grag Prime. She decided not to speak until spoken to. Krithhelm nodded to the guards and said, "Leave us." The order was in Grunthian, but Bloodstone's helmet translated it. Bloodstone then realized the Grag Prime was female. Grunthian men and women were virtually identical except for their genitals and their voices. The women had two sets of vocal cords, and when they spoke, it sounded like two people speaking at once.

The soldiers filed out of the room, leaving Bloodstone alone with the Grag Prime. Krithhelm then addressed Bloodstone in English. "Bloodstone. Born Datan Zareb Taush. Now Detanna Zephyri Taush. Daughter of Merrienna Torres-Taush and Corton Taush. Born on Earth. Former pirate. Galaxy's most prominent bounty hunter."

Bloodstone winced at hearing her deadname, but she bowed deeply. "And you are Grag Prime Krithhelm, supreme leader of Grunthar, slayer of Arathnon. It is an honor."

"Actually I defeated Pythoran to claim the throne," Krithhelm said. "He defeated Arathnon. Pythoran only kept the throne for a month before I challenged him." She smiled at the memory.

"I'm sure you dispatched him with great skill," Bloodstone said politely. "Why am I really here?"

"Straight to the point, I like that," Krithhelm said. "Then I will be just as blunt. You have secrets. So do I. I have acquired a rare blood disease. I have no symptoms yet, but as it progresses, my body will weaken."

"I'm sorry to hear that," Bloodstone said. Then the full impact of the statement hit her. "Oh."

"You understand. Any sign of weakness and my reign will abruptly end. But there is a cure."

"And this is where I come in?" Bloodstone asked.

"If I send a Grunthian to retrieve the medicine, they will suspect I am sick," Krithhelm said. "They might tell others. They might challenge me. They might poison the medicine. I have to send an outsider such as yourself. And even then, I have to send you under false pretenses."

"What do you mean?"

"Decades ago, a Grunthian artifact was stolen by archaeologists. The Chalice of Ginth. I will tell my people that I allowed you to live in exchange for this mission. They know I would never waste the time of Grunthian soldiers to retrieve an artifact, but it isn't unheard of to hire an outsider for such tasks."

"I see," Bloodstone said.

"Your crew will perform both tasks. Retrieve the Chalice and the cure. In exchange, I will keep your secrets, and you will keep your ship. But be quick – it won't be long before my soldiers notice my symptoms."

Krithhelm gave Bloodstone more details, then sent her back to the Bloodwind.

"We're going to split into two groups," Bloodstone told the crew. "Raven, Trenyn, Vik, and Dervish, you will take the Bloodwind and retrieve the medicine. Whisper, Yna, Panther, and I will get the chalice."

They took a warp gate to Haktet, where the chalice crew departed in a landing shuttle. Then the Bloodwind took the rest of the crew back through the gate, headed for the Cytrine system.

From a distance, Cytrine Delta appeared to be a futuristic wonderland of high-tech wizardry. But Raven knew the disappointing truth. The planet had been host to a Galactic Fair a decade prior, the kind that promised visitors an opportunity to visit the communities of tomorrow. It had attracted a huge number of sponsors from a variety of planets, all of whom were eager to show off their upcoming projects. The fair lasted a full year and hosted events that covered nearly a fourth of the planet.

But when the fair left, the planet's economy tanked. Those that stayed now lived in poverty, living in rundown smart homes that had long since ceased being smart. Their houses looked straight out of science fiction, yet the owners had to beg for food to survive. Crime rates soared, and it was dangerous to walk the streets at night.

That said, it still had a thriving scientific community. A great deal of lab equipment remained on the planet, including experimental machines that had been deemed too cost-prohibitive to relocate when the fair had ended. Scientists were relatively safe from muggers, partly because scientists never carried any money, but also because they often hired the homeless for research projects. Even non-scientists sometimes wore lab coats around town to avoid getting mugged.

Dervish stayed on the Bloodwind, in orbit over Cytrine Delta. Vik, Raven, and Trenyn took a landing shuttle to the surface. The landing pad was overgrown with grass and weeds, and they got several strange looks from the locals. Vik eyed them warily. "One of us should stay with the ship," he suggested.

After a quick discussion, they elected Trenyn to stay behind. They'd already agreed Raven would do the talking when they got to the lab, and Vik's police presence made him a good escort. The lab was only a few blocks away. They hoped to get back before nightfall, but the sky was already a dark orange.

Haktet was hot. Three-fourths of the planet was covered in orange sand, with the only surface vegetation surrounding the planet's single ocean. It was a windless day, and there wasn't a cloud in the sky. Bloodstone, Whisper, Yna, and Panther trekked through the desert, headed for a large pyramid.

It was the kind of heat that immediately sapped your energy, making a five-minute walk feel like a ten-day hike. The only one of them who didn't seem to mind was Panther, who pranced back and forth, pouncing on shadows, and batting the sand with his giant paws. He'd probably exerted twice the energy the others had, running in zig-zag patterns instead of a straight line, but he seemed no worse for wear.

They arrived at the base of the pyramid twenty minutes later. They could have parked closer, but landing directly on the sand was dangerous. This desert was prone to sinkholes due to underground caverns, so it was safer to park on rock when possible. They stared at the base of the massive black pyramid, looking for an entrance.

Sixty-odd years earlier, a group that called themselves the "Historical Artifact Liberation Front" constructed these pyramids to house stolen artifacts. The members of HALF held a variety of contradictory beliefs about the reliability of museums, the limits of cultural appropriation, and the best way to preserve ancient relics.

The organization had started with noble intentions – robbing from museums and returning the items to their original cultures. But sometimes the original cultures weren't around, or had no safe way of protecting the artifacts from the ravages of time. So HALF built their own protective buildings, with impenetrable defenses, on hostile planets. They even started robbing museums that only displayed their own culture's artifacts, on the logic that HALF's structures would keep the items safer.

No visitors could view the artifacts now, but at least they wouldn't be lost. HALF itself disbanded a few years later, due to infighting and lack of funds. But the pyramids remained, brimming with well-guarded historical items.

Bloodstone used her wrist computer to scan for tech, and discovered a hidden panel on one stone wall. The keypad was more than sixty years old, which oddly enough made it more difficult to hack. Modern keypads had interface ports, which Bloodstone could plug into and run her codebreaking software. But this one had no port. It had a slot for a keycard, but Bloodstone couldn't work with that. She removed the keypad's face and examined the circuits underneath.

Meanwhile, Yna and Whisper walked up and down the base of the pyramid, feeling the smooth black rock with their fingers, looking for more hidden panels. "Here's something," Whisper said, finding another panel. This panel was human-sized and slid aside to reveal a doorway. It looked like an emergency exit and had no handle on this side. Yna looked for hinges, hoping to burn through them with her energy power.

Bloodstone was making no headway with her panel, and was relieved when Whisper called her over to show her the door. Bloodstone scanned the door, looking for contact points. She directed Yna to a spot to burn, but it was plated with volcanic rock, and burning it was beyond Yna's power.

"Do we have any stronger equipment on the shuttle?" Whisper asked. "Maybe a large drill, or a high-powered battering ram?"

"On the Bloodwind, maybe," Bloodstone said, woozy from the heat. Her helmet contained an airflow system, but the rest of her body was about to collapse.

"If Trenyn were here, they could probably build something," Yna said.

"What's Panther doing?" Whisper asked.

The cat was digging hard, in a spot a few meters from the pyramid. Every once in a while he'd stop, sniff the air, and start digging again. The others walked over just in time to see Panther uncover the remains of a dried-out human hand. It looked like it had been dead for decades. Working together, the group unburied the rest of the body.

It was probably male, but it was impossible to tell how old. A sturdy old satchel was strapped to their waist. "Oh, please please please," Bloodstone said, rooting through the satchel. She pulled out a keycard. It was a bit faded, but it identified the owner as a man named Benjamin Farzen, member of HALF.

Bloodstone returned to the keypad, swiped the card, and a hidden door slid open. The group entered the pyramid, glad to be out of the blazing sun.

"So the Grag Prime's a woman?" Vik asked. "Weird, Grunthians are so, you know, masculine. I wouldn't think they'd want a woman in charge."

"There are many problems with the Grunthian society, but sexism isn't one of them," Raven said. "They have no concept of gender roles. For them, people are either strong or weak, and their sexes are equally strong."

"Still..." Vik said.

They had retrieved the medicine from their contacts. Raven now carried a steel briefcase. Inside were four syringes full of mycrozencrynalide sulfovaxxin, the only known cure for Grunthian Netalymphoma. Four doses, each taken twelve hours apart, and Krithhelm would be completely cured.

"Vik," Raven said. It was dark now, and only a few of the street lights still worked. Both Vik and Raven wore night vision sunglasses, but so did the people watching them. Several young men and women gathered, and were joined by others who trickled out from the alleys. They dressed in clothing that would have screamed "street gang" on just about any planet.

At first, they just kept pace with Vik and Raven. The followers kept their distance, while the people ahead just leaned against the wall with "I ain't doin' nuthin" expressions on their faces. Each person they passed joined the entourage. Vik and Raven stared straight ahead, showing no fear, as the crowd behind them grew. By the time they were halfway to the landing pad, they had more than twenty followers.

"Don't panic," Vik muttered.

"Have I ever?" Raven asked.

From ahead, one last ruffian leaned on an unlit lamppost. He looked human except for the four small horns on his forehead. He wore a torn leather jacket and denim jeans, and his spiky hair was dyed red, yellow, and orange in flame patterns. "Got a light?" he said.

"I don't smoke," Raven said, noting that the man wasn't even holding a cigarette.

"No worries," he said, his voice polite. "What's in the suitcase?"

"Nothing that you would find valuable," Raven said.

"Now I'll be the judge of that," the punk answered.

"I don't want to hurt you," Raven said. It was true. She and Vik were outnumbered at least ten-to-one, but Raven's biggest concern was that if it came to a fight, she might be forced to kill someone.

But the punk just laughed at her confidence. "I wouldn't lose sleep over that."

"That's enough," Vik said, flashing an expired badge. "Official police business. Move along."

They did not move along. Instead, they pulled out weapons. Mostly lead pipes and crowbars, but a couple of them had AON knives.

"Last warning," Vik said, drawing his gun.

The punks attacked.

The inside of the pyramid was overwhelming. It held rows and rows of pedestals and display cases, showing off ancient and rare items from countless cultures. Hundreds of worlds were represented. The electricity still worked after all these years. The outer walls of the pyramid were basically solar panels, and everything was automated. The air was stale at first, but as soon as the systems detected movement, the air conditioning activated. After a few minutes, it was much more comfortable.

Bloodstone looked for a catalog screen. She found one mounted to the wall, next to the stairwell in the center of the pyramid. As it turned out, the pyramid had thirteen levels, and the item they needed was on level eight. There was no elevator, so they took the stairs.

On the eighth floor, they checked the map again. As they moved between the rows of historical artifacts, Bloodstone noticed that there was no rhyme or reason to how the relics were ordered. All these items had come from different planets and different historical periods. A Glorkan ceremonial pauldron sat next to a Vhelran ritual glove. An amber diamond from Kartha lay adjacent to a clay pot from ancient Earth. The same weapons rack held a Cethervaan spear, a Galean claw hammer, and a Ken-Tith falchion.

Granted, it wasn't a museum. The collectors had probably just filled each floor as they acquired the items. But the lack of organization irritated Bloodstone, and she wanted to retrieve the chalice and leave as soon as possible.

After a few more minutes of searching, they found it. The Chalice of Ginth was made of dull gray iron and was shaped like an upside-down skull resting in a skeletal hand. The wrist formed the stem of the goblet, and the base was carved with Grunthian symbols representing strength and power. Several sharp spikes surrounded the cup of the chalice, so that it could be used as a mace if needed. It wasn't uncommon for Grunthian stemware to double as weapons. A Grunthian celebration wasn't considered a success unless there was bloodshed.

Like most of the smaller artifacts, the chalice sat atop a pedestal, inside a clear acrylic cube. There was another card reader in the pedestal, underneath a small digital readout. Bloodstone inserted Benjamin Farzen's ID card, and the readout displayed, "INSUFFICIENT AUTHORIZATION."

"Figures," Bloodstone muttered. She turned to Yna and Whisper. "When I open this cube, be prepared for anything." Bloodstone examined the cube. It was locked in place on the pedestal, just waiting for someone with sufficient authorization. She pulled out her AON knife and cut each of the contact points. Then she paused, looking around the room for any alarms, lasers, or murder robots.

She lifted the cube and grabbed the chalice. Again she looked around the room. Nothing but silence. "Looks like we're in the clear," she said. "Now let's get—"

Just then, alarms blared, red lights flashed, and hundreds of metallic discs detached from recesses on the ceiling.

Raven ran through the streets of Cytrine, the mob hot on her heels. Vik leaped from rooftop to rooftop, keeping pace with Raven and firing his stun pistol at Raven's pursuers. At first, he'd tried to carry Raven with him, but her robot body had proven just a bit too heavy.

A hand grabbed Raven's left arm, just below the shoulder. She was about to punch her assailant when they lost their grip, hit by a blast from Vik's pistol. Another mugger attacked her from her left side, and she clobbered him with the metal briefcase. Two more caught up to her, and she stopped running. *Fine,* she thought. She'd given them every chance to break off the chase, now they would face the consequences.

The attackers formed a circle around her, weapons ready. "Decided to give up?" one asked.

Raven set the suitcase down and put one foot on it. Then she took off her overcoat, revealing her flesh-colored robotic body. Finally, she took off her sunglasses, showing her white-irised eyes. She made a threatening pose, trying her best to look intimidating.

A few of the muggers took a step back, confused. Her fleshy body looked almost human but obviously wasn't. "She's a cyborg," one punk said with a wide smile. Cybernetic parts went for a fortune on the black market. This lady was a walking goldmine. The circle around Raven started to close.

Raven held out her arms. A panel slid open on each forearm, and small weapon barrels popped out. Once again, the circle hesitated, a few punks stepping back at this new development. Vik watched from above, taking aim at the leader. If Raven had a plan, he didn't want to interrupt.

"Who's going to be first?" Raven said, pointing her weapons at the crowd. "You? You? How many do you think I can take out before you take me down?"

"You're bluffing," the leader said, and charged. He didn't get two steps before Vik's energy blast knocked him unconscious. As the rest of the gang swarmed Raven, Vik dropped down into the fray.

Unfortunately, Raven had been bluffing. As much as she'd considered adding deadly weapons to her suits, she just couldn't bring herself to do it. She was a doctor, after all. One barrel fired fire extinguishing foam, which she now used to temporarily blind one of her opponents. The other barrel was the scope of a long-range sensor, which was of no use to her right now. But she still had her fists, and while she didn't have the martial arts skills of Bloodstone or Whisper, she could hit hard.

She heard bones shatter with every punch she threw, and her mind raced with data: diagnosis, treatment, approximate heal time. Broken nose. Fractured rib. Cracked femur. These were hungry people, scrounging to survive, and it made her sick to send them to the hospital. It went against everything she stood for. But she had warned them.

Vik fought his way through the crowd, trying to help out Raven. He'd already taken out at least twelve of them, but apparently the sound of fighting had drawn every desperate reprobate in the city. Three grabbed onto him now, and he used his Levatech power to push one way while he shot the other two with his stun pistol.

One mugger stabbed Raven in the left shoulder with an AON knife, and working with two others, they managed to wrench her arm free. Another jammed a crowbar into her knee joint, piercing the artificial skin and ripping into the servos. It dawned on Raven that after all that worrying about hurting her attackers, they were literally tearing her apart.

She lost it. Now prone, she grabbed the closest mugger's ankle, feeling no guilt at the sound of snapping bones or his cry of pain. She threw him to the side, knocking down two other people. She rolled onto her stomach and tried to stand, but more people jumped on top of her. They tore at her, using crowbars and AON knives at her joints. A man with a scar across his left eye held an AON knife to Raven's throat.

Then he vanished, pulled away backward by Vik's Levatech. Vik ran to Raven's aid, frantically pushing more punks away with his abilities. He had several deep cuts and bruises, but the attackers weren't done yet.

There was an electronic whining sound in the air. The landing shuttle, piloted by Trenyn, hovered overhead. A hatch on the side opened. Vik holstered his gun, pulled the suitcase to one hand, and grabbed Raven with the other. With Raven's limbs now gone, she was just light enough to carry. He leaped high into the air and through the hatch.

Some of the remaining muggers shook angry fists at the escaping shuttle, while others gathered up whatever pieces of Raven's suit they could scavenge.

"How did you know?" Vik asked Trenyn as they flew toward the Bloodwind.

I could hear her pain, Trenyn answered. Raven didn't lose her temper often, but when she did, Trenyn could feel her emotions from kilometers away.

Vik took over piloting so Trenyn could tend to Raven. They removed her from what was left of her robotic body and strapped her into a seat. Her suit had taken most of the damage, and she only had minor bruises on her face.

"I'm fine," Raven said, still angry at the mob. "Tend to Vik." While Trenyn's instinct was to protect Raven first, they had to agree that Vik's injuries were worse. As Vik flew the ship, Trenyn stood by and patched up a few of his cuts. When they were satisfied that no one's injuries were life-threatening, Trenyn decided to examine the briefcase.

The case opened, and Trenyn's face turned yellow. Despite the padding, two of the four vials had broken.

Bloodstone's party rushed toward the stairwell, as discus-shaped drones buzzed around them, firing blasts of energy. "Hide behind the artifacts!" Whisper shouted, ducking behind a pedestal. Since the drones were programmed to protect the priceless relics, they were reluctant to fire at targets that were too close to them. However, small blades protruded from each drone's outer edge. Spinning like buzz saws, the drones dove at their targets, attempting to slice them to ribbons.

Bloodstone took out several drones with her energy pistol, aided by the autotargeting system in her helmet. She held the drones off while the rest of her team made it to the stairwell, then she followed them down the stairs. When they reached ground level, they found hundreds more drones waiting for them.

And that was definitely all they had? Trenyn asked.

"Our contacts said they didn't even have the ingredients to make more," Raven said. They were back on board the Bloodwind, and Raven was currently scanning the medicine with a piece of lab equipment. She now wore her older body, which looked much more robotic than the one she'd lost on Cytrine.

Do we have the ingredients to synthesize more?

"It looks like we're lacking one ingredient," Raven said. "We need the calcified bone marrow from a Vikaran valecat."

Aren't they extinct?

"For a while now," Raven said, thinking. "But you can find them if you know where to look. The ancient Vikarans mummified valecats and buried them with their dead. I suppose we could set a course to Vikara, but their government won't like us going through their tombs..."

We should pick up the rest of our crew first. We're probably already halfway to Haktet.

"Haktet..." Raven said, and the next idea occurred to them simultaneously.

"This isn't a good time, Raven."

Raven could hear explosions and weapons fire over the comm channel. "I'm sorry, Bloodstone, but this is important."

"I don't interrupt you while you're at work," Bloodstone said.

"Just this morning you interrupted a patient consultation to hand out assignments," Raven countered. She heard more weapons fire, a buzzing sound, and a loud crash.

"Fine, make it quick."

"I need a mummified Vikaran valecat."

"This is no time to... OOF... complete your collection of... Ow! Look, I don't even have time to come up with a quip right now, can it wait?"

"It's for the current mission," Raven said.

"But we're almost to the door..."

"Is there a valecat in the pyramid?" Raven was insistent.

"One sec, I'm checking the catalog..." There were a few seconds where all Raven could hear were the sounds of battle. Then Bloodstone let out a long string of curses. "Six levels up? Are you kidding me?"

"Sorry," Raven said. "We'll be there soon to pick you up. Be safe."

Bloodstone let out a few more choice invectives before closing the channel.

By the time the Bloodwind reached Haktet, Bloodstone's team was ready to meet them. The minute the shuttle docked, Raven took the mummified valecat and went to work. The medicine wasn't quite ready yet when they reached Grunthar. Bloodstone decided that she would go ahead and meet with Krithhelm to return the chalice, and let her know the medicine would be ready soon.

Half an hour later, Bloodstone once again found herself in the throne room, standing before the Grag Prime. The Grunthian leader had no horns on his head nor spikes on his shoulders. Instead, thick bony plates ran up his arms and surrounded his face. The head of Krithhelm sat on a pedestal, in an acrylic cube.

"Welcome, Bloodstone," the Grunthian leader said. "I am the Grag Prime Velkime, successor to Krithhelm."

Bloodstone knelt and held up the chalice. "Grag Prime Velkime, it is an honor. I present to you, the Chalice of Ginth."

"Rise," Velkime said. "Your gift is most appreciated.

Though you made your deal with my predecessor, I will honor the agreement. Your ship is yours, and we absolve you of past indiscretions. You are free to go."

A few days later, the crew of the Bloodwind had an early holiday celebration. Christmas was still a week away, but Vik wanted to spend some time with the crew before he left for Earth. They met in the galley and exchanged gifts. Vik explained his favorite Christmas traditions for the benefit of those not from Earth. Whisper taught them about the holiday of Els-Mora - literally translated as "Family Gathering" – which was the closest thing her people had to Christmas. Navorans didn't have holidays per se, but Trenyn told them about Orva, the Day of Peace. It was an annual tradition where Navorans switched lives with their rivals in order to understand them better.

Dervish and Yna found Christmas fascinating, and wanted to learn everything they could about the holiday. Panther loved diving into the pile of discarded wrapping paper. Someone gave him a huge rubber cat toy, and it lasted nearly four hours before he managed to tear it apart. Even the usually stoic Raven was seen laughing and smiling with her friends.

Detanna watched her crew with a full heart. She had been a loner for such a long time. When she'd decided to team up with these people, she wasn't sure it would work. She never thought they'd still be together a year later. And she definitely never thought she would get so used to them. She couldn't exactly call them family, but that was only because the concept of family was tainted for her. The word brought up images of intolerant bigots shouting transphobic slurs.

But watching her friends, seeing the void they filled in her life... Detanna could finally admit to herself she needed them, and was glad they were here. Even Vik.

It was the first holiday they'd celebrated together as a group, and it could easily be their last. Once they caught

Alterra, would this group even have a reason to stick together? Detanna wasn't sure. At the very least, she hoped to stay in touch with Whisper. She was a fascinating woman, highly skilled and seemingly full of secrets to be discovered. Detanna couldn't wait to learn everything about her.

Detanna was beginning to wonder if Alterra would ever be caught. The trail had gone cold again. There hadn't been a verified sighting since the Mindwipe incident two months ago. And Detanna wasn't even sure that one had been reliable. There was a good chance Alterra had gone so deep into hiding that she would never be found.

But I will find her, Detanna thought, forcing those intrusive doubts from her mind. That reward money meant everything to her. With that prize, she could give up bounty hunting – if she wanted to - and live as her true self. It was going to happen. Looking at her crew, she was filled with confidence. With this team under her command, there was no way she could fail.

Soon, very soon, victory would be hers.

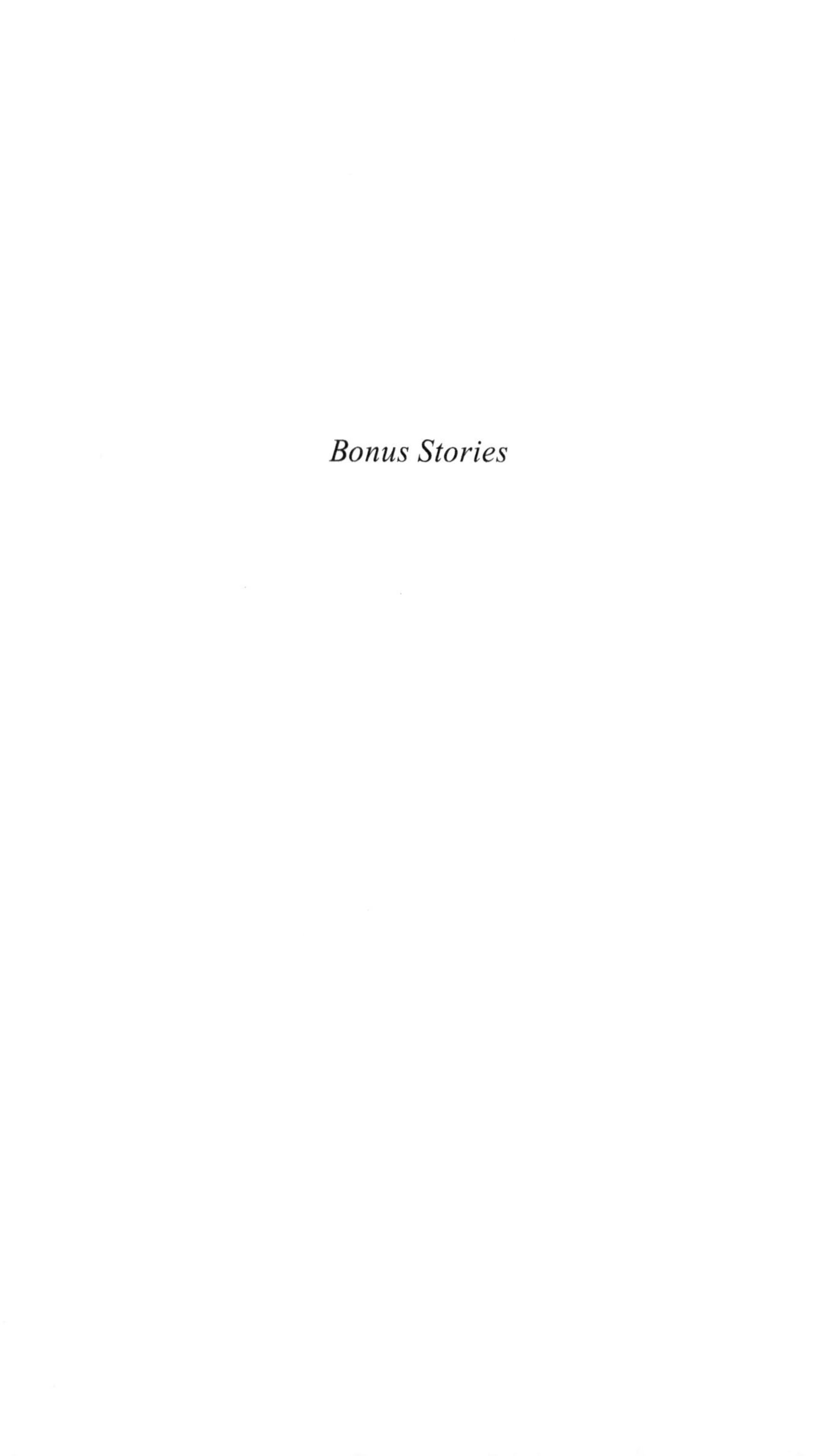

Bonus Stories

03.00   Introduction

The following is a collection of prequel stories leading up to the events of **Bloodhunters v1: Bad Blood**. These six short tales are unconnected and can be read in any order. They have two things in common: They all take place on the planet Cytrine Delta, and they all involve characters who later appear in the Bloodhunters novels. It is not necessary to read these stories before reading the rest of the Bloohunters series.

03.01 Blood Hunt

ED02499.08.02

The planet Cytrine Delta looked more advanced than it actually was. Once considered the technological center of the galaxy, now most of its citizens struggled to survive. State-of-the-art buildings, originally constructed to show off the latest breakthroughs, now served as homeless shelters and illegal drug dens. But despite the failed economy, the planet still had a thriving scientific community, mostly because the scientists couldn't afford to move anywhere else.

The SportsDome's flickering neon signage was the only thing illuminating Quantum Street, as the local gangs had stripped the solar cells off of the streetlights. The darkness and the frigid rain might have deterred a few customers on most worlds, but here, the line to the ticket booth stretched all the way down the block.

In a futile effort to boost the economy, the Cytrine government lobbied to hold major sports events at their stadiums. This drew in wealthy sports fans from all over the galaxy, whose off-world credits would trickle down to the local population. At least theoretically. So far it hadn't made a difference to the average citizen's wallet, but it did boost their morale. Locals were allowed to attend sporting events for free, to fill out the crowds for the cameras.

Across the street, in a run-down hotel, Detanna Taush got dressed. A successful bounty hunter like her could have afforded a nicer place to stay, but she wasn't in town to relax. She'd chosen her lodgings based on location, and the room's poor quality barely registered with her. Even when she saw a glyph-roach scurry across her mirror, she just ignored it and continued applying her makeup.

On most jobs, Detanna would have been more decked out, with weapons and body armor and dozens of hidden gadgets. But tonight she didn't want to be recognized as a bounty hunter, and she was dressed to blend in with the crowd. Besides, she couldn't have smuggled any weapons past the stadium's security.

She gave herself a final check in the mirror. She wore a black shirt, pants, and boots. Her purple vest matched her hair and lipstick, a bright contrast to her dark brown complexion. She thought she looked pretty good. Maybe a bit more well-off than the average Cytrine citizen, but not so much that she'd look out of place. The locals were mostly human like Detanna, and while they were poor, they still often wore bright colors. She'd fit right in. But... did she pass?

Detanna scrutinized her reflection, judging it as objectively as possible. Yes, she was here on business, and nothing mattered but her target. But it was still important to her to be recognized as a woman. It wasn't about vanity, it was about identity. Besides, she didn't want to run into any violent transphobes. She was confident in her fighting skills, and knew she'd win any potential altercation, but getting into a fight at the stadium would endanger the mission.

Looking good, she thought. Yes, the reflection was tall and muscular, but beyond that, she saw a woman looking back at her. She wasn't going to win any beauty contests, but no one was going to question her gender. Satisfied that she could complete her mission without being clocked, she locked up the hotel room and crossed the street.

The view wasn't bad, and if Detanna had actually cared about the sport, she would have been pleased with how well she could see the action. Currently in the ring, a six-armed wrestler called "The Ahraknoid" grappled with a beefy, yellow-scaled Vhelran. Most of the crowd was captivated by the exciting match, but Detanna's eyes were elsewhere. She knew her target would have the most expensive seats available, so she scanned the front row. She recognized several celebrities, but not the person she'd come here to find. Still, a few of the seats were empty, so maybe they were being fashionably late.

In the middle of the second match, she spotted her target. Arvanna Nethridge had just arrived, flanked by a pair of bodyguards. Nethridge was the founder and CEO of Aonic Industries, a company that mostly manufactured weapons and surgical equipment. But Detanna didn't care about her. The actual target was Lyon Kreet, one of the Nethridge's bodyguards.

Kreet was a Sethran, which was an offshoot of the human race. He looked human, but with pale skin and short, white hair. With his physique, he wouldn't have looked out of place in the wrestling ring itself. Nethridge looked like a child next to him. No wonder Kreet made such a good bodyguard. For Nethridge, it had to be like having her own personal brick wall following her around.

In addition to being a bodyguard, Kreet was also a criminal. Or at least, Detanna believed so. There had been eight robberies in the past two months, across three different planets. There was video footage of the perpetrator, but he was always masked. The IGP, bless them, had done their best at sifting through data and had come up empty. But Detanna had software of her own, programmed to look for patterns the InterGalactic Police wouldn't consider. And she'd discovered that each robbery had occurred while Nethridge was in town.

Nethridge had a sporadic schedule, hopping from planet to planet to visit her company's factories. It was too much of a coincidence for the robberies to have matched her itinerary so closely. The suspect in the video obviously wasn't Nethridge, but their musculature was certainly a potential match for Kreet.

The IGP had posted a reward of twelve hundred credits for the capture of the man in the video. Alternatively, they were offering two hundred credits for information that led to his arrest. The IGP had a sample of the thief's blood, but it didn't match any blood in their database. All it would take was one call, and Detanna could turn over her evidence and collect an easy two hundred credits. But that wasn't her way. It was all or nothing for her.

Detanna watched her prey from the cheap seats, waiting patiently for an opportunity. She couldn't just tackle him out in the open; she'd find herself fighting off all of the SportsDome's security, and probably wind up in jail. Besides, she didn't want to look like an idiot. She wanted to prove to herself that Kreet was guilty before she turned him in.

She'd already hacked the IGP database and downloaded their blood analysis. Tonight she would get a sample of Kreet's blood, take it back to her hotel, and analyze it. If her suspicions were correct, she would capture Kreet tomorrow. Nethridge was scheduled to deliver a speech at the Science Center while she was in town, so they wouldn't be leaving until tomorrow evening. It was a tight schedule, but Detanna was sure she could pull it off.

As she watched Kreet, she wondered why he would turn to a life of crime. Surely he was well paid. Maybe he just didn't want such a risky job anymore, and was trying to make enough credits to retire early. Detanna could relate. She enjoyed bounty hunting, but it had become a grind. She was saving up for multiple surgeries, and hadn't been taking any time for herself. She no longer even knew what she'd do with an actual day off.

Early in the fourth match, one of the bodyguards – not Kreet – got up and left. Ten minutes later he returned with some popcorn and a beer for Nethridge. During the seventh match, Nethridge herself stood up and left, and both bodyguards went with her. Detanna stood and headed for the lobby.

In the circular outer hall that surrounded the arena, Detanna spotted the two bodyguards standing outside the women's restroom, one on each side of the door. Detanna casually strolled towards the doorway, as if she were just another attendee who'd had one too many sodas. Before she could enter, the two bodyguards stepped sideways, blocking the restroom entrance. "Occupied," Kreet said.

"There's like, ten stalls," Detanna protested, trying to sound like it was really urgent.

"You'll have to wait," the second bodyguard said.

"Is there like, a celebrity in there?" Detanna asked, pretending to take a peek past the bodyguards.

"None of your business," Kreet said. "Step away from the door."

Detanna tried to push her way past Kreet and he grabbed her. She fought back, scratching him with her fingernails and drawing blood. Just then, three SportsDome security officers ran up and asked if there was a problem. Detanna apologized, and the security officers escorted her out of the building. Then she rushed back to her hotel room to examine the blood sample under her fingernail.

It was a match. Kreet was definitely guilty, even if his motives didn't make a whole lot of sense. Some of the objects that had been stolen had a niche market, the kind for which it would be difficult to find a buyer. Detanna wondered what Kreet's plan was.

Now that she could prove Kreet was the culprit, the ethical thing to do would be to pass the information along to the IGP. Detanna laughed at the very thought of it. Not only would it mean giving up a larger reward, but the police would probably screw it up, and Kreet would go into hiding. No, Detanna would be the one to bring him in, no question.

She considered going back out tonight. After the match, Nethridge would return to Georgina Suites, the only luxury hotel in this armpit of a city. Her bodyguards would stay in her suite, sleeping in shifts. Detanna considered stealing a hotel employee uniform, or taking a shuttle and parachuting onto the penthouse balcony, or even scaling the outside of the building.

But this was a job that called for patience. It wouldn't do to get herself arrested by acting too quickly. Security would be more relaxed at the Science Center tomorrow. She set out her clothing and equipment for the morning, in a meticulously organized pattern. Then she spent an hour exercising, while watching the news on the room's old-fashioned, non-holographic video screen.

The following morning, Detanna dressed more conventionally than she had the night before. She wore dark slacks with a professional-looking gray blouse, and darker makeup that complemented, rather than contrasted her skin tone. She wore a shoulder-length black wig over her short, purple hair. She wondered if Kreet would still recognize her. With Detanna's height and physique, she wouldn't be surprised. She briefly considered dressing as a man, but at this point, that would have been more work than she had time for.

She still couldn't wear her bounty hunter gear, at least not without attracting attention, but she was much more equipped than she had been the night before. While the SportsDome had prohibited all sorts of tech, the Science Center would only be checking for weapons. Detanna packed several high-tech gadgets, most of them disguised as other devices. Her comm unit was also a stungun, her wristwatch could fire miniature tracking devices, and even her boots had sound dampeners in case she needed to sneak around.

Convinced that she was ready for any situation that might arise, she locked up and headed for the Science Center.

It had once been a beautiful building, state-of-the-art in every way, with a retro-futuristic architectural style. But now it was covered in graffiti, its broken windows covered up with welded panels of sheet metal. Nine-year-old posters still advertised the 2490 Galaxy Expo, though the signs were now faded, torn, and defaced. A giant phallus was spray painted directly above the front door, and some rude words appeared on the doors themselves. There had been a few attempts to repaint and repair the building over the years, but the local youths always ruined it again within days, and the scientists didn't have the budget for round-the-clock security.

Inside, however, was a different story. The hallways were clean and brightly lit, and the many labs and showrooms were packed with cutting-edge technological breakthroughs.

Even though she'd already checked it online, Detanna looked over the lecture schedule to make sure there weren't any changes. She was a couple of hours early, but she wanted to get a feel for the place in case she had to chase Kreet through the building.

She walked through the hallways, nodding at passing visitors and scientists, reading the posters next to each doorway. Each room had its own display, showing off the latest inventions. Detanna wasn't a scientist, but she was into tech, and she didn't see anything she found particularly impressive. Most of it was just new applications of existing technology. A faster hovercar. A more precise AON scalpel. More durable types of cloth. More powerful Levatech emitters. Skirts with pockets. Binoculars that could see fine details on other planets.

Then she turned a corner and saw a poster that gave her pause. *What?* she thought. She read the poster three times before entering the lab. There was a huge metal cylinder against one wall, connected to several pieces of monitoring equipment. Three scientists – one man and two women, all human – stood in front of the machine. They wore white lab coats and were engaged in an animated conversation. One woman turned when she saw Detanna walk in.

"Hello," she said, with a big smile. "I'm Doctor Vartan. Would you like to take a look at our invention?" The scientist handed Detanna a flyer from a stack on a nearby desk.

"So, how does it work?" Detanna asked, almost unable to speak. She stared at the machine in awe.

"The True-U 3000 is the latest breakthrough in gender affirmation technology," Doctor Vartan said. "It actually rewrites the patient's DNA, changing their chromosomes from XX to XY or vice versa, altering every cell in their body. It's almost like cloning a brand-new body over their skeleton. No more hormones. No additional surgeries. After a few weeks in this tank, the patient won't even think of themselves as trans anymore. They'll emerge as their authentic self, and never look back."

"It changes… everything?" Detanna asked.

"Every cell," the scientist replied. "Face, genitals, you name it. Plus the patient can tweak it for their personal tastes. No more unwanted body hair. It can remove their Adam's apple, or give them one. The patient's vocal cords are calibrated to give them their desired voice. The machine can't change their height, and they won't be able to bear or sire children, but believe me, the True-U is going to be a miracle for those who wish to transition."

"Does… does it really work?" Detanna asked, her eyes transfixed on the tank.

"It worked on me," the woman answered, winking.

Detanna looked at Doctor Vartan, really seeing her for the

first time. She appeared to be in her mid-thirties, with short, brown hair. While she was a bit taller than the average woman, there was no way anyone would have mistaken her for a man. Her face, her voice, her entire body was perfect. Not a shred of masculinity remained. To be fair, Detanna had met other trans women who were just as beautiful, but they'd walked a hard road to get there, and some of them still weren't satisfied with the results.

What this machine promised was difficult to believe. Detanna leaned against the desk, feeling slightly dizzy. "How... how much does it cost?"

"Well, there's only one machine in existence so far," the scientist said, "so it's really not for sale yet..."

"The procedure, I mean," Detanna clarified. She'd already been saving up for several surgeries, but this device may as well have been sent from heaven. All her current transition plans vanished from her mind. She had a new goal now. It was this machine or nothing.

"Currently?" The woman tapped a few keys on her comm unit, paused, and tapped a few more. "We estimate the procedure would cost... just over six million credits."

Detanna felt like she'd been punched in the stomach. "Six... *million*?" she asked, hoping she'd heard wrong.

"For now," the woman confirmed. "Once we refine the process, we can probably get it down to half that. And eventually, who knows?"

Detanna took a few deep breaths, started to say something, then stopped. Her mind was reeling. Everything she'd ever dreamed of stood just a few meters away, and it might as well have been in a different galaxy.

"Are you okay?" the scientist asked, looking concerned.

Do you know a lot of transgender multi-millionaires? Detanna wanted to ask. Instead, she just said, "Thank you for your time," and stumbled back out of the lab. She leaned against the wall in the hallway. Six million. She'd saved up nearly two hundred thousand credits so far, and that had taken her entire bounty hunting career. She already lived as cheaply as she could, only splurging on tech that would help her catch fugitives. She took the highest-paying jobs, regardless of how dangerous they might be, and never spent money on entertainment or frivolities.

She looked at the flyer one last time, then folded it neatly and tucked it into her pocket. Then she took a deep breath and cleared her head. She had a job to do, and there wasn't any time for distractions.

Scientists, college students, and investors were starting to gather outside the auditorium. As they filed into the room, Detanna saw Nethridge and her two bodyguards come around the corner. Detanna turned her back to them as they approached, pretending to study a poster on the wall. Kreet didn't even glance in her direction. As they walked past, Detanna turned and pressed her thumb to her wristwatch. Then she walked down the hallway in the opposite direction.

After turning right at the next hallway intersection, Detanna stood against the wall and loaded up an app on her comm unit. She wasn't alone; several other visitors wandered the hall, killing time while waiting for various lectures to start. But while the others used their comms to play games or chat with friends, Detanna's attention was focused on a map of the building, with a red dot indicating Kreet's location.

She'd been right, the security wasn't nearly as pervasive here. There was an officer at the main entrance, checking for weapons, and at least one other security guard wandering the halls, but there just wasn't much call for police presence at a science convention. Detanna couldn't remember the last time she'd heard of a crowd of drunk science fans getting rowdy and trashing a venue. Nethridge would be more relaxed as well, and wouldn't require both bodyguards to stand by her side at all times.

The lecture was scheduled to start in ten minutes. The speech would take about thirty minutes, after which there would be another half hour of Q&A, and then Nethridge would tour the building to critique some of the projects. It was actually kind of funny; Nethridge was no scientist, just a trillionaire CEO who often invested in emerging tech. And yet, every scientist in the building would be swooning at her praise. Detanna felt it should be the other way around, with Nethridge bowing to the scientists' expertise. But if there was one force more powerful than science, it was money.

Detanna hoped Kreet would take the opportunity for a restroom break before the speech began, so she could catch him alone. She doubted she'd get that lucky, but anything was possible. She studied the red dot on her screen, watching it move back and forth in the auditorium, most likely helping set up equipment for the lecture. Then, about five minutes before the lecture was to start, the dot left the auditorium and began walking down the hallway.

Was this her chance? Detanna stood up straighter and started moving towards the intersection. But no, the red dot walked right past the restrooms, and continued moving in Detanna's direction. When Kreet reached the four-way junction, he looked left and right, until finally his eyes settled on Detanna. He stomped toward her, holding up the tracking device.

"Did you really think I didn't recognize you from the stadium?" he growled. He struck an intimidating pose, clenching his fists in anger. He was a full head taller than Detanna, and probably twice her body weight.

Detanna was unfazed. "Lyon Kreet, I'm here to collect the bounty on your head. Please come with me."

"You've got nothing on me," Kreet said, throwing the tracking disc to the floor and stomping on it. "Now get out of here before I tear you apart." Up and down the hall, visitors stopped looking at their comms and watched the drama unfold. Some of them started filming.

"Your blood was found at multiple crime scenes," Detanna lied. Technically they'd only recovered a blood sample from one location, but Kreet didn't know that. The crowd of onlookers grew, but stood at a respectful distance from the pair.

"Bull," Kreet said, but a flash of worry crossed his face. His eyes darted across the crowd of visitors, not liking how many of them had their comm cameras up.

"Don't make me use force," Detanna said. "It'll be so much easier to take you in if you can still walk, but I'll drag you if I have to."

Kreet laughed at her confidence. "Try it," he said. "I'll break you in half."

Up and down the hallway, people started chanting "Fight! Fight!" A couple of the onlookers left to find a security guard.

Detanna knew a fight was inevitable, but she didn't want to throw the first punch. "You'll do no such thing," she said. "Try it, and I'll pound you into the ground, like the pathetic little worm you are."

Kreet knew she was trying to goad him into a fight, but his anger overrode his common sense. Detanna easily sidestepped his fist, dropping to one knee and countering with a punch to his stomach. It was like hitting a wall, but Kreet still flinched at the impact. He tried to grab her, but she ducked between his legs, then kicked him in the back of the knee. By the time Kreet turned around to face her, it was just in time to get punched in the nose by the base of Detanna's hand.

Detanna had him on speed, but Kreet knew it would only take one solid hit to take her down. He pulled his arm back, then paused. A security guard was coming around the corner, led by one of the visitors. Instead of following through with the punch, Kreet turned and bolted. He pushed his way through the crowd, tossing people aside like ragdolls as he ran. He burst through an emergency exit, setting off an alarm that rang throughout the building.

Once Kreet was outside, he kept going, looking for a place to hide so he could come up with a plan. He crossed the street, ran through an alley, crossed another street, entered a parking garage, and hid between two parked hovercars. He took a couple of slow breaths, regaining his composure. He just needed to think things through.

The police had his blood. Could he come up with a rational explanation? Probably not. He'd been ordered to commit those robberies. Nethridge often had him steal new technologies so her company could reverse-engineer them. Would his boss stand up for him in court? Of course not. In fact, she'd probably plant evidence of her own, just to keep her reputation clean. For that matter, Nethridge might have been the one who planted the blood at the crime scenes. Kreet didn't specifically remember cutting himself during any of the robberies.

But if he was being used, he'd need to keep it to himself. He wasn't about to mess with Nethridge. Any attempt to link his boss to the crime, and he'd meet with some sort of "accident." If he were caught, he intended to plead guilty.

If he were caught. It wasn't too late to run. Could he evade the IGP long enough to get off this planet? Or that bounty hunter? He wondered if she was still on his trail. He risked taking a look at the street. Peeking underneath the bumper of one car, he could see all the way to the alley he'd come through. He saw no sign of his pursuer. He did, however, see intermittent spatters of blood, leading from the alley to his location.

Kreet's hand went to his nose, and came away bloody. It hadn't hurt before, but now that he saw the blood, his nose started to throb. He knew he couldn't stay here, not with the blood trail giving his location away. He reached into his pocket and pulled out a handkerchief, and held it to his nose. Then he stuck his head out from between the cars, looked left and right, and stood up.

ZZZ-ZAP! Detanna's comm/stungun caught him in the back of the head, sending wave after wave of electricity through his body. Kreet hit the ground, unconscious. Detanna hopped down from the roof of one of the hovercars, and looked him over. She still wasn't sure how she was going to get his massive form back to her ship, but at least he wouldn't resist.

Leaving a fugitive alone wasn't the best idea, but there was no other way. Besides, she'd left him unconscious and cuffed to a metal pole, with a tracking device clipped to his clothing. She returned less than ten minutes later, driving her rented hovercar.

She knew there was a problem before she even entered the parking garage. A man in a blue uniform stood in front of Kreet, attempting to unlock Detanna's bracers. For just a second, Detanna thought, *Cop*. But the uniform looked wrong; it fit too snug and held more weapons than IGP officers usually carried.

Detanna pulled into a space and got out of her vehicle. The interloper turned around, drawing his energy pistol. He wore modified police armor, but all the IGP logos had been painted over. He was a Canik, with Doberman-like facial features, pointed ears, and black fur. Detanna stayed informed about rival hunters, and she recognized him as an up-and-comer who called himself Darkhound.

He growled as he looked Detanna up and down. "Back off, he's mine," the dog-man said, holding his pistol on her.

"Carrion hunter," Detanna said. It was a serious accusation. Carrion hunters were lowlifes who followed more successful bounty hunters around, stealing their prey out from under their noses. It was considered bad etiquette among bounty hunters, and if proven, such conduct could even get one barred from the Bounty Hunter Registry. "How long have you been following me?" she asked.

"I don't even know who you are," Darkhound said. "I smelled his blood from a kilometer away. Matches the sample the cops have. Now beat it."

Of course. Detanna remembered reading that Darkhound had once been an IGP officer. The first Canik to join the IGP. But he'd been put on permanent leave for brutality. Apparently he still had access to IGP resources.

Detanna still didn't have any weapons on her, and her comm was currently charging on the front seat of the hovercar. She considered arguing with Darkhound, but she knew she wouldn't get anywhere. And if she reported him to the BHR, it would just be her word against his. But she wasn't about to let him steal her captive, either. She'd put too much time into this hunt to leave empty-handed.

"Fine," Detanna said, and turned to get back into her hovercar. As she did so, she pressed a button on her wristwatch. The tracking device on Kreet began to emit a high-pitched whine.

Darkhound's hands went to his ears, and he turned towards Kreet, looking for the source of the sound. Detanna tackled Darkhound from behind, knocking him to the ground and sending his pistol flying. The two wrestled on the ground, rolling over each other, each trying to gain the upper hand. The Canik was stronger, but Detanna was more agile, and she managed to twist her way out of several attempted holds. Finally Darkhound rolled on top of her, nearly crushing her with his weight.

But she still had one free hand. Detanna reached up, her hand moving up and down his side, until she found a weapon dangling from Darkhound's belt. Not caring what it was, she pulled it off of his belt and used it on him. The stun baton sent a powerful jolt of electricity through him, dazing him long enough for Detanna to wriggle herself free.

Darkhound started to stand up, but Detanna was already on her feet. She kicked him in the face, causing him to topple backward, and he landed on the cold concrete with a thud.

Then she stood over him, holding the stun baton to his face. "I give, I give," Darkhound finally said, holding up his hands in resignation. But as Detanna started to step away, he lurched forward and bit her on the leg.

Detanna whacked him with the baton. He released his grip, and she shocked him repeatedly until he was unconscious. "Bad dog," she said, unsure if that was a racial slur in Canik culture. Leaving Darkhound on the floor of the parking garage, Detanna dragged Kreet into the backseat of the hovercar and drove away.

Detanna Taush turned in her captive and her evidence. Twelve hundred credits were transferred to her bank account. She left Cytrine Delta, took her shuttle through the nearest warp gate, and returned home. While eating her bland but nutritious dinner, she did some math. After expenses and taxes, she'd made a net profit of just over eight hundred credits. She averaged about three bounties a week, some paying more than others. At this rate, it would take her nearly fifty years to earn six million credits.

To be fair, by then the price of the procedure might be lower. Perhaps it would only take twenty-five years. She didn't find that particularly comforting. Not for the first time, she wondered if she'd chosen the right career. Before becoming a bounty hunter, she'd mostly lived a life of crime, so she didn't have much to put on her resume. With her computer skills, she knew she could earn a programming degree pretty quickly, but the thought of spending the next couple of decades behind a desk was almost as bad as the thought of living as a man. And she doubted it would pay more.

She needed a big score. She didn't want to go back to crime, but she couldn't imagine earning enough as a bounty hunter to reach her goal.

Detanna sat on her bed and slowly exhaled, looking at the flyer from the Science Center. She wasn't given to flights of fancy, and that procedure on Cytrine Delta was just a pipe dream. It was time to be realistic. She folded the paper, and was about to tear it in half, but then she stopped herself. Instead, she stood up and attached the flyer to the wall, just above her computer screen. It didn't hurt to have a goal, even an unrealistic one.

Six million. She had a target number, and she'd take a day off when she reached it. Until then, a day idle was a day wasted.

She sat down at her computer and browsed the latest bounty listings.

03.02   Blood Bond

ED02499.08.06

"What's wrong with her eyes?" Mr. Venderson asked, examining the photo.

Every time, Lerveen thought. "Don't worry, it's just a genetic thing. She sees just fine."

"How old is she?" Mrs. Venderson asked.

"We don't have a birth certificate, but we think she's about eleven."

The couple looked at each other. Lerveen knew what they were thinking. They were actually hoping for a younger child, perhaps just old enough to already be potty trained. But Lerveen always showed clients Sekka first, because she knew Sekka would be the hardest to get rid of. *Get rid of*? she thought, admonishing herself for the thought. But it wasn't a lie. Raising Sekka required a lot more effort than the other girls, and while Lerveen truly cared about Sekka, it would be a great relief to see her get adopted.

"Just come meet her," Lerveen said. "I'm sure you'll love her."

Sekka sat in the fenced-in play yard. The other girls played in groups of three or four, but Sekka sat alone, on the grass, watching a bird build its nest. It was fascinating to watch the process. The way the bird wove twigs and grass into a stable structure was so impressive. Sekka knew the bird couldn't think like a person, and yet it seemed to know more about construction than most people did.

She felt a tap on her shoulder. "Sekka!"

"What?" Sekka asked.

"I've been calling you for five minutes," Lerveen said. "Come inside, there's a couple I want you to meet."

The Vendersons looked skeptical as Lerveen approached, Sekka in tow. The girl was pretty, but her clothes were covered in dirt, and she kept looking in every direction except at the Vendersons.

"I don't know," Mrs. Venderson said. "Does she play outside a lot?"

"Just ask her some questions," Lerveen said. "I know you'll love her."

Mrs. Venderson got down on her knees, looking into Sekka's white-irised eyes. "So, Sekka," she asked. "Do you like dolls?"

"No," Sekka said.

"Do you like flowers?"

"No."

"Do you like... boys?"

"No."

"Why is she so standoffish?" Mr. Venderson whispered into Lerveen's ear.

Instead of answering his question, Lerveen said, "Ask her about animals."

On hearing this, Sekka didn't even wait for them to ask a question. "I love animals," she said. Suddenly she was very animated, like a wooden puppet that had just been turned into a real girl. "There's a bird outside right now, building a nest. I've been watching it all morning. It's so smart! And there's this squirrel that visits me every day. I've been teaching him to dance. And there's rats in the walls here.

They're so cute! And..."

Lerveen watched the prospective parents carefully during Sekka's passionate rant. They seemed confused, and with good reason. Lerveen herself had been perpetually confused ever since Sekka was dropped off as an infant. She still had the note. "Please take care of this baby. She was my sister's. I don't know who the father was. I can't give her the care she needs. I'm so sorry. Please forgive me." Lerveen had reread the note many times over the years, and now had it memorized.

Sekka would require a special set of parents. Patient ones, people who didn't have any preconceived notions about what it was like to raise a child. Lerveen knew that Sekka was borderline... *something*, but the orphanage didn't have the budget for a psychological evaluation. Unfortunately, not a lot of people on Cytrine Delta were looking to adopt, and even fewer would be willing to take on a special needs child.

She knew she'd lost this one. She could always tell when a connection was being made, and the Vendersons just weren't into Sekka. They didn't want a kid they'd have to chase around the woods all day. They wanted a girl they could dress up like a doll, who would look cute in family portraits. That was fine, Lerveen knew just who she would show them next.

"You can go back outside now, Sekka," Lerveen said. Sekka smiled, and left without saying another word.

It was now after lunch, and Sekka once again sat in the dirt in the play yard. The rest of the girls were inside doing chores, but Sekka couldn't stand the sound the laundry machines made, so Lerveen allowed her to play outside whenever they were running. It wasn't exactly fair, but they made up for it by giving Sekka extra chores at night, while the rest of the girls played board games together. Sekka didn't mind. She preferred to do her chores alone.

Her favorite visitor had come by, a pink-furred squirrel she called Nutters. He was only about six weeks old, and Sekka had pretty much known him since birth. His family lived in the tree back by the fence. Sekka had been teaching him tricks lately, and he seemed to learn really fast.

But today he seemed agitated. He kept running up to Sekka, then running back towards the tree, as if trying to get her to follow. While the creature wasn't sapient, he was smart for a squirrel, and Sekka was the only human he trusted.

Sekka reached the tree, and Nutters climbed up the fence, looking out over the nearby street. The wooden fence was too tall for Sekka to see over, and there were no gaps between the slats, so she had to climb the tree to see what was wrong.

Across the street, another squirrel was in trouble. Two boys had overturned a metal trash can, trapping the poor animal. The receptacle was made of a wire mesh, with diamond-shaped holes too small for the squirrel to squeeze through. A red-haired boy sat on top of the trash can, while a boy with brown hair lit firecrackers and fed them through the holes. The squirrel ran in circles around the inside of the trash can, scared to death of the small explosions and desperate to escape.

Sekka was livid. It didn't even occur to her that it was against the rules to leave the play yard. The only thing going through her mind was, *Save the squirrel.* She used the tree to climb over the fence, hopped down to the ground, and ran across the street. It was a good thing the street didn't get much traffic, because she didn't even look both ways. She barged up to the boys, pushed the one off of the trash can, and lifted the can so the squirrel could escape. It scampered down the street and climbed up the side of a building.

"Hey, what's the big idea?" the brunet said.

"Leave the squirrels alone," Sekka said. She turned back

toward the street.

"Just having a little fun," the redhead said, grabbing Sekka by the shoulder.

She turned around and hit him, her fist catching him in the stomach. It didn't hurt, but it knocked the wind out of him.

The red-haired boy grabbed her from behind. "Now you've done it," he said. He trapped her in a bear hug, tightly holding her arms to her sides. Sekka fought back, but he was much stronger.

The other boy lifted the trash can. "Put her under here," he said.

Working together, they got her under the trash can, and set it down on top of her. Once again, the redhead sat on top of it. Sekka screamed, but no one was around. She was very cramped, and she pushed and kicked as much as she could, but the can wouldn't budge. The brunet started to light another firecracker.

"Boys!" came a man's voice, as someone came running around the corner. Sekka could only see his legs from her position. "Get out of here!" he shouted, and the boys ran. The man bent down, saw Sekka's predicament, and helped her get out of the trash can. "Kids these days," the man said.

"Thank you," Sekka said, and turned back toward the street.

"Wait," the man said. "Do you need a ride?"

"No," Sekka said, and kept walking.

"Just wait," the man said again, putting his arm on her shoulder. Sekka jumped. She didn't really like being touched, especially by people she didn't know. She turned and looked at him. He was in his mid-thirties, with black hair and a mustache. Sekka was pretty sure she'd seen him before. She wasn't good with faces, but his mustache looked familiar. "I really don't mind," he said. "My hovercar's just around the corner."

"So's my door," she said. Her phrasing perplexed him a

bit, going by his expression. Sekka was used to seeing that expression on people. What she meant was, there was no back entrance to the orphanage, so she would have to walk around the block to the front of the building. It might be a little farther than this man's hovercar, but it still seemed pretty silly to hitch a ride there.

"What's your name?" he asked.

"Sekka," she said.

"I thought so," the man said. "You're from the orphanage, right? I've seen you on my walks."

That's where she'd seen him. Sometimes Lerveen took Sekka with her when she ran errands, and she'd seen this man walking down the street sometimes. He seemed to hang around the orphanage an awful lot.

"I could never forget eyes like yours," he continued. "Listen, the lady that works there, oh, what's her name again?"

"Lerveen?" Sekka asked.

"Yes! She told me you'd gotten out, and asked if I'd give you a ride back."

"That doesn't make any sense," Sekka said. "It's right there."

The man frowned, thinking. Sekka was about to walk away again, when he said, "You're right, you should head on back. But first, can you help me with something real quick?"

Sekka cocked her head, genuinely confused. What could this man possibly need, that she'd be able to help with? "What?" she finally asked.

"I found a lost kitten," he said. "I need help finding its mother."

"Kitten?" Sekka asked. It was like flipping a switch. She was no longer distracted with trying to leave; the man now had her full attention.

Checkmate, the man thought.

* * *

Sekka woke up in a strange room. She couldn't remember how she got here. She knew she'd followed the man back to his hovercar, and he'd had her lean into the side door, but she didn't see the kitten. Then she'd felt a sudden jab, like a needle. She couldn't remember anything after that.

The room wasn't well-lit, but it was bright enough to make out the details. She was lying on a mattress on the floor. The room reminded her of the basement at the orphanage - gray brick walls, no windows. There was a washing machine against one wall, next to a sink and a toilet. Some stuffed animals and other toys lay against the opposite wall. One of the toys was a creepily realistic child-sized doll, its mouth open in a permanent O-shape. There were some posters on the wall, mostly of cartoon girls in schoolgirl uniforms. The room's light came from a single luminescent disk mounted to the ceiling, directly over the mattress.

In one corner, a wooden stairway led up to a door. Sekka stood up and climbed the stairs, then tried the door. Locked. She knocked at the door, and when nothing happened, she pounded on it.

After a few minutes, the door unlocked, and the man stepped through it. Sekka tried to rush past him, but he held her firmly by the shoulder and locked the door behind him. He grabbed her by one hand and pulled her back down the stairs.

"Where am I?" Sekka asked.

"This is your new room," the man said, smiling. He got down on one knee so he could look her in the eye. "Surprise! I adopted you."

"I don't want to be here," Sekka said.

"You'll love it here," he said. "Listen, you can call me Mick. I'm your new father, but I'm also your new best friend. Anything you need, let me know, I'll get it for you. Seriously, anything."

"I want to go," Sekka said.

"Anything but that," Mick said. "But believe me, you're not going to want to leave. I have some things to do right now, but I'll be back down in a couple of hours with dinner. And then we'll play together. I have a lot of new games I want to teach you."

"I want to see Lerveen," Sekka said.

"You will!" he said. "We'll go see her tomorrow, I promise."

"I want to see Lerveen!" Sekka wailed this time, and slapped him on the arm. It couldn't have hurt him, but a flash of anger crossed his face.

"Now that's just rude, little lady," Mick said. "I have feelings too. You need some quiet time. I'll see you in a couple of hours." He stood up, climbed the stairs, and locked the door behind him.

Sekka ran after him, but reached the door too late. As she heard the lock click, she pounded on the door, screaming. After five minutes of shrieking, she sat down on the stairs, put her head between her hands, and closed her eyes.

After a few minutes, she realized she could hear something moving. She walked down the stairs, only to see something scurry away. *Hmmm.* She walked over to the mattress and sat down. She sat as still as a statue, not moving a muscle. After ten minutes, she saw it. She remained perfectly still, not wanting to scare it off. A rat carefully crept along the far wall. Every once in a while it stopped to sniff the air. Finally it looked in Sekka's direction.

Bingo, Sekka thought as their eyes locked. Her eyes glowed for a second, and the rat was mesmerized. It scurried toward her, stopping about a meter from her, and sat at attention.

"Go get your friends," Sekka said. "*All* your friends."

Mick got back from the fast food restaurant, kicked off his shoes, and unlocked the door to the basement. "Dinner time!" he shouted down into the darkness. *Wait,* he thought.

Why was it dark? Kids don't like the dark. Was she taking a nap? He flipped the switch, but the light didn't come on. "Sekka?" he carefully stepped down the stairs, feeling oddly uncomfortable. Something didn't sound right, and he thought he saw odd shapes moving in the darkness. "Where are you?" he asked.

He reached the bottom of the stairs and stepped on the floor. Only it wasn't the floor. Something furry moved out of his way as he took that last step, and he could feel more somethings moving around his ankles. In the meager light that made it down from the kitchen above, the floor appeared to undulate, a great mass of moving fur. "What in the world," he said.

"Now," he heard Sekka say, though he still couldn't see her.

Rats swarmed over Mick, dozens, hundreds, probably more. He shrieked like a five-year-old, tried to run up the stairs, tripped, and hit his face on a step. Then he tried crawling up the stairs, but the rats were in his face now, squeaking and crawling on him. He tried to stand, but fell backward down the stairs. He got to his feet again, freaked out, fled in a random direction, and ran straight into a wall. He hit the ground, out cold.

Sekka called emergency services from Mick's kitchen. The police took her back to the orphanage, and Mick was taken to a hospital, where he would stay until he was well enough to stand trial.

A few weeks later, Lerveen was on her way to the grocery store when she saw a golden-haired woman walk out of a bank. Lerveen did a double-take. "Excuse me, ma'am?" she asked, tapping the stranger on the shoulder.

"Yes?" the woman said, turning around. She had gold-tinted skin that matched her beautiful blond hair. She had purple freckles across her face. She obviously wasn't human, yet she looked strangely like Sekka. Especially her eyes.

"Lerveen McTonnel," Lerveen said, shaking the woman's hand.

"Lemondrop Vermon," the gold woman said, confused. "Can I help you?"

"This is a long shot, but do you know a little girl name Sekka?"

Lemondrop shook her head. "I'm sorry, I'm here on business. You must have me confused with someone else." She started to turn back around.

"She has your eyes!" Lerveen blurted out. "And your nose. Please, I've been looking for her family for such a long time."

"That… sounds like someone I should probably meet," Lemondrop said, and the two walked back to the orphanage together.

03.03   *Blood Contract*

ED02499.08.13

"She's not going to make it," the male voice said.

"I'll call it," the woman's voice answered. "Time of death at… wait…"

Yeela gradually became aware of the heart monitor, beeping by her left ear. First it was slow, but it gradually picked up the pace.

"Looks like she's going to live after all," the man said. "Good work, doctor."

"You know this means you owe me five credits," the woman answered, and both voices laughed. "Let's stitch 'er up."

Yeela shouldn't have been hearing any of this. The anesthesia should have kept her out for at least another two hours. But part of her condition prevented her body from processing drugs consistently. Fortunately the anesthetic was still working against the pain – this time – but she could still feel the pressure of the tools moving around in her chest, and it seriously creeped her out. She wanted to scream, or at least politely ask for a stronger dose of anesthesia, but she was paralyzed.

This wasn't the first time she'd come back from the brink of death. Yeela had been dying for more than three years now. This was her third operation this month, and she'd woken up during every one of them. When she'd told the doctors of her experience, they'd laughed it off, and told her she'd dreamed it. The last time, after the operation was complete, the staff had used her seemingly-unconscious body as a teaching aid for some gynecology students. The memory still had her fuming, but she had no legal recourse. She was getting these operations for free, and part of the agreement involved signing away most of her rights. She could either be a prop, or she could die. There were no other options.

Karouc's disease was so rare that Yeela was only the third identified case. The other two victims, including Karouc herself, were now dead, and Yeela didn't expect to reach a ripe old age either. As her bodily functions took turns shutting down, her cyborg implants took over. The doctors were excited to have a living test subject, so they could try out their newly-designed implants. Having her around meant the hospital received tons of grant money. It was dehumanizing, being treated more like a lab rat than a patient, but at least the hospital had a vested interest in keeping her alive.

Until it didn't.

"I'm afraid we're terminating your contract," Director Leem said, not an ounce of emotion in his voice.

"My contract?" Yeela asked, incredulous. "I'm not some blastball player having a bad season. Your treatments are the only thing keeping me alive."

"Our investors are no longer interested in researching a disease that has so far only affected three people," the Director said. "They'd rather funnel their money into more... marketable cures."

Yeela wasn't sure what to say. Her skin went cold, and she felt like she was no longer actually present, but rather watching this discussion on a medical drama. "What am I supposed to do?" she heard herself say, though it was more to herself than to the Director.

"There are other research centers on Cytrine Delta," he said. "I'm sure if you send out enough requests, one of them will be happy to take on your case. And if not, they might be interested in buying your body for research purposes, once the disease runs its course. Do you have a next-of-kin who could use the credits?"

Once again, Yeela was speechless. The conversation felt so surreal. Director Leem spoke as if they were talking about a broken-down hovercar. Yeela couldn't look at his impassive face anymore, or she'd break down in tears. She glanced around his lavishly-decorated office, as if hoping the answer to all her problems resided on a knick-knack on Leem's bookshelves. He had a lot of baubles, and some of them looked more expensive than Yeela's most recent operation.

She'd known she was dying for a while now, and she'd thought she'd come to terms with it. She'd gotten used to being on borrowed time, living operation to operation. She tried not to entertain too much optimism, but deep down, a little ball of hope lived in her heart. Logically speaking, if a cure was possible, it would eventually be found. Every day she lived, the doctors were one day closer to finding that cure. All she had to do was keep breathing until then.

But that was ten minutes ago. With the breaking of this contract, there would be no more research into Karouc's disease. As of right now, Yeela had an expiration date.

Or did she? Yeela stood up, a look of determination forming on her face. "I want every bit of data you have on my disease," she said. "Every test you've run, every bioscan."

"That's your right," the Director said. "I'll have my secretary get you a data drive. But Yeela… you really should just accept the inevitable."

Yeela glared at him. Her eyes were wet, but there was fire behind them. "Not on your life," she said.

* * *

Yeela spent an hour every day looking up research centers, and sending them requests for consideration. Within a month, she'd contacted every medical facility on the planet. When there were no more options on Cytrine Delta, she sent requests to labs on other planets. She only got a handful of replies, and most of them started with the words, "We regret to inform you…"

But that was only an hour a day. She spent the rest of her waking hours studying medical textbooks. Yeela had been a mechanical genius all her life. Once when she was six, she stripped her father's hovercar for parts so she could build some anti-gravity skates. That hadn't gone over so well with her parents, but they'd still spent her youth encouraging her to learn more about computers and engineering.

Her parents were gone now, as was the family home. Yeela lived in her father's old business, an auto repair garage, sleeping on a cot. Though the building had once belonged to the family, she was basically squatting in it now. Fortunately, no one seemed interested in buying the property, or any other property on the street. Most of the buildings in the area had been claimed by squatters, and with the amount of time Yeela spent at the hospital, she'd had to rig up an elaborate security system to keep the garage from getting claimed by someone else.

She earned a meager living doing minor repairs on hovercars and small appliances, making just enough credits to buy food. With all her ailments, she just didn't have the strength to operate a full-time business. She was going to have to tighten her belt even further now, because she intended to put all her energy into conquering Karouc's disease.

She already had implants that manufactured the chemicals her body was no longer able to produce. Having studied the schematics of these implants, she could easily upgrade them. She wasn't going to cut herself open to install them, but she was more than willing to attach new devices to her skin, where they would be easier to tinker with. She'd look like a cyborg, but she was long past vanity at this point.

When you got down to it, the human body was just a squishier kind of machine. She'd spent her youth learning how engines and circuits worked, now she'd have to apply that knowledge to biological systems. Sure, the sight of blood made her nauseous, even after all her operations, but she'd just have to start thinking of it as bright red coolant.

As time went on, she would have to add more devices to correct for her loss of motor skills, and to replace any other functions her body could no longer do. If she reached the point that she was too weak to walk, she'd graft an exoskeleton onto her body. If her hands began to tremble so much that she was unable to perform her own upgrades, she'd build helper drones. As long as she had a functioning brain, she'd survive.

She'd do whatever it took. It was her only choice. She was only seventeen, and realistically, she probably wouldn't live to see twenty. But she wasn't going to go down without a fight. All she needed was data and time.

Well, that and credits. She would need lots and lots of credits. But she had a plan for that as well.

Villip Leem, Director of Operations at Starpoint Medical Innovations Hospital and Research Center, prepared for bed in his luxurious home. He'd inherited most of his wealth, and he'd used those credits to become a controlling stockholder at SMIHRC. In his self-appointed position as Director, he'd managed to steer the company away from financially unsound decisions, and damn the bleeding hearts who accused him of being "cold-blooded." His subordinates often praised him for his ability to make difficult decisions, but he didn't find the decisions all that difficult. The hospital was a business, not a charity, and a business had to keep its eyes on the bottom line in order to keep its doors open. Especially on Cytrine Delta, where so many companies went belly-up every day.

Dressed in his Kalaran silk pajamas, Leem slipped between the imported sheets of his emperor-sized bed and turned off the lights. He would sleep well tonight, knowing he'd spent another full day maximizing company profits. Just as he was about to drift off, he heard a crash from downstairs. He jumped out of bed, grabbed the comm unit off of his nightstand, and ran down the stairs.

As he reached the first-floor foyer, he heard buzzing from every direction. Dark shapes flew past his head, the size of birds. He turned on the light, and shrieked at what he saw. His house was swarming these... things. They looked like flying spiders, but much larger. As one flew past his head, he panicked and ran back up the stairs. From the second floor landing, he watched the creatures, ready to run if any came upstairs.

It was hard to get a good look at them because they were so fast, but the more he watched, the more details he was able to discern. They weren't bugs or birds, but many-legged drones. They looked like flying skeletal hands, with several jointed fingers hanging from a single Levatech ball.

As he watched, these intruders flew around the house, picking up expensive knick-knacks and carrying them away. They didn't appear to be armed, and they hadn't reacted to his presence earlier. Now feeling a bit safer, he called the police from his comm unit and carefully stepped back downstairs.

The drones swarmed past him, altering their flight paths to avoid his head, but none acted in a threatening manner. He followed their route into the dining room, where he saw a broken window. *Why didn't the alarm go off?* he wondered. He'd have to worry about that later. Drones continued to fly in through the broken window, while others flew back out, carrying valuables.

"Clever," Leem said out loud, standing up straighter. Whoever set this up had to have been a genius. Part of him wanted to hire this person for his innovations department, but he wasn't that forgiving. They'd be lucky if he didn't have them killed.

Stepping back into the foyer, he grabbed an umbrella from the stand beside the front door. Swinging the umbrella like a club, he tore through the foyer, trying to bring some of the intruders down. However, they were too fast for him, easily dodging his clumsy swings. Then he ran into the dining room and opened the umbrella, using it to block the hole in the window.

The drones paused for a moment, recalculating. Then Leem heard another crash from the other side of the foyer. The drones turned and headed for the living room, where another window had been broken. Now livid, Leem ran to the kitchen, where kept an energy pistol in the pantry. He returned to the foyer and started firing at the swarm.

He was a lousy shot, but he managed to bring a couple of them down. As soon as the first one hit the floor, new drones stopped coming in through the windows. The remaining drones fled the house, regardless of whether they currently carried any valuables.

Now out of breath, Leem sat down on the foyer steps and examined one of the downed drones. If its software was hackable, the police would be able to find its point of origin. And if they couldn't do it, Leem's own people could, guaranteed. Still breathing heavily, he set down the drone and waited for the police.

For all its flaws, Cytrine Delta had a decent prison system. Sure, the cells were cramped and the food was bland, but they had an excellent educational program, allowing inmates to learn new skills that would help them get decent jobs once they were released. If there were any jobs left by then, anyway.

But more importantly, at least to Yeela, was their medical program. Under planetary law, prisons were required to provide inmates with the highest level of medical care. They weren't allowed to cut corners, even if the prisoner had special needs or rare diseases. Yeela was put back on an experimental research program, with around-the-clock care. This time, her caregivers wouldn't be allowed to break the contract. As long as Yeela remained in prison, the treatments would continue.

Yeela sat in her cell, reading a book on rare diseases. She'd been given an eight-year sentence, and she wondered if she'd live long enough to see the end of it. Just in case, she was already considering ways to blow her parole hearings, and contemplating petty crimes that would put her back in prison. She didn't love prison life, but at least it was life.

And really, when you got down to it, how much freedom had she actually had before?

03.04 *Blood Ties*

ED02499.08.18

Zak stumbled through the alley, trying to find a dry spot in the downpour. He'd just been thrown out of a coffee shop for loitering. There weren't a lot of places in town where he could just sit without buying anything. Sure, there was probably a homeless shelter somewhere, but he didn't trust that idea. If his mom had the police looking for him, they'd probably start there.

He'd been on the streets for two days, and he hadn't eaten or slept yet. He hadn't been thrown out. Heck, he could go back any time he wanted to. But he'd have to follow his mom's rules. Wear dresses, grow his hair back out… betray his entire identity. And he wasn't willing to do that. Better to live on the streets than to live as someone else.

Of course, it had been easier to say that on a full stomach. He stopped at a trash can and pulled off the lid. Someone had thrown out some chili, but there were already maggots crawling in it. Zak quickly replaced the lid. He was hungry, but not that hungry. At least not yet. He'd been raised on foie gras and filet mignon, but he'd always preferred more common foods. Right now he'd kill for a bean burrito, or even an orange.

He found a set of stairs, leading up to the back door of a

restaurant. It was beneath a slight overhang, so he sat on the steps, his back against the door. He was still getting wet, but it wasn't quite as bad as being out in the open. He clutched his purse, which held the only possessions he still owned in this world. He must have looked pretty strange carrying a woman's purse, but right now that was the least of his worries.

He closed his eyes, thinking about his nice bed at home. It was soft, maybe a bit too soft, with a thick pink comforter and tons of pillows with those ridiculous lacy frills around the sides. Dolls and stuffed animals were lined up on his dresser and bookshelves, staring at him, judging him, asking him why he didn't appreciate the cushy life he'd been born into. Nothing in that room had been Zak's style, and he hadn't been allowed to redecorate. But at least he'd never had to sleep in the rain.

He was starting to snore when the door behind him opened, and he nearly fell backward through it. A man in a cook's hat held a gun on him, a double-barreled energy rifle that probably wasn't even legal in this city. "Get outta here," the chef said. Zak immediately stood up and backed down the steps, then ran out of the alley without looking back.

A few hours later he sat on a park bench. Lisbon Pointe was one of the nicer cities on Cytrine Delta, which was a bit like saying that weight loss was one of the nicer symptoms of molecular disintegration. The city still had well-maintained parks, a few nice restaurants, and a slightly lower crime rate than the rest of the planet. A few billionaires lived on the edge of town, in secure, gated communities.

These wealthy citizens kept the factories open, which was great because it meant there were still jobs in town. But they also exploited every possible legal loophole, bribed government officials to keep the minimum wage low, and made it so people lived in poverty regardless of how many hours they worked per week. Zak had first-hand knowledge of this, as his mother owned a robotics company, and he'd witnessed some of her underhanded dealings first-hand.

But at least the park was nice. The rain had finally let up, and while the bench was still wet, Zak barely noticed. His clothing was soaked through anyway. Once again he tried to take a nap. He couldn't lie sideways across the bench, because it had a couple of metal armrests dividing the bench into three sections. It looked pretty, but Zak knew the extra armrests were intentionally designed to prevent homeless people from sleeping in public. Nevertheless, Zak leaned back in his seat and closed his eyes.

He heard a scream in the distance. *What now?* he thought, visions of dancing citrus fruit dissipating as he opened his eyes. A man ran down the sidewalk, clutching a briefcase under one arm. A woman ran after him, but couldn't keep up in her heels. "Stop him!" she shouted. "That's my valise!" She slowed down, rooting through the pockets of her oversized trench coat.

Leaving his purse behind, Zak leaped up and chased the thief. The man was bigger than Zak – most men were – but Zak was faster. He caught up to him and jumped on him from behind. The thief stumbled and dropped the briefcase, using both hands to pull Zak off of him. He turned and punched Zak in the face, then reached down to pick up the briefcase again. Now on the ground, Zak got to the briefcase first and grabbed the handle.

"Let go," the thief said, trying to pull the briefcase out of Zak's grasp. He was much stronger, but Zak was determined to hold on. The thief pulled so hard, he lifted Zak off the ground along with the briefcase. He was about to punch Zak again when the briefcase's owner caught up to them. She now held a small energy pistol, and aimed it at the robber.

The thief let go of the briefcase and ran. Zak handed the briefcase back to the woman. "Thank you, young man," she said. "Oh, your poor face. Here, let me give you something." She once again searched her massive pockets, until she came up with a twenty-credit note, which she handed to Zak.

Zak smiled and started to thank her, but he felt sort of stunned, and the woman walked away before he could get any words out. The money was nice, it meant he could finally eat something. But what had really tied his tongue was being called "young man." It was the first time a stranger had referred to him that way, and it felt amazing. For just a moment, all his problems went away. It no longer mattered that he was wet, hungry, and bruised. She could have given him a hundred credits, and the validation would have felt like the greater reward.

Still in a daze, Zak wandered back to the park bench. His purse was now gone. He looked around and saw a blue-haired teenage girl running away, Zak's purse under her arm.

Vex couldn't believe her luck. The purse had just been sitting there, out in the open, no owner in sight. It wasn't even stealing, it was just a case of finders keepers. If somebody stopped her, she'd just act like it was hers. If somebody accused her of taking it, she'd just claim she was looking for the actual owner. Either way, she was free and clear.

So why was she running? Well, for one thing, she didn't want a confrontation, regardless of how it turned out. The sooner she was out of the park, the sooner she could look through the purse for loose credits, without having to look over her shoulder the whole time. She felt like she could talk her way out of any situation, but she wasn't about to push it.

But the main reason she was running? Because she was being chased. She could hear their footfalls behind her, too loud to be a jogger. And then she got a flash – a mild psychic premonition – showing her pursuer. Her flashes weren't very common, and weren't actually precognizant. She just saw the surface thoughts of nearby people, other park-goers who happened to be watching the chase.

It didn't look like it was the purse's owner. It was some guy, about Vex's age, maybe fifteen or sixteen. He had a bloody nose and a really bad haircut. But he definitely wasn't jogging; there was no doubt that he was after Vex. And he looked very angry. While Vex was pretty sure she could come up with a believable lie, this guy didn't look like he was in the mood to listen.

Vex briefly considered just dropping the purse, in the hopes he would break off the chase. But what if that wasn't why he was after her? She could be out the money and still have to deal with this guy. No, she wasn't going to give up so easily. She had more mouths to feed than just her own. She had high hopes for the contents of this purse. She imagined finally getting a less threadbare outfit, not to mention a couple of hot meals for the gang.

She was out of the park now. She crossed the street without looking, causing a hovercar to swerve around her. The driver shouted some angry invectives at her before driving away. Vex ran into an alley, but she could still hear her pursuer behind her. She was starting to run out of breath, but the guy didn't seem to be slowing down. She reached out with her free arm, and pointed at a trash can a few meters away. The lid flew off and into her hand. Then she turned around and threw the lid at the guy. He blocked it with one arm, shouting, "Hey!"

They were now face to face, about four meters apart. Vex reached into her pocket and pulled out a switchblade. "I will cut you, man," she said, making a couple of threatening slashes in the air.

Zak wheezed, trying to catch his breath. "There's not… any… money in there," he said, pointing weakly at the purse.

"I'll see about that," Vex said, rooting through the purse. *Damn*, she thought. He was right. Still, it was an expensive-looking purse, and while it wasn't in the best condition, it could probably fetch a few credits at a secondhand store. She looked up at the guy, who just stood with his shoulders slumped.

"Please?" Zak asked, looking like he was on the verge of tears.

Vex rolled her eyes. He really did look pathetic, with his banged-up face and puppy dog eyes. But how did she know he hadn't stolen the purse himself? "Look," she said. "If you can name me three things in the purse, you can have it. Not the lipstick or the tampons. Stuff that's not in every purse."

"A black book with a lock on it, a small rubber panda, and an ID card," Zak said.

"Lots of purses have ID cards," Vex said, looking through the purse. "What's the name on the card?"

Zak exhaled in resignation. "Charlotte Lisbon," he said.

"Lisbon? Like in 'Lisbon Pointe?' Is that who you stole the purse from?" Vex asked.

"Are you a cop?" Zak countered.

"No, but…" Vex began, but she got distracted. She looked at the ID card again, then back at Zak. Her eyes widened. "Oh," she said finally. She took a couple of steps forward and tossed the purse to Zak. "Sorry," she said.

"Thanks," Zak mumbled, and started to turn away.

Vex watched him take a couple of steps, then called after him. "Wait… do you have someplace to go?"

Zak turned back around. He was quiet for a few seconds, and finally said, "I… have no idea."

Vex hesitated, going back and forth in her mind. Another mouth to feed. Would the others even accept him? Zak was just about to turn back around when she said, "Come with me."

She led him to an old pizza restaurant, long since closed and abandoned. She knocked on the back door, and after a few seconds they heard a lock unlatch and the door opened. "Who's this?" asked a teenage boy. He had tan-colored skin, black hair, and looked about fourteen years old.

"He's one of us," Vex said, leading Zak down the stairs,

into the restaurant's basement. The room was poorly lit, with two ripped-up couches, and some wire shelves full of bottled water, old blankets, and random supplies. In addition to Zak and Vex, there were three other teens in the basement.

"Who are you guys?" Zak asked.

"We're the East Side Daggers," said the boy who'd let them in. "We're a gang!"

"We're not a gang," Vex said, turning to Zak. "We're just like you. We have nowhere to go, so we watch out for each other. Safety in numbers, or whatever. I'm Vex. And you are?"

"I'm Zak," he answered. "It's nice to meet you." He held out his hand.

Vex ignored it. "I'm guessing your parents threw you out for not looking enough like your ID card?"

"I snuck out, but yeah," Zak said. "I couldn't be who mom wanted me to be. She was about to send me to some sort of 'finishing school,' but I think that was code for 'conversion camp.' I'd rather starve."

"Well, you probably will, living with us," Vex said. "This is Hugo, Calix, and Keygan." They all gave Zak a quick wave. "Hugo ran away because his dad kept touching him. Calix is non-binary, which was a dealbreaker with their parents for some reason. And Keygan's dad used to beat him with a shock-stick every night."

"Wow," Zak said, then turned to Vex. "And you?"

Vex held out her hand, pointing it toward one of the shelves. "My parents freaked out 'cause I could do this," she said. A bottle of water flew off the shelf and into her open hand. She took a swig of water and offered the bottle to Zak.

"Weird reason to throw you out," Zak said, taking a drink. Telekinesis was uncommon in humans, but it wasn't unheard of.

"There's more to it than that," Vex said. "Some other time. You hungry?"

Zak opened his mouth to reply, but his stomach answered for him, groaning loud enough for the entire room to hear.

Vex laughed. "Well, we can't offer you much but…"

"Oh wait," Zak said, remembering something. He fished around in his pocket, pulling out the twenty credit note. "What can we get with this?"

The others stared at him like he'd just walked on water. "Welcome to the East Side Daggers," Hugo said.

The gang had been living on the streets for a while, and knew how to stretch their money. Rather than blowing all the credits on fast food, they sent Calix to the grocery store, where they picked up enough ingredients to feed the five of them for a week. The meals wouldn't exactly be nutritious, but at least they wouldn't starve.

Zak took a nap on one of the couches. When Calix got back from shopping, Vex boiled up some noodles using an old hotplate. They woke Zak up when dinner was ready.

"So, Zak," Vex asked, scooping the noodles onto five plates, "You cut your own hair?"

"I was… angry," Zak said, touching his hair. He hadn't looked in a mirror since he'd run out. Vex handed him a plate, and he started scarfing down food like it was the best meal he'd ever eaten.

"Dude, don't make yourself sick," Keygan said.

"Yeah, it's just a waste of food if it comes right back up," Calix added.

Zak paused, and forced himself to chew more slowly. "So, what do you do here?" he asked through a mouthful of noodles.

"We survive," Hugo said.

"What else is there?" Keygan added.

"We work together," Vex said. "We teach each other what we know. Calix here is good with tools. They managed to patch into the city's power grid, which is why we're not eating in the dark." As if on cue, the lights flickered for a few seconds. "For now," Vex added.

"My dad's an electrician," Calix said. "I guess he was hoping I would be too. He was always teaching me stuff. Then I came out to him, and he stopped talking to me at all."

"And that's when you ran away?" Zak asked.

"No, mom threw me out," Calix said. "Told me not to come back until I was normal."

"Yeah, 'cause it's so *normal* to throw your kids out onto the street," Vex said. "Just 'cause they want a different name or whatever."

"At least you could go back if you really wanted," Keygan said. "I had to get out of there. My dad hit me harder every time. He couldn't control himself. Sooner or later he was going to kill me."

"Did you ever call the police?" Zak asked, taking another bite of noodles.

"Dad *is* a cop," Keygan said. "They stick up for each other in this town. Now I'm worried about my little brother. Without me there, Koy's going to get hurt."

"Well, we need to go get him," Zak said. He looked around at his new friends, all of whom looked like he'd just suggested they go bungee jumping in a volcano. "...Don't we?" Zak asked, embarrassed.

Vex smiled sadly, shaking her head softly. "It's not that easy," she said. "We can barely take care of us. We can't fit more kids in this room. And Keygan's dad is tough. He has guns and crap."

"Yeah, but there's five of us," Zak said. "Surely we can—"

"Zak," Vex interrupted. "It's hard enough to get food every day. We can't just—"

"You always say that!" Keygan wailed, his face filling with tears. "Koy's going to die because of you!" Keygan stood up and ran out of the room.

Vex stood up. "See what you did?" she huffed, glaring at Zak. She turned and followed Keygan up the stairs.

"Sorry," Zak said, though he wasn't sure he'd done anything wrong.

A few minutes later, Vex and Keygan came back down the stairs together. "I have an announcement," Vex said, as she came into view. Everyone gathered around so they could hear better. "We're going on a supply raid," she said. "For food, first aid stuff, maybe some weapons…"

"Great," Hugo said. "What are we going to hit?"

Vex paused, biting her lower lip. "Keygan's dad's house," she finally said.

From the outside, the house looked like a monument to paranoia. It was surrounded by a two-meter-high chain link fence, and featured barred windows, security cameras, and guard dogs. One might have thought it was a military base rather than a suburban home. But this was how Keygan had grown up, and he knew how to bypass the security.

First, they had Calix shut off the power to the street. Of course the house had an emergency backup generator, but it always took a couple of minutes to come online. Keygan no longer had his keys, so Vex picked the lock on the outer fence. As they crossed the yard, two Rottweilers ran up to Keygan and started licking his face. They'd always preferred Keygan to his father, and with good reason. And in the dogs' eyes, Keygan's friends were innocent by association.

The gang ran around to the back door, where Vex once again picked the lock. The kitchen light started to flicker on as the generator finally kicked in. Now came the hard part. There was no way they could grab Koy and the supplies without waking up Keygan's father. Some of them would have to distract him, or subdue him, while the rest of the gang went to work.

Vex looked at her party. Everyone but Keygan wore makeshift masks made out of potato sacks they'd found in the pizzeria. Vex had suggested Keygan wear one as well, but he figured he had every right to be in his own home, and he didn't want the mask to scare his brother.

Vex was the only one armed, and her pitiful switchblade surely paled in comparison to whatever gun Keygan's dad kept on his nightstand. *We're here to save a life*, she reminded herself. Taking a deep breath, she opened the door.

Turk woke up when the power went out. He slept with a fan on, and the sudden silence put him on high alert. It could be nothing, but it could be the first signs of war. His father had always told him, "Assume the worst, and you'll automatically be prepared for everything else." Turk had tried his damndest to teach his own sons the same lesson. He demanded nothing less than perfection from them.

One of his children had already bailed on him. Keygan just hadn't been strong enough to keep up with Turk's daily regimen. But that was fine. He still had Koy. He'd been too soft on Keygan, he could see that now. Turk resolved to be extra tough on his remaining son, so that he wouldn't wimp out on him like his brother had.

Turk climbed out of bed, grabbing his modified energy rifle off the nightstand. First he peeked out from between his window blinds, and saw nothing. Even the street lights were out, which was a good sign. It meant that The Enemy wasn't targeting his house specifically. But that didn't mean he was out of trouble. It might just be a random power outage, but it could still be an invasion, whether city-wide or even planet-wide. If it was a war, Turk didn't intend to be a casualty.

He quickly pulled on a shirt and pants. As he slipped into his boots, he heard the thump of the backup generator coming on. From outside the bedroom door, he saw the kitchen light turn back on. He always kept that light on at night, so he wouldn't be caught in the dark if there was an emergency. But then he heard a familiar sequence of beeps. Someone was turning off the alarm. Someone who knew the code.

The hallway was still dark, so Turk crouched down and poked his head out the bedroom doorway. It was a home invasion. It looked like four, maybe five intruders. But Turk had the element of surprise. Still hidden in the darkness, he raised the barrel of his gun, aimed for the closest intruder, and fired.

"Augh!" Calix went down, writhing in pain on the kitchen floor.

"Calix!" Vex shouted, but before she could reach them, a man came running down the hall, shouting something about victory. The man was about to fire again, but he stopped when he saw Keygan.

"My own son?" Turk asked, his face contorting with rage. "You'd betray your own family?"

"Dad," Keygan said, holding up his hands. "Please put the gun down."

"My own son?" Turk repeated, louder this time. He held up the gun again, this time aiming at Keygan's head.

Vex threw her switchblade, and used her telekinesis to guide it through the air. It hit Turk in the upper torso, and he shrieked like a toddler.

Vex went back to checking on Calix, and the rest of the gang pressed their advantage. While Turk pulled the knife out of his chest, Hugo, Keygan, and Zak rushed him. Turk used his rifle like a club, swinging it at the approaching trio. The first swing hit Hugo in the head, knocking him down. Then Keygan tackled his father, or at least he tried to, but Turk was much heavier and shrugged off his son's attack. Zak tried to help, but Turk hit him in the face with the butt of the rifle.

Keygan punched his father in the stomach, but once again Turk was more annoyed than injured. Turk grabbed Keygan by the neck, picked him up off the ground, and slammed him against the wall. Keygan's face started to turn purple. He reached out, trying to grab his father's throat, but his grip was too weak to hurt him.

Attracted by all the shouting, the two Rottweilers burst in through the open kitchen door. They saw their two masters, literally at each other's throats. Two masters fighting. One master who always played with them, and pet them, and treated them with nothing but kindness. Another master who always beat them, and went out of his way to be intentionally cruel.

The dogs rushed forward, attacking Turk in a frenzy.

Calix woke up in a hospital bed. Their left arm was bandaged, from the shoulder all the way to the wrist. There was a huge patch of gauze taped to their ribs. It hurt to move anything on the left side of their body. They were still looking at the bandages when a nurse walked in.

"Oh, good, you're awake," he said. "Your parents are out in the hallway, shall I send them in?"

Great, Calix thought. "I don't…" they started to say, then they paused. What was Calix going to do, climb out the window? With one working arm? Might as well get it over with. "Sure," they finally said. "Send them in."

Keygan and Koy sat in a social services office. They were starting to get bored when their case worker finally arrived. A blond woman in her mid-thirties sat down at her desk, and read over their case file. "I'm Joyce," she said, and got straight to the point. "I just got word from the hospital. You're not going to see your father for a long time. He'll recover, but his injuries were pretty severe." She watched their faces, gauging their reaction.

The boys looked at each other. Koy smiled, a wide toothy grin that looked out of place on a face that currently sported a large, fist-shaped bruise. Keygan looked relieved, but also worried. The longer Turk took to heal, the angrier he'd be when he finally got out of the hospital.

Joyce leaned forward. "We have evidence that your father was abusive," she said. "A lot of it, actually. He had cameras all over your house, and he never deleted any footage. Talk to me, tell me everything you can. I promise you, I'm on your side. I don't care if he's a cop, I'll make sure he's never in the same room with you again."

"But what's going to happen to us?" Keygan asked. He didn't want his little brother begging on the streets for food like he'd had to.

"We'll try and find some relatives to take care of you. In the meantime, you'll be placed in a foster home. There's a couple waiting outside right now who will take you to your temporary home."

Keygan nodded. The thought of living with strangers made him nervous, but it was better than the streets. Another thought occurred to him. "What about the dogs?"

"We'll find good homes for them, I promise," Joyce said.

After getting their statements, she led them out of her office and introduced them to their temporary caregivers. It was two women, each in their mid-forties, with genuine smiles and a tendency to hug a lot. They seemed like nice people, the kind who wouldn't use shock-sticks to dole out punishment, though it was impossible to know for sure.

Outside the glass doors of the social services office, Keygan saw Zak, Vex, and Hugo standing around, just talking and waiting. Zak kept holding his hands in front of his face, wary of the building's security cameras. The caregivers were busy filling out paperwork, so Keygan asked if he could go talk to his friends for a minute. They told him it was fine as long as he stayed where they could see him. Keygan walked out the front door and approached his friends.

"How's Calix?" Keygan asked, after hugging each of his friends.

"They're doing much better," Vex said. "They're back with their family. We said goodbye to them this morning."

"But I thought—" Keygan began.

"Calix's mom was so happy to see them alive, she came around," Vex said. "She said she'd respect their name and pronouns. 'Anything to keep her child happy and healthy.' That's a direct quote."

"And their dad?" Keygan asked.

"He didn't seem as enthusiastic about it, but I think he'll get used to it," Vex said.

"I'm gonna miss you guys," Keygan said.

"We'll miss you too," Zak replied. "But I'm also happy to see you go. Frankly, I'm a little jealous. Your new moms look nice."

"They could probably find a home for you too," Keygan said.

"Maybe later," Zak said. "Right now, I can't risk being in the system, my mom would find me."

"But if your new moms don't work out," Hugo added, "you're welcome back any time."

Everyone hugged, and Keygan went back inside.

A few weeks later, Zak was walking through an alley – the same one he'd once sought refuge in, before being threatened by an angry chef – when he saw a teenage girl sitting against the wall. She had auburn hair, a fair complexion, and was wearing a dirty school uniform. Her face was buried in her hands, and Zak could hear her sobbing.

Zak crouched down next to her. "Are you okay?" he asked.

She nodded for a second, then stopped and shook her head no.

"What's wrong?" Zak asked. "Maybe I can help."

The girl looked up at Zak, her eyes red from crying. "I ran away from home," she said.

Zak nodded, his face full of concern. "What happened? Did they hit you?" he asked.

She shook her head. Through her sobs, she said, "They just don't listen. Look at this." She reached into her pocket and pulled out a brand new, state-of-the-art comm unit.

Zak practically salivated at the sight of it. He'd seen signs for this model in store windows; it cost enough to feed the East Side Daggers for an entire year. "Wow, that's a beauty," he said.

"But it's the wrong color!" the girl wailed. "I wanted the purple one. I never wear black. It won't match my ensemble!"

Zak was stunned. After a few seconds, he said, "So you ran away."

"And I'm never going back," the girl said, pouting.

Zak nodded slowly, an odd smirk forming on his face. "Good for you," he finally said. "Stand your ground. You're doing the right thing."

"You really think so?" she asked.

"Sure," Zak said. "You'll love the freedom of being on your own. Sleep when you want, stay out all night…"

"Damn right," the girl said, her face taking on a look of conviction.

"Never changing clothes, always bathing in the river, using old newspapers as toilet paper…"

The girl stared at him, her mouth open.

"Just this morning I had the best breakfast," Zak said. "I found a half-eaten hot dog in a garbage can. I had to shake the bugs off of it, but it was still the best meal I've had all week. What did you have?"

"Eg… eggs Benedict," she said.

"I'm sure that was good too," Zak said. "And you're going to love sleeping in the rain. It's refreshing. And efficient. You get to sleep and shower at the same time. And with your looks, you're going to love all the attention you get. Guys won't be able to keep their hands off you, if you know what I mean. And these guys won't take no for an answer."

The girl had turned pale. She started to say something, but Zak was on a roll.

"And I hope you're used to getting judged. Everyone who

looks at you is going to assume that you're an alcoholic. If you ask for money, they'll accuse you of wanting to buy drugs with it. If they see you sleeping, they'll 'accidentally' kick you on the way by. And it's a good thing you don't like that comm, since you'll have to sell it anyway. It's not like you can afford the monthly service charges. Say goodbye to texting your friends all night. But hey, it's not like you'll have time for friends, you'll be too busy looking for food all day."

"What... what do you think I should do?" the girl said.

Zak reached over and took the comm unit out of her hand. "Is this thing insured for theft?" he asked.

"I think so," the girl said.

"Go home," Zak said, tucking the comm into his pocket. "Tell your mother you were mugged. Apologize for how you reacted to her very thoughtful gift. Thank her for the privileged life she's given you. Appreciate your warm bed, and the roof over your head. Tell your mother you love her every day. Remember that listening is a two-way street. Pay more attention to what she says, and she'll probably listen to you more too. And if you have a problem, talk to her about it, don't just run out the door."

The girl nodded, and climbed to her feet.

"And just one more thing," Zak said, standing up.

"What?" she asked.

"The next time she won't let you go to a party, or buys you the wrong present, or yells at you for not making your bed or whatever, please try to remember that other people have it worse. Running away won't solve any of your problems, but it will give you a whole bunch of new ones."

"If that's true, then why don't you go back to your home?" the girl asked.

Zak smiled, shaking his head. "It was never my home, not really. It belonged to some girl." He turned around and walked away, headed back to the abandoned pizzeria.

It wasn't the life he would have chosen. Not for himself,

and not for his gang. But it was what it was. Family wasn't blood, it was love, and he loved his friends more than anything.

03.05   *Blood Frenzy*

ED02499.08.22

Personal Journal of Sierra Kearns, Lab Assistant
  Employee ID# 74263-145-02
  Tachyon Labs, Vertex City, Cytrine Delta

One of the first rules of lab work is, "Don't get attached to the test subjects." I honestly thought I was smarter than that, but that was before I met P-224B.

I'll never forget when they first brought him in. He was just a kitten, one of ten delivered to the lab that day. They were all leopards, but P-224B was the only one with solid black fur. I wanted to give him a name, but of course that would have been silly. They were lab animals, destined to receive experimental treatments, and naming them could make objectivity more difficult. And yet, in my mind, I kept calling him "Shadow."

I secretly hoped he would end up in the control group, but no such luck. Shadow, along with four of his siblings, was given artificial growth hormones. The formula had already been tested on smaller mammals, so we weren't expecting any complications with the leopards. As expected, they grew much faster and much larger than ordinary examples of their species. The experiment was deemed a success, and we were in the process of arranging a larger living environment for the animals, when we had a sudden change in management.

The new manager's name was Allin K'garr-Ott, but everyone called him "Doctor Shagg." I'm not sure how he got that nickname, and I never got up the nerve to ask. I don't know what species he was, but he had pale yellow skin and bushy red hair. The top of his head was bald, but he had a full beard that almost reached his waistline. He made a great first impression – always smiling, his deep laugh booming at even the mildest of jokes. He was like a palette-swapped Santa Claus.

But those early impressions proved to be deceptive. This man was no Saint Nick, he was no Saint anything. Krampus would have been a more apt comparison. It started slowly. He gradually replaced members of our staff, having them reassigned to other experiments. That wasn't too unusual, labs like ours often went through reorganizations, as people were placed where their expertise would do the most good. I was the only member of the original team who didn't get reassigned, probably because I got along so well with the animals.

Doctor Shagg (ugh) didn't want to retire the leopards. He wanted to use them to test other drugs, to see how the growth hormones interacted with other experimental enhancements. He tended to cut a lot of corners, and often ordered us to do things that contradicted procedure. On several occasions, I warned him that his refusal to follow scientific methods would invalidate the results of our experiments, but he just laughed. Only it was no longer the jovial belly laugh I'd heard so much in his first week. It was now a bark of mocking derision, a laugh that said, "Your opinion is worthless to me."

I also didn't like the way he kept looking at me. I could swear I felt him undressing me with his eyes whenever I walked away from him, but I told myself I was imagining things. Did his species even find humans attractive? I wasn't sure, and I didn't want to look like an idiot by making outlandish accusations.

It became more blatant as time went on. He'd make a double entendre, and if I called him on it, he'd claim he meant it some other way. And yet, he never seemed to use such phrases around the other staff. I made it clear that I was in a relationship, and he backed off for a couple of days.

But apparently he spent those days asking around about me, and found out I was in a polyamorous relationship. From then on, he ran hot and cold on me, and both temperatures made me uncomfortable. Some days he'd be overly nice to me, inviting me out to dinner, giving me a guilt trip if I refused, claiming he was just being friendly. I guess he figured that if I was open to multiple partners, that must mean I had room for one more. Other days he'd give me playful nicknames, which I won't repeat here, but they rhymed with "glut" and "bore."

I should have filed a report with HR. I seriously considered it, but I was afraid it might lead to me being reassigned. And I didn't want to risk being separated from Shadow. He was now as big as a lion, and his growth seemed to have stopped. Doctor Shagg had given us a slew of new formulas to try on the cats. No more control groups, just "try one of these on each leopard." Some of them seemed riskier than others, so I picked the one I deemed most benign to give to Shadow. I know I shouldn't play favorites, but if Shagg wasn't going to follow procedure, why should I?

One of Shadow's sisters was given an experimental steroid, which greatly increased her muscle mass. Unfortunately, her heart couldn't handle the demands of her new size, and she passed away. Another sister was given a serum that made her fur as hard as chitin, basically giving her natural armor. But then she developed breathing problems, and she, too, died. I didn't even know what some of the other formulas were supposed to do.

Shadow received a treatment for increased cognitive reasoning. I thoroughly researched the serum before administering it. The experimental concoction was designed to combat dementia. In earlier studies, it had been successfully used on animals, including felines. There were no reported side effects so far. It wouldn't go so far as to turn Shadow sapient, but it would improve his memory, and potentially boost his problem-solving skills.

Despite the two deaths, Shagg was extremely pleased with our progress. He even demanded we start experimenting on the original control group, the previously-untouched leopards in Habitat Two. Once again, I seriously considered filing a complaint against Shagg. If nothing else, for animal cruelty. He treated the poor cats terribly, often using shock prods on them so they'd learn to fear him. But he claimed to be under orders from the highest authorities on the Science Council, and for some reason I believed him.

Yes, I know. Looking the other way when animals are being mistreated… it's not something I'm proud of. All I can say is that well-paying jobs are hard to come by on Cytrine Delta. I had every reason to believe that Shagg would have me blacklisted if I confronted him. And if I got the shaft, Shagg would just hire another lab assistant, someone who would obey his orders without question. For the animals' sake, I needed to stick it out for as long as I could.

Another week went by, and a tech crew was assigned to upgrade our equipment. We had to consolidate some of our computer systems, as the techs kept dismantling our old hardware and carrying it away. The upgrades weren't scheduled to come in until the following day, so we would be stuck with minimal systems for the rest of the day. That was fine, it wasn't a particularly busy week. For the most part, we were just observing the leopards through their window, and noting any unusual activity.

After a while, several things started to strike me as odd. First off, the only female tech – I think they called her "Eena" – was treated as if she were a slave. She never spoke unless spoken to, she followed the others around at a respectful distance, and she just had this shrinking violet quality about her, like she was afraid to do anything that might offend the other techs. I tried talking to her a couple of times, but she just stared at me with a frightened look in her eyes. Her specialty seemed to be welding, as that was all they had her do, when she wasn't helping carry things. Oddly, I never actually saw her welding device. I could have sworn I saw her using her finger to burn through one metal panel, but that's just crazy, right?

I also noticed that the tech crew was doing a really sloppy job. They'd rip panels off the wall instead of unscrewing them, roughly unplug equipment in a way that could damage the cables, and generally seemed to care more about getting the job done quickly than carefully. I suppose it's not too strange; this equipment was being replaced, after all. If the old equipment was destined for recycling, then it didn't matter if it still worked when it got there.

But then, some of the equipment they took didn't need to be upgraded. I saw one tech walk by with our emergency backup generator. That generator was only two months old, and a newer model wasn't even on the market yet. I stopped the tech and asked him about it.

That's when I noticed the tattoo on his wrist. He'd tried to cover it up with his sleeve, but I could see enough of it to recognize it immediately. It wasn't the kind of thing most people would notice, but one of my partners is a true crime buff. It was the symbol of the Loothawks, a team of space pirates.

That's modern piracy for you. They hadn't come in with guns blazing, oh no. They'd come with fake credentials and stolen uniforms.

I like to think I'm an intelligent person. I may be a lowly lab assistant at the moment, but I'm doing well in my studies, top of my class in fact. I'm not arrogant about it - I hope - but I am proud of my mind. My social skills, on the other hand...

Before I could stop myself, I blurted out, "Pirate?"

The pirate didn't hesitate. He pulled out a gun and shot me in the chest. I looked down at my smoking torso, my mouth open in terror. I could hear the blood rushing in my ears, my vision blurred, and I couldn't breathe. I fell to the floor and watched as he barked orders to the other phony techs. They gathered as much equipment as they could haul, and headed out into the hallway, leaving me for dead. As the world faded away, my last thoughts were, *Who's going to feed Shadow when I'm gone?*

I've had a cybernetic heart pump since I was thirteen. In fact, that's what jump-started my interest in science in the first place. My heart isn't one of the more advanced models. My parents were poor, but not quite poor enough to qualify for government medical assistance. We were in that one specific income bracket where you can't get aid, but also can't afford anything after you pay the bills each month.

It was the kind of life that seemed to invite judgment from every direction. People looked down on me for wearing patched-up, second-hand clothes. One time my cousin got a new comm unit, and she gave me her old one. Whenever I used it in public, I heard whispers of, "Her parents won't buy her new clothes, but she has her own comm." My parents made sacrifice after sacrifice, doing everything they could to scrape by, but in everyone else's eyes, they were lazy and irresponsible.

And then I developed heart problems. My dad would have gladly sold himself into slavery if it meant saving my life. But he couldn't even get a loan. With his poor credit, the insurance company wouldn't approve the procedure.

But if there's one thing that Cytrine Delta has plenty of, it's opportunities for test subjects. A nearby lab actually paid *us* money for the opportunity to replace my heart. My heart pump isn't pretty. Instead of a normal surgery scar, there's a fist-sized metal plate in the middle of my chest, with an access hatch leading to the pump. Since it's experimental, they wanted to keep it easy to access in case there was a problem. Every couple of years they give me a free upgrade, as they come up with ways to improve the device. I hope they add a coffee maker someday.

It's not the implant I would have chosen if I'd had unlimited money. But so far it's saved my life twice – first by replacing my defective heart, and later by protecting me from the pirate's gun. The energy blast hit me right in the access plate, but didn't go any deeper. The skin around it got singed, and the jolt was enough to knock me out for a couple of minutes, but I survived. While I don't believe in miracles, I have to admit it was an improbable stroke of luck.

As I regained consciousness, the door reopened. Two pirates came back into the lab, dragging Doctor Shagg behind them. I played dead, keeping my eyes nearly shut and trying not to breathe. They opened the door to Habitat One, shoved Shagg into the enclosure, and locked him in. Then they left again.

As soon as they were gone, I climbed to my feet and ran to the window. Shagg stood, his back to the wall, as three giant leopards slowly approached him. The doctor was in a blind panic, shrieking and holding his hands in front of his face. The leopards seemed confused. He'd come into the habitat before, but he'd never shown fear.

Shagg turned and banged on the transparent door, staring at me with wild eyes. I pulled on the door, but it was locked. There used to be an emergency lever inside the habitat, which could unlock the door if someone got locked in. But a few days earlier, Shadow figured out how to activate the lever, so Shagg had us disable it. A more complicated lever was on back order.

I tried to remember the keypad combination, but my mind had gone blank. I used this code almost every day, but I swear, I just couldn't bring it to my mind. Shagg started yelling numbers at me, but I couldn't hear him through the window. I did my best to read his lips, but I've never been good at that. I typed in a number, but the screen flashed red.

The leopards stalked closer. Shagg cringed away from Shadow and his litter mates, P224-C and P224-E. This was the longest he had ever been in the habitat without using his shock prod on one of them. Shagg turned back to me, frantically making numbers with his fingers, trying to show me the correct combination. But he was so nervous, and his hands were shaking so hard, it was hard to get what he was saying. I noticed that he'd wet himself.

I typed another number, but again the code was rejected. I only had one more try before it would lock me out. I took a deep breath, cleared my mind, and tried to remember the code. It just wouldn't come. I'm usually good under pressure, but between getting shot and knowing the pirates could come back at any moment, I just couldn't get past the mental block.

And then I remembered it. Five nine three seven eight two. I had typed the first two digits when P224-E's eyes started to glow. They'd never done that before. I hesitated, unable to believe what I was seeing. The leopard fired a pair of energy beams out of her eyes, hitting Shagg in the stomach. He fell down, holding his scorched stomach, and crawled away from the door.

Then P224-C approached him. The leopard opened his jaw, and some sort of mist sprayed out, hitting Shagg in the face. Whatever it was, it must have burned, because his face turned red and started peeling. He howled so loud I could almost hear it through the soundproof window.

I finished typing the last digits, and the door slid open. I was about to rush in and help Shagg, but C and E were already tearing into him, ripping him apart for meat. Only Shadow seemed uninterested in taking part in the feast. He gingerly stepped out of the habitat and nuzzled my hand.

"I'm sorry," I told Shadow, bending over and hugging

him around the neck. Then I turned and ran out of the lab, taking the hall opposite from the direction I'd seen the pirates head. I didn't stop until I reached the police station.

The project was scrapped, and the Science Council declared Doctor Shagg's data to be useless. An investigation eventually discovered that he'd been trying to develop biological weapons, in the hopes of selling them to the militaristic Grunthians.

The remaining animals were taken to a wildlife habitat where they could be studied for long-term effects. After I submitted my final report, I was transferred to another lab, where I worked with a much friendlier staff.

Shadow was not among the animals recovered. Since the pirates had taken the data drives, there was no security footage to show where the cat had gone. Nor were there any sightings by Vertex City's citizens.

About a week later, I remembered that I had my own private feed. Because sometimes I'd needed to check up on the leopards from home, I'd set up the cameras to transmit their data to my personal cloud as well as save it to the lab's drives. I examined the footage.

I had just fled the lab. Shagg's killers were still feasting on his corpse, while Shadow walked around the outer lab, sniffing things. Further down the hall, another camera showed the last three remaining pirates carrying away large pieces of equipment. The woman, "Eena," was having trouble dragging a large metal device down the hallway. She kept stopping to rest.

There wasn't any sound, but one of the other pirates was clearly angry with her. He appeared to yell at her, and finally he punched her in the face. And then Shadow pounced on him. The third pirate pulled his weapon on the cat, but Eena stepped between them. He looked like he was about to shoot through her anyway.

But then the other pirate, the one on the floor, yelled

something. He didn't appear to be hurt, just restrained under Shadow's massive paw. Eena said something to the cat, and he appeared to be soothed by her words. She petted him, he nuzzled her, and he finally released the pirate.

There seemed to be an immediate bond between Eena and the cat, similar to the bond I had with him. Maybe we smell alike, or it could be our demeanor, or maybe he just only likes women. I don't know. But the other pirates seemed to recognize it too, and they allowed Eena to lead the leopard away.

And that's the last I ever saw of Shadow. As far as I know, he left with the pirates, and is now living on a spaceship somewhere. I don't know what they're planning to do with him, but I hope he doesn't get hurt. He was truly one of a kind, and I miss him every day.

Shadow, I hope you live a long, happy life, wherever you are.

03.06 *Blood Guardian*

IGP Officer Zhari Ze-Rastt was sick of EarthStation 1. For every four hours she spent on the streets, she spent another four filing paperwork at the station. It was also where she slept, ran her training exercises, and ate most of her meals. And while the station was beautiful, a true testament to the power of engineering, she wished she could spend more time in the sun, breathing non-manufactured oxygen. She was getting married in a few months, and was greatly anticipating her honeymoon. She wasn't sure where they were going yet, as it was supposed to be a surprise. The important thing was, she'd be spending a couple of weeks planetside.

But which planet? Earth was nice, but she was hoping she'd get to visit her homeworld of Galea. She hadn't been there in years, and she looked forward to showing Vik her favorite landmarks. She'd been dropping hints for a while; had Vik picked up on them? She wasn't sure. He was keeping it close to the vest, but she could tell he had something big planned. Even if it wasn't Galea, it was going to be a spectacular trip.

She glanced at the picture of Vik on her desk. They couldn't be more different. He was human, square-jawed and duty-driven. Zhari, meanwhile, had cat-like facial features and a more relaxed attitude. Not that she didn't take her job seriously, but it seemed like Vik stayed in officer mode even when he was off the clock. Nevertheless, she loved him. She wanted to talk to him, right now. She didn't have anything to say, really, she just had to hear his voice. She grabbed her comm, and her thumb was hovering over the call button when a message flashed.

Duty assignment. But not just any work detail. This one would keep her off the station for a couple of days, at least. She grabbed her things and headed for the landing bay, practically skipping with glee.

"You've all read the briefing," Officer Tannish lectured. "And you know why they picked us for this assignment. Each of us has dealt with this fugitive before, and our unique insights give us the edge in recapturing him. Time is of the essence here. We believe he's headed to Cytrine Delta to get black-market facial reconstruction. If he succeeds, we might never get our hands on him again. It is vitally important we get to him before he goes under the knife."

Zhari looked around the cockpit. In addition to Zhari and Tannish, there were two other officers on board. Officer Blake had close-cropped red hair, and always looked like she was bored. She'd been the one to process the crime scene after the murder. Agent Renn was bald, with olive-brown skin. He was a profiler, and he'd interviewed Hezler in prison. Zhari was the only non-human. She'd been the one to recapture Hezler after his first escape two months earlier.

"But there's something else you should know," Tannish said. "Something that wasn't in the briefing. Against my recommendation, they've posted a bounty on Hezler." Blake and Renn sighed with disgust. "I know, I know," Tannish continued. "As if Hezler wasn't enough, we also have to deal with bounty hunters getting in the way. But with such a tight time limit, they didn't want to take any chances."

Zhari understood the reasoning. As long as Hezler was a danger to society, it didn't matter who brought him in. But she also understood the reactions of her fellow officers. If the bounty hunters got to Hezler first, it would make the IGP look bad. And there was always the chance the bounty would attract carrion hunters – unscrupulous mercenaries who would have no compunctions about killing an officer if it meant they got the reward.

"I know what you're all thinking," Tannish said. "But don't worry. We know more about Hezler than any bounty hunter, and I'm confident that we can bring him in without incident. We land in two hours, be ready."

The IGP shuttle sped toward the warp gate that would take it to Cytrine Delta. No one in the galaxy stood a better chance of apprehending Hezler than the ship's five passengers. The real question was whether Hezler would be caught by one of the four officers, or the stowaway.

The sun was sinking on the horizon when the ship landed in Silicon Bay. Most of Cytrine Delta's major cities had science-themed names, because the planet was known for its high-tech research centers. The local scientists were annoyed by this sort of pandering, but the tourists ate it up. Unfortunately, there were fewer tourists every year, as more and more cities became slums. The tech-themed names of the world's cities and streets seemed increasingly incongruous as the years went on.

With an entire planet to pick from, choosing a landing site could have been a major decision. Fortunately, someone matching Hezler's description had been spotted in Silicon Bay. Their informant swore that they'd only notified the IGP and no one else, so hopefully they'd be in and out before any bounty hunters got wind of Hezler's presence.

The officers disembarked from their shuttle and headed for the local police headquarters. A few minutes after they left, the shuttle's door opened again. A shadowy figure slipped out the door and vanished into the dusk.

Reylund Hezler paced in his tiny motel room, wishing time would pass faster. He was supposed to meet his contact in three hours. He couldn't be early, or his contact wouldn't be there. He couldn't kill time in town, or he might be recognized. His best bet was to stay put until it was time to go.

But this room… it was smaller than his cell had been. He could barely breathe in here. He'd only been here an hour, and he already felt like screaming. Three more hours seemed insurmountable. What was he going to do?

He sat down on the bed. It was old, and the mattress sagged in the middle, but it was much softer than the beds in prison had been. He briefly considered taking a nap, but he didn't think he'd be able to get any sleep. And if he did, he might sleep through his alarm and miss the rendezvous. He stood up again, and thought about ordering some food.

But he was too nervous to eat. What if the surgery went badly? What if the doctor put him under, then turned him in to the IGP? What if the police found him mid-surgery, leaving the procedure half-finished? Scenario after scenario whirled through his mind, and he began to feel nauseous.

He wasn't cut out for this lifestyle. Hezler was no criminal. He'd taken the rap for his boyfriend, Vinz Kacy. It was a complicated set of circumstances, almost a comedy of errors, that had led to Hezler's conviction. At least… that's what he'd thought at the time.

A year earlier, on a Friday morning, Vinz gave Hezler a stuffed platypus as a surprise. Hezler took it to work to show his coworkers, and left it on his desk. But it turned out that inside the platypus was a second surprise, tickets to a play on Saturday night. The office was closed on weekends, but Hezler had keys, and offered to go get the platypus. But Vinz still wanted to keep the title of the play a surprise, and was afraid Hezler would peek, so he offered to go to Hezler's office instead. It was against the office's security rules, but Vinz convinced Hezler it would be fine.

While Vinz was in Hezler's office, he found the body of Hezler's boss, Virra Spinner. While trying to revive her, Vinz got Virra's blood all over his clothing. Rather than call the police, Vinz panicked and returned home. When Hezler heard the story, he called the police. But he didn't want to get in trouble at work, so he told the police that he'd been the one to go to the office, and that Vinz's bloody clothes were his.

Things spiraled out of control from there. The killer had taken the office's data drives, including the ones that held security camera footage. Hezler wasn't fond of his boss, and his coworkers knew it, so there was motive. Even if he'd wanted to tell the police the truth, that Vinz had been the one to find the body, they wouldn't have believed him at that point. There was simply too much evidence against Hezler.

At first, Hezler was content to bide his time in prison, sure that more evidence would come out, and the real killer would be revealed. After a few months, he realized no one was still looking for the truth. Vinz never came to see him in prison. When Hezler escaped the first time, he tried to pay Vinz a visit. But Vinz had moved on, and was dating someone else. He'd sold off all of Hezler's possessions, and had somehow made it rich by buying stocks. Vinz had never shown any interest in finance before; how had he gotten so lucky?

Once Hezler was back in prison, he started putting the pieces together. And now he had a theory. It was Vinz who had suggested that he go to the office instead of Hezler. Once there, Vinz found data that gave him insider information on stock tips. But he was discovered by Virra, and he killed her. Finally, he convinced Hezler to take the blame for breaking into the office, assuring him that it looked less suspicious.

And I fell for it, Hezler thought angrily. That was the worst part about it. If he'd known he was being set up, he would have fought harder in court. He would have thrown Vinz under the bus, instead of protecting him with lies. But it was too late to do anything about that. If he were to bring it up now, he'd just be a twice-escaped convict desperate to stay free. No one was going to believe him without hard evidence.

But how was that going to happen? Hezler was having a hard enough keeping the cops off his trail. He didn't have the time or resources to play detective, too.

He checked the time again. *Damn.* For all his brooding, only ten more minutes had gone by. He sat down on the bed again, pulled his knees up to his chest, and tried to calm his breathing.

Whisper was practically invisible from her vantage point. Her species had the ability to manipulate shadow, allowing her to blend into the dark recesses of the building. She crouched on a ledge on the second floor, in one of the building's many exterior alcoves. From a bystander's point of view, the alcove might have looked a bit darker than it should have, but they probably wouldn't question it.

She was familiar with police procedures. The four IGP officers would be scattered across the city right now, first questioning known informants, then every local surgeon, starting with the ones who specialized in facial reconstruction. But Whisper knew better. Hezler wasn't dumb enough to hire a surgeon listed online. No, he'd go for someone experienced, but no longer practicing. So while the cops and other bounty hunters were on a wild goose chase, Whisper had an actual lead to follow.

The guy's name was Ryfush Weglan. He was a Vhelran, with dark orange scales, and a scar across his left cheek. He'd once been an expert in the field of body modification, but he'd abandoned the career after some malpractice suits. But he still had connections, and now made a living illegally procuring painkillers for people who didn't qualify for a prescription.

He'd also gone to the same high school as Reylund Hezler. Maybe it was just a coincidence, but Whisper's intuition told her that this was the guy she needed to watch. She'd headed to Weglan's place immediately after leaving the IGP shuttle, staked it out until he left, and followed him to this alley. Just a few minutes later, another man showed up. This newcomer wore a hood, but he was about the right build to be Hezler.

The two spoke for a few minutes, and Whisper strained to hear their conversation. Some bounty hunters could afford fancy tech that would have allowed them to hear them from a distance, but Whisper didn't have that kind of money. But then, she wasn't in it for the profit, she just wanted to keep violent criminals off the streets.

Whisper considered leaping down from the ledge and grabbing Hezler, but she couldn't be sure it was him. If she was wrong, and Weglan was planning to meet Hezler at a later time, acting now would blow her whole plan. Weglan would cancel his meeting with Hezler, and Whisper would be back to square one.

After a few minutes, Weglan gestured farther down the alley, and the duo walked away. Whisper followed, keeping her distance, blending back into the shadows whenever one of them started looking around for witnesses. They ended up at a nearly abandoned office building, its doors closed for the night. Weglan unlocked the door and led Hezler inside.

"So, what do you want to look like?" Weglan asked. The office had originally been used by a talent agency, and some of their posters still hung on the wall. The room was poorly lit, illuminated by a single hanging lamp in the center of the room. The partially-open doorway also let in a strip of light from the hall, but it was still unusually dark for a doctor's office.

"I don't care," Hezler answered softly. They were the only

ones in the building, but Hezler still kept his voice low. "I'm only doing this so I don't get caught."

"Sure, but you're going to have to live with this face," Weglan said. "Might as well get one you like."

"Can't you just change it back once I prove I'm innocent?" Hezler asked.

Weglan laughed. "You make it sound like I'm going to store your old face in a freezer somewhere. Doesn't work that way. Look, some time down the road, if you want to look like your old self again, I can recommend a surgeon who might be able to get you there. It'll be expensive, though, and it won't be perfect. And that's only if you actually manage to catch the real killer, which is a big if. My advice is to accept reality, and pick a face you can live with."

Hezler's mind reeled. Before, facial reconstruction had seemed like a nebulous idea, something he'd seen fugitives do in the movies. It was just one of those things people do when they're on the run. But now that he was sitting in Weglan's eerily dark office, surrounded by medical equipment, the full weight of what he was about to do hit him. He was going to change his face, permanently. He was going to look in the mirror, and see a stranger staring back.

He liked his face. He'd never really thought about it before, but it was a decent face. Not super handsome, but clean, average, the kind of face you might see in commercials. He'd never looked in the mirror and thought, "I wish my nose was narrower" or "I wish I had fuller lips." There were no celebrities he envied, nobody he wanted to emulate.

"Do you have a book or something I can look through?" he asked.

Weglan grunted in annoyance and handed Hezler a tablet. It contained thousands of pictures of noses, eyes, chins, and other facial features. As Hezler scrolled through the images, Weglan asked him a few questions, trying to narrow down what face would make him happiest. Weglan knew Hezler wasn't getting this done out of vanity; he just needed to keep from being recognized, and to fool facial scanners. But they were friends, even if they hadn't spoken much since high school, and Weglan wanted to do the best job he could.

Whisper watched them from a dark corner near the doorway. She could absorb sound as well as light, so sneaking in when their heads were turned had been easy enough. Fortunately there were plenty of shadows to hide in, the office's hanging light leaving the edges of the room in darkness.

This was it. Whisper could easily subdue Hezler from here. With her skills, she'd have him tied up in seconds. Even if they fought back, she'd be able to take them without a scratch. She'd handled crowds of armed criminals before, so two average joes would be a cakewalk.

And yet, she still hesitated.

As Hezler thumbed through the tablet, their conversation drifted away from the surgery, and back to Hezler's conviction, incarceration, and escapes. Weglan explained how he unjustly lost his medical license, due to false claims of incompetence. Whisper listened intently, studying Hezler's posture. Aurorans were raised to read body language in addition to spoken words, a skill they used to predict their opponents' moves during hand-to-hand combat.

Hezler was telling the truth. Whisper could tell by his shoulders, his breathing, his eyes, and even his speech patterns. Either he was innocent of his crimes, or at least he believed he was. Weglan, meanwhile, was embellishing his own story. The former surgeon believed some of what he was saying, but he was definitely keeping some significant details to himself. The contrast between the two was undeniable.

Most bounty hunters wouldn't have cared. Money was

money. Whisper was paid to bring them in, and the courts could work out the rest. But that just wasn't how Whisper saw the universe. If this man was innocent, she wanted to help him, even if it meant giving up a reward.

But what if she walked away, only for Hezler to get caught by another bounty hunter? There was no way he could stay on the run forever, even with a new face.

Whisper was still debating when there was a loud crash from down the hall.

"This is the police! Come out with your hands above your head!" Zhari didn't have a warrant, but police procedure was pretty lax on Cytrine Delta. Her team's leads had been dead ends so far, until an informant gave her a hot tip that led her here.

Having just kicked open the outer door, she now stood in a long hallway, lined with numbered doors that led to long-abandoned offices. She jogged down the hall, gun drawn, looking for any indication of which office to investigate first. She reached a side hallway and peeked around the corner, wary of any potential danger. Halfway down the hall, she saw an open door. As soon as she spotted it, it slammed shut.

"What exactly is your plan, here?" Weglan asked bluntly, as Hezler pushed the operating table in front of the door.

"Shut up and help me," Hezler said, in a panic. He turned around and grabbed a chair, and started pulling it towards the door as well.

"There are no other exits from this room," Weglan said. "You don't have any weapons, and I don't think you'd use them if you did. You think that cop's going to go away just because she couldn't push the door open on her first try? No. She's going to call for backup, they're going to bring in the drones, and you're just going to make things worse for yourself."

"I can't go back to prison," Hezler said, wedging the chair under the operating table.

Weglan sighed. "Fine," he said. "Hide behind this chair, and let me do the talking."

There was a pounding on the office door. They heard a muffled voice shout, "Open up, this is the police!"

Hezler dragged the chair back to the far corner, and hid behind it. "One minute," Weglan shouted, pulling the operating table back from the door.

The officer kicked the door open. She was Galean, with a catlike face. She had light gray fur, and her face was framed by a blue mane. She wore a navy blue IGP uniform with lightweight armor plating. She quickly looked around the room, then turned to Weglan. "Where's Hezler?"

"Behind that chair," Weglan said, pointing.

"Jerk!" Hezler shouted, emerging from his hiding spot.

"Realist," Weglan countered.

The officer stepped forward, her right hand pointing the gun a Hezler, her left hand reaching for her bracers. She paused when she saw Hezler's shocked expression. He wasn't looking at the cop, but past her.

From the corner closest to the door, a figure emerged from the shadows. It was as if the darkness itself coalesced into a feminine, humanoid shape. Then the shadows dissipated, revealing a woman dressed in black and gray. She wore a tight-fitting jumpsuit, with a black vest and boots. Her helmet featured a mirrored faceplate.

The officer was about to turn around when this shadowy newcomer grabbed her from behind, pinning her arms to her sides. "Run," the shadow woman said. Hezler didn't have to be told twice. He ran past the two women, past Weglan, out the door, and down the hallway. He didn't stop running until he was back in his motel room.

What is this thing? Zhari wondered, trying to break free of the creature's grasp. She couldn't turn to get a good look, but it felt humanoid. Zhari had checked the corners upon entering the room, as per her training. Where had it been hiding? Zhari couldn't move her arms enough to aim her pistol, no matter how hard she struggled. Instead, she lifted her right leg and stomped hard on her captor's boot. The woman gasped, momentarily loosening her grip, enough for Zhari to break free.

Zhari turned, but only got a glimpse of her attacker before the lights went out. The dark woman had thrown something into the air, smashing the room's only light. While the light from the hallway still illuminated the room enough to see Weglan and the furniture, the dark woman seemed to completely vanish in the dimness.

The officer raised her weapon, only for it be kicked out of her grasp. Then Zhari lunged forward at where she'd last seen the woman. Grabbing her foe around the waist, Zhari wrestled her to the ground. She still couldn't see the woman, which was confusing. Galeans had excellent night vision, but all Zhari could see was blackness where she felt her opponent to be.

Weglan carefully stepped backward, away from the women, and out the door. He pulled the door shut as he left, leaving the two in total darkness.

"Whoever you are," Zhari grunted, trying to get a better grip on her invisible opponent, "You're under arrest for aiding and abetting a known fugitive..."

The dark woman didn't answer, she just kept trying to hold Zhari still. Although Zhari couldn't see her opponent, she could tell that it was a woman, probably human, stronger than average, with formal martial arts training. The woman seemed to sense every move Zhari planned to make before she made it. But as they wrestled and fought, another realization dawned on Zhari – this woman wasn't trying to hurt her, only delay her. She had passed up several opportunities to deliver crippling blows, going for grabs and holds instead.

Zhari wrestled herself free again, and slowly stood up. Instead of attacking, this time she backed up until she felt the wall at her back. "You're protecting a murderer, you know," Zhari said, breathing heavily.

There was no response, but Zhari thought she heard a drawer open.

"He'll kill again," Zhari said. Her firearm was lost in the darkness, but she had a few other tools at her disposal. But what did she have that would affect this woman? She'd felt a helmet while they'd grappled, so that ruled out mace. She had gas grenades, but the woman's helmet might have its own oxygen reserves. She had a stun baton, but her opponent might be wearing a shock-resistant flightsuit.

Finally she reached for her AON knife. She didn't want to use lethal force, but it was the only weapon guaranteed to breach her attacker's defenses. Plus it gave off light, which was what Zhari needed most right now. She held up the weapon and clicked the switch on the hilt. The blade immediately started to warm up, giving off a blue glow.

Zhari jumped, seeing her own blue-tinted face reflected in the woman's visor. The shadowy woman was leaning towards her, mere centimeters away. Before Zhari could even register what the woman was doing, she felt a prick in her shoulder. She thrust her knife forward, but the woman jumped back and disappeared into the shadows once again. Zhari touched her shoulder, already starting to feel dizzy. What had she...

Of course. It was a doctor's office. It had to be some sort of fast-acting sedative, taken from the drawer. Zhari knew she only had seconds of consciousness left. She sheathed her knife and pulled out her comm unit. "Tannish," she said. "I need... need... baffllezerrrrm..."

As Zhari fell forward, the dark woman caught her and gently set her on the floor.

Someone spotted Hezler leaving the planet, but after that the trail went cold. The four officers returned to EarthStation 1 and filed their reports. They were given a stern lecture, but ultimately it was determined that they'd done all they could. A few days later, a surprise piece of evidence arrived at the station. It was the stolen data drives from Hezler's office. An accompanying note apologized for the interference on Cytrine Delta, and claimed that the drive had been found in the possession of Vinz Kacy. While the drive had since been wiped, a data recovery team managed to restore most of the deleted files, including security logs.

It was all there, in full color, high definition, pixel-perfect video. Indisputable evidence that Kacy had entered the office, accessed restricted files, and killed Virra Spinner. Kacy was quickly arrested, and Hezler turned himself in. Hezler was still sentenced to probation for the minor crimes he'd committed while on the run, but he would soon be able to resume a normal life.

In Zhari's report, she described her attacker as a "woman seemingly made of shadows." For a couple of weeks, she took a fair amount of ribbing over it. Her fellow officers joked that she'd been attacked by the boogeyman, and one of them even gave her a night light as a gag gift. But then Agent Renn fell into a vat of relish while chasing a suspect, and Zhari's story was immediately forgotten. "Agent Pickles" became a sensation, the most joked-about officer on the force, for the rest of the year.

Right up until the disaster. After that, nothing seemed funny anymore.

Author's Notes

These notes contain spoilers, so please read the book first.

I started writing this story in the late nineties. Well, no… It's actually based on comic books I drew in high school in the early nineties. Well, no… those comics were based on the stories I played as a kid in the eighties.

My friend and I didn't play like typical boys. Instead of reenacting scenes from our favorite movies and cartoons, or even just making our action figures pew pew pew at each other, our play sessions felt more like romantic comedies. We played stories about bounty hunters with secret identities, who then fell in love and got married, with lots of sitcom-esque misunderstandings. Later, in high school, I drew some of these stories in comic book form. It was just a big free-for-all fanfiction, using existing characters from dozens of movies and cartoons. I'm a terrible artist, but it was all for fun.

Sometime after high school, I read through my old comics and thought, "Wow, you take out all the famous characters, and there's a lot of creative, original ideas in here." So I took some of my favorite characters and storylines, removed any connections to existing properties, and started over. I wrote a novella about how these characters came together and decided to work as a team. I even drew a comic adaptation.

And then I sat on it. I sat on it for more than two decades.

The story was there, but it just felt like it needed something. Something to make it stand out from all the other "misfit team of space mercenaries" stories out there. The characters weren't completely out of my thoughts during that time. Occasionally I'd think of a short story involving one of the characters, and type out some notes. So if Part 2 feels like some of the short stories are written differently than others, that's why – some of them were written years apart.

Sometime in the mid-2000s, I realized I was transgender. I went through some terrible bouts of depression, made some questionable financial decisions, and my marriage suffered. I never transitioned, and probably never will, but my wife and I worked through the other issues and we both came out stronger on the other side.

A few years after my egg cracked, I developed an interest in LGBTQ+ literature. I grew up thinking I hated romance novels, but as it turns out, I like romance just fine – it's just that I find straight couples boring. Still, I did find it a little off-putting that most of the lesbian books I read were just modern-day romances. Whenever I came across a lesbian sci-fi novel, I read it with great fervor.

I knew I couldn't be the only one who wanted more LGBTQ+ sci-fi to exist. And that's when I started thinking about my bounty hunter story. I knew it needed some polish; what if I gave it a coat of rainbow-colored paint? Would that be pandering? Would it look like rainbow capitalism if I tried to fill that hole? Would I get some details wrong about LGBTQ+ culture, and wind up offending the very people I wanted to embrace? That worry alone was enough to put me off doing it for a few more years.

But eventually, I realized that it didn't matter. I would make mistakes, no doubt about it. My book would not please everyone. But the bottom line was, I just wanted to write the kind of story that I would want to read. If someone else happened to enjoy it too, that's just gravy.

I didn't even have to change that much. Trenyn was agender from the beginning, though originally they went by he/him pronouns. Raven was originally meant to be asexual, now she's more questioning. The biggest change was Bloodstone herself. She went from being a white straight cis man to being a trans woman of color.

It pains me that I had to misgender Bloodstone for most of Part 1. For the twist to work, I also had to take out a lot of her internal monologue. I needed the reader to see her as the galaxy saw her – as an inscrutable male of indeterminate species. I couldn't out her to the readers until she was out to the characters.

Each of the main characters, in their own way, is an author avatar. Some represent my ideal self, some represent my struggles and/or goals, and some represent specific aspects of my personality. A couple of characters were almost cut, but I left them in to represent past versions of myself that I've mostly left behind.

I know this book isn't much. I know it won't win any awards or inspire a blockbuster movie. But it is a piece of my soul, with origins tracing all the way back to my childhood. If I accomplish nothing else in life, I hope someone finds this book and it makes them smile. And maybe, just maybe, it will inspire them to write a book of their own.

- Xine Fury

Special Thanks

I would like to thank:

...My wonderful spouse, KJ, who supported me and gave me the encouragement I needed to finish this.

...Alan K. Garrett, author of *Brain Child*, who walked me through self-publishing in a digital world.

...Cyanimations, for the fantastic cover.

...My childhood friend, J.S., who would hate this book and everything it stands for, but who nevertheless inspired me in ways he'll never know.

...Kaius Coolman, who helped me find typos, gave me tips on making the story more LGBT+ friendly, and showered me with encouraging words.

...Mike, who gave me some useful advice, some of which I even followed.

...Paula Offutt, author of The Soliloquy series books *To Sleep* and *To Dream,* who gave me some excellent in-depth feedback, even if some of it was hard to hear.

About the Author

Xine Fury is a mammal.

Also By Xine Fury

The following books by Xine Fury are also available:
    Bloodhunters v2: Blue Blood
    Bloodhunters v3: New Blood
    Nomads of Zyden

Random Xinery (Short Story Collections):
    Geek Cutes
    Rainbow Nightmares
    Gender Rolls
    Side Quests

Find them here: bit.ly/XineFury